Anne Christine Ostby is a Norwegian journalist and author of nine books. Her stories frequently depict women's lives and struggles in various cultures around the world. When *Town of Love* was released in Norway in 2012, it was supported by FOKUS, the Norwegian resource centre for international women's issues which partners with the Coalition Against Trafficking in Women. Since 1990, Anne Ch. Ostby has lived in Denmark, Malaysia, Pakistan, Kazakhstan, the United States, and Iran. She currently resides in Fiji.

By the same author

Tegn (Signs) 2012

Forbannet Velsignet (Damned Blessed) 2008

Asif, Asif, Asif 2005

Snorkeprinsen (The Snoring Prince) 2004

www.veien_videre/Anna (www.way_forward/Anna) 2003

S for Lengsel (S for Longing) 2002

Anna+Framtid… Søk (Anna+Future… Search) 2000

Anna@verden.com (Anna@world.com) 1999

TOWN OF LOVE

ANNE CH. OSTBY

TRANSLATED BY
MARIE OSTBY

AFTERWORD BY
RUCHIRA GUPTA

First published in Australia by Spinifex Press, 2013, Reprinted 2014
Originally published in Norwegian by Schribsted, Norway as *Kjærlighetsgata*

Spinifex Press Pty Ltd
504 Queensberry St
North Melbourne, Victoria 3051
Australia
women@spinifexpress.com.au
www.spinifexpress.com.au

Copyright © Anne Ch. Ostby, 2013
Afterword © Ruchira Gupta, 2013
Translation © Marie Ostby, 2013

This translation has been published with the financial support of NORLA

All rights reserved. Without limiting the rights under copyright reserved above, no part of this publication may be reproduced, stored in or introduced into a retrieval system, or transmitted, in any form or by any means (electronic, mechanical, photocopying, recording or otherwise) without prior written permission of both the copyright owner and the above publisher of the book.

Copying for educational purposes
Information in this book may be reproduced in whole or part for study or training purposes, subject to acknowledgement of the source and providing no commercial usage or sale of material occurs. Where copies of part or whole of the book are made under part VB of the Copyright Act, the law requires that prescribed procedures be followed. For information contact the Copyright Agency Limited.

Cover design: Deb Snibson
Typesetting: Palmer Higgs
Cover photo © Uri Baitner uribaba2010@gmail.com
Printed by McPherson's Printing Group

National Library of Australia
Cataloguing-in-Publication
Ostby, Anne Ch, 1958-.

Town of love / Anne Ch. Ostby.

9781742198477 (pbk.)
9781742198521 (eBook: ePub World)
9781742198514 (eBook: ePub North America)
9781742198538 (eBook: ePub UK)
9781742198484 (eBook: PDF)
9781742198491 (eBook: Kindle)

839.828

To Meena

AUTHOR'S NOTE

This story begins and ends under a mango tree in Bihar. It is told through many voices in many places – some real, some fictional. Some of these houses I have actually visited; others I have not. Some of the stories lie extremely close to the truth; others do not. I have let some characters who are alive and well in reality die between these covers; others have been conjured out of thin air.

But everything that is important in this book is true. That human beings are bought and sold; that young girls are kidnapped and hidden away; that children are assaulted, abused and raped. That there are mothers who cry tears of desperation over their newborn girls' cribs because they know the vicious cycle that awaits them – the same fate that lay in store for themselves, their mothers and their grandmothers. That those who reap the benefits of the human flesh trade, with its violence and brutality, mostly walk free.

But this story also finds a glimmer of hope for the women who walk the streets of the Town of Love; the girls on display in doorframes and on balconies. A hope brought by those who care. Those who do not turn away, but enter the tiny rooms of Prem Nagar, push back the curtains, breathe in the same air as Rupa and Salma, share their pain. Like Tamanna and Fauzia there are those who reclaim the governance of their own lives and their own bodies.

The hope of this book is that there will be more of them.

PROLOGUE

Tamanna's house consisted of three rooms, neither big nor furnished. The walls were woven from bamboo leaves, easily penetrated by sound and sight. Thin, flimsy walls, no match for anyone who might want to tear them down– but what she did have was a door. A door with a padlock – the paradoxical symbol of her freedom – and one single key that rested safely inside the short, tight blouse of her sari. Squeezed against the nipple, the cool metal burning reassurance into her skin. *There are no other roads to me. Only I decide when this road is closed or open,* she thought to herself.

The fruits dangling from the mango tree were still green. Tiny, dense, heart-shaped fruits of hope that would one day grow ripe and heavy, juicy and swollen with yellow pulp. A ray of moonlight bounced off the water pump beneath the tree, the metal gleaming dully where the paint had worn off. The pump was a triumph, a monument to victory, one that she had paid for herself: access to life-sustaining water, to cleanliness, to the smothering of fire and the drowning of shame.

Muted evening sounds echoed through the darkened streets of Prem Nagar, the Town of Love: a barking dog, a crying baby. An oil lamp swung back and forth in a doorframe, its yellow light flickering over the face of a young girl motionless in a chair.

1

'I won't be long!'

Tamanna shouted, giving Amina a quick wave as she squeezed the black handbag under her arm and hurried down the road. It was a good turnout this morning, twelve or fifteen toddlers had spent the past few sun-baked hours crawling or taking tiny, clumsy steps around the brown dhurrie they called the kindergarten, a coarse rug spread out over the dusty front yard of the schoolhouse. A few worn plastic toys lay in a woven basket; a couple of little cars missing their wheels, a tractor that had once been painted red, a tired brown and white plastic dog that probably used to have eyes. Tamanna hurried out into the hot, dusty thoroughfare of the Town of Love, carrying twenty rupees in her handbag.

Fauzia with the long, stern face sat perched on the elevated wooden platform of her paan-stand – *like a queen on her throne*, Tamanna mused as she momentarily slowed her steps to admire the intricate handiwork. Fauzia's things lay strictly organised in front of her: betel leaves soaking in their tub of water; small jars of lime, katha, and betel nuts; tobacco for zarda paan; fennel seeds and other sweets for meetha paan. Her experienced hands smeared the lime paste across the betel leaves with a wooden stick; she sprinkled and spread, squeezing and folding the mixture into a neat, triangular packet: 'Here you go, one rupee!' Biscuits, cigarettes, teabags, chips and chewing gum lined the shelves behind her, two for a rupee. The cash register was a small plastic container with the lid securely fastened, never resting more than a few inches from her lightning-quick right hand.

Fauzia looked up from her work briefly and gave Tamanna a quick nod as she passed by. The paan saleswoman's eyes were always half-closed, but Tamanna was well aware that Fauzia took note of everything. In a kinship none of them would ever publicly acknowledge, Tamanna knew that the work of Fauzia's swift fingers – those moist and tempting green triangles soon to be shoved behind dark lips and chewed until the juices came gushing out, colouring the gums and the corners of the mouth unabashedly bright red – that work was what made her sit proudly upright on her throne. The knowledge that the customers approaching her were buying only the work of her hands. That when dusk fell over Prem Nagar, Fauzia could close her shop, wrap the woollen shawl around her shoulders and go home. Go to bed under the mosquito net, pull her blanket up, and contemplate the miracle that the two women shared without ever speaking about it: that the lumpy mattress she lay on belonged to no one but her, the whole night through.

But neither Tamanna nor Fauzia could go home just yet. It was still afternoon and the heat visibly vibrated in the air of the shanty town consisting of a single, dusty street. The Town of Love, on the outskirts of bustling Forbesganj, where roaring trucks thundered past day and night on their way north to the India-Nepal border. The Town of Love, where being a Nat meant calling these lopsided sheds home, carrying on a century-long caste tradition behind dirty curtains. The Town of Love, with its own life and its own law. Its own ways and its own woes.

The traffic in Prem Nagar was mostly made up of bicycles; a handlebar bell rang abruptly, startling Tamanna, who scurried to the side of the road when one of them nearly caught her sleeve. Laden heavy with jute sacks drooping to the ground on each side of the rear wheel, the cyclists ambled slowly past the houses. Some had walls of painted brick, cement finishing on the outside steps, and openings that could pass for windows; others displayed an outward respectability of red brick; but most had simple walls of interwoven mats of sticks, haphazardly reinforced with lumps of grass and straw. Tamanna stayed close to the edge of the road as she passed a group of men making small talk while they wheeled their bicycles by hand, their dark upper bodies gleaming with sweat, rags around their heads to protect against the heat, shovels or picks over their shoulders. Just like the rickshaw drivers, stoically weaving their worn two-wheelers in and out between vegetable vendors, tea stalls, the dispensary and the open-air butcher, they didn't cast a glance at the girls. Girls sitting on chairs in doorways, on covered wooden platforms, or on benches under the thatched roof, in the semi-dark entrance to what they called home. Dressed in dazzling, sequined saris, tight blouses in feisty red or elegant peacock blue, with their shining hair oiled and newly combed. Heavily made-up eyes fixed in a distant gaze, long earrings gleaming in the afternoon sun, aggressive, pink lipstick. Slouching shoulders over small, pointy breasts. The workforce of the Town of Love.

Tamanna was headed across the bridge, the cracked cement passageway that linked Prem Nagar and its inhabitants with the rest of Forbesganj. She planned to visit the big vegetable market downtown, where she would take advantage of the cheap okra, in season right now. The Town of Love had its own grocery shops and counters with plentiful tea, rice, and oil for purchase, but today Tamanna wanted to go over the bridge, to cross the putrid river that served as sewer, garbage dump, and bathwater, but more than anything acted as a border between the citizens of the Town of Love and those who would rather keep them at arm's length. The border between the Nats and those who shuddered to touch them, but who still comprised the most loyal customer base for the girls in the doorways. Tamanna plodded resolutely ahead, her wide chin jutting forward; she was in a hurry and didn't stop to say hello to anyone. The twenty rupees in her purse would cover a pound of okra and a couple of tomatoes, more than enough for just her. Tamanna forced the thought: *Just her*. She had no one else to worry about. She pushed away a shadow of a thought, a flicker of a face in darkness behind a window.

As Tamanna passed the last house on Prem Nagar's main street, something happened. Salma jumped up from the bench halfway covered in shade and planted her hands on her hips. Her slight but firm body in its yellow salwar kurta trembled in protest, her sharply painted lips quivering. The man next to her raised one hand right above her face, sparks of anger shooting from his eyes. 'You'll take Lalita to the hospital afterwards. I said *afterwards*! After the passenger is gone!'

The 'Passenger', as the customers were known in Prem Nagar, stayed in the background – the price was set, he was just waiting for the children to be ordered outside so he and Salma could make their way inside towards the lumpy mattress in the innermost corner of the house. Salma ground her teeth silently behind lips squeezed shut as she cast one last glance at the wiry old woman in the brown sari resting on her haunches, rocking slowly back and forth with her head in her hands. Softly, she touched her hair before turning to lead the passenger across the inner courtyard and further in through the house.

Tamanna pressed her palms swiftly together. 'Namaste!' she said, greeting Lalita, who was still sitting curled up against the wall, her head in her hands. Salma's mother did not budge, her brown sari coated in a grey layer of dust from the road.

The racket from the motorcycles intermingled with the rickshaw-wallahs' shouts and the blaring horns from trucks and buses, the endless background tapestry of noise in the heart of Forbesganj. The balls of jute, lifeblood of the economy in Bihar, were stacked high in teetering pyramids on the backs of unsteady, cheerfully painted trucks that gridlocked the main street day and night. Tamanna skillfully dodged the cars and wove her way through the maze of cardboard boxes, baskets covered in burlap sacks, piles of purple eggplants, bright white cauliflower, tomatoes, carrots, beans, gnarly brown ginger, fragrant green bunches of coriander. And okra. The market overflowed with the narrow, pointy 'lady fingers'; okra was in high season and Tamanna concentrated on picking the best of the produce: firm and medium-sized, not too slimy, not too dry. The squatting peddler in front of her was just about to fill the bag when a noise, a quick motion of a rustling garment, spun Tamanna around. A narrow arm with unusually light skin brushed against her own; the young woman's long braid whipped against her shoulder as she pulled away. The fine eyebrows that nearly touched at a point right above her long, straight nose – Tamanna jerked back and gasped sharply for breath. Then she saw the look, the one she was so used to getting, a haughty scowl of pity and disdain. The young woman gathered her sari around her with a quick motion and disappeared behind a tower of vegetable baskets. Tamanna tried to calm herself, taking the okra from the peddler and paying him. Repeating to herself, again and again, as she hurried back across the bridge, *It wasn't Rupa. She looked nothing like her. Nothing at all.*

Tamanna scurried down the path towards the little schoolhouse a short distance away from the other dwellings in Prem Nagar. She felt guilty about making Amina cover the end of the kindergarten shift alone; should she offer her some of the vegetables in the bag slapping against her calves? No, Tamanna decided, her friend was better off than her, she had a husband, Kasim, who even had a job, at least in theory. If he had been sober enough to drive the rickshaw around for a few hours this morning, he might come home with some money in his pocket, and just might give Amina a few rupees so she could buy her own okra.

The last of the small children were being picked up now. Tamanna nodded to a couple of the mothers in distracted greeting. Amina had already shaken out the dhurrie, folded it and placed it back on its shelf in the classroom, and was sitting with Aftaab on her lap. The two-year old kept his head hidden under the upper part of his mother's purple sari, smacking his lips and lazily drinking as Amina let her gaze roam the fields behind the schoolhouse. Flies buzzed around her face, an incessant nuisance; she waved them halfheartedly away as her eyes followed a black water buffalo waddling slowly forward, its muzzle to the ground. It stopped, lifted its mud-caked tail, and deposited a sizeable pile of dung before continuing to fill its stomach with the dusty grass. Tamanna plopped down beside her friend in the shade by the front steps, neither of them speaking as Aftaab finished nursing.

Roshan was alone inside the classroom. The soft-spoken teacher, who always wore a woollen hat pulled snugly over his ears, sat at the corner table with a stack of papers in front of him. The schoolchildren had run home for a while, firmly clutching the two slices of white bread distributed to them at lunchtime. In an hour they would be back – at least some of them – for two more hours of arithmetic or Hindi or Urdu. If there was any bread left over, Tamanna and Amina allowed themselves a slice as well, but today provisions had run out before it was the grown-ups' turn. Roshan somberly shook his head, fetching two metal cups of tea and handing them to the women. Tamanna received the cup and drank deeply, savoring the steaming liquid and its notes of ginger and cardamom, the fatty pearls of milk skimming the surface. She closed her eyes and inhaled the steam through her nose, filling her lungs with the sweetly spiced aroma, trying to ignore the stomach pangs that told her it had been far too many hours since she last ate. An expectant tingle arose on her tongue at the thought of fried okra with tomatoes and onions over steaming hot rice.

'Heena's moving in with you today?' Amina asked and set her half-asleep son upright in her lap, tucking her breast back in underneath her blouse and pulling the shawl back over her head.

Tamanna shrugged her shoulders. 'Maybe tomorrow, unless her brother changes his mind again. When he wanted to throw her out last week, he was furious that there was no food in the house; the women had only had three passengers all day. And Heena….'

She stopped helplessly. Amina gave her a nod, knowing well what Tamanna was about to say. Heena, who was almost fifty and whose powers of attraction and earning ability had long since dwindled, was the one who would suffer. She had a roof over her head as long as she was careful not to step on any toes, take less food than the others, help out around the house, and cook the meals. But she was also the first to feel the beatings if she didn't make herself scarce when the mood soured, as it had a few days ago when her brother screamed at her to *'Get out, there is no room for you here. I can't keep feeding you, you ugly old hag; no one wants you anymore. Get out, you can take care of yourself!'*

Neither Heena nor her brother were surprised when Tamanna was the one to throw her door wide open. Or, as the case may be, that it was Tamanna's door Heena came knocking on that night, with bloodied lips and her hair in a bedraggled knot. Of course, Tamanna knew what had happened; in Prem Nagar there was no such thing as privacy or secrets. Soft, worn washrags, ointment, a few leaves from the genda plant soaked in water. Eyes that were all-seeing, hands that had nursed a thousand wounds before, sewn together ripped blouses with tiny, patient stitches. 'You can live here with me,' Tamanna had said. It doesn't have to be harder than that.

The relief in Heena's eyes, the gratitude in her trembling, swollen lower lip, was answer enough.

'And her daughter?' Amina asked, looking away at once, fully knowing the answer to her own question. Tamanna didn't bother to reply, but let her thoughts linger for a few seconds on the teenage girl with the vacant, slightly cross-eyed gaze. Everyone knew that Heena's daughter was mentally disabled, a fact that hadn't stopped her uncle from putting her round, heavy body to work in the door frame. Amina didn't need to ask. As long as the girl made money she would stay where she was.

Tamanna stood up, collected the teacups, and went to rinse them at the water pump behind the school building. Squeezing the worn black handbag under her arm and pinching Aftaab's cheek, she turned to walk away. She hoped Heena would bring something with her – a blanket, a cooking pot, a box of spices or lentils. Tamanna had no idea what they would eat, knowing painfully well that no one in Prem Nagar would donate as much as a handful of rice to help her. The pigheaded Tamanna Khatoon, who thought she was different, thought she was above them. The randi, or prostitute, who considered herself too good for passengers! An exotic bird, native to Bhutan according to her own story, but a bird who refused to land properly and find her place. Why on earth should they lift a finger for her?

When Heena moved in, she would be in exactly the same situation.

Fauzia swiftly counted the money in her plastic box, removing a few of the rupee notes and slipping them into her blouse. She peered over in disdain at her eldest brother. The patriarch was reclining on a rug in the shade a few yards away, half-asleep in his usual foggy alcoholic stupor. He grunted as he turned onto his side; the blue and grey checkered lungi fell open, revealing a dark, hairy thigh. Other patriarchs sat dozing on the bench next to Fauzia's platform: lungis wrapped around their waists, dirty grey undershirts under unbuttoned collars, cigarettes drooping from trembling fingers. Young boys swarmed around them, some with amulets dangling from black woollen strings around their necks. Tiny metal boxes carrying Quranic verses for strength and protection, meticulously folded by the fingers of proud mothers.

Fauzia shut the lid on the moneybox and tucked it under her arm as she stepped down from the platform. Closed her shutters and clicked the padlock shut around the little shop that was her livelihood. She had seen no trace of her niece today, and set out towards her eldest brother's house. Without knocking Fauzia entered the first room, which was empty apart from an elevated brick bench covered by a mosquito net and a few clothes hanging from a clothesline by the wall. She ducked past a couple of large shawls at the far end of the room and emerged in the backyard. Her sister-in-law was sitting by the water pump, scrubbing her feet under the trickle of water. By her side was a cooking pot resting on glowing embers; plastic boxes full of yellow and brown lentils were stacked inside a large basket in a corner. Fauzia continued inward along the labyrinth of her brother's house, making her way through the narrow passage with a brick wall on one side and a flimsy thatched straw wall on the other. She stopped in the doorway to the innermost room, where a bed with a crumpled blanket rested against the wall. The bed was empty. No shy, long-legged eight-year old in sight, no oversized front teeth in the middle of a solemn face.

'Where's Rozy?'

She yelled over her shoulder.

'At school.'

A tiny smile flickered across Fauzia's face as she turned and went back out into the street bathed in whitish-yellow sunlight. She reopened the paan-stand with swift motions and began folding the betel leaves.

The moon shone full and round over Prem Nagar. The windows in most of the little lopsided shacks were dark; here and there an occasional light bulb burned naked and bright. In Tamanna's room the light from an oil lamp with sooty glass flickered by the bed where she rested, eyes closed, her body entirely still. She placed a hand on her satiated belly, savouring the blessed feeling of being full. Reminded herself how fortunate she was, how far she had come. She could sleep in peace, alone; no one would wake her up with demands for her body and her company. Mustn't think about what it had cost her. What she had to sacrifice. Who she had to sacrifice. The padlock securing her bedroom door at night was priceless.

2

Rupa had always known that Dolly wasn't the one. Dolly with the ugly words, the calloused hands, the frizzy grey hair peeking out from underneath her dupatta – she couldn't be Rupa's mother. This in spite of the years of calling Dolly *Amma*, as she had been taught from a young age. Deep inside she had always known that a mother was something else. Someone with gentle hands and kind eyes telling you that you meant the world to her.

Even Jabbar was afraid of his wife. Dolly was smarter than him, and he knew it. Smarter than both him and his brothers. But Jabbar was the one with the knife, the long knife with the curved black handle that he always kept close by.

The others said he had killed two girls with it. 'They tried to escape,' Rupa's friend recounted in a hushed voice, 'but someone on the street saw them and warned Jabbar. They got as far as the station in Katihar,' she embroidered the story further, 'but just before they could jump on the train' – her friend stood up for dramatic effect, one foot lunging forward – 'Jabbar came running onto the platform! He grabbed them by the arm, and no one's seen them since!' she whispered quickly, her eyes bulging wide.

Dolly said it was all nonsense. 'Stop that ridiculous talk,' she always snapped when Rupa was younger and asked where her real mother was. 'Of course I'm your mother! Jabbar is your father, you have a sister and a brother, we are your family and that's that.'

But Rupa knew. She knew it every time they slapped her while her younger siblings sat calmly watching, every time a belt or broomstick beat her skinny spine into a chain of bluish-green lumps. Jabbar was no father to her.

'Stay out of the sun; we don't want you getting too dark!' His voice echoed perpetually in the background, shouting and commandeering. 'Don't go outside! Stay in the house, go help your mother in the kitchen!'

She knew, of course she knew what kind of house she lived in. She had always known. The uncles who came and went, the women who closed the doors, drew the curtains shut. Who drew them open again after a little while with deadened eyes and stooping shoulders. But she had somehow believed she would be the exception! She was the one they trusted, the one who helped out around the house, the one who always did what they asked! When Dolly and Jabbar were out, when even old Mumtaz Begum took off to visit her sister in Forbesganj, it was Rupa they entrusted the keys with. It was she who collected the money from the girls when the passengers had all gone.

Anger flared up inside her, mixed with a gnawing sense of shame that it had taken her so long to understand the cost of it. She hadn't fully comprehended until the night she lay beside one of the older girls and heard her sobbing. Sobs of an entirely different nature than those of sibling squabbles, or fear of beatings. The sobs she had heard that night were the sobs of someone who had lost all hope.

It had to be Tamanna, she was sure of it. A desperate comprehension deep inside Rupa: *It's her. It's Tamanna, with the broad face and the slightly protruding lower lip, the golden stud in her nose shaped like a flower.* She was the one who had showed up outside when the crown of the gulmohar tree bloomed into full, golden-red maturity. The one wailing and crying for the police and finally being chased away by the policeman armed with a baton and a few extra rupees in his pocket. It had to be her.

'That crazy woman,' Dolly had said disdainfully. 'She's filthy! She's mad, something is wrong with her head. The way she screeches and hollers, you'd better not believe a word she says. All she wants is money. Don't you dare listen to her.'

But something inside Rupa knew that it was true, what the crazy woman was screaming. 'I want my daughter! Let Rupa go! Let my daughter go!'

She knew Tamanna was the one; the tone of her voice was like no other. No one else screamed as recklessly, with no concern for who might hear or what might happen. No one else could spit and screech the most terrible curse words, threats so grotesque they would border on the ridiculous had they not been deadly, dreadfully serious. Only a mother could swear by her daughter's name, her white-hot curses emanating straight from the heavens. She knew Tamanna was the one. And she hated her more every day for having left her behind. Left her behind in the blue house in Katihar, where no girl could ever hope to be an exception to the rule.

A cloud covered the afternoon sun and cast a cooling shadow over the four women surrounding the water-pump in the back courtyard. The noise from the trucks roaring to and from the Katihar railway station was reduced to a murmur here in the red light district of Kuli Pada, where the blue-painted house of Jabbar Aslam joined countless others in the same line of business. The four young women talked softly as they washed their hair, scrubbed their feet. The preparations somehow seemed less threatening when they were all together.

Sona's weeping came out of nowhere. Her sobs were quiet and clear-voiced, like the thin spurts of water from the pump just before it dies. The others tried to comfort her, tried to turn it all around. 'It'll be a boy. Just imagine it, a boy!'

Sona shook her head, her neck craned so far over Rupa could see the thin spiral of hair trailing all the way down her spine. A tiny breeze touched the women in the backyard, the wet hems of their saris hanging dark and heavy around their calves. As one of

Jabbar's brothers strode through the courtyard, all four of them unconsciously turned their backs to him as he passed by. The oldest of the women grabbed Sona by the shoulders: 'Pull yourself together, girl. You knew this was bound to happen, sooner or later.'

But Sona found no comfort in her words, her shoulders shook violently as she sobbed. The others understood her well. If only Sona had a babu! Someone to let her child bear his name, someone who paid her regular visits and kept an eye on her. Surrendering her body to him for free would have been a small price to pay, all things considered. He might even have been introduced as 'my husband', had the opportunity arisen.

But Sona had no babu. She was dark, her face bore acne scars, and her broken nose had healed in a crooked way after the blow from a passenger who was really angry with himself – bloody girl who didn't open up fast enough! Sona's only advantage was her low price. Few other girls in Jabbar's love house went for as little as fifty rupees. She had been there so long that she was now adhia, fifty/fifty, meaning Jabbar Aslam only took half of every paisa she brought in; the other half she got to keep.

'Just think of it,' the other girls said encouragingly, trying to sound bright and optimistic. 'You get to keep half. You can save for the baby! You should set up a bank account!'

For Sona's sake they all pretended to believe it. Pretended to visualise a world with roads leading out from here, bank accounts, doors that could be opened. But Sona was not so easily deceived. 'What if it's a girl?'

Her words trickled out, diluted, transparent, like water dripping slowly out from the faucet.

'If it's a girl....'

Rupa held her breath for a moment before saying what had to be said.

'Then they'll be happy. She'll be taken good care of.'

They let the words sink in. Sona's sobs were no longer reticent. They grew into a flood. *She'll be taken good care of.*

Rupa squinted as she focused her gaze on the thin spurts of water from the faucet. Soaked herself in the cascading, glittering rainbows that burst at her when the sun hit the droplets. Imagine it's a girl. A girl who would be taken such good care of she could never, ever leave.

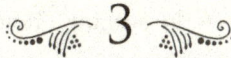

3

Heena didn't bring very much with her when she arrived at Tamanna's door – a mattress, a blanket so threadbare it was nearly transparent, a tiny metal box containing a comb and a few medications, a packet of tea, a set of extra clothes. These were the wages of thirty long years of service under her brother's roof, of thousands of men lying in the same bed, year after year. She had let it happen, staring up at the ceiling, repeating the same mantra to herself over and over: Open up, steady breathing, let him finish. Then, listening for the footsteps until they vanished, getting to her feet and heading out to the pump, filling the aluminum bowl with water, washing herself, delaying the dreaded trip out between the bushes for as long as possible.

'But look what I have brought!'

A triumphant look spread out over the tiny, wrinkled face as she lifted up a plastic bag in the tight grip of her wiry hand. Precious white flour, enough for two chapattis each. Heena smiled, flashing discoloured teeth stained by paan above a jaw line made crooked by many rounds of well-placed punches. 'Do you have any oil?'

Tamanna didn't, but decided she would ask Amina to risk giving her just a few drops. She knew her friend would be punished if Kasim got word of it, but Amina had never cowered under the threat of a beating. Tamanna called out to one of the little girls in the street, one who knew there might be a punishment waiting in school tomorrow if she didn't do as she was told. 'Can you go see if Kasim is home? If he's not there, tell Amina I need to talk to her!'

A miracle occurred and the oil appeared. Heena and Tamanna ate the humble bread and sipped their tea. Neither of them breathed a word about their daughters.

Salma came by in the early evening. Tamanna lifted her head, startled, when the young woman poked her small, obstinate face in through the gate – Prabir's women didn't usually roam the streets freely at night, and Tamanna knew that she was not in Salma's father's good graces herself. Tamanna and Heena nodded hello, and Salma took a seat in the vacant chair under the mango tree. Minutes passed; nothing was said. Salma sucked on a lump of paan with all her strength, then turned her head aside and spat, blood red, before locking eyes with Tamanna.

'Amina's got quite a beating coming her way in the morning,' she blurted out.

Tamanna turned around sharply, the tiny cup of oil that had been her friend's sacrifice glistening in yellow flashes before her eyes. 'What do you mean? What is it this time?'

Salma threw an anxious glance towards the gate. 'Her mother has come to visit.'

'Her mother? All by herself?'

Amina's parents lived a few hours' rickshaw-drive away, on the other side of the porous border with Nepal – at least most of the time; Tamanna knew that they 'travelled,' as all Nat families did. But why did a visit from Amina's mother mean that she would receive a beating?

Salma nodded. 'Mmm-hmm. She wanted to drop by, say hello, see Aftaab and the girls. But the big girls weren't there.'

She looked meaningfully into Tamanna's eyes, as if the weight of her words was crystal clear.

And Tamanna understood. Strong-willed Amina had managed to convince Kasim to let the two older daughters go away to boarding school. Eighty rupees a month for each of them paid for food, uniforms, reading and writing and a bed behind a tall double gate that was locked at night. A shield of white-painted metal, an incomparable security. Tamanna knew how much this had cost Amina, and still cost her. When Kasim had had just the right amount of tharra, homemade liquor brewed from rice husk, when he deemed his meals acceptable and Amina avoided asking for money at the wrong time, then days and even weeks could sometimes go by before he was reminded. Before he remembered how his daughters' studies were draining his income, how he was a Nat just like everyone else and damn it, his brothers didn't get stuck with wives who whined and complained just for doing the job Nat women everywhere else went along with. But when the liquor didn't set in fast enough, when the scornful words from the men on the bench by the paan-shop hit him where it hurt, when his brothers' daughters and daughters-in-law had had a lucrative day – Kasim would see red. And Amina had to pay. For the ridiculous pretension of sending her daughters to school so their heads could be filled with crazy ideas. For being nothing but trouble from the day she came into his house, a disgrace and a disaster of a wife. A complete calamity, a fury who hit back, biting and spitting. A woman who had escaped, fought back, denied him, escaped again, denied him again, and had never brought in a single rupee!

Nights like these were not good for Amina. When Kasim's anger flared up it was time for the stick. Or the belt, or whatever was closest to hand. Tamanna was confident that Amina knew how to protect herself. Her young body with its strong, angry limbs; her coarse, curly hair; her teeth still white as chalk – Amina never chewed paan – no, Kasim's wife was not afraid. But even Amina's jaw could be crushed if battered from just the right angle; even her hair could be yanked out if there were enough hands pinning her arms to the ground.

Amina has been beaten more times than any other wife in Prem Nagar, Tamanna thought to herself. She'd had to fight for her life – literally – but she had never let them sell her. A proud, pained wave of exhaustion rolled through Tamanna at the thought of her friend.

She knew Salma was right. When Amina's mother went back across the border early tomorrow morning, to avoid the scorching midday heat, Amina would need more than luck and her lion's courage to avoid a black eye and a swollen lip.

Salma jumped to her feet and opened her mouth halfway, as if to say something. Then she changed her mind, and disappeared without saying goodbye.

There was nothing she could do. Tamanna knew very well that she couldn't come anywhere near Kasim's house, it wouldn't help Amina in the slightest, might even make things worse for her. Still, an unsettled feeling pushed her out the door, out into the street that felt so different at night, without the muted hush of the yellow dust rendering everything ordinary. The nighttime street was illuminated by a cold moon, its bluish light washing the small, lopsided dwellings clean. Tamanna stood frozen still for a moment, unsure of her feelings. The Town of Love had given her a roof over her head and a door to shut behind her. But it never let her forget who she was, never let her scrub the dirt off her body. The street where she lived but didn't belong.

She turned instinctively to the left, her feet marching on autopilot towards the schoolhouse, her daily commute to work. But a sound somewhere down the street made her head snap back. A man in a light-coloured shirt ducked out from Fauzia's gate. He threw a glance at Tamanna before pulling a cigarette out of his front pocket, lighting it and vanishing along the houses, in the opposite direction. Tamanna turned away disinterested, it was only a passenger who had just visited Baby. The slender girl with heavy eyeliner renting a room from Fauzia was one of the few prostitutes in Prem Nagar not living under a patriarch's roof. But the connections were there regardless, the threads of the spiderweb: the road to Baby's door went through Prabir, Salma's father, a few houses up the street. Prabir brought in the customers, took his cut, and visited Baby once or twice a week. And Fauzia, who kept her distance and safely reigned from atop her platform, could add a few extra rupees to her meagre paan-business income. Principles were a luxury that no one in Prem Nagar could afford.

Tamanna remained standing still. If Baby had just let a passenger go, chances were that Fauzia would still be awake. Maybe she'd heard something about what was happening at Amina and Kasim's house tonight? Fauzia's paan-stand wasn't the only one in Prem Nagar, it wasn't even the biggest. But there was always a buzz, always a sense of excitement surrounding her platform, gossip exchanged and drama discussed. The queen herself never deigned to participate, never indicated that she was listening. Still, Tamanna knew that Fauzia remembered every word. If Kasim's brother's children had come by for paan after the evening meal, they might have leaked something about what was going on. Tamanna made up her mind. If anything had happened at her friend's house tonight, Fauzia would know about it.

She paused to press her ear to the gate, the thin woven frame was left ajar. She pulled back as she heard quick footsteps approach from the inside, it was Fauzia coming to lock up for the night. 'Namaste, Fauzia, sorry I'm coming by so late.'

The long face remained motionless as usual, the eyes that sized Tamanna up revealed neither surprise nor irritation. 'Namaste,' Fauzia replied.

She didn't invite Tamanna in, Fauzia was not famous for her hospitality. So Tamanna jumped straight to the point: 'I heard that Amina's mother has come to visit.'

Fauzia gave no reply, but nodded her head almost imperceptibly.

'Do you know…' Tamanna didn't usually stutter, but Fauzia's silence always caught her off guard. She pulled herself together. 'Do you know if there's been any trouble there? Have you seen Amina today?'

She saw it right away. Fauzia knew something, but had no intention of sharing. From the moment Fauzia wrinkled her long nose and took a tiny step back, narrowing the crack in the doorway even further, Tamanna knew that the next day would not be a good day for Amina.

Fauzia opened her mouth, parcelling her words out slowly. 'I haven't seen her. She must be busy, now that her mother is here.'

Tamanna walked alone through the streets of the Town of Love, passing her own house, Salma's, the intersection where the path curved off towards the school. The house belonging to Kasim and his brothers was hidden behind a grove on the right, just before the bridge across the river. A dizzying labyrinth of stairs and corridors and back rooms where everyone knew each other's whereabouts and exactly who was being punished for what. Tamanna held her breath to listen, but walked on by without stopping. A dim light in one of the windows, but not a sound. She crossed the bridge, walked all the way up to the rickshaws under the streetlight on the corner, where the street of shame met the main thoroughfare in Forbesganj. She bought herself a paan from the sweets vendor; it was not as good as Fauzia's. Sucking and nibbling it mournfully, she slowly made her way home.

4

Her first memories were of the mountains. Tamanna remembered how the colour green, the grass itself was different in Bhutan, as if the soil nourishing it were richer, more fertile somehow. And she remembered the monkeys. Chattering and squawking macaques and langurs, with their silvery-grey fur blending into faint white hoods circling their faces.

Tamanna lay flat on her back in bed, staring out into the soft darkness of night. She travelled hundreds of miles, shuttling light-years back in time. Another village, another country. Another name: *Hasina*. She inhaled deeply and let the comforting warmth of those perfect days fill her lungs. The days when they weren't travelling, when they stayed in Chhukha with her uncle's family. When her father worked in the fields and came home every night. When she could run around on the dusty roads with the others, ride an old bicycle, play.

They had to pass through seven doors to enter the gumpa. It was at the top of the mountain; the path leading there wound slowly up the hillside in a spiral. It cost them five rupees to get into the monastery. When she closed her eyes and listened closely, she could still hear her mother's voice echoing. 'This is a very ancient place. This is a place for quiet.'

She didn't want to think about it. Tamanna had packed the past away, she had long since passed the point at the end of the road where every memory starts to lose its scent and colour. *It is what it is*, she told herself firmly, squeezing her eyes shut against the images that forced their way in. But the avalanche of sorrow that poured over her tonight, thinking of Amina, had cracked her own facade as well. It had been so long since she had thought, 'if only'. She knew that it amounted to nothing. Still, it was always there, that little voice that told her everything would have been different if only she hadn't been out on the road that day.

Tamanna sat up on the thin mattress, hearing Heena tossing and turning on the other side of the flimsy wall. She was in her own house now, grown up and living in Prem Nagar. None of it mattered anymore. But the thoughts refused to listen; they wound their way back to the dark corners of her mind: *If only you hadn't been so nosy! If only you hadn't been friends with Jannati!* One of the older girls, a few years older than Hasina, who dressed up and wore makeup and seemed exciting, who took the time to pay attention to an eight-year-old. Tamanna could still remember Jannati's glittering eyes when she leaned close to her, the smile when she asked her if she wanted to come along to Bihar, 'just to see what it's like.'

I had no idea where it was, Tamanna thought wearily. Her shoulders sunk down as she succumbed to the wave of defeat and exasperation flooding over her. *How could I have known she was talking about crossing the border into another country?* The eight-year-old went straight to her father and asked if she could go, she seemed to remember a peal of laughter from his lips as he said no to the wide-eyed little girl running around in a pair of shorts and no shirt.

Did it ring a bell for him when I asked?

She whispered the question out loud into the darkness. *Should he have understood?*

But Jannati was definitely going. She had stood there calmly at the bus stop that morning, surrounded by parents and siblings and stray dogs and neighbours, the curious and the envious – she was going to Bihar, India, to work. Tamanna spotted Hasina at the blurred outer edges of the frame, her mouth open and her eyes filled with admiration, Jannati looked so beautiful! A playful breeze stirred a lock of her heavy, oiled black hair and swept it down in front of her eyes; she laughed and brushed it back behind her ear. Her white teeth gleamed in the sun, and Hasina had never seen anything as pretty as the short, pink jacket she had on.

Driver had been in the village for a few days. *I knew his face,* Tamanna realised – *did I know, even then, that he was from Bihar? Had I seen him coming out of Jannati's house? Did I know that he had talked to them, agreed on a deal?* What did an eight-year-old see, after all? How much could she have understood?

She didn't remember Driver being there when the bus arrived and Jannati was saying her goodbyes. Or, maybe he'd been there after all, in the background, in the shadow of the trees across the road, keeping a watchful eye to make sure everything went ahead as planned? But why would he be doing that? His work was done at that point, the money already in his pocket. Some of it had changed hands and found its way into another pocket at the bus stop, one belonging to the man who would handle the first leg of Jannati's one-way journey.

Tamanna was strangely puzzled that she couldn't remember what Jabbar was wearing or what he had looked like at all that day. A child's extraordinary ability to erase the atrocious, to give it different faces and new names. What she did remember, though, was his firm grip around her arm. For years afterwards, she would pull up the sleeve of her blouse and inspect her right upper arm, time after time amazed at the absence of a deep, dark scar. No five-fingered stamp, no mark of the thief. Five fingers closing in around a naked upper arm, pulling an eight-year-old girl onto the bus as it accelerated and sped away from the cluster of barefoot kids, dogs, waving relatives, and young boys running to catch a free ride a few yards down the road. The quick flex of a strong bicep, a sudden sweeping motion. In the midst of the commotion, the shouting and the laughter and the frenzy, no one noticed.

Tamanna was so cold she was trembling. She hugged the threadbare blanket closer to her with frozen-stiff fingers. *What went through my Mother's mind? Did she frantically run around searching for me; was she screaming? Did she plead and cry, or shout my name? Did she feel the roaring panic fill her head, paralyse her thoughts?* Tamanna had always pictured her in such a state, had wanted to keep framed in her mind the image of her mother running from door to door, shouting, her rubber flip-flops thudding beneath the soles of her feet. Desperately shaking her big brother by the shoulders: 'Where is Hasina? Why didn't you look after her?' Squatting by the side of the road, weeping, left alone in the dust which had long since settled, the bus already miles away.

She was wearing nothing but a pair of shorts. A pair of dark blue shorts and no shirt. The bus was teeming with people, and she sat on Jannati's lap feeling horribly shy and embarrassed about the missing shirt. 'Don't be sad,' the older girl said, Tamanna could still hear the lightness in her voice. 'Don't worry. We'll buy you a dress when we get to Siliguri.'

The prospect of a new dress, and of going to Bihar with Jannati just as she'd wanted, was enough to keep the first wave of tears at bay – and the dress was gorgeous. Yellow with puffy sleeves, white piping, and a piece of transparent material just below the collar, embroidered with tiny white flowers. Tamanna was no longer struggling against the memories; she was inside the store now, remembering Jannati and Hasina, remembering how the shopkeeper had to climb onto a plastic stool to reach the dress where it hung. Jabbar wasn't a part of that picture. Maybe because it was the very last picture it had been possible to keep him out of, Tamanna thought. The last one before he started to fill every image, every room. Like breathing in rotten, contaminated air.

The border between Bhutan and India had never been easy to cross. Nothing like the toll-gate in the middle of the street in Jogbani in Bihar which was always open, letting you believe that India glided into Nepal with no friction, and vice versa. Entry from Bhutan was much more severely restricted, or at least it had seemed that way on that particular day in Phuntsholing. Hasina had stood next to Jannati in the blazing sun; she had been thirsty and had asked Jannati for water, but the older girl hadn't listened. She had looked concerned and hadn't answered.

We must have been standing across the road when I spotted the truck, Tamanna thought. Suddenly a crystal-clear picture grew larger than life: Jannati on the verge of tears, averting her eyes from the truck driver who had been walking towards them. His shadow had come closer, growing larger and larger until it covered the two girls completely. Hasina had clutched Jannati's hand tightly, still immersed in happy thoughts of her new dress, when the moment had suddenly struck: Jannati had let go of her grip and started walking towards the truck. Her graceful, swaying gait had been slow but resolute as she headed straight for the looming vehicle.

Tamanna sobbed as she gripped the blanket tightly between her fingers, feeling the desperation spread through the chest of the little girl trying to follow a few steps behind: *Take me with you! Don't leave me behind!*

The grip around her arm, the same grip once again. She had tried to free herself, a pathetic tug against a powerful steel claw. She remembered screaming Jannati's name wildly, panicking as she watched what happened. There was no one holding Jannati's arm, no one pulling her forcefully into the truck. She had opened the door and climbed in all by herself.

I didn't know what they meant then, Tamanna thought as the nausea rolled through her, dark and heavy. The big letters across the side of the canvas tarpaulin covering the back of the pickup. Now she knew that the writing on these trucks always reads the same. *Goods Carrier.* Carrier of goods.

Until that point it had all seemed like an adventure, sort of. A new dress, an exciting road trip with a girl she looked up to, someone enveloped in an air of excitement and mystery. But now the colours had started to fade, the fumes from the trucks lined up at the border crossing had formed a repulsive film on her tongue. Hasina had looked up and peered straight into his face: his flaring nostrils, big and black and scary; his steely eyes had towered someplace way up there. She had seen her own reflection in them, the brown and gleaming mirror image of a girl in a yellow dress. A very little girl in a yellow dress.

Mayee? The word filled her head. 'Mayee!' Mother!

Suddenly an old woman had appeared, her hand large and dry, with long nails pinching Hasina's shoulder.

'Mayee! I want my mother!'

She hadn't understood the answer. It was too brief, too simple to grasp. 'You are not going back to your mother. We have bought you,' was the old woman's curt response.

Tamanna rolled out of bed, staggered towards the door, made her way outside and over to the water-pump. She grabbed onto it as she crouched down and vomited up the memories in gut-wrenching heaves.

※

The stifling heat in the classroom was unbearable. The ceiling fans were heavy with layers of dust and old grease, like giant frozen insects, their stiff legs stretched out above the heads of the twenty schoolchildren. The only audible sounds were the scratching of pencils on paper, a knee shifting slightly on the concrete floor, now and then a grunt from the two black water buffalo visible through the open door. Roshan had promised them that the fans would be working again at some point today; an electrician was shuffling across the red-hot tin roof with his cables and tools. The students were learning their multiplication tables by rote, page up and page down of 3-6-9-12-15-18 in more or less legible handwriting.

Birbal had one lazy eye, the pupil lying motionless at the outer edge of the white. He slowly swivelled his head to the right as his good left eye followed his writing hand, completed the line, and turned his buzz-cut head back to start over on the left side of the page. Roshan the teacher, sitting on a red plastic chair at the front of the room, closely followed the nine-year-old's hard work with the pencil.

'Let me see, Birbal!'

The boy pushed aside the low wooden desk, got to his feet and made his way to the front of the room. Roshan's gaunt face unfolded into a smile as he checked the notebook. 'That's very good! Now let's see if you can do the five-times table.'

Tamanna appeared in the doorway with a message. 'Birbal, you have to go home!'

The boy asked no questions, grabbing his notebook and pencil and following her outside. Amina was seated on the brown dhurrie with the kindergarten kids, throwing a stone at one of the water buffalo that had strayed too close. As she bowed her head, her hair falling across her face, you could barely see the dark purple shadow casting a shroud over one of her eyes.

Birbal began to walk down the path that led away from the school building and its single multi-purpose room that served as classroom, office, kitchen, and community centre. The path turned a corner and merged with the main road just as it reached his house, where his father stood in the doorway with rolled-out-of-bed uncombed hair, one hand shielding his eyes from the piercing sun. 'You have to look after Nila,' was all Prabir said before heading straight for the shady bench by the paan-shop and the card game waiting there. 'Your mother is going to the hospital.'

Birbal's big sister Salma wore the same yellow kurta as yesterday, but her painted lips weren't set in the usual half-pouting, vacant expression. Her eyes darted around quickly, anxiously, as she dumped the baby girl into her brother's arms. 'I'm taking mother to the hospital,' she said, turning away before Birbal had a chance to respond. She gently scooped her mother up from her half-lying position against the wall, as Lalita whimpered, hands clutched over her stomach. Prabir had already disappeared, so it was the rickshaw-wallah who helped Salma shuffle her mother onto the cracked green vinyl seat.

Technically the name was Referral Hospital, but most of the patients had found their own way there. The front of the two-storey building still had a touch of the original red paint, but mostly the grimy, grey facade showed the telltale wear and tear of rain on raw concrete: sad-looking splotches and stripes running down from the roof onto the windows, some shielded by bars, some with clothes lines stretching out to wrap around the branches of nearby trees. Rickshaws scuffled for the best parking spots in the front yard, among black goats rummaging through piles of garbage. Wiry stray dogs, their coats covered in blood-swollen ticks, lay half-dead in the heat alongside people squatting while eating their lunch, purchased on the spot from the man deep-frying samosas in the large pan on his homemade wooden cart. Salma dragged her mother along the corridor towards the bare, unmanned reception desk, past the rows of squatting people lining the walls, some clutching foil-wrapped strips of tablets or brown bottles of liquid medicine.

She began to ask the nearby patients for help, trying to keep the panic out of her voice. 'Where is the receptionist? Why isn't there anyone in charge here?'

No one offered an answer, though a few faintly shook their heads.

'My mother needs help, I have to ... Where can I find a doctor?'

She helped Lalita gingerly lean up against the wall, carefully wedging the dupatta in between the dirty concrete and her mother's head, which flopped back and forth in her fevered daze. Salma arbitrarily chose one of the doorways leading out from the reception area and hurried along the corridor. Suddenly a tiny, official-looking woman in a blue and white sari blocked her path, stern glasses resting on the bridge of her nose under the tight, grey bun in her hair. 'Where do you think you are going?'

'My mother, she's sick! You've got to help her!'

The woman took her in with one sweeping glance, from her dangling earrings to the sparkly, sequined patch on the front of her sari. Her nose instantly wrinkled up in a face that read 'Dirty Nat whore', but after a moment her sense of duty took over and she pushed the glasses further up her nose, squaring her shoulders back. 'Show me where she is!'

Salma had followed her mother through it all: the registration paperwork, the waiting in two different reception areas, the examination by the weary, soft-spoken doctor, the inevitable questions about payment. Through the X-rays, Lalita's frightened whimpers, her emaciated body exposed under probing, prodding fingers.

Stones. She comprehended the word as they showed her the X-ray images of the telltale white shadows. Salma didn't know how different body systems interacted with one another, but she did understand that these stones were not supposed to be there. The doctor avoided eye contact as he explained that the pancreas was inflamed because Lalita had developed gallstones. This was the cause of her stomach aches, and the persistent fever was due to infection in the biliary passages. He wanted to try giving Lalita medication to dissolve the stones within the body, but if that didn't work, she would need an operation. It could be done on location, but the better option would be to bring her mother to the district hospital in Katihar, three hours away, which was equipped with a blood bank, in case anything went wrong. Salma would have to arrange her own transportation since the hospital had no ambulance at its disposal, and to attempt the trip by bus or auto-rickshaw, she was told, could be 'very tough for your mother.'

Salma softly stroked her mother's head, smoothing down the limp, matted tangles of hair. She heard the doctor loud and clear: *It's a question of how much your family is willing to invest in Lalita.* Nowadays her earnings added up to barely twenty rupees a day, no one wanted to pay for a few pathetic minutes on the mattress with this broken body, this crooked, scrawny frame. She read the words in the doctor's mind. *It's up to you. I know what kind of people you are, your business is no secret to anyone. The decision is yours, I'm merely telling you the cost.*

'How much is the medication?' Salma asked, staring unflinchingly into the doctor's drained face. Turning to her mother, her voice took on a different tone. 'Amma, why don't I wash and oil your hair when we get home?'

※

Tamanna had decided to give Habib a try. The feeling of unease she had had since the day the young woman in the bazaar brushed close to her had grown stronger. It was seven months since she had last been there. Seven months since she had stood outside the wretched blue door, crying out the beloved name over and over. The sickening panic of what might happen, what might already have happened. The desperation she had become so adept at stifling simmering just below the surface. Rupa was thirteen now. Tamanna didn't have a choice. She had to give Habib a try.

Having a husband is supposed to provide some small measure of protection, isn't it? Tamanna asked herself. It had to mean something, even if she was only his second wife and would forever carry the stamp of randi, prostitute. It had been more than a year now since Habib was last seen in the Town of Love, and she hesitated before setting out on the journey across the fields, past the putrid greenish creek, and along the paved road for a few miles until she could make out the houses of Uttari Rampur in the distance. *Please, oh please let him be sober enough, please don't let him be in a bad mood.* Tamanna wasn't scared – fear was a useless, limiting emotion – but if Habib was having a bad day or if Nafiza, his first wife, was there, then making the trip would be pointless. And Rupa wasn't even Habib's daughter. If only he would just give her money for the bus fare to Katihar, a few rupees to cover food for a couple of days, or – should she allow herself to hope for a miracle? – enough to pay off a policeman or two.

Tamanna's courage began to falter as she crossed the fields, past rickety houses even more dilapidated than her own, with roofs cobbled together from torn pieces of tarpaulin held in place by logs and frayed car tyres. The odds of Habib giving her anything at all were minimal: Nafiza despised her husband's 'dirty whore' of a second wife to begin with, and disaster would ensue if she suspected that even a single paisa from Habib's pocket was going to Tamanna's bastard child, who had nothing to do with him. The money he made from running the dispensary in Uttari Rampur didn't reach very far, and most of it went to tharra. Tamanna knew where Nafiza was coming from, she would have done the same thing in her position: she would have made sure that every rupee she could get her hands on was spent on her own children.

Tamanna passed a tree that was bent low and obligingly across the dirt path, a few kids were scampering playfully up and down its trunk. 'Tamanna didi, where are you going? Hey, Tamanna didi, look at me!'

'Go home and help your mothers with the housework,' she replied automatically, a half-hearted strictness in her voice. These kids had been coming to school, they had that fragile safety net stretched out for them, at least for now. She was all too familiar with the parents' rationale, knew all too well the perfectly valid reasons not to send the Nat children to the unassuming little schoolhouse, which couldn't award them any sort of diploma or open any doors to the public school system. *The girls, what on earth should they go to school for? No need to know the alphabet to be able to show a passenger the way to the mattress. Mastering the multiplication tables isn't necessary in order to get undressed and lie down on your back.* The boys ... for them, of course, the ultimate dream was a desk job with a collared shirt and an office door to open every morning. But forget that – the ridiculous vision was dismissed with a wave of coarse laughter in a fog of cigarette smoke – *who would give any of us a job? Who would even accept a glass of water from our hands? Our boys are Nat, their job is to look after their women, that's how we do things.*

Still, Tamanna reminded herself, it hadn't all been for nothing. Didn't twenty children show up at school every day, however informal and unofficial it was? Didn't they have a teacher who kept coming to work despite the threat of violence and a salary impossible to live on? At least there were some in the Town of Love who dared to hold their heads high. Who dared to believe that karma could be improved upon, that new roads could be paved, even if it took time. Like trying to crack open a rock with your bare hands, an immobile mass of clan and caste. *We are Nat, this is our livelihood. This is what we do.*

Tamanna tried to hold on to the thought of the school. The kindergarten that at least got the little ones out of the house for a few hours at a time. Sitting on the dhurrie with her and Amina, singing a song, counting aloud the numbers from one to ten. Throwing the brown and white toy dog down in the dust over and over again – she was happy to pick it up time after time, chastising them mildly, pinching their round little cheeks. It was a hundred times better than the alternative: a sharp 'Get out now, stay outside!' before the tattered curtain was drawn shut and their mother or sister or aunt disappeared.

Twenty kids in the school, somewhere between ten and fifteen in the kindergarten. A considerable victory, Tamanna told herself and straightened up as she walked along the bumpy road, staying clear of the blaring roar of trucks and buses, the perpetually sputtering, honking rickshaws. A warm little nugget of pride in her chest quickened her steps, the faint trace of a smile travelled across her face. She, Tamanna, knew that it could be done. Living off the 3,500 rupees a month from her job at the kindergarten was an impossibility, but she made it work. She held her head high as she passed by the group of women working to widen a stretch of the dirt road – even the majdoors, the daily wage labourers with hands cracked from carrying stones and the soles of their feet tough as buffalo hide, looked down on Tamanna from Prem Nagar spitefully.

We know who you are. Go ahead, hurry past us, we wouldn't have responded even if you'd said hello.

Tamanna pulled the end of her sari tightly over her head, feeling the sweat spread at her armpits. If Habib didn't give her any money, how was she going to get to Katihar? A stubborn voice in her head flared up: she would walk there if she had to! Deep down inside her core, in Rupa's room that was painted a heavy and desperate red, the familiar sense of hopelessness knocked on the door. Why should she have any more luck this time? What could possibly convince Jabbar to let Rupa go, force Mumtaz Begum to unlock the deadlocked door and make Dolly give up her investment without a fight? Seven months since the last time she came and stood outside the accursed gate, screaming her daughter's name in heaving sobs. She knew it was Rupa's face she had seen for a split second before the shutters slammed closed, it was her unmistakable light skin she had glimpsed for just an instant.

Tamanna stopped for a moment amid the yellow dust in the road. Prayed, to every god she could think of, *Please, please say it hasn't happened yet.*

5

Sona could feel her belly growing. A little bulge of life under her sari, which she had to tie a little tighter every day now, a lump of despair just below her heart. There were no abortions in Jabbar Aslam's house; somehow he managed to make the breeding of new human capital sound like empathy and concern. 'Don't worry, we'll take care of the baby,' he told Sona.

She commanded herself not to feel, not to hope, not to get attached to the growing mass of cells inside her uterus. *Please let it be a boy. Oh please, please let it be a boy.* He might be stuck in the blue house anyway, but she could learn to cope with that. She would refuse to feel a thing when he learned how to despise, was taught how to raise his fist without a trace of shame or compassion. She would let him look down on her, let him force her and mock her and finally throw her out onto the street. *Just as long as it's not a girl.* The only thought she couldn't endure. To give birth to her silky smooth body. To clean and wash the small, pink folds of skin with deferential hands. Knowing that they'll soon be ripped apart, slit and slashed with hateful force.

Sona rocked back and forth in her chair. Once again reliving the extraordinary moment: the stirring, the kicking, the soft thumping inside her uterus. She smiled a wordless hello to her baby, carefully stroking the growing cocoon and whispering in her mind: 'Namaste.' *The light in me welcomes the light in you.*

Sona didn't know whose baby it was. It made no difference anyway. It could be anyone's. The boy wheeling the cart loaded with animal carcasses for the butcher. The taxi man who owned two auto-rickshaws. One of the soldiers from the Dinapur platoon. The policeman. The truck driver. Anyone.

Sona tried to tell herself she was lucky. She had heard stories, gruesome tales of what had happened in other blue houses. How the girls were forced to jab wooden poles and metal hooks inside themselves and flay the nascent life to shreds. Sometimes they were helped by the dais, the local midwives; some of the nurses at the hospital might also be called upon for a token fee. Or they could use medicine, as far as Sona had understood. Drinking mashed-up carrot or cottonseeds, cooked in milk and mixed with palm sugar. Injecting scum from the biskhapra plant up into themselves, or forcing open the throbbing orifice with a speculum, slathering the cervix with contraction-inducing cream. And if the foetus latched on, held on tight and refused to let go, there was always a chemical last resort. Pregnil, Mensurite, Pregno, she had heard the names over and over in whispered conversations.

Jabbar wouldn't pressure her to kill the baby, on the contrary. She would carry it to term, her body would shield and nourish it. Until the day it was ready to leave her. Until it had to emerge from its cave and meet those who sat waiting outside.

Sona cradled her belly with both hands, spreading a shield of ten spindly fingers over the tiny bump. *Please let it not be a girl.*

Deep down, Tamanna had hoped she wouldn't have to enter the village of Uttari Rampur. That she would somehow run into Habib by chance, on the road, on his bicycle, or come upon him by some kind of miracle. But miracles didn't happen to the Tamannas of the world. People like her walked the whole way on foot. Endured the beatings until the hand holding the belt dropped down after the final lash.

She walked into the village, hearing the silently slithering rumour winding its way down the main street, a gleeful murmur from house to house, 'She is here. Habib's whore is here. Just wait till Nafiza finds out, this is going to be good!' Tamanna's impassive face masked the struggle between steeliness and resignation. She had just as much of a right to walk on this street as they did; she was Indian, just like them! *Who do they think they are?* The question flared through her. *I am not Nat, I am not Tamanna! I'm Hasina, the girl who was stolen and sold to them. How dare they call me dirty?*

Of course, Habib was drunk. Standing there with bloodshot eyes behind the counter in the dirty little dispensary, his wiry frame looked ridiculously pompous against the backdrop of shelves stacked with dusty boxes and sticky glass bottles.

'Salaam!' He had no choice but to greet her formally, there were customers in the store.

'Salaam.'

She gave it a second, waiting for him to take the initiative, even though she knew it was useless. The other customers drew closer and the chatter faded away; she could practically hear them unfolding their big ears, fine-tuning their antennae.

'What do you want?'

No more politeness now. She stood up straight, this was what she had expected.

'You have to give me some money.'

No point in stalling or skirting around the issue.

'I have no money.'

So that was the one he was going for today.

'I have to go to Katihar.'

'I have no money for you to go to Katihar.'

But she had caught it. His split-second glance over her shoulder, towards the door. Tamanna turned around and the sunlight from outside transformed the figure in the doorway into a black backlit shadow; but she knew, she knew it before she turned around. Nafiza's hysterical voice shrilled through the room, 'What is she doing here?

She belongs in the whore village, not here! Get back to your whore village! Don't you dare come here and pollute our village! People like you give us a bad name! A whore's name!'

She took a menacing step forward, but Tamanna knew Nafiza would never hit her. She was substantially smaller than Tamanna – she might be strong and sinewy, but no way would she dare to physically attack the taller and heavier woman, even if she was a whore. Neither would Habib, but the fear of a beating was the furthest thing from Tamanna's mind right now. There was only the thought of Katihar, nothing else. She had to get to Katihar. Had to stand once more outside the walls with flaking blue paint, had to pound and rattle the gate she herself had been locked inside for so many years, had to scream Rupa's name. Had to never stop screaming Rupa's name.

There was nothing more she could say to Habib. Tamanna had put all her eggs in one basket; just ask for the money, nothing else. She hadn't seen him for over a year, and hadn't missed his company. Tamanna had known about Nafiza when she accepted her former passenger's marriage proposal four years ago, had known that she would be staying in Prem Nagar no matter what, that being accepted as Habib's second wife in Uttari Rampur was out of the question. Even if she had had a birth certificate, some form of proof that she, Tamanna Khatoon, wasn't born a Nat, it still would have been meaningless. The stamp of the brothel in Katihar, the ten-year-deep scar of Jabbar Aslam, could never be wiped away. So why had she said yes? Why had she agreed to give him free access for so little in return? She knew full well why. Even inside a randi there was a place for impossible dreams. A vague notion that his status from running the dispensary, despite the drinking and the cowardice, would somehow reflect onto her slightly, give something back to her in the form of ... fewer threats? She searched for the word. Protection?

That this was an utterly empty dream had become grotesquely clear on their wedding day itself. A simple civil ceremony, just to get the registration taken care of. Tamanna hadn't dressed up, knowing all too well that there was no talk of celebration or festivity. When you have no friends or relatives, and your neighbours barely tolerate your presence – that is, when they are not busy sneering disparaging words at you over the fence – you lower your sights and concentrate on just getting through the day.

The relationship between Uttari Rampur and Prem Nagar had been one of uneasy ceasefire for many years, their forced and unhappy truce merely a result of proximity: the women of Uttari Rampur walked through Prem Nagar on their way back from visits to Forbesganj, it was the easiest route home. But having to bear a catcall or a leering glance, real or imagined, from the customers cruising through Prem Nagar, alongside their sacks of beans and vegetables – that was an offence the Uttari women wouldn't stand for. And the bitter resentment often grew ominous and physical: there were countless threats, occasional fist fights, and more than one instance of arson in the Town of Love. When Habib's liaison with Tamanna moved from being spitefully but silently accepted as that of a passenger and his prostitute to a lawful union of man and wife, tempers had flared in both camps. Tensions were already running high, and a formalised relationship was something neither side wanted.

Three days, Tamanna mused as she left the dispensary and the village, heading back towards the main road. It had taken three days to have the papers laid out on the table in the town hall and to get them signed. She had travelled on foot from her house alone, past Fauzia's paan-shop, across the bridge where the Nat women did their laundry in the murky brown water. She had walked into the main street of Forbesganj, holding her head high as she passed the rickshaw stand where the wallahs' gobs of red spit landed at her feet. With steely resolve she had marched past the hotel, the restaurant, the melon vendors, without once turning over her shoulder to face the menacing mob that formed behind her, hollering insults and threats. Outside the town hall there had been the usual commotion: self-important assistants trotting in and out with stacks of paper, beggars, various food and drink vendors, people standing in endless queues for an official stamp, a signed form, a licence, a letter of permission. Habib had been there waiting next to a guard in uniform, and Tamanna had been quickly ushered along a corridor, hearing the roar of the heaving crowd that tried to follow them inside more than actually seeing it. A sharp cry had caught her ear through the teeming, deafening chaos, 'You can't marry a man from that village!' And another shrill voice, straight into her ear as she had felt a hand grabbing at her sari, 'Get out of here!' Moving through the heated throng of people pushing and shoving, she had been terrified, trying to stay close to Habib and the guard as the policemen entered the town hall corridor. In a blur of beige uniforms and batons thrashing, Tamanna had found herself pressed against the wall as Habib cried out in panic next to her, his glasses crashing to the floor.

The next thing she remembered was standing in a small storage room with two policemen. The groom had disappeared, and after a while they had quietly sneaked her out through the back door. 'Go home! Come back tomorrow, but make sure you're alone!' *Make sure you're alone?* Tamanna had certainly not invited any wedding guests, but there was nothing to do except slink home, take a long detour to enter the Town of Love from the other side, tiptoe into her house as invisibly as she could and just lie there, immovable in the dark, with an empty stomach and no marriage certificate.

She had taken the same detour back early the next morning. But the crowd was already in position; she immediately recognised the hateful faces from the day before in the mob gathering outside the town hall. The memory brought an angry sense of shame: she had turned around and walked away. Couldn't bear to face it. She had been far along the street, past the sugar stand and nearing the truck stop by the time the panting policeman caught up with her, 'Get here an hour before we open tomorrow. We'll take you in through the back door.' She hadn't even stopped while he was talking, had merely nodded as her feet continued their thankless march back over the bridge. Back to her place.

On the third attempt, she had shown up long before opening hours, when only the corn-wallah was there with his rickety wagon parked under a tree in the corner of the well-trod square. She had hid herself behind the cart, wishing she had some money to buy one of the hot, sweet-smelling cobs spiced with red masala. On the guard's signal she took a few hesitant steps towards the door, and quickened her pace when she caught sight of Habib, who was also glancing nervously over his shoulder. Three policemen had hastily led them away from the crowd that had followed him from northern Rampur, and in through the back entrance, into a room where the door was slammed and locked behind them. She still didn't know who the witnesses were; they might have been acquaintances of Habib, she had never seen them again since. The groom had signed on behalf of both parties, Tamanna had pressed her inky fingerprint on the piece of paper, and they were married.

She stood by the dusty roadside, thinking back on her wedding day. And the wedding night. The police had been expecting trouble now, and had approached it head on: Those gathered outside waiting for the happy couple were given the choice between tasting the batons and getting themselves home. Tamanna recalled the absurd moment, the blunt warning to her neighbours, 'Touch her, and you're going straight to jail!' For once, it had been her they protected. But it didn't help much: Habib and Tamanna had managed to complete their hurried return down the main street of Prem Nagar, had safely reached her door without the heckles turning violent, but their tea water hadn't even boiled before the first shouts from the pursuing town hall mob had begun to penetrate the walls, led by the men from Uttari Rampur who wanted Habib out. 'Get out of the whorehouse! Go home to your wife!'

By then an all-consuming fear had gripped her – *They'll burn down my house*, she had thought, *right now, they'll set my house on fire* – and she had begged him to leave. The only thought in her mind, *please, please let them go away. Please let them take him away and leave my house unscathed.* A wedding night spent in terror, bolt upright in a chair, with her nostrils flared, sniffing after the faintest whiff of smoke.

Tamanna had stopped walking; she was hot and thirsty and wished she had the money to stop one of the rickshaws rolling by with a canvas roof shading the back seat. Getting to Katihar today was a lost cause anyway, she should probably wait till Sunday when the kindergarten would be closed. She really couldn't afford to lose a single rupee of her monthly salary. But Rupa's name pulsed through her veins with every heartbeat. *Is it happening now? Now? Is today the day when it's too late?*

She pulled her dupatta over her head as a shield against the merciless sun and didn't immediately hear the footsteps approaching from behind. They were quicker than her own, the running footsteps of a child, slowing down just a few steps behind her. 'Didi! Namaste, didi!'

The little boy addressing her as 'elder sister' wore a plaid shirt that might once have had sleeves and buttons. He was breathing hard after sprinting to catch up with her, and handed over a small, flat, folded-over paper square. She peered down into his sweaty face, the dirt and dust melting away as he flashed her a radiant smile, 'From Habib Sir, didi.'

He turned around and took off before she had a chance to unfold the paper. Three crumpled, bluish-green, blessed hundred-rupee notes.

6

'You can't go there!'

Amina stood squarely at the end of the dusty road, hands on her hips. 'Don't you know how dirty it is? How drunk they are? They come in droves and pay as little as possible, try to push two passengers on you for the price of one. Don't go there, Baby, don't do it!'

The girl who lived in Fauzia's house shrugged her shoulders. She and a group of other girls had prepared themselves to travel to Dharam Ganj, an hour's drive away. The annual mela was in full swing at the fairgrounds, with its bright lights, the ferris wheel, the amusement park with the rusty old rides. But the main attraction had no printed admission tickets and didn't go round and round to tinny melodies. It lay in the shadows, in the background, inside the thirty or forty small thatched-roof huts where the girls sat on display all day and all night. Their clothes were a little flashier than those in the Town of Love, their eyeliner more sharply drawn, the tempo slightly more charged. This was window shopping in the truest sense of the word, before any exchange took place: Groups of leering young men took turns back and forth along the rows of huts, making several rounds before they decided, discussing loudly amongst themselves before the haggling began. Three hundred rupees? A hundred? Two hundred and fifty? The girl in the doorframe sat silently with empty eyes, listening to her owner as he negotiated the price of renting her body for a few minutes. The first customer went in, his friends' tense, sniggering laughter trailing behind him. The others waited. Seven minutes, maybe ten, before the hero re-emerged and was met by gleeful hollering from his friends, who slapped the next man on the back on his way in.

'You don't want that, Baby; you don't want to go there!'

Baby was embarrassed by Amina's outburst, which drew all eyes to her. Amina knew as well as she did that there was no arguing with Prabir once he had decided who was going to the mela! He stood at a distance now, his large hunched frame casting a shadow over the girls close by, some of whom had already climbed into the motorised rickshaws. Amina's husband Kasim was in one of the driver's seats, clearly wishing he were somewhere far away.

Amina was a lioness in the sunshine. Her red-and-black patterned dupatta had slid down around her shoulders, strands of hair slipping out of her braid and curling up above her ears. The plastic bangles on her arms jingled aggressively; she lifted her son higher up on her hip and looked around, narrowing her eyes in a challenge.

'You have a husband,' Baby said at last, uncomfortably, she had to say something. 'I need to get food on the table.'

Lightning flashed in Amina's eyes. 'Do you think *we* always have food on the table? Kasim doesn't make much, the kids often go to bed hungry.'

Prabir's eyes sneered at Kasim, who sat behind the steering wheel of the jalopy, 'You really let her talk to you that way?'

Salma stood at a distance, taking in the conversation. She herself wasn't going to the mela, someone had to attend to the passengers here in town this month, and she felt a vague sense of gratitude towards Prabir for letting her stay behind with her mother. But the outburst from the woman in the red-and-black dupatta set off a stinging pang of irritation in her: *who does Amina think she is?* Amina knew just as well as she did that the girls didn't exactly go to the mela craving excitement and adventure! Salma snapped back, 'Well, if you'd only listened to your husband, there might be food on your table too!'

An avalanche of shame and betrayal hit Salma as soon as the words tumbled from her mouth. She knew Amina had received just as many beatings as her, for refusing to do what she herself did. Lalita's pain-drawn face flashed before her eyes: *my mother*. Passenger after passenger, year after year. Food for everyone, oil and rice, the water pump finally installed behind the house. The impossibility, the inevitability of it all: her mother's hospital bills, medications, all the mouths to feed every day. Someone had to keep driving the bus, keep picking up new passengers.

Of course, she knew how Amina felt. But it was a question of filling stomachs, day after day. Fill stomachs and avoid being beaten to death. And so Salma stubbornly lifted her chin, 'You're a Nat, just like the rest of us.'

Amina whipped around, seething, 'My father is a Dhunnia! You know just as well as I do, I came here from Jogbani when I married Kasim! We don't work in the flesh trade, I've never been part of that! My children will never eat rice that's bought with flesh money! We'd rather starve!'

She fumed, spitting out the words. Kasim had drawn himself further and further back into the shade of the rickshaw roof, but this was too much. He felt Prabir's scornful look jab at him sharply, and glanced around at the surrounding group of girls going to the mela, his brothers' women among them. Kasim knew that every word said here would travel right back to his brothers, to his mother, his mother's sisters and their omniscient, omnipresent network of men: husbands, pimps, babus, sons, sons-in-law. He reluctantly climbed out of the driver's seat, walked over to Amina and slapped her in front of everyone. 'You go home now! Don't just stand here bothering the travellers!'

Salma shrunk back, the slap stung just as hard as if it had landed on her own cheek. She looked at Amina, a quarter-second's pleading glance: *I'm sorry. You're right. But we don't have your courage, the same fire behind our dreams.*

Amina's gut reaction was to hit her husband back. She had done it before, and she was strong. But the child on her hip held her back, and for once she saw her immediate future in a flash: this evening, tomorrow, few girls left in the Town of Love, little traffic. The men would be irritable, boiling points would be low. Kasim's brothers, his mother, they would all be there complaining about her: the troublemaker, the impossible rebel, the babysitter in that ridiculous school, making a fraction of what she could have earned by taking passengers. Forcing Kasim to work hard, driving another man's rickshaw for a bare-bones salary, stirring up trouble among the other women with her wild talk and her crazy ideas. Amina knew beyond doubt what lay in store tonight if she released her anger and fought back against her husband in front of the others.

She glared hatefully at Kasim. Accepted this beating, the lesser of two evils. Turned on her heel and stomped angrily over the bridge to Forbesganj, but not before firing another salvo in Baby's direction, 'Don't think they'll beat you any less over there!'

Amina put down the bag of onions on the little table by the door. Placed her son on the floor, automatically starting to peel the onions, chopping with swift motions. Aftaab made tiny babbling noises to himself, playing with the onion skin that had fallen to the floor. Amina sifted spices out of plastic boxes and poured the lentils swimming in a bowl of water into a pot. Her movements were deft and rapid, the fingers worked independently of her thoughts. Her rage still burned black in her eyes, *Does Salma really think it's easy for me? That I haven't paid a price to share my bed with no one but my husband?* Three daughters in a row before the son finally arrived. Did Salma think Amina got off easy from that? Her mother-in-law's contempt and obvious disappointment, she couldn't even produce a son! Sure, she was pretty, the girl they had bought for their son when she was eleven years old, but they hadn't seen much of a return on their investment!

Amina had lost count of how many times she ran away those first few years. How many sequined, glittery saris she ripped to shreds, how many bracelets she tore off her wrists and hurled violently to the floor. 'You have to dress up, look presentable.' Never, never! Randi – she hadn't even understood the word. That it was a curse word, something shameful, something she had heard all her life, yes. But not that it was what they expected of her. As a wife, married into the Nats' town of love in Forbesganj. She knew Tamanna's story, knew that her starting point could have been a brothel with a deadlocked door and a much larger apparatus keeping her in check. *But still, I would have fought back!* Amina thought to herself. *I would have taken all the beatings in the world!*

Kasim had already had two wives when Amina was brought from Jogbani, the border town up north. She hadn't thought much of it; the only thought in her head had been that she had to escape. Back to playtime, her sisters, running, flying kites. Her rebellion against her new life as a wife in the Town of Love had been loud and strident, with biting and spitting, wild pounding with her tiny clenched fists. They all had instructions to keep an eye on Amina; time after time she was spotted heading north along the highway, adamantly stomping forward, time after time Kasim had gone after her and dragged her home.

Amina let her hands sink onto the table; the even rhythm of the onion-chopping ceased. She hadn't seen much of her husband in the beginning; it had been his mother and sisters who had kept a watchful eye on the wildcat from Jogbani. She didn't remember being scared, exactly. It was anger that dominated the memory of those days. Anger that she hadn't been allowed outside, that they wouldn't let her go home! The senseless escape attempts blurred together in her mind, but the first time she had succeeded, remained crystal-clear: Amina had been woken up in the middle of the night; she remembered streaks of white moonlight across the face of the girl shaking her, the lower lip split open by a swollen red gash. 'I'm leaving, come with me!' Stumbling barefoot, they had slipped out of Prem Nagar in the darkness and set out through a field of jute. She remembered her exhaustion when they had sat down to rest, how the other girl had brought a piece of chapatti to share. And how she woke up, the sharp morning sun burning her eyes, and found herself alone. The older girl had vanished, but Amina had not had a moment to lose. She had made her way up to the roadside and resolutely flagged down the first rickshaw that drove by. The old rickshaw-wallah, she remembered the kindness etched into his wrinkled face, had pulled over for the bewildered girl with no shoes and no money, and had miraculously brought her back to her parents' house, pedalling for several hours up to the border with Nepal for the crazy little girl who said she wanted to go home.

Amina's gaze trailed over to her son on the floor, her hand with the chopping knife resting motionless on the table. Her parents had not been happy to see her, she knew that. Still, they had hidden her away when Kasim showed up, had managed to scrape together a few rupees somehow, bought her a year's reprieve. Twelve more months of childhood, twelve months to convince herself that it had all been a dream, a nightmare, something that had happened to somebody else. Playing with her sisters, flying the kites their father made for them, searching for firewood in the forest for hours every day, this was what was real. She had never been to Forbesganj, and she certainly didn't have a husband. So when the dark, gargantuan shadow had reappeared in the doorframe one day, she could barely comprehend who it was. One of his brothers had driven the auto-rickshaw, and Kasim had kept her upper arm in a vice-like grip the whole way back.

But the girl-wife's temper had not been subdued when she was foisted back into the mother-in-law's house: her lion's mane had bristled just as furiously; there was no way she was staying here! Neither the belt nor a shoe nor a hairbrush could shake her resolve. *I am not one of them. I will never do what they do. Never!*

Amina picked her son up off the floor absent-mindedly, hugged his restless body against hers as she thought of her two oldest girls, in blessed safety behind the boarding school's gates. Struggled against a feeling at once of empathy and anger towards her own mother – couldn't she simply have said no? The small, withered woman with dark lips and few words. What choice did she have? And her father – Amina knew it was her father who had put his foot down a few months later, when she had dragged herself back north to the border town with a broken wrist and her back one continuous blue bruise, and had appeared in her parents' doorway once again. The desperation in her mother's eyes, the dark determination in her father's as she told them everything. About the tears and the threats, the days with no food, the rage they planned to starve out of her. About the night before, when Kasim had come stumbling home demanding food and satisfaction. About her mother-in-law who had barked out an order in the kitchen and come out carrying a tray, insisting that Amina bring it up to her husband and 'obey him'. 'But I refused, Amma, I wouldn't do it. I was so mad! They're not good people, Amma!' The beating that had followed, her mother-in-law's howling rage, Kasim who had come lurching down the stairs to knock some obedience into his young wife once and for all.

Her father had sent her out of the house when Kasim showed up in Jogbani the next day, it had been her sister who retold the story for her in whispers that night: how Kasim had accused her of being a thief, impossible and useless, just another household expense with nothing to contribute. Her father, polite, but with an elder's authority, 'We know she is the property of your family now, but it pains us to see that you all beat her so horribly!'

Now Amina understood the dilemma, of course she understood. The money they had sold her for was long gone, they had no way of paying it back. But she couldn't help measuring it against the rage she summoned in the fight for her own daughters. For Kasim's daughters! How could it have been any harder for her parents to fight for her? How could any price be too high?

Amina's eyes were dry as she wearily placed her son back on the floor. The mental images she would never be able to rid herself of: her father who looked the other way when Kasim grabbed her arm, a tiny, whimpering sound from her mother. Her sisters' desperate shouts, the ice-cold thought shooting through her as she met the younger sister's gaze, *That you have to see this! You're next, soon it will be your turn*! The jaded knowledge that darkened the room, *This is how it is, I won't get any other life. Kasim is my husband, this is what lies in store for me. But dressing up, putting myself on display to be sold, I'll never do that. I'd rather be beaten to death.*

They didn't beat her to death. One day the blows came to an end and a ceasefire of sorts was established. She remembered that night well. She had turned fourteen and was spending most of her nights in her husband's bed. When he was too drunk and didn't care, when he passed out early and didn't notice, she crept outside and down the stairs. To the floor mats in the big room downstairs, the soft undulation of baby noises and women's breathing. A safe and peaceful darkness, full of whispered stories about playtime and laughter, about full bellies and loaded dinner plates.

They had hit rock bottom with her that night, the same day as today, the opening day of the mela. Both of Kasim's brothers had witnessed her kicking and screaming as he hauled her from the house towards the waiting pickup, his humbling defeat when he couldn't get her into the back of the truck. She could close her eyes and still feel his fists pummelling her, a wall of punches. The shrieking and uproar all around her, and finally her mother-in-law's cold voice, full of contempt, 'Take her inside! She'll never be worth anything to us.'

One of Kasim's nieces was pregnant and would be staying home. She had dragged Amina inside, had got her into the room and down on a mat. Had fetched some water – Amina had no idea where she had found the courage, but the woman had come back with a piece of chapatti and fed her bite by bite. Each time Amina had opened her eyes the room had grown darker and darker, quieter and quieter around her, until she had drifted off to sleep, her head pressed against the woman's warm, rounded bosom, breathing in sync with the foetus inside the darkness of the womb.

Amina shut the kitchen door tightly. If Kasim came back tonight, she'd be safe if it was late enough and his food was waiting for him. She pulled Aftaab onto her lap, feeding him slowly, her thoughts in an entirely different place.

7

Tamanna knew the trip would take all day, and it was possible she wouldn't make it back that night. She had confided in Amina, no one else, knowing her friend would cover for her at the kindergarten. True, she couldn't afford to lose a day's wages, but there was no way around it. Roshan was the one who took note of the teachers' attendance, which was closely monitored by Pukaar. The two kindergarten employees had been thoroughly trained in the rules of the workforce: only those who showed up and worked their hours would receive their allotted wages.

Pukaar – the name of the organisation said it all: a cry for help, a beacon flare. A call to action, an outstretched hand. To the women of Prem Nagar and their children. To those who believed that karma could be reversed and lives could be transformed. In the meagre early days three years ago, when Rukmini and Darya had walked from house to house in the Town of Love and doors were slammed in their faces, no one could have predicted this, Tamanna thought as she headed towards the bus station.

The two kajas, the outsider women, had become familiar faces in the Town of Love, but it had taken time. The aid organisation had its headquarters in Delhi, and had slowly and deliberately worked to get a foothold in Prem Nagar. Had taken baby steps towards trust-building and cooperation, not least through employing local staff, both men and women. *Saleem*, Tamanna thought. She couldn't quite decide whether she thought hiring Saleem had been a mistake or an inspired move on the organisation's part. The young Nat man from

Khawaspur had plenty of baggage; no one knew and understood the inner workings of the flesh trade quite like Fauzia's brother. Saleem's insider's knowledge was a huge asset for Pukaar, no doubt, Tamanna thought. Still, Prem Nagar had branded him a traitor, a heavy and inescapable burden to bear. Saleem's name on Pukaar's payroll might be both a curse and a blessing for them.

But Rukmini had been sure. 'We need Saleem,' she had said. 'He knows the system inside out, who could help us more than him?'

Pukaar's managing director was based in the capital city, a lawyer by background. After the intense initial months when she had been here in Bihar full-time, Rukmini was now constantly on the road on the organisation's behalf. In and out of Delhi, back and forth to the offices in Kolkata and Mumbai, her daily agenda always full of the struggles of the women bought and sold, a plea for assistance always on the tip of her tongue. There was a bed ready for her at all times in the tiny second-floor room above the Forbesganj office whenever she came to visit; but it was Darya, the short, energetic aid worker with the thick eyeglasses, who had the Prem Nagar dust truly ingrained in the fabric of her clothes. *She is the one who knows everything about us*, Tamanna thought as she turned the corner and entered the bus station where the massive vehicles stood revving their engines, engulfed in their own exhaust. *Darya didi, Rukmini didi*, she thought, surprised by the tears welling up within her. *You lifted me up. I won't forget it.*

The three hundred rupees in Tamanna's purse let her buy a bus ticket to Katihar with a carefree heart. She was used to going without food, and the feeling of urgency had turned her stomach into a hard knot anyway. She couldn't feel hunger this morning. She was wearing her green sari, greyish-green with tiny embroidered flowers, the closest thing to a modest, suitable outfit that she owned. But she knew that walking through the streets of Kuli Pada in Katihar, she would still feel like a randi. The dirt she could never scrub off, the stench of the past.

The bus driver was old and asked no questions. The woman beside her wore a dark purple sari; she dozed intermittently, her head softly thudding against the window. Tamanna knew she would be stuck on the clammy plastic seat for the next several hours, and she closed her eyes too, yearning for sleep. Kicked her sandals off – they were pinching her feet – and gingerly curled her aching toes. The road was pothole after pothole, and the driver carefully wove between the gaping pits, patiently putting the miles behind them one by one, rarely exceeding the pace of a slow stroll. Still, the occasional slam on the brakes jerked her awake. At one point the entire surface of the road was cracked open in a ten-foot-wide chasm, and everyone had to step off while the driver manoeuvered the dilapidated bus along the very edge of the road, ensuring safe passage.

It was the end of May and time for rabi, the first harvest. They drove past enormous fields of tall, thin jute stalks, maize and wheat, lush yellow meadows of mustard oil plants. There was plenty of traffic despite the poor upkeep of the roads, trucks roaring past with double axles in long rows under their garishly painted bodies. Weary cyclists, with rags wrapped around their heads to shield them from the burning sun, pedalled unrelentingly forward on black metal frames, bony legs jutting out from the folds of their lungis. Occasionally, overflowing piles of yellow maize were spread out on the road, laid out to dry in meticulous rectangular patches on the asphalt. The traffic veered politely aside into the oncoming lane for a moment, leaving the boy assigned to guard duty alone with his harvested riches.

As the hours went by and the bus inched closer, the knot in her stomach began to ache more and more. She tried not to think of how many times and in what condition she had travelled on these roads before. Tried to become another Tamanna, a stranger to these places. She had no wish to revisit the little girl ferried back and forth between Jabbar Aslam's relatives and acquaintances, always in secret haste, always with the feeling that something worse was still in store.

She didn't want to look out the window, but couldn't stop herself. Knew that at the next bus stop on the left a small road curved in towards Basantpur, the town that reeked of homemade liquor, where she was held for months at the age of ten. Here, where the river flooded each year, the paddy from the fields yielded plenty of husks: waste for the farmers, raw material for the Nats who produced cheap liquor from it. Tamanna remembered a bed under a window, a red blanket she had called her own.

She had got used to the name Tamanna by then, as well as to Hindi. The eight-year-old Hasina, who had been dragged onboard the bus at the outskirts of Chhukha, spoke only Nepali, but after a few months the wooden cane on her spine had made it clear that not a word should leave her mouth unless it was in Hindi. For Jabbar Aslam, as for all Nats, religion was a cape to be turned in the wind: those at the bottom of the ladder could not afford the luxury of firm convictions, with gods or with people. The neighbours would be sure to notice a strange, new little girl who said daily prayers in the blue house where everyone knew what went on.

She remembered Mumtaz Begum's hands best of all. It was Jabbar's mother who had kept the girl under close and constant scrutiny with her beady black eyes. No rod or hairbrush had been needed to keep Tamanna in check; the crooked fingers with yellowed fingernails had served as both threat and punishment. Bony, rock-hard fingers that pressed bruises into her skinny upper arms, yanked bread out of her hands, delivered lightning-quick slaps across her face. *Even now,* Tamanna thought, *twenty years and an eternity later, I still remember the feeling that followed the slap: my stinging cheek, my hand automatically flying up to my face. My throat still burns dry because I just don't understand. Standing in an unfamiliar kitchen with an old woman slapping me across the face. I didn't understand why, and I didn't want to be there.*

After a few weeks – or was it months? Tamanna wasn't sure – Mumtaz at last felt sure that the girl wouldn't try to run away, and took her out grocery shopping. The nearest little market lay just around the corner: a vegetable stand or two, oil sold in reused plastic bottles, a few dusty packets of candy and chewing gum. The butcher had been their last stop of the day and Mumtaz had pulled the girl's tiny hand hard, 'Come on now, hurry up!' The tug had made Tamanna stumble, and as her knee hit the ground she let out an instinctive cry, 'Allah!' A suspicious glare had dissolved the courteous shopkeeper's smile in the face of the large man with the meat-cleaver, 'Who is that girl with you, Mumtaz Begum?' Another tug of the hand as the old woman had hurried her along without missing a beat, 'A relative. She's just a relative.'

Many years later Tamanna found out that the butcher was not so easily fooled: What was a little girl so obviously raised in a Muslim house doing with the brothel madam? Only now did she know that he had gone to the police and reported his suspicions, only now did she realise that it had led to a raid on the blue house – what else could the chief inspector have done? But with money comes friends in high places, and Jabbar had been tipped off by one of his very best and well-positioned: the sergeant in the anteroom, who supplemented his modest policeman's salary with a monthly bonus from the blue house. And free access to soft, frightened young bodies.

She remembered the days that followed, at the Doms', with painful clarity. Jabbar had shoved a wad of rupees into the hands of the lowest-of-the-low family, whose daily bread consisted of dirt and sewage, and had ordered them to keep her hidden away, out of sight. The revolting stench that had wafted through the house, clinging to their clothes, the blankets they had piled on top of her, the kitchen reeking of filth – Tamanna couldn't remember eating a bite of food in the week she had spent there.

The bus rolled on and on, buildings appearing more frequently now in between the fields and pastures, and traffic began to accumulate. Katihar was the only town with railway access for hundreds of miles, and many of the trucks were headed for the big cargo depot below the train station. Tamanna clutched her purse in her lap and swallowed drily, wishing she had a little water or a piece of candy to suck on. She wouldn't, couldn't bear to follow little Hasina further along these roads, but this unstoppable journey of memory surged forward.

New hasty escapes, new hiding places, new aunts and uncles to house her 'for a little while.' On her dark inner voyage Tamanna stopped for a moment at a place filled with sunshine: at Mister's house, that was what she had called him. A tall, nearly bald man with kind eyes and a hand that stroked her hair quickly when no one was watching. Tamanna recalled listening to the voices of Mister and his wife coursing through the kitchen as he tried to find a way to get her home – she was sure of it, Mister was trying to get her home to Amma. 'A mistake!' She could still hear his voice, deep, insistent. 'The girl was a bad investment in the first place, her family will never stop looking for her. We should let her go – she'll never be of any use to Jabbar Aslam!' Tamanna had sat on the floor rinsing beans in a metal bowl, she remembered how she had forced her fingers to keep working: snap-pling, snap-pling, without stopping, even when the wife had hissed back furiously, 'Are you crazy? They are paying us good money to keep her! If they don't find her here when they come for her, Jabbar will kill us.'

The bus jerked over to the right to avoid hitting a man pulling a wooden cart. Had she invented it in the rosy haze of hindsight, or had they really formed an alliance, Mister and her? Had she dreamed up the stories he told, the plans the two of them made for getting her safely home? The dreams that turned out to be just that, on the day Jabbar was back on their doorstep with a message for the couple whom he had paid handsomely to hide his precious investment. 'Mother is sick, I have to take the girl to go see her at once!'

She still didn't know whether Mumtaz Begum really was ill that day, nor did she remember how she had avoided being shoved into the car – was it Mister who had sent her out the door with a whispered command to go hide, just before Jabbar's entourage arrived? Was it a secret glance between them that told her: 'Hurry, go, run off into the woods?' At least she didn't have to hear Jabbar's rage when he found out she was missing, or witness the subsequent retribution. Only much later had she found out that Mister had been beaten black and blue when his wife sobbingly revealed her husband's soft spot for the girl from Chhukha. How, pleading forgiveness for Mister's foolish sentimentality, she had promised that the girl would not be left out of her sight for a minute, day or night. Tamanna swayed with her eyes closed, the old fear shooting up inside her as her thoughts jumped to the moment a few weeks later when Jabbar stood in the doorway yet again, the familiar cold gaze down on her, the hand that never, ever released its iron grip on her arm. As always, he took her, snatched her up, shuttled her farther and farther from home.

Two years, three years, four years, running from place to place. Much later, Tamanna learned that the people looking for her had sometimes been only a day or an hour behind them, but Jabbar Aslam had always stayed one step ahead, month after month, year after year. Hasina, 'the beautiful one', had grown paler and paler and disappeared entirely. Tamanna had taken her place, speaking Hindi and, in spite of herself, had grown into the pretty young girl he had invested in. The fruit had finally become ripe for harvest.

Had she always known what was in store? Dhanda, the flesh trade, prostitution – Tamanna had never once said the word out loud to herself. She had accepted even the myth of the money tree wholesale; had sat wide-eyed and absorbed the words dripping like honey from the lips of the woman in front of her. 'Do you know what we'll do in Katihar, Tamanna? We'll plant a money tree. A golden money tree that bears fruit all year round. We'll water it and prune it; we'll look after it and make sure it thrives every day. A money tree that grows gold, Tamanna. Don't you want a share of that?'

The woman who had come with Jabbar to pick her up had glittering threads woven into her dupatta, and full, shimmering lips. Her henna-dyed fingertips were soft, with no cracks or calluses, and the strappy sandals on her feet were adorned with sparkly rhinestones. She had stretched out her hand: 'A money tree, Tamanna. In Katihar.'

A money tree, who wouldn't want to help harvest that? How could she have known that she was to be both the tree and the gardener?

But with one eye we always see what lies in shadow, with one ear we always hear the silent words that fall between sentences. So when Tamanna stood facing Mumtaz Begum's quivering jowls once more, hearing the money tree explained to her in no uncertain terms, her emotion was one of dreaded recognition, not shock and surprise. 'We are Nats. Our daughters all take passengers. That's what you'll be doing now too.'

The answer she would keep repeating to herself, year after year, found its voice: 'Never! I'll never do it!'

First, they had simply locked her in; then the beatings had started. Was there anything in the house that hadn't been used to hit her? Poles and canes, shoes and tools and chairs, belts and electric cables – once Jabbar's brother had beaten her so long and hard with a screwdriver that she stumbled and fell into a wall, knocking her shoulder out of its socket. Later, a tray of food had been shoved into the room where she had sat locked up, all alone. Tamanna remembered sitting on the floor and refusing to eat with her left hand, the dirty one – the right one hung forward at a grotesque angle, dangling limp and useless from the dislocated joint; she couldn't lift it. In tears, she had lain down on her stomach and tried to slurp the food from her plate without using her left hand. She had been beaten black and blue, but she wouldn't be dirty.

Rumours of Mumtaz Begum's new girl had spread quickly in Katihar, and the passengers had come, their pockets bulging with money. An auction offering up the right to tear a hymen apart. Time after time, they had come to fetch her from the girls' room on the second floor, had paraded her around in heavy makeup and dangling earrings. Tamanna could still hear Mumtaz Begum wheezing as she shoved her towards the crowd. 'Smile now! No one likes a sad-faced girl!'

She had never got to know her final sale price, what the highest bid had been for the body of a 12-year-old. Tamanna squeezed her eyes shut and clenched her fists, pressing them down into the yellow bus seat. Didn't want to remember, couldn't ever forget the night they let the victorious bidder into the room with her, the door slamming shut behind him. She had screamed, a loud, sharp scream, like an animal warning its enemy not to come any closer. He had tried to approach her with words at first, with assurances and persuasions. She had responded with noises, sounds of rejection, hatred, and fear. He had finally got tired of it and had pressed her into a corner, grabbing at her forcefully, roaring at her to shut up. Tamanna had grown four arms, eight, twelve, had hit back as hard as she could with all of them, screaming and kicking, her knee in his groin, biting, digging sharp fingernails into his hands with a piercing, unbroken wail.

It had been the passenger who was left with his back against the wall and a sheepish, embarrassed look on his face when Mumtaz Begum unlocked the door. Tamanna had thrown herself at the old woman and burst out into the hall before the madam had even stepped into the room, pounding her fists against another door until somebody had let her in. She needed water, needed to wash herself, right away! There were traces of his skin under her fingernails.

She had fought harder, screamed louder the next time. And the next time. Part of her had almost started to believe it: as long as she could get stronger, punch harder, grow bigger than them, it wouldn't happen. If she could keep this room as her line of defence, complete with warning screams and called-off fights, she could handle it.

But the price was raised, the stakes got higher. Tamanna struggled against the memories with her eyes closed, jumped in her seat and fumbled for her shoes when the driver turned around to ask if this was her stop. She stumbled out of the bus, planning to walk the last few steps on foot.

She had heard of Coke, but had never tasted the sticky brown drink. They had left her alone for a few days as she nursed her wounds, rubbing them with arnica cream and steely denial. When Mumtaz

Begum had brought her the glass and told her to drink up, she had taken it, tasting it slowly. Hadn't realised that everyone suddenly grew quiet, that no one else had been given anything to drink. It had tasted funny, not quite what she had expected, but what did she know? Tamanna had been thirsty and drained the glass, and soon had felt limp and drowsy, realising she couldn't walk straight when Mumtaz Begum had suddenly reappeared, leading her into the next room.

She had recognised him at once, the man standing there beside Jabbar Aslam. She'd seen him in the house before, knew he was rich, had overheard his mocking nickname, 'little grandpa'. The knife in Jabbar's hand was waving in a blur before her eyes as he lifted his arm: 'If you don't do what this man says, I'll cut your head off!'

Through the waves of dizziness, the familiar click of the door locking behind her, she had steeled herself for another battle, sharpening her claws, baring her fangs. But this time her arms had refused to obey her; she was too heavy and too slow, felt sick to her stomach. And the fear, her best ally in battle, had failed to stoke the flames and raise them high and wild inside her; instead it had paralyzed her, had frozen her into a mute, white block of ice.

It was morning when she awoke. A throbbing stillness in the room, in her head. As her eyes slowly opened, she had noted with hazy surprise that her hair lay pasted against her cheek, smeared in orange-yellow, matted clumps that smelled so bad that she had to vomit again. Shaking, she had tried to sit up as her stomach turned inside out in uncontrollable spasms. Her hands had found something soft, a piece of cloth, she had pulled it towards her and wiped her mouth and her breasts with the ripped sari as her gaze moved frantically down her naked body. Blood between her legs, dark, dried-up shame smeared along her thighs.

She hadn't shed a single tear that morning. Had accepted the defeat with dry, cold eyes. Had filed it away on the bottom shelf, buried beneath the two thoughts that would drive her every action since. Two oaths, two darkly pledged vows she had sworn to herself that morning.

One day I will get out of here.
One day I will get revenge.

Tamanna paused outside the tailor's shop in the intersection that marked the entrance to the labyrinth. Straight ahead, and you would stay on city streets, unscathed, filling your plastic bags with vegetables and oil and soap, maybe even peeking into Elegance Tailors for a quick browse, checking out a few yards of flowery or striped fabric. Turn left into the alley, and there was another life. A life of closed doors, unaired, musty rooms, mattresses with stained blankets. White talcum powder in dark armpits, red henna on fingertips, the sour smell of homemade liquor. The endless washing of genitals that never felt clean, the senseless scrubbing to remove stiffened clumps of semen in the hair around the opening that was never left alone. Five times a day, or ten, or fifteen, money changed hands, but for the women here, everything stayed the same. The same callused hands, the same desperate wheezing, the strain in the feeble grunts before they emptied themselves out. A left turn into the alley, and there you were.

The first year, it wasn't every day. Tamanna was still new and attractive, and the price stayed relatively high. She never knew how high, she never saw any money, the passengers came through Jabbar and Mumtaz. They just suddenly appeared, and owned her for a half-hour or an hour at a time. The brothels lay wall-to-wall in Kuli Pada, eventually she had discovered that the Aslam family owned and ran several of them. Girls were always moved back and forth, but Tamanna had mostly stayed in the blue house – Mumtaz Begum had kept an especially sharp eye on her.

She had remained a novelty for a while, but eventually Tamanna was told she had to help advertise her services. Another round of kicking and screaming had followed: she would never, ever go sit on the balcony voluntarily! She had refused to put on makeup, furiously wiped off the red lipstick they smudged across her mouth, kept tearing off the oversized nose rings. But drops of water slowly, slowly erode the rock as the stream runs down the mountain. The fists, the daily beatings, beatings so hard it had hurt just to sit down, ensured that she at last relented – the hours she sat out on the balcony were at least free of slaps and kicks.

A thirteen-year-old with a defiant lower lip, all alone on the balcony. Always on the balcony, not on the street, the fine print of the business was critical: A girl standing outside the house was an easy target for the police – the blatant solicitation was a crime, 'Come with us, please!' And a suitable wad of rupees would have to change hands before the girl could be released. The balcony was the perfect spot: off and above street level, a private but still fully public display. The first time they had placed Tamanna out there, she had known the battle was lost.

Tamanna was still standing on the street corner in Kuli Pada, oblivious that she was blocking the path of a man trying to get past her with his wide vegetable cart. Oh, but she had to hurry, she had come here because something in her felt desperately urgent! She made a decisive left turn and entered the first narrow alleyway as the light immediately dimmed and turned into thin, dull strips that stifled sounds and deepened shadows. Her feet found their own way, all her muscles were tensed now. How many times had she walked here? How long was it since the last time she had stood outside, watching the balcony girls disappear behind the upstairs door as she started to shout? The same cry, always. 'Rupa! Where are you, Rupa? Let her out, I want my daughter!' Mumtaz Begum's head appearing in the window, older but always the same. 'Go away, you filthy woman! You have no business here, you have no daughter here!' How many times had she stood outside the police station, crying for help, demanding they come with her down to the brothel, shouting about her rights as an Indian citizen, about the atrocities taking place under their noses, about their duty to stop this? It was not as if she had been unaware of the phone receiver being lifted as soon as she had convinced the reluctant sergeant to go with her, 'She's back again, we have to come over for a visit.' She had heard Jabbar grumble in irritation and dig out his wad of rupee notes, close the doors to the rooms, go through the ritual exchange with the policeman: 'There are no minors living here; we rent rooms to grown women who can have whatever visitors they want.'

She had stood in the doorway and screamed Rupa's name, screamed in vain, her body telling her that behind one of these doors was her daughter, the child she had had to leave behind in order to make her own escape that night. To be able to make the perilous jump into the swamp, the desperate dive that maybe, just maybe, could lead to a new life far from here.

Since then, not a minute had passed without her thinking of Rupa. The weary nineteen-year-old who jumped had a child who grew up in the opposite side of the house, a child who called Jabbar Abba and Dolly Amma. A child they had rejoiced over when Tamanna gave birth to her, a child they had celebrated and called their own. They had bought sweets and decorated the house, hired musicians and invited relatives, had showed Rupa off and praised her light skin, her big, beautiful eyes. Tamanna remembered the party well. She had sat in the corner, an incidental bystander, the fourteen-year-old mother of a life for whom she hadn't been able to fathom a future. She had been relieved of duty these past few months, had been left alone with her swelling body for several weeks. But she had been strong and healthy and they had had other uses for her, housework and laundry and other, more important duties: When the owners left the house for a few hours, it had fallen to the pregnant fourteen-year-old to keep the keys and collect the money. She, who had had no place to go, had been tasked with making sure that everyone else stayed where they were.

It was Mumtaz who had delivered the child. Tamanna had thought she had experienced all the world's pain, she couldn't fathom that her body could hurt any more. But this stretching and tearing, this pain from the inside, ceaseless, unyielding, hour after hour – this time she had really thought she would die. Had grasped old Mumtaz, as if there were relief to be found in the crooked fingers with gold rings embedded in the skin. Tamanna had wanted to get up, run away, but was shoved back into bed time after time. 'Shut your mouth, girl, this won't kill you! Lay still and let the baby come out!'

She didn't think she'd even heard the first thin cries. Had felt such relief when she realised it was over, had only dizzily registered the voices of approval, Mumtaz's pleased lip-smacking when she confirmed it was a girl. A nice, light-skinned girl with all her parts intact. A new branch on the money tree.

Tamanna had never been called Amma. But in the eight years since she ran away, this had been the desperate dream she had clung to: They had kept Rupa in their house, fed her and let her sleep in their room – they couldn't possibly be doing this to her? The eternal argument in Tamanna's head between two voices, the first holding on to a forlorn hope, the second laughing scornfully, saying *can't you see, that's just it? Their investment, keeping your daughter clean, healthy, clothed, and well fed. Did you think that was all for nothing?*

She had to hurry, had to hurry! Rupa had been five when she jumped, she was thirteen now. That she gave birth to her! That she left her behind! That she was back here now, running through the streets with her heart pounding in her throat, knowing it could be too late!

The house hadn't changed at all. The same dirty blue colour, had it once been meant to look cheerful, beautiful? Bars over the windows, gently curved as on all the other houses in town, nothing about them revealed that there were lifelong prisoners behind these windows. She nearly tripped over a flea-infested dog, its long, drooping teats dragging mournfully underneath its stomach. A cloud of flies took off in a swoosh around her feet when she carefully stepped over a blood-coloured clump on the ground; she held her breath against the stench.

Tamanna stood outside the front door, taking it all in: the pile of worn plastic sandals, the stains around the door knob, the bicycle with the seat that was just a rag draped over the springs. She knew only too well the room on the other side of the closed door: the dark hallway that opened out to the kitchen on the left, the stairs straight ahead leading to the rooms where they kept the girls. Her hands rose to pound on the door when a sound behind her froze the motion. Just one brief shout, the man in the white shirt didn't have the loudest voice. Tamanna couldn't even identify his word; it was the tone, the way he spat it out, that she recognised. She spun around with hatred in her eyes, an arsenal of poisoned arrows on her tongue. Until she saw that he wasn't yelling at her, his eyes were fixed somewhere else. Tamanna staggered two steps into the street, following his gaze up to the balcony. The balcony on the second floor, where sinless items of clothing swayed on the clothesline tied to the banister. A single chair up there, a white plastic chair in the afternoon sunlight. The girl in the chair wore a pink salwar kurta and sat with one leg folded underneath her. The dark red lips shimmered against her pale face, her hair was pulled back in a thick braid that let the sunrays catch the sparkling earrings, scattering tiny patches of pastel across her cheeks. The dupatta hanging loosely from her shoulders was thin and sheer. A slight breeze lifted it up and gently let it back down over her face, like a riddle.

It was Rupa on the balcony. She didn't move. Staring straight ahead; no life, no light in her eyes.

8

She must have screamed. Must have charged towards the man in the white shirt. A long scratch ran down the length of his cheek and he looked at her in shock before he yelled something in anger and pushed her hard, knocking her down. Tamanna staggered to her feet, her head was pounding, her body heavy with unspeakable pain. She had come too late. It was Rupa up there. Rupa for sale on the balcony. She had come too late.

Tamanna ran back into the street, screaming her daughter's name against the blind, pale sun that saw nothing, did nothing. Screamed up to the balcony and the flapping garments on the clothesline.

Suddenly her cry was lodged in her throat. She was frozen stiff, arms dangling by her sides, heaving for breath. The chair up there was empty.

Rupa walked slowly down the corridor, passing one doorway after another, some half-open, others with their flowery curtains drawn. Walked down the stairs, through the kitchen, entered the inner room where Mumtaz Begum lay sprawled on the couch. Dolly sat on a mat on the floor with a little girl beside her, braiding her hair. 'She's here,' Rupa mumbled.

'Who?'.

Dolly's head jerked upwards, like a watchful hawk's: 'Who's here?'

She released the girl's long, dark hair and stood up. Shuffled into the kitchen, gasping sharply as she peered through the window onto the street: 'Rupa, go upstairs and stay there. That crazy woman could go get the police, they could throw you in jail!'

Dolly shoved her towards the staircase and slammed open the bedroom door to wake her husband. 'Jabbar! Tamanna is here again!'

Muttering curses from the bed in the corner, her husband dragged himself into the hall, pulling a shirt over his head. 'Where is she?'

He opened the door, raising his voice, 'Get lost, you wretched hellcat! Your daughter is nowhere …'

No Tamanna there. Just a man in a white shirt across the street, his hand pressed against a bloody gash on his cheek.

Tamanna knew the way to the police station by heart. She had been here countless times, she was younger than Rupa was now when she first came running in through this door, screaming that she wanted to go home. She had been beaten by Jabbar right here in the waiting room, had wailed her complaints to officers who would beat her later on, out of sight from the station. So Tamanna didn't have high hopes for help as she charged in through the open door at the Katihar police station. It wasn't her trust in fairness and equality in the eyes of the law that made her walk straight past the man in the anteroom, who kept pecking away at his computer without lifting his gaze. It was the knowledge that all hope was gone. That was what pushed Tamanna further in through the corridors. That everything was lost and too late and in vain. She hadn't got there in time.

Chief Inspector P. Laskar was a diminutive man; he threw her a curt glance as she showed up in the doorway and barked out from under a heavy moustache, 'What is going on?'

Nothing fazed her, she wasn't afraid of anything, there was nothing to fear anymore. 'They have my daughter up for sale. She's thirteen. Jabbar Aslam. I know you know it.'

The fleeting looks between the policemen, the imperceptible shrinking, the glances deferring to the boss: who would have to deal with this annoying episode in the afternoon shift? He made it easy for them, pulling out a drawer, retrieving a manila folder. 'Let me see … Tamanna Khatoon, yes? Resident of Forbesganj? Your husband is Habib from Uttari Rampur?'

She stomped her foot, reaching the point of livid. 'Yes, yes! But you have to get Rupa out. They're holding her prisoner, selling her to men. She's a minor!'

The chief inspector slowly shuffled his papers. 'You've come here with false accusations against Jabbar Aslam before, yes? Of coercion and captivity? Why don't you bring your husband with you, shouldn't we hear what he has to say about all this?'

This was the last straw, the only card they hadn't played yet. But she couldn't give in, wouldn't give in. 'You have to come with me! Don't you see, they're holding her prisoner!'

He looked at her with weary eyes, sick and tired of this screaming, hollering mess of a woman who brought nothing but trouble. One of his deputy sergeants was assigned to the blue house and other houses like it in Kuli Pada; he didn't personally deal with these arrangements and intended to keep it that way.

'Come back tomorrow. Jabbar Aslam leases rooms to young women who pay rent, that's all. We will look into the matter, but it's too late for today. Come back tomorrow.'

He smoothed the creases in his beige shirtsleeves before turning away from her and shutting the office door behind him.

Rupa sat on the floor mat; her eyes slowly tracked a fly buzzing around the ceiling in tiny circles. Her thoughts were blank, no emotions. She felt nothing for the screaming woman on the street below, nothing but a vague uneasiness. Like something scratching the back of her throat, a stain on her shirt she could easily look away from. She had no mother, this was just unwanted background noise. Rupa lay down flat on the mat. Eyes closed, she heard Mumtaz Begum open the door. 'Don't go out on the balcony again today. Stay in here. You never know what that crazy woman might do.'

There had been no missi mehndi. Rupa had never actually seen the ritual, only heard about the 'wedding ceremony' where you were married to your future, where the streak of vermilion was painted down the parting in your hair. Where they decorated your hands and feet with intricate swirls of henna, smeared your body full of tamarind paste to bleach your skin. You would sit alone, dressed in your most beautiful sari under a wedding canopy while the other Nats surrounded you, admiring you, singing. The elder would give a speech of honour, present you with a gift of jewellery, and everyone would applaud when he finally declared you nath utrai, ready for your first man. The nathia, the large ring, would be stuck onto your nose. The age-old signal that the auction of a virgin can begin.

She could have kicked herself. How could she have been so stupid? How could she possibly think she'd get off so easy? Hadn't she always known what lay in store for her? How could she have pinned her hopes and dreams on laughable details, thinking that a gift from Jabbar meant anything? A plastic doll, a candy bar, trinkets from a day in town?

But she had believed she was the exception! That she was surrounded by a golden cloud of perfection, an inborn, invisible amulet that would forever keep her away from it all: the haggling, the money, the panting old men.

There had been no missi mehndi. One day the message simply came to her. 'We've fed you and clothed you and taken care of you, covered your expenses from the day you were born. It's time for you to start paying us back.'

Rupa would never forget Dolly's face as she uttered the words. Her small black eyes had flashed as she handed over the new clothes and instructed Rupa to bathe and oil her hair. Rupa had cried, begged, stammered to Dolly that it was her time of the month, how could she do such a thing? The woman across from her in the stained sari had sneered and shoved her out of the room: 'Good. That means it will hurt less.'

Tamanna didn't know how long she'd been sitting on the steps outside the tea shack. She cradled a teacup in her hands; had she bought it? The cup was empty, women in patterned saris hurried past, see-through plastic bags of beans and tomatoes slapping against their legs. Here, two blocks from the brothels in the alleyway mazes behind Elegance Tailors, normal life absurdly ran its course. Vegetables were bought, chapattis were made, the paan-wallahs assembled their stacks of green triangles that would be in high demand after the evening meal. Children were called inside, bottoms were spanked, school uniforms were washed in time for tomorrow.

Two blocks away, Rupa lay on a mat on the floor in a room. Wearing a very different kind of uniform.

※

Lalita was not feeling any better. Salma dutifully gave her the medication and her mother hobbled through day after day, dozing in and out of sleep most of the time. Deeba, Prabir's second wife, cooked and looked after the children. Pregnant, and far along by now, she spoke even less than usual. Surely her father would leave Deeba alone now, Salma thought to herself. Or maybe not. In any case, it was Salma and her sister who now had to compensate for their mother's earnings. Not that it had been high the last few years, but Lalita had still had a few passengers now and then, despite her missing teeth and her frail spindly body. But anything could happen now. Tamanna had taken Heena under her wing, but Salma had no intention of putting Lalita on her doorstep like a beggar. Tamanna Khatoon always expected something in return, demanded a kind of courage Salma knew she herself couldn't afford to have. She had no idea whether Prabir would give her money for her mother's next round of medications. Right now she needed to block out all thoughts beyond putting up her hair, hanging the glittering chain around her neck. Plumping up her lips, redder and juicier than ever. Needed to sit straight-backed on her chair in the doorframe, averting her eyes to hide her contempt when the passenger approached.

She wished her little brother could go to a real school. Birbal was a smart boy, Roshan and the others all said it. Salma had told her father, 'What if Birbal could graduate and get a job in Forbesganj? Or maybe in Katihar, or even farther away? He could sit behind an office desk somewhere and get a salary every month!'

Prabir had simply looked at her and scoffed; she couldn't believe he had even bothered to answer. 'Have you forgotten where he comes from? Do you really think anyone would hire a Nat from Prem Nagar, even if he travelled a thousand miles from home?'

Her father had turned his back and added over his shoulder, 'And why should he anyway? He has you and your sister, doesn't he?'

She had said nothing in reply, there was nothing to say. Why should Birbal work, with two older sisters as breadwinners? She had merely nodded. Yes, of course he had his sisters.

And Nila, she had thought to herself. Deeba's youngest child, Salma knew what awaited the plump, healthy baby. Nila, who would be allowed to share her mother's bed for a few more years still. Salma had never touched anything so exquisite, never allowed herself to love something as glowingly content and perfect as little Nila. Her beautiful baby half-sister, or stepsister – in the Town of Love it didn't much matter what she called her. Nila was hers just as much as she was Deeba's. Cranky, unpredictable Salma, with her tart remarks, would sometimes introduce the warm body in her lap as 'my daughter' to an unfamiliar passenger walking by. She was just as fit and unfit as Deeba to offer Nila any protection. Just as helplessly vulnerable to everything that could happen to her. Everything that most certainly would happen to her.

Fauzia looked Saleem straight in the eye. Could she really believe what her brother was saying? A house? A real house, up in town? Was she really going to cross the bridge with her trunks and bags; pile her mattress, her blankets, the black pots and pans, in the back of a rented pickup, cross the bridge, leave Prem Nagar and never come back? Close down the glass counter with the assortment of paans, get up and walk away without as much as looking over her shoulder?

Her long face with the perpetual half-sardonic expression bore a strange, feverish glow; her gaze fixed on her brother.

'A house, Saleem? For you and me?'

Oh – but what if he was thinking of getting married? It didn't matter, she made up her mind before even completing the thought. She'd be more than happy to keep house for him and a sister-in-law, and for the children she'd never had herself. In Saleem's house there would never be passengers – the thought spread like sunlight in a clearing, among other hopeful rays that peeked through the dark woods one by one. A house, a door, a neighbourhood, a garden? Oh, what if they could have a garden!

The pictures in her head flickered back, far back to the little shed in Khawaspur. Her and her sister, the three brothers, the sick father with the perennial cough, the mother who brewed homemade liquor and sold it to keep them alive. Had she ever imagined there could be another way? A real house in a real neighbourhood? A man, a brother, coming home with daily wages, giving her money to buy the groceries and run the house? Did she dare imagine it now?

Fauzia had come so far. The mattress in the inner room had yielded two hundred rupees, a hundred rupees, fifty rupees each time she had lain down on it. Had provided for her father's medication and food to fill the belly. She had come from Khawaspur to Forbesganj and the Town of Love, had gone from being an enticing prey for lustful passengers to a successful merchant with her juicy paans – an upheaval more groundbreaking than any earthquake. She had Saleem to thank for that, too; it had always been the two of them. They had taken responsibility, each in their own way. As for the brothers who had taken over the liquor business, what else was there for them to do? And then there was Basanti, the little sister Fauzia didn't think about. She didn't know, and had no wish to imagine, where Basanti was. She couldn't go there. She had already come so far.

'A house, Saleem? A house across the bridge? A house for you and me to live in?'

Her brother looked at her solemnly.

'I've been thinking about this for a while. You should get out, it's not safe for you here.'

Fauzia felt a weary smile spread across her face. Her little brother. She'd lived here much longer than him. Seen passengers she wouldn't breathe a word about, received beatings she would never share with him. But it had been his money that had rescued her from the adhia, had bought her the little paan enterprise. She knew she owed him everything. Knew she would give her life for him in a heartbeat.

'Saleem bhaiya,' Fauzia said, at once maternal and keeping a respectful distance. 'It would be a great honour to move into a house with you.'

Saleem saw right away that something was wrong with Tamanna. He had just crossed the bridge and was on his way home to the bed that wasn't really a bed, just a plastic-wrapped bundle of sheets stashed behind some boxes in the office, to be draped over the couch at night. He could have spent the night at his sister's, but Saleem knew he had enemies in the Town of Love. His brothers couldn't protect him from this kind of rancour, and not just because their alcoholic daze made them rather ineffective helpers; the loyalties they were navigating, were many and conflicting. Better to sleep on the threadbare couch in the Pukaar office; everyone knew he used it as a bed, but no one spoke of it. It was easier that way.

Saleem had just crossed the bridge and was heading for the rickshaw-stop lights when she appeared, staggering towards him unsteadily, like a drunkard. Her face was lit up by the dangling bulb over the corner kiosk, something in her features was broken.

'Tamanna didi, what's wrong?'

The nausea, a brownish green lump wedged deep inside her, the words she couldn't find. Rupa on the balcony, her dark red lips. The swamp she had jumped into, the child she had left behind. Past and future in a blind, thundering maelstrom of impossibility.

'Rupa.'

He couldn't recognise the voice rasping out the breathless words. 'It's too late.'

Saleem grabbed her arm, not knowing where to lead the delirious shell of a woman. They stood still in the middle of the road until a pickup truck came roaring past, honking them off to the side with angry blares.

'Come on,' he said at last and pulled her back with him over the bridge.

He knew he shouldn't be seen here, not now. Not outside Tamanna's door late at night, her key in hand, jiggling the padlock. Heena had been gone for days; if she were here, he could have left Tamanna with her. For him to bring Tamanna home was a risk to both of them. But there was no other way. He could have brought her to Fauzia, or to Amina's house – no wait, Kasim was at home, it wouldn't have worked. But the bond between him and Tamanna was one of a kind, they both were and weren't Nat. She had spent years trying to fit in here, not wanting to be like them for a second. He was one of them and wanted to be, but had decided to change what it meant.

Tamanna lay on the bed, senseless with grief. He stood by her side and dragged it out of her, the meaningless words, the broken sentences. Finally, he saw enough to put the pieces together, a picture blurry around the edges and murkier still in the centre, where Rupa sat on her chair.

A long silence ensued. He hoped she wouldn't say what had to be said so that he wouldn't have to tell her what had to be told. At last, she did say the words.

'Pukaar.'

Her voice was still hoarse, a thin fracture in the darkness.

'Pukaar has to help. You have to get Rupa out. I want Jabbar Aslam in jail. Mumtaz Begum and Dolly, too.'

His turn.

'It won't be easy, Tamanna didi. You know that.'

There was no need to mention the spider's web, they both knew it all too well. In the centre: Jabbar Aslam, waiting and ready. In the corners, up against the ceiling, the three old crones: Mumtaz Begum, mother of Jabbar; Saleem's mother, nothing but a faded memory. And Kasim's mother, Amina's mother-in-law. Three sisters. Three times Nat. *This is our business. This is what we do.*

She hoped there would be biryani in the cardboard boxes. The spicy aroma wafted enticingly over from the stacks in the corner, little containers stained with greasy patches where the yellow sauce had seeped through. Basanti sat on the floor near the back of the room with her legs crossed; she gathered the sheer folds of her chocolate brown sari over her shoulder. She was exhausted. There had been little time for sleep last night, the last passenger had slipped out through the curtain at around three in the morning. She glanced around, nodding at some of the familiar faces nearby. There was no hint of glamour in the prostitutes congregating in the multi-purpose room of the Pukaar shelter in Kolkata this afternoon, only heavy, dejected bodies, hair in dishevelled buns, drooping bellies, rubber sandals and shapeless T-shirts. Basanti went to these gatherings every Thursday, although they were mostly meant for the mothers whose children slept at the shelter, because there was always food. Sometimes other things were handed out too, clean sheets or toiletries.

They always began at two o'clock sharp, but a half-hour later there were still footsteps scuttling up the stairs, bodies gliding in quietly and sinking down along the walls. Manjira was speaking, Basanti liked her. The stern face with glasses perched on her nose was oddly lopsided thanks to the sizeable lump of paan she always kept lodged inside her cheek, but that didn't stop her incessant stream of words. She had launched into an explanation of the organisation's newest initiative for the girls:

'We all agree that safety is our first priority. When your girls spend the night here at the shelter, they're safe behind locked doors, watched by trustworthy adults. During the day they go to school, and they come here for meals and help with their homework. In many ways they've already come so far, they've taken the first steps out of the life that none of you want them to be stuck in.'

Manjira broke off for a moment, trying to catch her audience's eye, making sure she had their attention before she continued.

'But you know just as well as I do, it's not enough.'

She spoke slowly now, choosing each word carefully.

'Your kids, both sons and daughters, they've seen far too much violence – haven't they?'

A slight pause brought a few nodding heads in the front row.

'They've seen their sisters and mothers and friends and neighbours get all dressed up and stand on display in the doorways; they've seen the pimps and the passengers; they've seen the violence and the beatings you've had to endure.'

More nodding heads.

'It's frightening and traumatising; it breeds bitterness, it creates powerlessness and despair. That's why we have therapists, counsellors who are here to talk with your girls and help them process the experiences they've had.'

No one said anything. They had been over this before, and many of the mothers had witnessed changes in their kids, heard them articulate the things they had been through, express their anger in words and pictures. That was Manjira's next point. 'Look at this, for example.'

She pointed at the wall, to a drawing in green marker where a group of stick figures stood stiffly assembled in a row, their genitals the most prominent part of the picture.

'We think this kind of therapy is important, we believe it has an effect.'

Basanti was only half-listening, distracted by the aroma from the cardboard boxes in the corner. She hadn't had anything to eat since yesterday morning. But her focus snapped back when Manjira continued.

'And that's why we now plan to begin using dance as an added form of therapy.'

The word sparked a shift in the crowd. Glazed eyes blinked attentively, stooped shoulders were squared back, sluggish folded hands tensed up in their laps. Dance! A glimpse of something forgotten, music, movements the body once made from pure joy. Releasing yourself in lighthearted pleasure, in something with no demands, no strains on your body.

In other faces: other reactions, other associations. Tightening corners of the mouth, a shadow of disgust wrinkled across the nose. Recalling something they had seen, maybe been part of, and had no wish to return to.

Manjira lifted her arms defensively, pre-emptively shielding herself from the storm.

'Of course, this is just an offer. *You're* the mothers, *you* decide if you want your daughters to take part. It won't affect their schoolwork – only those who keep their grades up will be allowed to participate.'

A small woman with a skeptical face was the first to raise her hand:

'Who will get to watch them dance?'

Manjira was unflappable, she knew exactly where the question was coming from. Laxmi used to be a dancing girl in one of Mumbai's infamous dance bars. No doubt better than the life she lived today, but to her it had been a gateway leading straight to the little room with the flowered curtain and the endless series of fifty-rupee intercourses that made up her current existence. A few years ago, when the authorities had shut down Mumbai's dance bars by the dozen and Laxmi had found herself desperately searching for her next meal, she had been offered the amazing chance to go to Kolkata, 'where the rules are different and the dance bars are still open'. There might be dance bars here somewhere, but Laxmi had never set foot in one. The job she had been promised did not exist, had been replaced with the abrupt offer of a forty-square foot room with a bed shoved in the corner and a loyal customer base. And her daughter needed food – what else could she have done? Laxmi wouldn't be the first to sign her daughter up for dance therapy, the memories were too fresh, too many, too muddled and bewildering. Even Manjira's answer didn't lower her guard, 'No one will be watching your girls dance, they'll be dancing for themselves, away from prying eyes and clawing fingers.'

Manjira looked at Laxmi entreatingly, but no. Laxmi was deeply and eternally grateful for the shelter, she would gladly get down on her knees and sing praises to the organisation that paid her little girl's tuition and gave her one hot meal a day. She fully understood what Manjira meant when it came to processing painful memories, she was sorely aware that her daughter could remember. The times when there had been no one around to look after the girl and a passenger arrived, the street was too dangerous, and she had been forced into the last resort. Shoving her daughter underneath the bed with an urgent whisper, 'Be quiet now! Don't move! Go to sleep!'

But dance? The hands, the eyes, the cash thrown after her like gobs of spit. She wanted her daughter to stay in school, become a teacher – Laxmi could barely admit to herself all the big dreams she had for her six-year-old with the pigtails and missing front teeth. If her daughter ever needed to learn how to dance, Laxmi would teach her herself.

Basanti's thoughts were somewhere far away. She was oblivious to the voices of Manjira and the others who joined the discussion, she had even forgotten the delicious scent of the biryani. The smell that filled her nostrils now was raw, acrid, and yet somehow calming. The smell of burning cow dung, gathered by her and Fauzia and dried in long rows of splotches along the outer walls of the house in Khawaspur. The dried cowpats burning in the brick oven – as a little girl she had always thought of it as bringing home a piece of the solid, warm cows, their hefty bodies bulging with fatty, yellowish milk. At the edge of the comforting smell of dung: another, sickly sweet, simmering odour. The black, cylindrical contraption on top of a wobbly stack of bricks behind the house, the shiny metal containers, the pipes, the liquid dripping into small buckets, the firewood piled high next to the still. They had always been told to stay away, it was dangerous, precious drops would go to waste should something be knocked over by accident. The men who'd come and go, sometimes they would send children carrying dirty rupee-notes; the plastic bags full of clear liquid changing hands.

But behind the smells, behind the bubbling and clattering noises in the backyard, she heard her grandmother. Her creaking voice, gnarled after a lifetime of shouting and weeping, yelling and singing, the night she had told her who she, Basanti, really was. Had spun her life story like a thread trailing out through her son's miserable coughing fits on the mattress by the oven, the shuffling steps of daughters and daughters-in-law behind the curtain, out and up above the heads of sons-in-law and grandsons weighed down by alcoholism and apathy.

'People call us dirty. You'll hear it your whole life, trust me – dirty, whores, criminals. That being Nat is something to be ashamed of, that we're not even a real caste. People won't let you into their homes, they'll refuse to drink from cups that have touched your lips, they won't let their children come near you. Ignore them. They have no idea who you are. The ones who are teachers, priests, or potters – have they ever danced for kings and princes? Have they performed for the emperor in all his splendour, dazzling him with their breathtaking acrobatic skills? Have they walked the tightrope high above the ground and been admired for their bold jumps and fearless leaps? Have they made generals and rulers roar with laughter at their clowning tricks, made them clap their hands in sheer delight? That's who we are, Basanti! Those were the ancestors you can be proud of! Did you know that 'Nat' comes from natak, Basanti? In Rajasthan, it's the word for the nimblest acrobat, the one who jumps the farthest and climbs the highest. The one who stands at the top of the pyramid with his head held high and his arms in the air!'

She had let herself be swept away, taking her grandmother's hand and gliding down the roads of fantasy from place to place, town to town, through past years and generations. Dancing with the other girls until her hair puffed out like a cloud around her head, gasping enthralled from the sidelines while the young men performed death-defying acrobatics on the tightrope, somersaulted on platforms high up in the air, balanced on top of human pyramids many times her height. Watching the old men repair pots and pans and kitchen tools, bartering food for special herbs and other secrets the old women knew well. She had closed her eyes, inhaled the pungent air of cow dung fuel, and wished she could have been born a hundred years ago.

There had never been any question of going to school. Not for her and Fauzia, that was a given, but not even for her brothers had the possibility ever been mentioned. Her grandmother's proud fairy tales – no matter how badly she had wanted to believe in them, live in them – had been worlds away from the dirty little shack in Khawaspur, the homemade liquor, the passengers visiting her mother and her aunts behind the innermost curtain, passengers her older sister eventually had taken over. The court jesters' singing, the acrobatic flights of fancy, she had found a place within herself for the history she knew she had inherited, but had never had a chance to live. Had repeated it as a silent mantra whenever she had been confronted by scorn and derision: 'Thieves! Whores! Criminals!' Had stepped into that sanctum, closed her eyes, and taken her grandmother's hand.

Basanti turned back towards the narrow room where too many people were sharing far too little air. If she had had a daughter, she would have let her dance. But the meeting had moved on to the next item of business, a reminder of the shelter rules. The girls were only allowed to visit their mothers every Sunday, mothers could come visit every Thursday. 'There's just not enough room,' Manjira apologised, gesturing to indicate the obvious lack of space. These two rooms furnished thirty-five girls with a place to sleep, eat, and do their homework; there was simply not enough space for mothers to come and spend their days hanging around, no matter how much they might need a break or a place to catch a few hours of sleep.

'In Mumbai we run a centre for the mothers,' the fiery speaker continued, 'and we hope to build something similar here in Kolkata soon. But we need funding; it's expensive to rent a house, to set up electricity and running water, make sure there is food and security.'

The women met each other's eyes throughout the room. It always boiled down to money. To having enough for at least one meal a day, rice and vegetables, some egg or fish on a good day, or if a passenger happened to leave a few extra rupees as a tip.

Manjira adjusted the paan with the sharp, red tip of her tongue and launched into her next chapter about the centre in Mumbai. 'For the girls, it's the same as here: we give them opportunities to learn some skills, show them ways to make a living: embroidery and sewing, basic computer training …'

A stocky woman with vivid red henna streaks in her hair interrupted, 'How about the boys? Our sons need to learn too!'

Manjira hurried to add, 'Yes, yes, we have classes for the boys too, carpentry, locksmithing, bricklaying – wait, isn't your son already training to be a carpenter here?'

The henna-red head nodded contentedly, she had made her point. But Manjira wasn't finished. 'We have many plans, we just need the financial backing to get started! We'd like to have a teacher here once a week to give lessons in basic arithmetic – so you can manage your own money without getting swindled.'

The room nodded in assent, this would obviously be useful. But the woman with the henna-red hair had more to get off her chest:

'We need a place to sleep!'

Manjira's mouth remained open, the blood-red tongue facing the crowd for a moment. For once, she did not have an answer prepared. More than anything, what the tired, exasperated women needed was a place to get a few hours of uninterrupted sleep. Manjira knew that many of them didn't even own their room all day. They rented it for eight out of twenty-four hours, and lived the rest of the time on the street. In those eight hours, they were expected to see passengers, look after their children, bathe and do laundry, cook and eat their food – and sleep. For the other sixteen, they were stuck in the streets, sitting on sidewalks, snoozing against a house wall. They had no place to go. What they needed more than anything was a safe place to get some sleep.

'I know', she said at last. 'I know it's not easy for you to get the rest you need.'

Then she pulled herself together and launched into a well-known rehearsal of the HIV/AIDS information speech, noticing the quickly waning attention as the group's focus honed in on the aromatic cardboard boxes in the corner. 'We are continuing the campaign for condom use …'

The only reaction to this was a few disheartened shrugs. What use was that? Their purses and pockets were bursting with free condoms, but having the power to make the passengers put them on was another story. 'If he says no, that's fifty or hundred rupees out the window, who can afford that?' the henna-red head asked bitterly.

At last, it was time to hand out the clean sheets, and today there was a bar of soap for each of them as well. Basanti knew that if she was going to ask about the dancing, now was the time.

'Manjira didi …'

Exasperated sighs from those who had already stood up halfway, stiff-limbed after sitting cross-legged on the floor. Blood rushed to Basanti's head, she was sorry she had spoken up.

'The dancing you were talking about, is it … will it be every week?'

She rattled her question off quickly, it wasn't what she had meant to say, but her courage failed her. She had meant, *is it just for the kids, for our daughters, or can we come and dance, too?*

Can I come too? was the question reverberating inside her. Transported from her grandmother's fairy tales by the fireside in Khawaspur, through unbearable days and evenings with passengers.

Through all the years without a trace of a tune or a dance step in her life. The girl who had danced for princes and emperors; the leaping, singing Nat girl who climbed to the top of the human pyramid and laughed in their faces, a big, brash belly laugh – that was who Basanti wanted to find. That was who she wanted to dance her way back to.

She barely registered Manjira's reply. 'Yes ... we'll see how many people sign up the first time around, and we'll figure it out from there ...'

The rest was drowned out by rustling dupattas and footsteps scurrying across the floor, cardboard boxes torn open by eager fingers, the scent of brownish yellow biryani-sauce with rice, meat and potatoes saturating the room.

The girls from Prem Nagar did their best to keep in touch at the mela. Tried to keep an eye out for each other, bringing each other food, dropping by to check up if one of them hadn't been seen for a while. It was almost a week since the mela began, the weekend was fast approaching and Baby and the others expected an influx of passengers in the coming days. Prabir had made several trips to Forbesganj and back that week, he had other things to look after there, but tonight he had settled down good and drunk in a daru ka adda, liquor shop, playing a game of cards. Maybe he would find himself a girl tonight, or maybe he would head over to Baby's to get it for free. He planned to sleep there in any case. But the night was still young, the cards in his hand felt lucky and he threw down a higher bet. More tharra!

Baby had made a new friend. It had started the very first night, when the other girl had jumped in to save her. Prabir had rented her a room, she had set herself up and got started, and Prabir had just left when the man had showed up. Drunk and even more foul-mouthed than most. Baby preferred the ones who paid up front, finished quickly, talked as little as possible, and left. This one had been different; it was as if he got a thrill from bombarding her with the dirtiest insults he could think of. She had sat there quietly for a long time, not looking him in the eye, wishing he would just pay the money, do his business, and disappear. An hour had gone by, an hour and a half, he had drunk some more and sworn up a storm. She had watched the girls around her taking in two or three passengers while she was still sitting with him; this wasn't making her any money. So she had inched closer, told him that he could touch her if he wanted, or did he want her to touch him? She had been pushed back by a cascade of curse words and had felt the panic begin to stir. Prabir expected a profit, he wouldn't be sympathetic when he heard that she had spent the whole night patiently listening to this idiot mouth off.

'Maybe you'd like to come back tomorrow instead?'

She had barely finished her question before the red-hot slap singed her cheek.

Baby had leapt to her feet with a shout, but he towered above her, fingers clutching her throat.

'You shut up, I'm not paying to hear you talk!'

Crimson waves had rushed through her head, flickering dots dancing before her eyes as she had tugged at his hands frantically. 'Let go!'

He had let go, but only for a moment. She had managed a desperate gasp of air before he grabbed her arm and brutally forced it behind her back. She had bent forward, wanting to scream, but his hand had clamped down over her mouth as he hissed, 'Quiet, slut!'

Trembling, Baby had tried to breathe, sucking in air between the fingers that were squeezed over her lips. 'Oh, I'll touch you all right, when *I* feel like it!'

She had known she was in serious trouble. Baby had sometimes had five, even ten passengers a day in the room in Fauzia's house, but they had never acted like this. She didn't know everyone who cruised through the streets of the Town of Love, but she was sure no one had ever behaved this way. The walls in Prem Nagar were too thin, the houses too close together, the networks too close-knit. Despite having no babu, no husband, no brother or father, there was always someone she could call for help if she needed it.

And suddenly she had needed it. Baby had desperately needed help, and wildly struggling, she had twisted her head away and bit him as hard as she could in the fat part of his palm, screaming as she let go. Screaming at the top of her lungs, no words, not a *Help!* or a *Come quick!* just a shrill, savage scream that had stunned him instantly. He had cursed aloud and torn his hand away for a moment before slapping her hard across the mouth. A sharp jolt of pain as her lip split open, she had taken a few steps back, stumbling out through the curtain. Had heard a shout, a voice from the room a few yards away, '*Behen*, sister – what's the matter?'

Baby had run over to her instinctively, feeling the other woman's hand on her arm.

'You're bleeding! Come here, let me take a look at you!'

The thought had flashed through Baby's head, 'Did I leave behind anything he could steal? Destroy?' But all the little shack had contained was a bag with a change of clothes, some makeup and a pair of sandals. She had earned a few hundred rupees earlier that night, but they were tucked away in her blouse; she never kept her money far out of reach. So she had followed the other woman, pausing a moment under the dangling lights festooned between thin wooden poles alongside the road, so they could examine her lip. Cautiously, she had nudged each of her front teeth with her tongue, no, none of them felt loose. Had forced a careful smile without too much pain: 'Thanks, I'm okay. What's your name, didi?'

'Jannati.'

'Where are you from, Jannati?'

'That's a long story. Now, first, let's see what we can do about your mouth.'

Jannati had fetched water and gently tended to the split lower lip. Had kept an eye on Baby's room until they had seen the passenger slip out and walk away in the opposite direction.

Baby had done pretty well for herself the first week, and so had the other girls. Prabir was happy. He had been back in Prem Nagar yesterday and checked with Salma, who had claimed there was barely a passenger to be seen in the Town of Love. It might be true; the mela in Dharam Ganj had new, exotic girls, and it was not that far away. He suspected that Salma was spending too much time on Lalita and not enough on passengers; he had asked the other women to keep an eye on her. So Baby was the one to bring in the profit this month. Prabir had also brought one of the neighbour's girls along, the one with the deformed foot that you didn't notice when she was sitting down. The girls in Kasim's brothers' house were also in his charge, and Heena's daughter, who still lived with her uncle. Prabir made the rounds several times a day, collecting the money, one meal a day was plenty for the girls. He finished his drink, staggered to his feet; Baby would have to do for tonight, he needed to get some sleep.

Prabir left the adda, sauntering past the merry-go-rounds, the horses and mythical animals, no longer moving now that the families had gone home. The circus tent nearby was a sad, drooping tarpaulin with greyish flaps, the music had stopped, the clowns had washed off their makeup. He turned in the direction of the row of grey sheds, lit with strings of red, yellow and green lights. It had rained this afternoon, the smells were stronger than usual, the air musty. Prabir slipped on a muddy patch, cursed and got back on his feet.

Isn't this Baby's place? The room was dark, the curtain hung lopsided. He tore it open – empty, nobody inside. He swore loudly, stomped around in circles with his muddy feet, shouted her name a couple of times. Finally he flopped down onto the mattress in the corner and fell asleep, mouth gaping wide open.

Baby was running, running, and she knew this was the dumbest move she could possibly have made. Had she seen anyone around as she stormed out, she would have shouted, but there was no one. No one to catch her panicked eye, no one whose arm she could grab and scream *Help me!* Baby had lost her bearings, her feet slipped and slid in the mud bordering the field; she should have run the other way, towards the central fairgrounds where there were still people around. Was he following her? She didn't turn around, kept on running in the impossible gold sandals. The hem of her sari dragged further and further down into the squelchy mud, making every terrified leap over stones and tufts of grass more treacherous.

She cursed herself for not thinking of it. For having failed to ask the other girls about the foul-mouthed man with the flaring temper and the brutal hands reaching for her throat. He would have visited some of the others as well, there must have been a red flag raised somewhere? She kept running, aimlessly, senselessly, still feeling his hands around her neck. He had appeared in the doorway without warning, saying nothing, not even a curse word had spilled out from his contorted, raging lips. Two long strides across the floor and he had been right in front of her, strangling her before she could raise her arms in self-defence, 'You goddamn dirty whore!' She had thought of Prabir, of Jannati just a few yards away. But there had been no time, she had had no voice to shout out that it was happening, *he's killing me, now, now!*

She had no idea how she had broken free, but she must have torn herself away somehow, she was here after all, she was running. In the wrong direction, a frantic voice echoed through her head, there was nobody here, she was running straight into nothing! Baby noticed that she had lost one of her sandals, the sound of her feet pounding the earth had changed all of a sudden: click – swoosh – click – swoosh. But losing a shoe didn't matter, she tried to listen for other footsteps behind her own deafening click – swoosh rhythm, too terrified to turn around. Click – swoosh onward, not a second to lose. A cluster of trees across the field, she had to make it there, she was too visible here on the open plain. A sharp turn to the right, heading straight for a low fence. She leapt over it and heard the fabric rip as the soaked, heavy sari got caught. In between the trees she saw a house, a little farm, she heard her own sobs of relief as she sprinted towards the dim light in the window. Didn't see the brick wall until it was too late. A low wall, two or three stones high, with a rough-hewn, homemade lid meant to keep the well safe for children and cattle. A lid that was not in place. A heavy, grey lid lying off to the side when Baby tripped over the edge and dove into the well headfirst, without a sound.

Jannati was the first to notice. She was outside in the morning, not early, but earlier than the hung-over man in the shed a few yards away. She had returned from the roti-wallah's cart with a piece of naan for herself and one for Baby; maybe they could sit together awhile, eat and talk and believe that life had things like friendship and laughter to offer, good things. She stood perplexed outside her friend's room, hearing the snoring, maybe Baby hadn't been able to make her last passenger leave? Alarm bells started ringing in her head, something was wrong! Jannati poked a finger gingerly past the edge of the curtain, pulled it aside. The man lying there was Baby's pati, the one who owned her, the one who brought her here. But where was Baby? Her bag was there, her shawl draped across the chair. Had she gone over behind the sheds by the field to relieve herself? Jannati waited patiently, the bread turning cold between her fingers. Still no Baby. She sat down on the chair in her own doorway and started to eat the fresh, fluffy piece of bread, munching slowly.

Prabir threw a fit of rage. Jannati heard him rummaging around in there, cursing, kicking the chair over. She had already seen her first passenger of the day when he came out, she spied him out of the corner of her eye and acted as though nothing was wrong, pretending to be busy brushing her hair when he shouted.

'Where is the girl who lives next to you?'

She didn't have to answer, she could pretend not to hear. But she was anxious, too, she wanted to know the answer to his question. So Jannati walked out into the sunlight and told him she hadn't seen Baby since early last night. It had been a busy night for them both, the last thing she had seen was a group of young boys, college students, she believed, talking to Baby outside. But then Jannati had been pulled away, and she hadn't seen or heard from Baby since.

Prabir cursed again and looked as if he was going to slap her; she reflexively took a step back. But he spun around and stumbled down towards the trees by the field, his wrinkled shirt flapping behind him. Jannati took one more glance into the empty room and walked slowly back to her own doorway, steeling herself for the questions from the other Forbesganj women.

10

Saleem woke up on the couch in the office and instantly knew whom he needed to speak to. Tamanna's despair had followed him into his sleep; he had spent all night flailing through bewildering dreams of her sitting on a balcony, surrounded by clothes flapping in the wind. He sat up straight and rubbed the sleep out of his eyes; he needed to speak to Roshan. The schoolteacher was in touch with people in the Town of Love every day; he knew who was preoccupied with what, sensed what new conflicts were brewing. The quiet young schoolteacher from another village, skinny and prematurely balding, was accepted and yet still an outsider – just like himself. Their association with Pukaar made them helpers as well as sources of irritation.

Still, there was a difference, Saleem weighed silently in his mind as he put the teakettle on the lone hot plate on the corner table. In their eyes, my betrayal is worse. My father and mother, brothers and sisters, they all did what was expected of them. Homemade liquor, the flesh trade. *We are Nat. This is what we do.*

Perhaps he couldn't stay the course simply because he was the youngest son? All Saleem could remember of his father was a coughing shadow on the corner mattress by the stove. One day it had been empty, and that was that. His mother and eventually his brothers had driven production and sales by the simmering distillery out back; his sisters' fates had long been sealed. Surely, Fauzia had spoiled him, as big sisters did; he remembered drifting off to sleep many nights with the heavenly taste of candy in his mouth, his sticky hands happily clutching the paper bag with the rest of the colourful gumdrops she had brought him when she hobbled in through the door, bleary-eyed and exhausted. *I wasn't that old*, Saleem thought to himself, *when I knew, someplace deep inside, that the candy had a bitter aftertaste. That it had cost Fauzia more than money to buy it for me.*

When had it finally dawned on him? That his sister's work, the work of the women all around him, was different from selling nuts or balloons on the street, different from folding betel leaves and peddling paan for a rupee apiece? He didn't know for sure. But he remembered the emptiness in Fauzia's face that night, the sluggish listlessness of her movements as she fetched water and brought it behind the curtain, the dark stains on the salwar she had carried back out. He remembered how he had struggled to get the words out as he approached her. 'Didi, what's wrong?' And then, her rocking back and forth as she sat down on the stool and told him.

Roshan's motivation was different, Saleem concluded to himself as he prepared the tea. The teacher's scrawny build and chronic cough made him an unattractive job seeker, and his background didn't help either. His papers would hardly make him a frontrunner for a job at one of the better schools, or any school for that matter, in Forbesganj or elsewhere. Still, Saleem had seen it. Had seen it clearly the day he sat in the Pukaar office in Forbesganj, tasked with interviewing the young teacher who wanted to introduce the concept of school to the children of Prem Nagar. The love children of hope and futility, of joy and despair. Saleem had seen the fire in the eyes of the wiry man with the hat pulled down over his ears, had seen his yearning, so much like his own, to make a difference. Had seen his willingness to accept the laughably low salary, the impossible working conditions, the lack of textbooks. Had seen that he was perfect for the job.

Roshan had been a pillar of strength, a steady force through expected and unexpected storms: the resistance to sending kids to school (*Why bother? What good is a school that's not even recognised by the government? We need the kids to help out at home! Why should the girls learn to read, they'll end up just like us anyway!*); the complaints about their limited means (*What kind of school is this anyway, with not even enough books for everyone?*); the unrest when mothers had begun to see a glimpse of possibility – just a glimpse – that even a Nat girl could dream of a future somewhere beyond a chair in the doorframe (*This will lead to nothing but trouble among the women, are you trying to snatch the food from our tables?*).

The schoolhouse was far from grand, just one big room, but from nine o' clock each morning the desks were lined up in rows, they had twenty of them now, and more often than not there were children seated behind all of them. Scratched, well-worn desks, but even so, proof that someone, somewhere, wanted the kids in the Town of Love – Birbal with the lazy eye, Rozy who always sat by the door, studious little Hirkani with her gnarled Hindi letters – to learn to read and write, to know about the outside world, to hear that opportunities and possibilities belonged to them as well. Those who supported the organisation, responded to the letters and appeals, sent donations of cash or notebooks or mats to spread over the cold stone floor. Saleem knew that that was what got Roshan out of bed in the morning. Got him out onto his bicycle, an hour's ride in the raw morning chill with the scarf bundled tight around his neck: The certainty that he was not alone in believing that even the children of love stood a chance.

Saleem waited for Darya to arrive at the office before climbing onto his bicycle. Decided not to tell his colleague anything yet, though he knew Tamanna would most likely be sitting in the visitor's chair facing Darya's desk when he returned. As distraught as she was right now, she would throw herself at Pukaar and desperately plead, no, *demand* that they did something, right now, to get Rupa out. And who could blame her – where else could she go?

Tamanna's place in the Town of Love was tenuous; she was left mostly alone in her little house, but at a cost. The timeline of the three months between her leap into the swamp that night and suddenly showing up in Forbesganj was vague. Her story changed periodically, like the sun moving across the sky, casting different shadows in the morning and the afternoon. She might have made it back across the border to Bhutan and gone back to her parents, she might have not. They might have taken her back, they might have not. It might be true that she had lived a few months among the Nats in a village near Saleem's own, just as true as her occasional claim that she had sought refuge with a Hindu family in Katihar.

The truth is whatever story you need to get through the day, Saleem thought. Those needs could be different tomorrow.

So when, one day, Tamanna had suddenly landed in the midst of the Town of Love, angry and free with her bottom lip jutting forward, it hadn't taken long for the rumour mill to start churning. Jabbar Aslam's relatives in Prem Nagar had unleashed their fury in bitter remarks: *Who did Tamanna think she was? She still owed Jabbar and Dolly for the investment they made years ago. How dared she come here, thinking she could settle down and live freely on her own?*

The news had reached Katihar before day's end, and the hearsay had grown: it was only a matter of time before Jabbar would come back to get her.

Saleem picked up speed, the bike shook and rattled along the bumpy road. Had he really just thought of Tamanna as 'free'? A bitter grimace drew the corners of Saleem's mouth downwards as he continued down the street, ignoring blaring truck horns and curving gracefully around an ugly, black boar with tufts of coarse hair protruding from its thick scruff. Tamanna was nowhere near free, and had been even less so when she first arrived. Saleem knew there had been no freedom in her choice to come to Forbesganj and the Town of Love, it was no carefully chosen alternative that had driven her to mount her most stubborn defense and insist that she had just as much right to be there as they did. She had known that Prem Nagar was the best she could hope for, Saleem thought, angrily pedalling away to keep the hopelessness at bay. The only achievable resolution. This was where the only profession she knew was practiced; if there had been anywhere she could hope to get back on her feet, it would be here. Tamanna had never explained how she had managed during those first few months in Forbesganj, before she got involved with Pukaar and got the job at the kindergarten. Saleem thought he knew, but there was no need to talk about it. What counted was that she had come to Prem Nagar to make a better life. To be able to close her own door behind her at night and know that there was no menacing knife on the shelf in the next room.

Saleem knew how wrong she had been. Tamanna had been beaten in the Town of Love, just as much as any of those who lived under 'protection'. But she had always picked herself up, always fought back, used words just as fiery and just as foul. Tamanna had been the first to seek out Pukaar when they opened the modest office in the old rice mill in Forbesganj three years ago. Been the first to come forward when Rukmini and Darya took the initial cautious steps into the Town of Love to start a conversation about change, possibility, another kind of life.

Saleem hadn't yet heard of Pukaar then. He was still studying at the university, painfully aware that every mouthful he ate, every pencil and notebook he used, every night that he spent in his dorm room lodgings in the district capital of Patna, was paid for on his sister's mattress. The pact between him and Fauzia that surreal night long ago: she would work, he would study. He would go to school, would cling to the conviction that something else was possible, that the roles could one day be reversed. Someday he would provide for her, get her out of it.

When he graduated and joined Pukaar, it wasn't without a fight between him and his sister. Instead of using his diploma from Patna as a ticket to a job in the local administration, or maybe in the police corps, Saleem chose a different way. Chose an alliance with the kajas, the outsiders. Joined hands with those who came in and said they wanted 'what's best for you'. He knew the objections by heart: *How would they know what's best for us? Is it best for us to declare war on our only means of survival? Is women talking back to their husbands and causing nothing but turmoil and grief, what's best for us?*

He knew Fauzia would rather have seen him follow the stream of white-collar young men into some office building every morning, so that he could slowly but surely climb the ladder towards greater dignity and safety with a salary jump every year. But he had to do what he did, for him there was no other option. Fauzia had bled her way through the days and the years to keep him in school. He had managed to buy her the paan-stand, had her seated firmly on the platform with her legs crossed. The past was what it was, unchangeable; her sitting there folding paan with red-splotched fingers was a victory for him, for both of them. No one was as painfully, lovingly close to him as Fauzia, no one more deserving of a house across the bridge.

His sister's constant half-ironic expression told Saleem nothing about what she really thought of the cause he had dedicated his life to. Was it merely a naive dream to her? A ridiculous idea which she smiled at sadly and knew to be futile? Or did she hide a conviction burning as brightly as his own behind those bottomless eyes and the pointed, sardonic smile? Saleem didn't know. All he knew was that he had to seize the opportunity when the organization needed someone to take charge of its finances and administration. He had to team up with those who confirmed what he had realised that night in Khawaspur, in the shadow of his sister scrubbing blood stains out of her clothes. First, get the tools. Then use them for what you believe in.

Saleem was not afraid, although the threats were always looming large. He received the same ominous warnings that were thrown in Roshan's face when one of the wives, daughters, sisters or daughters-in-law spent her time picking the kids up from the kindergarten or going to meetings in the schoolhouse. What could any of this be good for? If passengers were kept waiting by an empty chair in the doorframe, this would have to be dealt with! There wouldn't be a bone left unbroken in any of their bodies, and their so-called school would be burned to the ground! The children would be kept at home, they'd make sure of that!

Saleem knew the way they looked at him. The hung-over men in the shadow by the paan-shop despised and scorned their relative who sat behind a desk at Pukaar thinking he was going to turn the world around. *Their* world, the one he came from, before he went off to the school where they puffed up his chest! If only he'd used his schooling, the years Fauzia had paid for him, to help *them*. He could have taken a job that meant something, that gave him some influence. Could have made sure they had water and electricity, a sewage system, good roads. Why couldn't he get them jobs, well-paid jobs in the public sector? That's what he could have used his fancy education for, instead of getting behind those who wanted to snatch the food away from their children's mouths!

Saleem let out a long sigh and kept pedalling.

Everything was quiet when Saleem arrived at the schoolhouse. He leaned his bicycle against the wall, peered in through the window. Roshan sat with his back turned, facing the children, reading aloud from a book. A warm scarf was wrapped around his neck in addition to the usual woollen hat. His voice was low, but the kids, even the younger ones, soaked up every word. Saleem turned the corner, passing Amina who sat alone on the rug with the kindergarten kids. She nodded. 'Namaste,' he returned the greeting before continuing in through the open door.

Roshan nodded to him and resumed reading aloud, and Saleem took a seat on the uneven brick window ledge. Looked around the classroom, thinking how unfathomable this would have been just a few years ago. The colourful posters on the wall with animals and birds, the Hindi alphabet with a picture for each letter. The ceiling fans that whirled lethargically round and round, the teacher's chair that creaked every time he moved. The box of books at the back of the room, the world map on the wall with countries none of them had been to and might never visit, but nevertheless would learn about. The room was quiet, six-year-olds and twelve-year-olds calmly seated in rows on the floor with their legs folded under the low desks. Sunlight struck the wall behind Roshan at an angle through the window, the dust danced in the soft beam of light in front of his feet. He read Tagore to the children, his words trickling free and clear into the room:

> *Where the mind is without fear and the head is held high*
> *Where knowledge is free*
> *Where the world has not been broken up into fragments*
> *By narrow domestic walls*
> *Where words come out from the depth of truth*
> *Where tireless striving stretches its arms towards perfection*
> *Where the clear stream of reason has not lost its way*
> *Into the dreary desert sand of dead habit*
> *Where the mind is led forward by thee*
> *Into ever-widening thought and action*
> *Into that heaven of freedom, my Father, let my country awake*

'I need to talk to you. It's Tamanna,' Saleem said when Roshan had put the book away and got the kids started on their arithmetic.
'She didn't come in today,' the teacher nodded, 'is she ill?'
'Not ill,' Saleem said, and recounted the story from Katihar. He left out the details from the night before, the hours in Tamanna's house, the sobbing refrains, the uncompromising demand that they had to get her daughter out – now!

Roshan's face was slender, his angular cheekbones protruding under the sparse beard. As he listened it shrank inward, tensing into a narrow scythe of worry. He sat in silence for a long time.
'Rupa's just one girl,' he said at last.
Saleem knew exactly what he meant. One girl. And to Tamanna she was the whole world.

Saleem knew this would be the core issue. What were the risks, what were the costs? It had taken them three years to build up the flimsy framework of trust in which they operated in Prem Nagar. Three years to get the children into the schoolhouse, to make their parents send them out the door every day, or at least not hinder them from leaving. Three years of prodding and coaxing to get the women to the community centre in the evenings to talk, to share experiences, to see that solidarity could chase away fear. Three years of reassuring them that their courageous choice would lead to something, that it was the first step on the road to something better.

Can we risk all this? Saleem asked himself, rubbing his temples. Can we gamble with the fate of the school, the fragile women's group just finding its footing? Can we compromise the trust of those who have left their daughters in our hands, letting us send them off to boarding school? Can we – should we – place all our credibility and clout behind saving this one girl? Demand a full police raid and the arrest of people closely related to members of our panchayat, our village council?

This was where the battle lines would be drawn. This was not about boys and girls learning to read and multiply. Not even a question of putting crazy ideas in the women's heads. This was asking the Nat to betray their own. Not actively, of course – it will be Pukaar making the phone calls, Saleem thought. It would be the organisation demanding that the police take action, it would be the Pukaar staff taking the physical, actual risk. *But we will be asking the Nat to accept it. Accept that some of their own kin will be thrown in jail, will be convicted and put behind bars for years if we get our way.*

This wasn't just about one girl. This was a huge leap forward from a place most of them had yet to reach.

Saleem looked Roshan in the eye for a long time. 'Yes,' he said at last. 'She is just one girl.'

'You're asking a lot from us, Tamanna.'

Rukmini's face was serious and drawn. The organisation's director had been summoned from Delhi, these were high stakes and fateful decisions.

A spark ignited in Tamanna; her broad jawbone turned to steel.

'*A lot*? How can you say that I'm asking a lot? I'm asking you to save my daughter's life, that's what I'm asking. How could that be too much?'

She gathered her sari around her and sat straight-backed in the chair, glancing at Amina for support. It was late evening in the narrow Pukaar office, and everyone was tired. They had turned the subject back and forth, up and down, inside out, over and over again. Tamanna understood it would be complicated, acknowledged that it was a risky bet. She had been part of the slow work herself, convincing each one of the women in the mahila mandal, the fledgling women's group, to suffer through the beatings, the mockings and derision, and still show up at the meetings. Had persuaded them to sit down on a threadbare carpet and listen to people whom they didn't even trust tell them that the life they lived, the work they did, following their mothers and grandmothers, was something they could flee. Should flee. She had argued against the unarguable. 'If you can find me a job that earns as many rupees a month, I'll gladly give it up. But not before.'

Still, for Tamanna it was blessedly simple. She held one single picture in her mind, had one cry in her throat. Rupa. *Her tiny, sacred body in my arms.* This was clear as day. They had to get Rupa out.

Rukmini took a deep breath. She had never met Jabbar Aslam, but she knew he was a dangerous man. The dhanda, the flesh trade, was a wide network stretching across villages in Bihar and West Bengal, across the borders to Nepal and Bhutan. Rukmini knew that the monster they risked awakening had heads and arms everywhere. Had accomplices and profiteers in the transportation and hotel industries, in the police and the judiciary, had eyes and ears at every truck stop and every tea shack along the roads.

'Tamanna ...'

But when she saw the dogged, despairing depths of the woman's face across from her, the sentence died in her throat. If Tamanna could keep fighting, if she could stay the course, how could they not support her?

She looked over at Darya, running through the logic the two of them had been discussing for hours. The organisation was better established in Forbesganj than in many other places. Not as firmly rooted as in Kolkata or Delhi, but still they had achieved something here. They called it mobilisation, awareness-raising, self-esteem building. Piece by piece: your husband has no right to beat you, learning how to read is just as important for your daughter as for your son. Rukmini collected the positive results, the slow signs of progress: the girls who were allowed to stay in school for another year; the women who had coaxed or sneaked ten rupees with them to the meeting; the core of the joint bank account the women's group had set up. Not much by the standards of the world she herself came from, but an opening of new, infinite possibilities for those who had lived their whole lives in this joyless pleasure town.

Amina's face looked wounded the way it always did when she was upset – her lips tightly pursed, her gaze towards the ceiling. Wasn't this what Pukaar was always talking about? Put an end to the sex trade, no one has the right to hurt you, people are not goods to be bought and sold. Exactly! She knew Rukmini didi had the backing of a whole other caste; she was educated, she had relatives and acquaintances throughout the invisible power lines of society they call politics. Then why were they hesitating? Amina threw her hair over her shoulder, her lion's mane flaring – if *she* wasn't afraid, if Tamanna wasn't afraid, what was there to consider? At last, she opened her mouth:

'Rukmini didi – you're not the ones who will be beaten when we get Rupa out. It's us. It's me. My mother-in-law is Jabbar's mother's sister, don't you think I'll be punished for being on your side? It's the other girls in his brothel who will suffer, they'll be beaten even harder. If *I* want you to go through with it, what do *you* have to lose?'

Rukmini folded her hands, weary of the conversation. 'We know that, Amina! Don't you think we know that? That's exactly what we're worried about! What will the backlash be, for you, for our work, for all of us?'

She leaned forward.

'Have you considered that even if we try to get Rupa out, we might not succeed? What if we can't find her, what if someone tips them off and they have time to hide her away? What if we get Rupa out, but fail to catch those behind it all? What if we manage to save one single girl, but have to close down all our other work in Forbesganj? Even if we try, there is no way I can guarantee the outcome. Even if I mobilise every resource within my power, I have no way of knowing whether it will work!'

She threw her hands in the air, exhausted by the final decision she must make. Silently challenged the others in the room: Darya's knitted eyebrows, Saleem staring into his lap, Amina's stubbornly pursed lips. And Tamanna, unwavering, unshakable. The fate of the life she had created would be decided in this room. Tamanna looked into Rukmini's eyes, fixing her gaze: *This is what matters. No risk is too great, no price too high.*

Rukmini nodded, got to her feet. Inhaled deeply and pulled out her cell phone.

'We'll get Rupa out.'

11

She couldn't do it anymore. It was too painful, she was scared for the baby. Sona lay huddled in a corner of the large room adjoining the balcony. Her face turned against the wall, she tried to keep her back from convulsing as she sobbed. If they thought she was sleeping, they might leave her alone. It was early afternoon and she had just washed herself. Again. Scrubbing with the washcloth, rubbing herself raw and red. *No one is as clean as I am*, Sona thought. *No one scrubs herself to such odourless nudity. No one is as infinitely dirty.*

She had positioned herself as usual. Squatting halfway, her legs far apart so that it would drip straight out of her, trickle straight out without getting her thighs sticky. She had taken the time to make sure it was all out, emptying herself. She didn't know why she had looked down, following the watery slime with her eyes. A cry from the baby, she thought. That's what I heard. A faint, pinkish scream of blood.

If there was any threat to the baby, she thought, they wouldn't force her. The child would be useful to them, no matter what it was. Preferably a girl, of course, and a bonus if she happened to be light-skinned. If there was any threat to the baby, they definitely wouldn't force her. She had watched the others keep working until just a few weeks before giving birth. Seen them waddle back to their mats afterwards, arms wrapped around their bulging bellies' secret worlds.

Actually, it was incredible that it hadn't happened to her before. Like all the others, she always asked the passenger to wear a condom; like all the others, she got a 'no' nine times out of ten. She thought her body had been acting in self-defense. Sona had never dreamed of running away, never imagined an escape from the streets of Kuli Pada, Katihar. So, she thought, her womb had sealed itself off. The dark, rich soil inside her had refused to let the seed take root. Hadn't wanted to nourish a plant only to see its stem broken as soon as it reached sunlight.

Now, Sona had no idea what to believe. Would this be the only time, her sign from the gods? Should she blindly trust that this little life that had fought so long and so hard, would make it through? Her hand reached down between her legs, under her sari. She needed to feel that it was dry, that nothing was trickling out. Every drop of blood inside her belonged to the baby, every ounce of nourishment her body could squeeze out – *it is for you, little one.*

Mumtaz Begum appeared at the door: 'Sona!'

She didn't stir, her hand wedged between her thighs.

'What's wrong with you? Why are you just lying there?'

She squeezed her eyes shut, knowing the old woman knew she was awake.

'Get up, you lazy girl, come help me with these buckets!'

Sona sat up slowly, staring hopelessly straight ahead. Not a prayer for help in her eyes, there was no one to pray to. She got to her knees, dragged herself wordlessly across the floor, took a pail of wet laundry in each hand. Walked stiffly out onto the balcony and began hanging clothes on the line.

Rupa had kept her light skin, only the half-moon shadows under her eyes whispered of something lost and too late. Her eyebrows were narrow and smooth, nearly joining over her straight, longish nose. She met her own gaze in the small mirror, picking with her forefinger at the freckle on the left side of her mouth. Was she pretty? She didn't know, and it didn't matter. It mattered little what she looked like, what she did, what she said. Rupa spoke as few words as possible. Her voice was the only part of her body she could keep to herself.

She knew what was sending her in behind the glass wall. A dangerous journey, administered by Jabbar following the instructions from the doctors at the hospital in Katihar. When was the last time she was there? Three months ago? Four? Each time the light blue pills appeared, she was torn between the fear, the knowledge that she wouldn't be able to fight back, and the wish to disappear. Sail, alight, glide away from the fingers, the bodies. She saw it, she knew they were there, but it was only happening to the part of her that she could switch off and put away on the other side of her eyelids.

'Rupa!'

Every muscle in her body tensed when she heard Mumtaz Begum's voice down the hall. Footsteps shuffled closer, the old scowl appeared in the doorway.

'You'd better behave yourself if Rahul sahib comes to visit today! Behave yourself, sit down and chat with him if he wants a drink!'

She waved a stern warning forefinger at the thirteen-year-old sitting on the floor, hunched over with no makeup, hair trailing down her back in a droopy ponytail. How pathetic this girl was! The rings on Mumtaz's plump hand glinted as she scolded her: 'Don't forget, he pays well! Make yourself look good, this could be two thousand rupees, maybe even more!'

The numbers whizzed past Rupa's ears; it made no difference to her what Rahul sahib paid or didn't pay. She would never see the money anyway. The passengers made their payments directly to Jabbar, or to Mumtaz Begum if her son had gone out. Occasionally a passenger might hand her a few extra rupees before leaving, but Rupa had no place to hide them, Dolly found them every time. 'I need these to buy more rice,' she would say, tucking the bank notes into her blouse with quick fingers. 'You girls are eating me out of house and home.'

Jabbar's knife lay on a shelf within reach of his bed. He stared at it for a moment, leaving it there as he hitched up his pants and walked out to the kitchen. Said nothing when Mumtaz placed the dish in front of him, warm roti and dal, a big ladle of thick, brown stew. He rested on his haunches, slumped over, the muscles in his neck bulging in rhythm with his chomping jaws, his stout fingers shoving the food impatiently into his mouth.

'Where is Rupa?'

He wiped his hand across his mouth, shoving the clean-scraped metal plate away.

His mother shot him an abrupt glance:

'Upstairs.'

'How is she?'

Mumtaz shrugged with her back turned, her voice stayed flat: 'The usual. I've given her something to calm her down, so she won't get worked up.'

He had considered going after Tamanna again. Not to get her back in traffic, he wasn't that stupid, he knew she had friends and she was nothing but trouble anyway, always had been. Just to knock some sense into her, shut her mouth, let her know that next time she showed up at his door with her spectacle, next time she dared to go to the police in Katihar, she'd have more than a beating to worry about. Much more. He could always have someone in Prem Nagar take care of it, of course, didn't he have relatives there who could deal with her? He knew his khala, mother of Kasim and his brothers, was enraged at the closeness between Tamanna and her daughter-in-law Amina. The hellcat from Jogbani that his weakling cousin had never been able to tame. No, he refused to waste his thoughts on Kasim. He knew the Tamanna issue had been argued all the way up to the panchayat before, where his aunt's family was well connected. The consensus was that Tamanna wasn't welcome in the Town of Love, that she poisoned the women's minds and told wild lies about him and his business in Katihar. That she was an asset to the outside meddlers, those who did nothing but spread grumbling and discontent. Jabbar wasn't worried for himself, or for his business – he was too well established for that and paid good money for his protection. But Tamanna had to stop coming here;

the noise she made was getting on his nerves and he was sick of hiding Rupa away for days whenever she showed up.

It was no use asking anyone in Forbesganj to take care of it for him. He stood facing his bed again, eyes fixed on the knife on the shelf. This had to come to an end.

✳

It was never a question of whether it was the right thing to do, Tamanna knew that. She saw in Rukmini's eyes that she shared Rupa's pain. Felt Saleem's anger bubbling under the quiet, helpless surface. Still, she could not believe that the Pukaar leaders needed time to consider it. They knew what was going on. How could they hesitate? Tamanna didn't know what she would do with Rupa if they managed to get her out. Where she would sleep, what she would live off? The few rupees she herself got each month were barely enough for one meal a day, and conditions in the Town of Love were far from safe – not even for her, let alone for a girl taken by force out from Jabbar's house. But she couldn't think of that now. Just get Rupa out.

Tamanna sat under her mango tree, fists clenched in her lap, knowing she couldn't afford to be discouraged. Still, the dread of failure was always there, a constant buzz at the back of her mind: She had run away with her daughter before. In another life, long ago, long before her own leap into the swamp. She had tried to escape with Rupa once before, and she had failed. How could she even imagine that they would make it this time?

Rupa had been young, about three years old, a blurred image of the skinny toddler fluttered through Tamanna's mind. She herself had been ill for months, stricken by jaundice, burning with fever day and night; she remembered only flashes of Mumtaz Begum's complaints as doctors had been summoned and medicine obtained. Tamannna hadn't been contributing to the income, she was nothing but a burden, and Mumtaz had better things to do than nurse a worthless girl in a sickbed. And so Jabbar Aslam's network had been activated once again: Tamanna was to be sent away for a while. To be kept under close watch somewhere else until she regained her usefulness and could once again contribute to the money tree harvest.

Why they had let her bring Rupa along she had no idea. Her own pleadings were hardly what had yielded results, and Rupa had long been far closer to Dolly than to her. But Dolly was pregnant with her own daughter at the time, Tamanna recalled, could that have been the reason she wanted both of them out of the way?

She remembered the long journey with the child on her lap, one of Jabbar's brothers had been there to escort them. His face with the heavy jowls, his huge hands that would not have hesitated to slap her or her daughter had she tried to pull any trick. A train, a bus, another bus, the stifling heat, she had felt weak and had not expected a warm welcome, wherever they were heading. Still, a glimpse of the blue sky through the bus window, a hint of something nameless bordering on freedom: A young woman on a bus, a mother on a journey with her child. A vast, dizzying thought.

Tamanna buried her head in her hands in the shade of the mango tree, shut out the everyday noise from the Town of Love. Recalled the anxious murmur in her chest that had lasted the whole journey – why were they sending her away? What would happen to her, to her daughter? Would they take Rupa away from her? Tamanna had been seventeen years old, no longer expecting anything from anyone.

She had been so accustomed to not knowing what was happening that it had never occurred to her to ask questions. She and Rupa had been given a bed and a blanket and were left alone. She had helped out around the house, that was all, no one had seemed to expect anything more from her. As the weeks passed, her strength had returned. Rupa had been happy too, with plenty of space around the house for a little girl to play. Tamanna's hopes had ballooned; what if she never had to set foot in the blue house in Katihar again? And along with her hopes, her courage had grown, she had felt bolder. She had gathered information, one small piece at a time. She had eavesdropped when people talked, had picked up the name of the town where she was being held, and more importantly, where the nearest police station was. The seventeen-year-old had made a note of the name Rupauli and had started to dream big dreams at night. About how she would march into the office of the chief police inspector in Rupauli, tell him everything about Jabbar Aslam, demand that he be arrested and thrown in jail. And then the best part: how she would walk out of the police station, head held high and proud, carrying her daughter on her arm.

She had overheard the conversation that forced her fantasy into action by sheer coincidence. It was only by chance that she had walked by the two men smoking in the shade in the backyard just as they happened to mention the name Jabbar Aslam. Sheer luck that she had picked up which day they were talking about: Jabbar was coming here – *here* – the day after tomorrow. The dream suddenly had to become a plan, it was now or never, she had to flee before he arrived! The familiar terror of the steel grip around her arm, of the knife on the shelf. Tamanna's plan had consisted of one single point: She would make the journey to Rupauli. With the slim, shining hope that the Aslam network didn't reach quite that far.

She remembered that early, pinkish dawn, the flight from the house. She had given Rupa a cup of warm milk with sugar and a dash of liquor, and brought with her an oversized shawl to wrap the child and carry her in when she fell asleep. She hadn't known the way or how far it would be, but still couldn't risk following the main road. Tamanna had run and wept and shushed her daughter when she awoke, behind clusters of houses, across fields, along pathways and hills and through patches of dense forest. Had crossed streams and small rivers and, late in the afternoon, had dared to approach a main road. Exhausted and clutching a whimpering Rupa in her arms, she had struggled to stay on her feet as a rickshaw slowed down next to her. Without turning her head Tamanna had again forced one foot in front of the other, desperately pushing herself forward to give the impression she was going somewhere. A woman's voice had reached her from the rickshaw, a voice with the softness of trickling water, swathing her in kindness: 'Where are you going? Do you need help?'

Tamanna had been uncertain whether the woman with the gentle voice was real. Was she hallucinating from exhaustion? Fighting to form the words with her dried-out lips, she had held Rupa tight as she met the woman's eyes. 'I'm on my way to Rupauli. Is it far?'

The tender smile had lit up the dim interior of the rickshaw: 'You're here, behen. This is Rupauli.'

She remembered thanking the woman, sobbing, thanking her again, and finding the courage to ask for directions to the police station. Tamanna had thought of her many times since then, the woman in the dark red sari, a messenger from the gods, sent to greet her and show her the way. The first of many miracles that afternoon and evening, where carpets had rolled out and doors had opened for the worn-out young girl with the child swaddled on her back. The sergeant at the police station who had offered her water and listened to her story with a serious look on his face. The chief inspector who had been summoned and had spoken to her with measured gentleness. 'What do you want us to help you with, beti, my child? You're far away from them now, and you have your daughter with you.'

Tamanna, her clothes torn, sweaty and in disarray, but with majesty in her voice: 'I want him to sign a paper saying he has no rights to my child or me. And I want him go to jail for what he has done.'

The chief inspector's knowing gaze, her heart had raced in her chest until he nodded, slowly. The phone calls he made, his authoritative voice speaking on her behalf, she had sat right there and heard it all. Tamanna hadn't eaten all day, and her eyes had widened when she heard the chief inspector send a messenger home to his wife to have his meal brought to the station, and to send a little extra. She had sat there – she, from the whorehouse in Katihar, with her fatherless child on her lap, eating roti and dal from the chief inspector's kitchen in Rupauli.

When he had at last hung up the phone with a contented click and explained the plan to her, she had understood that like her, the chief inspector had risked everything on a single hand: Jabbar would be apprehended when he showed up the next day, and would be brought to Rupauli. Tamanna was to come back tomorrow afternoon, when the first interrogation would be completed. She had stood up, numb with exhaustion, Rupa sleepy and sulking in her arms. He had paused by the door, about to pull on his uniform cap when a thought had struck him: 'Where are you sleeping tonight?'

She hadn't had the strength to try to invent an answer.

The chief inspector had turned to the young sergeant who had welcomed her, who had nodded, not enthusiastically, but had nodded nevertheless. He had brought Tamanna two blocks further into town, had spoken to the receptionist at the modest-looking hotel and slid some money across the table. She had been so tired that it had physically hurt to climb the stairs, she had no energy left for fear. Had taken in the bed and the deadbolt inside the door. Had tucked Rupa in towards the wall and curled up next to her. Had thought to herself, 'I've made it.'

She had known she only had a few hours' head start on those sent out to track her down, but Tamanna and Rupa's path had been lit by smiling gods throughout their whirlwind flight. She had thought it would last. Had believed it so strongly that she had been unfazed by the meeting with Jabbar the next day. At the chief inspector's office in Rupauli, with less than three feet separating her from him, she had sat without flinching. Had avoided looking at him while the pensive-faced chief inspector did the unthinkable, made the impossible happen; he got Jabbar to sign his name on a piece of paper that said she, Tamanna, and her daughter Rupa, were free and belonged to no one.

She had wanted to demand he be thrown in jail for life and never be allowed out again! But she had had no strength to do anything but collapse in a chair when she saw him walk out of the police station a few minutes later, turn the corner, and disappear in a cloud of dust behind a honking bus.

She really had believed it. Had believed she could take her daughter and go back to Chhukha, had believed she could reverse the accursed journey and jump off the bus where she had once been yanked onboard, back when she was Hasina in just a little pair of shorts. The chief inspector in Rupauli had done her one last favour; she had always thought of him in hindsight as someone who had truly, honestly wanted to help her. Perhaps he had never even found out what happened? He had sent a police sergeant to accompany her and Rupa on the train to Siliguri, where they were to board the bus to her childhood village.

'Do you have relatives there?'

How could she have known, nine years later? She had nodded. Had pushed all other thoughts out of her head and nodded firmly.

She remembered how her heart had soared as they sat on the train. The young policeman dozing off in the seat across from her, Tamanna cradling Rupa on her lap. Feeling the warmth slowly unfold within her, looking around at the families, the young men, the noisy children eating and bickering and nagging their parents. She remembered thinking that none of them could harm her. Wishing she had a little money to buy some jalebi for Rupa.

She had been counting down the minutes in her head as they neared Siliguri. *The road home, the road home.* Wonder if it still went past a clothing store that sold yellow dresses for little girls? Dresses with ruffles on the sleeves and white piping? Two more stops to Siliguri, one stop – Kursila! Next station Kursila! Her eyes had glided across the platform at the tiny station: passengers overloaded with luggage, snack vendors with their shiny pots and pans and raspy voices, towers of boxes and crates stacked in the middle of the platform blocking everyone's way. Her calm, sluggish gaze had seen nothing, had realised nothing, not until Rupa jerked awake in her lap had she looked up and into the aisle. Among the teeming crowd of passengers pushing on and off the train, dragging suitcases down from the overfilled baggage racks, there he was. Rupa had whimpered and curled up in her lap; Tamanna had gasped in panic and turned towards the policeman. 'He's here!' she had wanted to cry. 'Jabbar Aslam is here! Get him away from us!'

But it had been the police sergeant who had opened his mouth. He had got to his feet slowly, adjusted the brown beret on his head and ordered her with authority, so it was clear to everyone onboard: 'Go with this man! Get off the train immediately and go with this man!'

Tamanna felt the rough tree trunk scratch her back as she sat on the ground, arms folded around her knees. She got up and brushed the dirt and dust off her clothes, stood for a moment under the unripe mangoes, listening to Heena's light snoring from inside.

She remembered how Rupa had screamed when Jabbar picked her up, how she had wanted to vomit when she saw his hairy underarm wrapped around her daughter's skinny brown thighs. Her voice had returned, the words had spilled out, her arms had begun to spin like windmills: 'Let go of her! Give me my daughter! You have no right! You signed the papers!'

The sergeant had grabbed her from behind, scooped her up from the floor and carried her towards the narrow doorway as the train snorted impatiently, scraping its hooves along the rails, anxious to keep moving. Just one more station.

She had screamed the whole way along the platform, down the stairs, over to the car where one of his brothers sat waiting. People had stopped and stared, children asked their parents, perhaps a woman's face had even turned away in unwilling recognition. But the legitimacy of the brown uniform had rendered any objection or intervention impossible; the sea of people had parted, stepped aside and let the kidnapping happen. In the gleaming afternoon sun, car doors had been opened and Rupa had been placed in the passenger seat. The quick nod exchanged between Jabbar and the policeman, his back quickly vanishing among rickshaws and grocery-shopping women in the narrow street behind the station. Tamanna had sat in the back seat with Jabbar, the knife resting on the seat between them.

Could she believe once again? It was already too late. Something had been shattered forever. All she could do now, all anyone could do, was to wrap gentle arms around what was left. Cradling, rocking, softly kissing the wound.

12

Not a word to anyone. Beside herself, only Rukmini, Darya, and Saleem knew. What would happen from here on was outside Tamanna's control, she had nothing to offer in the form of money, contacts or services. Deep down she could hear a small voice protesting, asking the troublesome questions: *Why would they do all this for you? What are you to them, what is Rupa to them? Why should they succeed where everyone else has failed?* But Tamanna knew what she had seen in Rukmini's face. In the solemn features of the young woman carrying so many burdens, shouldering so much responsibility, Tamanna had recognised the firm conviction that was to save her daughter's life: *No one has the right to buy or sell another human being.*

Tamanna had to trust they would find a way. Her helpers in Pukaar were all she had. Nothing to do but wait until everything was ready.

Amina slapped a bottom here, yanked an earlobe there, half-heartedly begun a well-known nursery rhyme which the children joined in unison. Tamanna sat on the edge of the rug, her mind somewhere else. Amina had spoken a few words with Roshan when they arrived this morning; his narrow, scraggly-bearded chin had been even more tense than usual. There were fewer kids in school today; the threadbare brown dhurrie they called a kindergarten was emptier. Birbal wasn't here, nor was Rozy. Fauzia hadn't even said hello when Amina passed the paan-stand on her way here, hiding her long face in the folds of her dupatta. Just like everyone else, Amina couldn't quite seem to figure out Saleem's sister, with her half-arrogant facial features and eyes never completely open. *Who does she think she is?* Amina asked herself tersely and pulled her dupatta closer around herself. Fauzia had been a prostitute for a long time when she arrived in Prem Nagar with her brothers! Amina had heard rumours of another sister somewhere, a girl no one talked about; she had never mustered up the courage to ask Saleem about it. Fauzia had no children of her own, no husband, why did she stick her nose up in the air like that? Why didn't she come to the meetings in the mahila mandal, the women's group? *She should be supporting us,* the warrior in Amina thought. Fauzia had her own income and her own living space, with no one to harass her at night.

Deep inside, she knew that Fauzia had paid her dues. That Saleem's sister had wept and suffered and stayed silent just as much as they all had. But she had a brother, Amina thought, suddenly envious. Fauzia had a brother who acted like a brother, someone who protected and defended. Someone who knew where you came from and who you used to be.

'Why isn't Rozy here?' Amina asked when Roshan appeared in the schoolhouse doorway. Fauzia's young, skinny niece was the only one who could bring a spark to the imperturbable face of the paan-saleswoman. The daughter of one of her eldest brother's wives, the plain, bony girl bore a striking resemblance to Fauzia. None of the other kids from that house came to school; Amina had been surprised when Rozy first started showing up a few months ago. Once in a while at first, then more and more regularly, and now they had grown used to seeing her shy, unsmiling face in the corner seat at one end of the back row. She almost never said a word, but her eyes were alert, and Roshan said she was close to breaking through and starting to read. But today Rozy was absent, and Amina's gut feeling told her that was no coincidence.

The schoolteacher simply looked back at her with patient eyes and shook his head.

'I don't think Rozy will be coming to school anymore.'
'Why not?'

Amina's retort was quick and sharp, but she felt the hopelessness lurking in the pit of her stomach. She threw a glance to Tamanna, whose eyes were still glazed over in another world, and wrinkled her eyebrows as if to ask Roshan: is it …?

He nodded. So the talk had started. Something had been let loose. She didn't know what Roshan knew, and she herself only had a vague notion of what was in store. But something was brewing in Prem Nagar; Amina had felt it all day long. The Town of Love was a sensitive creature, a thin-skinned animal despite its crude brutality. Nothing went unnoticed here, everything was seized upon and scrutinised. Rozy wasn't at school today, and that meant something.

Amina got to her feet and tapped Tamanna on the shoulder: 'I have to go use the woods.'

Tamanna replied with a distracted nod and Amina plopped her son, the kindergarten's youngest member, into her friend's lap. She didn't go to the woods. She walked around the houses at the end of the street, holding up her sari as she stepped over muddy piles of garbage, making her way towards Salma's house. Please, please let Prabir be out … but come to think of it, she was pretty sure he was still at the mela.

Salma was in her usual spot, sitting cross-legged on the woven-bottom bed that she had dragged into the doorway. Her kurta was turquoise today, she wore eyeshadow of a matching colour.

'How is Lalita doing?'

Amina sat down.

Salma shrugged, distractedly stroking Nila's head as the baby drifted in and out of sleep. Her eyes scanned up and down the well-trodden street, she paused to eye the overweight man across the road, the two young guys walking by the tea shack.

'The same.'

One part of Salma had already said goodbye to her mother and made her peace. When Lalita wasn't wincing in pain she just lay there and dozed; all Salma could do was bathe the feverish body and bring her a little water or tea if she could stomach it. The hospital in Katihar was out of the question, Prabir had made it clear enough that he 'didn't trust them'. An unbearable tenderness when she thought of her mother, her eyes that could stare straight into your soul, as they still sometimes did in her rare lucid moments. *She never wanted this for me*, Salma thought. *She has felt the same way for me as I feel now for Nila. She didn't want this for me.*

Amina sighed. Salma always knew everything there was to know in the town, but today she obviously wasn't going to give away any handouts.

'When will they all be back from the mela?' she asked, just to say something.

Salma took a long pause before she responded, her hands occupied with the child in her lap, stroking and cuddling the dark little head.

'In a few days …'

'Baby's disappeared,' she suddenly blurted out and clamped her eyes down on Amina's.

'What?' Amina leaned forward. 'Why? How long ago?'

Salma shook her head, her gaze drifted away once again. 'I don't know. Prabir was here yesterday, he said no one has seen her for days.'

Amina wanted to shake her – *That's what I told her! Didn't I warn Baby not to go to the mela?*

But shaking Salma wouldn't do any good. It didn't matter that Amina was right, that she had warned Baby. Prabir had been asking around at the mela, searching high and low. Jannati had quizzed the other girls about the ominous passenger from that first night, but no one had seen anything. Even if he had done something to Baby, there was nothing they could do.

Amina stayed seated, staring straight at Salma without actually seeing her. Was this what had been lurking under the surface in the Town of Love? What could this have to do with Fauzia ignoring her, Rozy not being at school? Baby was missing, what might that mean? Amina wanted to ask, but Salma spoke again before she could summon her breath. The gaze behind the heavy turquoise eyelids fixed on Amina without emotion:

'Tamanna Khatoon should watch out.'

Amina held her breath, her heart suddenly pounding. What was Salma saying? An impatient jolt flashed through her, but she knew Salma would say only as much as she wanted, when she wanted. The slender hand with dirt under the fingernails continued to caress the sleeping baby's head. Then it stopped; Salma leaned forward to whisper and Amina could feel her breath like a warm wind across her face:

'Jabbar Aslam is not happy that she was in Katihar again.'

Amina ran the whole way back to the schoolhouse, dying to find out what Roshan knew. She hadn't decided whether to tell Tamanna about Salma's cryptic message; frankly, she didn't think her friend would have much of a reaction. Tamanna had shut herself in behind so many doors, it would take more than this to prise them back open.

Roshan had just sent the kids home with a slice of bread in each hand, plus a bonus delicacy this morning: a hard-boiled egg for each. Several of them stopped by Amina on their way out to show off their precious white trophies, to be transported safely home and shared with siblings and mothers. No, come to think of it, Amina realised – the mothers would never accept even a fraction of the protein-rich white, the ripe saffron yolk. The best piece, the biggest portion, always belonged to the sons, the husbands, the brothers.

She told Roshan about her encounter with Salma. 'Where is she getting this? What have you heard?'

Amina had to get to the bottom of this. How many times had she sensed that even Pukaar, for all its broken barriers, still moved too slowly? That they were too cautious? Someone was finally daring to speak out about the unthinkable, call it by its real name, and at Pukaar they were still moving forward with such painstaking baby steps!

Roshan squirmed under the eyes that tried to pin him down; he wasn't sure if sharing what he had heard with Amina was a good idea. Still ... she was in a better position than him to help Tamanna, should it be necessary. He cast a quick glance around him and motioned for her to come inside the schoolhouse. Tamanna was busy picking up toys left by the kindergarten kids, chatting with a couple of the mothers.

'Some people think Jabbar Aslam might come to Forbesganj,' he said in a low voice.

Amina shifted Aftaab further up on her hip.

'Jabbar Aslam? I haven't heard anything like that! Why?'

'He might be getting sick of Tamanna coming and causing trouble outside his house.'

'Causing trouble? She was looking for her daughter! She ...'

Then she remembered Roshan was not the enemy, he was on her side. He had no wish to see Tamanna beaten up by Jabbar Aslam once again. Amina bit her lip and thought it through. She usually avoided all contact with her mother-in-law, happy that she and Kasim had part of the second floor to themselves in the house they shared with his mother and his brothers. She knew that they were talked about, the curses muttered at her, the sympathy shown towards him; although her sisters-in-law greeted her with feigned respect, they never failed to sneer at her. She had preferred it this way, distance had been her best defence. God knows, her marriage to Kasim was far from an ideal alliance, but Amina was proud regardless: Kasim was both weak and violent, a dangerous and unpredictable combination, but she had managed to stay out of the flesh trade, and would keep her daughters away from it. She knew her mother-in-law was sitting downstairs, weaving her net of conspiracies together with her sister, Mumtaz Begum, and the rest of the Aslam family, planning investments and calculating profits. What were they planning now? What was in the works, with Jabbar, with Tamanna? Amina's strategy was not to lurk in the background with her ears open, her usual mode was full steam ahead, with her head bent forward, ready to charge. Even if she tried, she wouldn't be able to pick up what they were whispering in the inner rooms downstairs. If they were keeping secrets from anyone, it was from her.

And from Kasim, she realised. If it was Tamanna they were after it might well spill over onto Amina, too. The useless, unprofitable daughter-in-law who, on top of everything else, was now waging war on her own people, their traditions and their livelihood. Amina stiffened, drawing her son closer: Could Salma's warning have been meant for her as well? With Tamanna and Amina out of the way two risk factors would be stamped out at once. And dear, poor Kasim – they'd find him a new wife. One who could provide an income so he wouldn't have to work himself to the bone driving another man's rickshaw for laughable wages. One who would serve him dinner and rub his feet without making trouble every step of the way.

'What else do you know?' she asked Roshan at last.

He shook his head. 'I don't know anything. But neither Rozy nor Birbal were here today, so I'm guessing that was a message from their families.'

Amina stood still for a while, the sun filtering in through the doorway and warming her back. She could hear Tamanna with the broom outside, sweeping the ground near the water tap at the back of the house, moving pots and pans around, putting things in order. Just as Amina was about to leave, she appeared from around the corner: 'See you at the mahila mandal meeting later today.'

Tamanna's wide, placid face did not betray the slightest tension. The women's group's meeting would go forward as planned. They had to go on, what else could they do? Amina knew that Rukmini's cell phone was buzzing, sending pleas for help and calls to action to everyone who might possibly be willing to assist. Their minds were made up, they would get Rupa out.

But the meeting in the mahila mandal didn't go quite according to plan. Roshan was like a vigilant guard dog, his nostrils nervously flaring – Tamanna later thought that it was as if he had known what was coming. More than half an hour earlier than he usually sounded the gong, he grabbed the stone and struck the round metal disc. None of the kids had a watch, nor did they care about the time; rattling the desks as they jumped to their feet, they stacked the chalkboards in a pile on the windowsill. *That's it for today*.

Tamanna had stopped by her house for a little while, enjoying the spicy dal and the handful of rice that Heena had somehow managed to conjure up. The two women arrived slowly, chatting, ducking into the dimly lit room where Amina already sat waiting.

The last time they were together, Amina had argued that those who didn't come to the meetings – or came late – should be fined ten rupees! The suggestion had sparked considerable debate, but no conclusion was reached. Heena had been chosen as the group's leader, mostly due to seniority and respect, but that was how it should be. Everyone was aware that Amina was the real driving force behind it all, in her insistent and often exhausting way. Participation had gone up and down, reflecting in its own manner the volatile opinions in Prem Nagar, depending on the flow of passengers and subsequent incomes in the Town of Love. Some of the members, including the leader, were too worn-out to reap any profit in the flesh trade, and their last station was usually a merciless one: thrown out on the street, unceremoniously, with no compassion.

All these things would be dealt with in due course, Rukmini thought. In Bihar they were still in the early stages, building trust, building awareness. Lobbying for political causes in Delhi corridors was one thing, painting new dreams before the eyes of the love-women out here in Bihar was quite another. Out here in dirt-poor, heartbreaking, miraculous Bihar. Every single day Rukmini asked herself whether this was right: Should she, who was from another caste, a whole other world, be at the frontline of the Nat women's battle against forced, institutionalised prostitution? Should she, the academic from the capital city, be the one to incite rebellion among the untouchable women raising their daughters to attract and serve customers?

She knew the theory; she herself had played a part in developing it. It was people like her who *shouldn't* lead, lasting change could only come from within, from those who needed it and would live with it. And they did want and need it here, Rukmini had no doubt of that. She sat on the steps of the schoolhouse with Darya, waiting for the rest of the women in the mahila mandal and sensing the afternoon sun slowly relax its scorching grip on the village.

The thought would not let go: the impetus, the will towards change had to come from the inside. She could not alter century-long traditions, she could not uproot what had been nailed down and cemented through systems and contracts, spoken and unspoken. Change had to come from within.

But what was she supposed to do when they came to her with every little issue? Came to her when they thought the doctor had given their baby the wrong medicine. Came to her when there was a squabble over the washing posts by the river. They came with complaints about the boarding school headmistress, that she was shaving off the girls' hair, their crowning glories, to combat the spread of head lice. They came to her and Darya with disagreements about who had the right to gather wood where, which tools should be shared between those who had secured some work on someone else's land. Rukmini had tried to explain again and again that she wasn't here as a judge or mediator; she was here to challenge them to solve their own problems. The deepest, toughest issues, the ones that lurked beneath everything else. She was not here to listen to who had stolen milk from someone else's goat in the middle of the night, or who had taken the cowpat which someone else considered her rightful property.

Exasperated, Rukmini shook her head. Awareness raising, was that what this really was? And where were they, anyway? She glanced at her watch.

And then she heard it. Not the chattering down the street, not the slow trudging accompanied by the whining of the children some of the women inevitably brought to the meetings. These were other footsteps, angry, stomping footsteps, an ominous muttering that was approaching fast. She lifted her head, stood up in a hurry and pulled Darya with her into the school building. Amina and Tamanna sat bolt upright on the rug, they had heard it too. Heena had her back against the wall, not moving a muscle, her eyes glued to the door.

Heena's brother was the one heading the procession. Behind him they spotted Kasim, Prabir's brother, both of Saleem's brothers, there was the telephone man, who supplemented the sale of calling minutes by trafficking a couple of girls. Rukmini glimpsed the women right behind them, clenched fists, angry shouts. The men barged into the schoolhouse, loudly yelling at the two kajas, 'What do you think you're doing? Leave the women alone! No one asked you to come here, you're nothing but trouble! You're not welcome here! If you don't get out of Prem Nagar, we'll burn down your office, we'll cut your throats!'

In a hazy flicker Rukmini saw Amina's face beside her, her white teeth glinting as she shouted back, unafraid, 'All they've done is help you! Don't you want your kids to have a better life than this? Don't you want your sons to have real jobs, instead of sitting here all day like you, like useless drunkards? Do you want your wives and daughters to keep selling themselves, keep spreading all kinds of diseases?'

Her voice drowned in the fray; she shoved away her husband who charged at her, lunging for her arm. 'What have *you* done to make a better future for your children?'

Kasim grabbed hold of his wife, gripping her flailing arms tightly as he dragged her towards the door. Behind him, Heena's brother had zeroed in on his sister, pressing her against the wall, wheezing menacingly into the face of the gaunt woman with sunken cheeks, 'What are you doing with these people? Aren't you ashamed enough that you've moved in with *her*? Haven't we always had an arrangement under my roof? Those who earn their keep get to eat their share!'

An unexpected sound from Heena startled those around her, made them spin around to face her. A hoarse and eerie laughter, one that she couldn't stop. The voices around her quieted down and the spine-chilling sound filled the room for several seconds before Heena did something totally unprecedented. The tiny figure straightened her back, steeled herself and spoke straight into her brother's face: '*You* have eaten, that's right. Because *I* have earned. All those passengers. Every day I have earned for you, my entire life. I never got to keep a single rupee. And then ... then you took Tiya!'

As she voiced her daughter's name, Heena's strength vanished. Her knees buckled and she fell to the floor, offering no resistance to the hands pushing her brutally against the wall. What more could her brother possibly do to her? Heena closed her eyes, feeling her knees buckle and her legs give way.

They didn't lay a hand on Rukmini or Darya. Loomed around them in a threatening circle, but no one wanted to be the first to touch the foreign women. The outsiders, whom they would gladly have beaten out of town but who somehow remained protected by a force they couldn't quite name. Another caste, another religion – it was not just that, the two women themselves preached that such things didn't matter in their modern India where everyone was equal and everyone had rights. That was not the reason why the men didn't shove and push and kick Rukmini and Darya out. Ingrained in them was the strange, nameless distance, the distance made of time and full stomachs, of land ownership and cattle counted and carefully recorded. Of generation upon generation living under stable roofs. Of feelings articulated, discussed and put to rest. This was the chasm separating the two women from Delhi from the raging men in the Town of Love. This was the threshold that the fathers and brothers with their wooden sticks couldn't make themselves cross.

Rukmini stood in the middle of the room as the hurricane of chaos stormed around her. This wasn't her area of expertise, this wasn't the type of conflict she knew how to resolve. Theory and logic would do no good here, a discussion of innovative models of progress would be irrelevant. The air was shot through with fear and bitterness, pride and rage. But she had to do *something*, what could she do? She had to ensure that the women's group, everything they had worked for, didn't end this way, in a spectacle of threats and blows. Rukmini pulled herself together and took a few steps forward. The men closest to her stepped aside as she proceeded to the window, climbed up on the windowsill and clung onto the frame. Her voice didn't carry very far amidst the frenzy that roared through the schoolhouse; the dhurrie Amina had spread out was bunched up and trampled in a corner. But Rukmini hung on, and somehow the sight of her up there on the narrow brick ledge in her green kurta, feet firmly planted, had some kind of dampening effect and the shouting died down. Heena lay curled up on her side, knocked down against the wall, Tamanna stood stiff as a tin soldier on the floor.

'This will lead to nothing!'

Rukmini's voice carried through the room.

'I know you think that Pukaar is out to ruin your lives. That we're trying to tear down everything the village was built on. You say we cause trouble and commotion among the women, that we're making your children go hungry.'

The mumbling around the schoolhouse grew feverish, the shouts were like stones pelted at the woman on the windowsill. 'We were doing fine before you came here! You know nothing about what it means to be a Nat, we've always lived this way!'

Rukmini took a deep breath, refusing to take the bait. The Nats had most certainly not always lived this way. She had spent years studying the Nats' history, she knew there were many stories of origin, numerous myths and legends. Some said the Nat caste descended from two brothers assigned to collect and assemble firewood for funeral pyres. Rukmini, however, favoured the theory that the word *Nat* was a kind of professional label that had over the years become associated with various tribes and families descending from the Dom caste at the very bottom of Indian society. Nomadic people who made their living as dancers and jesters, and through different forms of simple handicraft. And by prostituting their women.

But right now Rukmini didn't breathe a word of this. It was not her job to lecture the Nats in Forbesganj about their genealogy, and it certainly wouldn't help to calm this storm. Instead, she continued down the same path of argument. 'We're not here to make trouble for anyone! Why would we want to do that? Indian law says there is no such thing as an 'untouchable', no one can be denied opportunity on the basis of their name or caste. We want everyone in Prem Nagar to have a better life, a good life!'

'How can we have a good life if we have to go hungry?'

It was Saleem's elder brother asking; he wanted her to say it out loud. So she did:

'There are other ways to feed a family than to sell your own wives and daughters!'

She knew this would refuel the flames. Still, she stood firm, like a pillar of sheer, stubborn will cemented to the window ledge, as evening darkness crept into the room.

'What other ways? Do you have jobs to offer us? You know just as well as we do, no one would let us in at the door.'

The perennial argument. And this time it was bolstered by a scornful kick in the direction of Saleem, the absent traitor: 'You don't have fancy office jobs to offer *us*, do you? Only Saleem, huh?'

And another voice: 'He thinks he's a big, posh office man. But he wasn't too good to take the money his sister earned the Nat way when he headed to his precious school in Patna!'

This was the last straw for Tamanna. Her anger was slow to alight, but enough was enough. She spun around and lashed out at Heena's brother, the closest one to her:

'All you care about is drinking and playing cards. What do we need you for anyway? We're the ones earning the money, why should we share with you? We work the hardest and eat the least, and you think you have the right to beat us up. There's no reason we should put up with it anymore. The women in Prem Nagar have finally started to get it, and that's why they come to meetings in the mahila mandal!'

Tamanna had taken it a step too far, and she knew it. She clenched her powerful fists, preparing to hit back when the slap she expected from Heena's brother would sting across her face. But it didn't happen. Something popped up between her and the raging man, a slight figure, it was Heena, on her feet and swaying feebly. A parody of defence, a joke not to be laughed at.

'Don't touch her!' Her voice was a croaking whisper. 'She's the only one who has treated me like a human being. Don't you touch her!'

And he didn't. He stood there paralysed, marvelling at this desperate flash of courage, his arms dangling, his breathing heavy. Tamanna wrapped her arms around Heena's waist and gently led her towards the door. The commotion in the room came to a halt, only Kasim jabbed his fist in the air once more before joining the others in a wavering procession along the path leading out from the schoolhouse into the Town of Love.

13

Rukmini simply had no idea what to do, how to go about it. But she had promised that Rupa would be rescued, and knew painfully well that she alone had the resources and the connections to do it. Her own life, and that of her daughter, who was driven safe and sound to her school in Delhi every day, had had a different set of circumstances from the start. Born into a family of well-educated politicians, businessmen and lawyers, the question for Rukmini had never been whether she had opportunities, but which one of them she should choose.

So how did I end up here? Rukmini asked herself. I'm no good at fieldwork. Theory and politics are my strengths, that's what I know. What am I doing here in a small town in Bihar, far from home and family, where amenities consist of cold water and a few sporadic surges of electric power? How did I end up here, where bookstores and restaurants are replaced by muddy streets swarming with black pigs and hand-drawn carts? Why are we even trying to get through to the Town of Love when all we get in return are threats? When the turmoil at the schoolhouse might well have ended with someone being beaten to death?

'Because you had to,' she answered aloud, startling herself when her voice broke the stillness in the room. Because once you've heard Tamanna's story, seen Amina's lightning-bolt rage behind the bruises, you can't simply nod in sympathy, turn around and walk away. Once Salma's eyes have met yours as she sits on display in the doorway, you know that life shows you some stops on the journey where you are actually forced to get off.

Rukmini had connections within the police. Pukaar had been cooperating with some of the local police stations for some time; she knew that several chief inspectors had been grateful for their sensitivity-training programmes for officers. None of them denied the fact that the brothel owners had their own well-established contacts in the police force. Many of them would even be glad to see the legal provisions that allowed for punishment of sex trade beneficiaries carried out, instead of seeing girls thrown in jail following arbitrary raids against those 'soliciting attention and inviting indecent conduct'. When Rukmini talked to the police she was met with sympathy, unanimous condemnation of the flesh trade, agreement on common goals. But could she convince them to instigate a raid, a rescue action in true guerilla style, all for one girl? For a girl from a caste and a background that made them wrinkle their noses in disdain, one from a class they had been brought up to despise?

Rukmini had no idea. She had arranged a meeting with Chief Inspector Laskar in Katihar the day after tomorrow. What he didn't know was that she planned to bring along the deputy superintendent from Patna, who outranked him on the police ladder. Rukmini had plenty of ideas on who should eventually be part of the team that would go in search of Rupa. She had good contacts in the media, should she get a few journalists to come along? Should she rope in a doctor, a gynaecologist? Should Saleem come along, in a surprise raid against his cousin Jabbar? How many police cars, how many officers? And what if a fight erupted; what if they were armed?

She sighed and leaned her heavy head back against the pillows, shutting her eyes. She had never meant to become an activist! But maybe activism wasn't something you chose, she thought drowsily. Maybe it chose you. All the travelling, the days and weeks away from home. The same appeals, the same letters and funding proposals drafted time and time again. The same discussions, the same feeling of powerlessness when she once again was forced to explain that no, she didn't have all the answers, and no, she couldn't do this alone.

But with every girl who wasn't forced to sell her body for food, with every man who refused to treat another human being as a purchase, a small victory was won.

She called home to Delhi and said goodnight to her family before curling up in bed again, lying still and gazing into the darkness. Listening to the trucks' endlessly blaring horns in the street below and wondering if one person could ever have the power to stop or change anything at all.

The surprise visit from Patna to Katihar didn't work out. Deputy Superintendent Vatsavani called Rukmini from Patna early the next morning to inform her that plans had changed. 'It's better if we meet here. I've requested the chief inspector from Katihar to come here at four o'clock tomorrow afternoon, it would be best if you could be here then.'

That was all he said, but she understood. The distance between the police station in Katihar and the blue house with the girls was too short; the grapevine reached too close. She sighed, pulled a sweater over her nightgown and went to make herself a cup of tea. One hundred and fifty miles to Patna. Hours and hours on horrible roads, braking, clutching and shifting gears every few seconds. Better start the preparations right away.

It was a week now since anyone had seen Baby, and Prabir knew she must be dead. This just wasn't the way it happened when a girl escaped, or ran away with a customer, or got beaten so badly that she ended up in hospital. First of all, the other Forbesganj girls would have known something. They might have sworn to cover for her, but he knew how to make them talk, and he was convinced they really had no idea where Baby was. A couple of them even started to cry hysterically when he asked, saying they wanted to go home, that they were scared, that whatever had happened to Baby, they might be next. He had told them clearly that no one was going anywhere until the mela was over, they had to work as hard as they could and think of their families at home in Forbesganj, 'Remember, they're counting on you to put food on the table!'

Baby's room had obviously been deserted in a hurry; her bag, her clothes, her makeup had all been left behind. This was not the room of a girl who had planned her escape. Jannati, the girl in the next room who said she was from Patna, was older than his own girls. Prabir didn't like her eyes, they were too curious, even when she lowered her lids. Strictly speaking, she was a little too old for this mela, she looked tired, with a hardened face. Her skin was darker than the desirable hue, the insides of her lips were stained bright pink from katha, and her thick, limp hair was streaked orange with henna. Still, there was something attractive about that firm, plump skin and those rounded arms. Prabir judged that she probably had another five years' worth of income left.

He had heard about the trouble at the schoolhouse meeting in Prem Nagar, and was glad he didn't have to worry that his own wife, Deeba, would get mixed up in the noisy women's group. But Salma was a different sort; she had talked back to his face more than once. It was a shame, but beatings were the only language Salma seemed to understand; thankfully her younger sister was easier to deal with. His first wife Lalita had done well for him in her day, providing him with two daughters and a son. Both daughters were earning their keep and the boy was all right, although he had a funny eye and was quiet and diffident.

Now Lalita's earning days were over, and he knew he could no longer afford more doctor's fees and hospital visits. Maybe her illness would run its course quickly. If he had to put a sick woman out on the street, it would be with a heavy heart. *But what am I supposed to do?* Prabir asked himself, gripping a mug of tea in one trembling hand and a bidi, a self-rolled cigarette, in the other. He couldn't let Salma and her sister spend time on their mother, they had income to bring in, many mouths to feed. And Deeba couldn't afford to tend to

Lalita, she was responsible for the cooking and housekeeping, with yet another baby on the way. Prabir shook his head. And now this goddamn Baby disappearance!

Prabir had no qualms about his business. The women were his property, that was the way it was and always had been. They did their job in safe surroundings, the system worked out for everyone: The customer met the girl at home in a relaxed atmosphere, the family set its own price, the girls were protected from abuse when he or another male relative was around. No middlemen, no unnecessary price hikes, he could keep an eye on his daughters and daughters-in-law directly. Baby was the girl he took on as an extra; she originally belonged to his youngest brother. But when his brother died in a fire two years ago he had had no choice but to take the girl under his wing, and luckily had come to a quick agreement with Fauzia. Baby hadn't been much trouble, and although she had an annoying tendency to get pregnant, he had managed to deal with that. But now, the first time he brought her to the mela, she had to go and disappear!

Prabir emptied his tea mug, shaking his weary head. Shielded his eyes from the sun: What was going on down there by the side of the road? People were gathering around two young men, the bearers of seemingly alarming news, he saw a few of the girls erupt into wailing and screaming. Prabir got to his feet and hobbled down the hill. Started to pick up a few words here and there as he approached the crowd: '... young girl ... dead in a well ... the water was poisoned ... a rancid smell ...' He stopped a few yards from the throng, meeting Jannati's eyes for a second as she turned and looked straight at him.

※

Rukmini tried to find a comfortable position in the back seat. How would she approach it? She knew threats wouldn't get her anywhere, and what leverage did she have anyway? She could express disdain, but to what avail? It would be the disdain of an intellectual, urban elite whom a policeman in Patna had no reason to identify with. Earnest pleas? But these officers were surrounded by destitution on a daily basis, why should anything *she* said make a particular impression? No, she decided and leaned her head against the edge of the seat, an emotional approach wouldn't do her any good. She couldn't do anything beyond what she always did, insist that this was inhumane, demeaning and degrading. And illegal. Against the ITPA, the Immoral Trafficking Prevention Act, the law that prohibited the trafficking of human beings for commercial sexual exploitation. She knew it inside out: the articles addressing administration of or complicity in running a brothel; use of private property as a brothel; knowing sustenance from prostitution-generated income; purchase, initiation, or manipulation of women into prostitution; imprisonment inside a brothel or other locale where prostitution took place. And so on. She knew the law. The police knew it too. They knew especially well the section that listed the girl as the criminal, the one article that bullied a frightened girl who never saw a single paisa of her earnings, into giving the policeman the only thing she had to offer when he threateningly waved Section 8 in her face: a fine of five hundred rupees or a prison sentence of up to six months for anyone who 'offers or solicits prostitution in a public place'.

Rukmini closed her eyes. Thought of the ups and downs. The joy of a successful group session with policemen in a provincial town. The despair over the phone call the next morning from the sentry girls at the Nepal border, with news of yet another truck loaded with human cargo under the tarpaulin covering. They had accomplished so much. And so much still remained.

Deputy Superintendent Vatsavani in Patna was friendly and approachable, and stood up out of respect when she entered his office. The corridor and the adjoining rooms were teeming with people; tea boys, police officers in uniform, clerks behind wobbly desks overflowing with stacks of paper, defendants with downcast eyes, women with their faces hidden behind the corners of their dupattas. Mr. Vatsavani's office was calmer, with just one assistant stationed by the door, awaiting his orders. And the chief inspector from Katihar had already arrived. The short and square P. Laskar with his heavy moustache also got to his feet, greeting her courteously, but Rukmini could feel his dark, reticent gaze sizing her up. She even spied a flash of impatience in Mr. Vatsavani's eyes, he had other critical matters to deal with, more important meetings to attend. Issues more pressing than sitting here across from a woman young enough to be his daughter, listening to yet another sob story about some poor girl selling her body in a brothel in Katihar. There were hundreds of them. Thousands! Nevertheless, he politely offered Rukmini a chair and a cup of tea and made small talk for a few minutes before leaning back in his chair with an inviting 'So, how can we help you?'

She was slightly stunned – he knew full well what this was about, hadn't they already gone over the details of a possible rescue action in Kuli Pada over the phone? And then she understood: She had to be the one to break the news to the chief inspector from Katihar. She had to be the one to explain the whole plan to P. Laskar, so that it wouldn't be his superior implying any corruption or defection within the ranks. So she chose her words carefully. Took her time to tell not only Rupa's story, but Tamanna's as well, to recount how the mother of the girl they aimed to rescue had also been captured and sold by the same family. She explained how Tamanna had appealed to the police in Katihar on several occasions, taking care to avoid direct accusation that they had neglected their duty. Pointed out, wary of irritating the two policemen, article by article which sections of the law were broken daily in the blue house with the girls on the balcony. She took a breath and calmed herself down before sketching out the suggested rescue action she had in mind, and watched Chief Inspector Laskar's eyes cloud over as she outlined the details. She met his gaze unflinchingly. 'Jabbar Aslam and his brothers have several houses full of girls,' she said. 'Many of them are minors. And everyone in Katihar knows about it.'

Maybe she shouldn't have said that last part, giving Mr. Vatsavani an obvious opening to interrogate the chief inspector from Katihar on what had been done to address the problem. When he fortunately didn't seize it, she understood that he was willing to help. Somewhere behind the long face, with eyes bordered in deep wrinkles, she saw that he agreed, that he was willing to do this.

The deputy superintendent in Patna leaned forward in his chair and arranged two pens on his desk into perfect parallel lines before addressing his colleague.

'How quickly can you mobilise the personnel for a rescue action?' he asked. 'We'll provide backup support from here, of course.'

A weighty, warm relief washed over Rukmini. The decision had been made.

Chief Inspector P. Laskar had left them and started his return trip when Rukmini was offered the chance to speak to someone located elsewhere in the building. The feeling of disillusionment clouded her joy over the support for Rupa's rescue as Mr. Vatsavani told her about the raid in Patna's own red-light district a few days ago, when twenty-four girls were brought in. *This is exactly what we want to stop!* she thought, exhausted. That it was the girls, the frightened children with no knowledge of the law or their own rights, who were seized. That those behind the scenes, pulling the strings and filling their pockets, never saw the inside of a prison cell. Rukmini took a breath and began to feel the old rage fill her lungs, letting it seethe back out as she exhaled wordlessly. She was here for Rupa. She was here for Tamanna's bruises, Tamanna's humiliation. Today she was here to save just one life.

'Of course I'll speak to them,' she said.

She was left in a waiting room, in an upholstered leather chair across from a sergeant fastidiously typing some report. He hacked away at the keyboard with two fingers as if to underline the importance of the words. When Mr. Vatsavani at last returned he had four girls in tow, none of whom looked a day over fifteen. They clumped together by the door, each of them trying to shield herself behind the others.

Rukmini began by introducing herself, explaining that she worked with an organisation (*Did they know the word?*) whose goal was to get girls out of prostitution (*Did they understand that she was talking about them?*), and that there were alternatives to the situation they were in. Her heart began to sink as she realised that she was not getting through to them; their eyes flickered, nervously glancing in Mr. Vatsavani's direction. She changed her tactic, trying a more direct approach:

'How old are you?'

'Eighteen.'

The voice was barely audible, but the answer was clear enough.

'How many children do you have?'

'Two.'

'Do you know why you're here?'

The girl nodded vigorously, her thick black braid bouncing up and down.

'I'll never do it again. It was a very bad thing to do and I won't do it again.'

The girl recited her sentence without meeting their eyes.

Rukmini waited a moment before trying again.

'Have you been looked at by a doctor?'

The girl hesitated a few seconds before nodding. Rukmini sought out Mr. Vatsavani's eyes; he immediately took the hint and gave her the facts in English: 'Eight of them have tested positive for HIV.'

The girls stood still where they had been placed, immobile as the conversation continued in English above their heads:

'What do you do with them?'

He gave her a long look.

'What can we do?'

And now the deputy superintendent spoke directly to the girl:

'Did they offer for you to go to the rehabilitation home here in Patna?'

The girl nodded, it was irrelevant that she had no idea what a rehabilitation home was.

'But you said no?' To Rukmini, in English: 'They said no, all of them.'

The girl's gaze shifted to a point above his head as she repeated: 'I'll never do it again, it was a bad thing.'

Rukmini shook her head in frustration and tried to shoot the girls an encouraging smile before they were led away from the room. She could have asked them how they were being treated, how the food was, if they had a place to bathe. That might have triggered a complaint, might have led to slightly more or slightly better food today. But it wouldn't lead them out of the life they undoubtedly were headed back to, when their pimps had paid the price to get them out of jail. Back to what always lay beneath. What made them lie about their age, insist that they were not minors, that they were married, that they had never done this before and it would never happen again. The children. Their children, who were left in the brothels and whom they would never see again if they didn't recite the answers precisely as instructed.

When she asked him what would happen to these girls, she knew the answer before he even opened his mouth. 'When the fine is paid, they'll go back to where they came from.'

Focus on Rupa, she repeated to herself on the car ride back. We're going to get Rupa out.

Tamanna didn't at all look overjoyed when Rukmini saw her the next morning. Mournful shadows encircled her eyes, and the voice thanking her over and over again was heavy with anxiety. Rukmini's own apprehension over what she had promised on everyone's behalf overflowed into exasperation:

'What is it? Why aren't you happy? I traveled to Patna and back yesterday for this!'

The broad, resolute lower lip quivered just a little when Tamanna simply and perfectly put it all into perspective: 'Rupa won't be saved even if we manage to rescue her.'

※

The moon was uncommonly large the night Tamanna herself ran away. Yellowish white and nearly full, it had seemed much closer than usual, so close that she had been able to see every wrinkle in the face of the man on the moon. Was it this clarity, this radiant white light, that had given her the courage to jump? She had known they suspected her; she had been beaten for it many times. Jabbar wasn't stupid; he had understood that four vanished girls were no coincidence. But they had never caught her red-handed, it had always been when he was asleep, or in a drunken stupor, that she had helped a girl prise open the gate out to the balcony. Let the one who had had enough and had banished all thoughts of the consequences slip away into the night. Either down in the swamp behind the house, a fifteen- or twenty-foot fall, or the path of less physical peril but with greater risk of being spotted, from roof to roof along the neighbouring houses.

Each time she had unlocked the gate to the balcony with sweaty palms and a racing heart, she had thought to herself, next time. *Next time it will be me.* Next time they entrust me to watch the store while they drink themselves senseless, I'll do it. But then there was Rupa. Rupa who called Dolly *Amma* and Jabbar *Abba*, who addressed Mumtaz Begum as *Dadi*, grandmother. Who looked at her, Tamanna, as just another woman in the blue house. Since the five-year-old slept behind locked doors in another part of the house, since she wouldn't be able to throw herself off the twenty-foot ledge into the swamp cradling Rupa in her arms, she had never jumped. But the light of that strangely close moon had made everything look different. That night, it was precisely because of Rupa that she had had to jump.

It had been surprisingly easy, actually. She had brought nothing with her and sneaked out onto the balcony without arousing any suspicion. Had hesitated for just a second before leaping over the edge.

The moon had stayed with her the whole night, she had talked to it as she gasped for breath through her tears, running at a stumbling pace. '*What have I done, what have I done now? Oh Rupa, what have I done?*' She hadn't let her feet rest until she was out of Katihar, standing there feeling the blood throb at the back of her throat and a whirring, dizzy awareness, a wave pouring through her head: 'I've made it.'

Once again, she had sworn the two solemn vows a brutalised twelve-year-old had made herself one morning an eternity ago:

'*One day I'll get out of here. One day I'll get revenge.*'

Tamanna pulled herself together and returned to the neat, ordinary office of Pukaar and the all but ordinary decision that had been made.

'I'm not unhappy, Rukmini didi,' she said. 'I, too, have travelled a long way for this.'

14

Salma had known it all along: the hospital in Katihar would never be an option for her mother. She had had the doctor at Referral Hospital examine Lalita again a few times, but the only result had been meaningless talk of surgeries and price tags so high she hadn't even bothered to mention them to Prabir. Lalita's body had a swollen protrusion on the left side of the abdomen, a tender lump they said came from bacteria lodged in the tissue surrounding the inflamed gland.

Salma sensed that her mother had given up. Lalita knew that there was no money, knew she was getting worse, that the end was near. And that, in spite of everything, this might be the best possible end. Passengers had almost stopped coming even before she fell ill, and the few that came paid very little. Now, she was only filling time and space and draining money for medicine, keeping Salma from earning and keeping Deeba from taking care of the family. Lalita had seen fates like hers and Heena's play themselves out before. Prabir might not be as heartless as Heena's brother and throw an old woman out on the street, but she couldn't be completely sure. And she had absolutely no desire to become a charity case for Tamanna Khatoon. She took the cup from Salma's hand, swallowed the tablet dissolved in water, lay back and closed her eyes.

Lalita was unconscious when Baby's body was brought back to Prem Nagar the next day. She lay in the shade on the bed Salma normally used – today her eldest daughter had no intention of moving from her chair in the doorway. With her usual shocking pink lipstick and earrings dangling below her pulled-back hair, Salma sat stone-faced when her father came by after Baby's body had been delivered to Fauzia's house and he had spoken to the imam about the funeral arrangements. A few remarks about who would wash and prepare the corpse, and then he actually asked after Lalita. 'How is your mother doing?'

Salma took the time to look into his gaze, watching for his reaction. 'She is getting ready to die.'

Did she catch something in his eye before he nodded sharply? No, probably not. Just a shadow across his face as he turned away from the door.

A small group of women stood in the background at Baby's funeral, outside the low fence surrounding the graveyard behind the mosque. The dilapidated, once-painted-red house of worship was the centre for the religious necessities, governed by the need of the Nats to blend as seamlessly as possible into their surroundings. The prayer for the dead had already been recited at Fauzia's house; the ceremony at the mosque took place mostly in silence. The body wrapped in its white shroud was sunk into the earth, carefully leaned on its right side. Three handfuls of earth were sprinkled, followed by a few words from the imam about life and death, the good deeds to be done before leaving this world behind.

Had Baby done any good deeds? Probably, Amina thought as she gathered Aftaab and her youngest daughter, turning her back on the graveyard as the setting sun slipped behind the dome of the mosque. At least, she didn't know of any bad things Baby had done. Foolish things, no doubt, and the most foolish of all had been going to the mela.

She turned to Tamanna and Heena, slowly plodding along beside her: 'I told her, do you remember? That the biggest mistake she could possibly make was to go to the mela?'

Heena looked back at her with weary eyes. 'Did she have a choice?'

They both turned to Tamanna, waiting for her response. But her focus was elsewhere, her gaze following a strange woman slowly making her way up through the Town of Love. Was this the same woman hanging back alone behind a grove of trees at Baby's funeral, so far away that she couldn't possibly have seen or heard anything? Tamanna had thought her a mirage, for when she had turned back to look at her again a moment later, the woman had vanished. Tamanna strained her eyes, trying to connect the faint dots between the figure disappearing up the street and a memory someplace deep inside her. The blue sari stretched taut across wide hips, something in her swaying gait seemed familiar. Smooth, shiny hair and a short, pink jacket.

For a moment Tamanna's lower lip seemed to be quivering, just for a moment, before she lifted her hand to tuck a strand of hair in place behind her ear. 'Sometimes,' she asserted, 'Sometimes, I think the biggest mistake we make is being born.'

They passed by Salma on her chair in the doorway, but she turned her head away without saying hello.

※

'But don't you think it could backfire?'

Darya nudged her glasses back up on her nose.

'What do you mean?'

Rukmini looked inquisitively at her colleague before taking a long sip from her teacup. She shuddered and made a face. 'Ugh, it is cold. Why would taking the TV-team with us backfire?'

'I don't know ... I guess I'm just nervous. The whole rescue operation ... there's so much that could go wrong!'

'Of course things could go wrong. That's a given.'

The Pukaar leader from Delhi walked over to the sink and emptied out the cold tea.

'But it's the right thing to do.' She turned abruptly to Darya, 'You agree with that, don't you?'

'Well yes, of course, but ...'

Darya was struggling to find the right words.

'Of course it's the right thing to do, but ... the consequences could be catastrophic! Both for those involved and for our entire network! And dragging a TV-team along –'

Rukmini interrupted before she could finish the sentence.

'But don't you see – getting the whole rescue on video is what will offer Rupa the best protection! If we document everything that happens, things are much less likely to turn violent, and the police will be forced to stay the course and do their job!'

The idea had occurred to Rukmini out of the blue last night. She had been scanning old e-mails for some other reason when the name of a journalist friend had suddenly popped up. An old acquaintance from another life, a time when media contacts had been part of her job in the Department of Justice. Before she had realised that those who most needed a spokesperson had none at all, and had ventured down the path that had led her here, to this tiny office in Forbesganj. Her journalist friend was working with a private TV network in Delhi, had kept up with Rukmini's work, and had greeted her impulsive phone call this morning with encouragement. 'Of course we'd be interested, this could be a great story. When are you going in?'

There was no doubt in Rukmini's mind that they needed all the help they could get. It was only Darya who wasn't completely sure, not a hundred percent.

'It's just ... it's something about the exposure. It seems so cruel for Rupa to have her humiliation unfold on television – do you know what I mean?'

Darya looked helplessly at her colleague, who still stood by the sink. Of course she could see how on-site recording, minute by minute, would protect Rupa; it might even increase the chance that Jabbar was jailed and punished. But still?

Rukmini nodded. 'I see what you're thinking. Exploitation is all Rupa has ever known, and obviously we don't want this to become yet another freak show.'

Darya nodded, too; this seemed to echo what she was thinking. Things had been done to Rupa her whole life, they had to make sure the rescue didn't become one more free spectacle for anyone who wanted to see. She sighed again, wiping her glasses clean.

Rukmini sat down next to her.

'Listen, there are two things we have to accomplish here. The most important one is to get Rupa out, and I really do think the TV-team will be an asset here. The other issue is our work in a larger context, getting more girls out after Rupa, bringing this whole flesh trade to an end. And for that to happen, we have to spread the word about what really goes on, and what better way to do that than through television?'

Everything Rukmini said was logical and meaningful. Every step that helped them push in the right direction was good. But still, there was something lurking, something to do with ... dignity?

Darya replaced her glasses and gave another decisive nod. It was settled. 'And we'll need access to a doctor,' she said. 'We'll have to be able to document any injuries. For evidence in court.'

The door creaked open, they both looked up. Saleem poked his head in, he had just come back from an hour with his sister. Sharing a cup of tea and a dream that no one else knew of. Darya and Rukmini exchanged glances. They had been unsure as to what extent Saleem should be involved in this. A rescue action in pure guerilla style was a far cry from Pukaar's usual approach. And for Saleem there was so much more at stake. The fine line he walked was already razor-thin, the constellations of his family grouped in the most difficult ways possible. Should he now participate in a direct effort to arrest his own cousin?

Rukmini knew that Tamanna didn't see it that way. On the contrary – to Rupa's mother, those who knew the degradation of the dhanda way of life firsthand had an even greater obligation to do whatever they could. And Saleem knew. Knew more than he had ever let on to his colleagues at Pukaar.

So the question of whether to let Saleem in on the plan had been left hanging. The unspoken verdict was that he could decide for himself, take the initiative and jump in if he thought the risks were worth it. He sat with them in the office all day, overheard the phone conversations, talked to everyone who stopped by. He knew what was in store, but whether or not to participate would have to be his decision.

'Hello,' he greeted them from the doorway. The street lamp outside turned him into a silhouette with no features.

'I just wanted to let you know, I'm coming with you to get Tamanna's daughter.'

Sona had made up her mind to believe. Believe it was a boy, believe that she would get to keep him, believe that everything would go well. Believe that he would stay protected there in the dark, that he would come out healthy and strong. She opened up completely and smiled a big smile with crooked teeth under her misshapen nose: a healthy boy, and he would be good to her, he would love her. Of course he would! She would have a wonderful boy with no father, only a mother. He would grow up to be tall and robust, he would go to school and become a doctor, he would build her a house and she would care for them, just the two of them. Sona squeezed her eyes shut again, pushing away the tiny room in the blue house, with bad air and the doors bolted shut. She was going to believe. Believe her child through all the fears, protect it beneath the bulging veins and the translucent skin, swear it into life and happiness. It was a boy. It had to be a boy.

Jabbar Aslam had cancelled his plans to go to Forbesganj, at least for now. He had managed to contain the damage done by Tamanna's last visit; it had cost him a few extra gifts and favours here and there, but everything seemed to have calmed down now. The knife rested on the shelf by his bed. He was more concerned about the news leaking out over the past few weeks that Saleem, his cousin on his mother's side, was doing his best to actively undermine the business. The passengers were talking, his friends in the police were talking, others in the business from Kuli Pada were talking. And the latest rumour was that Saleem was working with Tamanna, no less! That someone was paying that wretched woman to spread her evil lies about him and his family in Katihar, and that Saleem was in on it! 'Dhoka,' he sneered to Mumtaz, fuming. 'Traitor, what a traitor! Turning his back on his own family, how could he do this?'

His mother looked back at him, her lips pursed tightly. She agreed completely. It was nothing less than a betrayal, the way her deceased sister's youngest son was acting. As for his two elder brothers, at least they had wives and daughters-in-law working and making money. Saleem wasn't married, didn't even have a keep, a girl to cook and clean and keep him company at night! His sister working to put him through school was one thing. But was this what he was using his education for? She shook her head, scowling at her son. What a betrayal.

'Sona isn't feeling well,' she said, changing the subject. 'Complaining that she's in pain.'

Mumtaz didn't go into detail. Headache, swollen legs, these were women's issues not worth whining about.

Jabbar's eyes clouded up in anger. The last thing he needed was more problems. Hadn't he provided for these girls? Didn't he give them a safe roof over their heads, bought medicine to treat their endless aches and pains? Jabbar snapped:

'We can't afford her whining and snivelling. She can put in a few more weeks of work.'

Rupa was ill as well. She had a fever, and she was bleeding. Not in the usual, normal way, but because of what he did to her. The old creep, she thought with a shuddering grimace. Drank too much, and couldn't perform. Rupa had long ago figured out that the most dangerous ones were those who drank too much and then got furious when they couldn't make it work.

Sometimes, when they drank so much they fell asleep, she would get a second to rest. If she just let them lie there, they wouldn't always remember whether they had done it once they woke up, and best to let them believe they had. But if they recalled the sad charade, and if they were greedy enough, they would go to Mumtaz demanding their money back, claiming the girl was 'worthless'. And then she would be beaten, with the belt or the rod, but she would much rather have that. Much rather have that than his relentless pushing and struggling in spite of both him and her knowing the futility of it. Like the night four days ago. He had demanded that Rupa make him perform. And he hadn't wanted it the regular way, but the other, unnatural, painful way she hated more than anything. He wouldn't give up, screaming and shouting, pummelling her back with his fists as she stood on all fours sobbing. She didn't know what he used in the end, she had refused to turn around. But it had felt cold, and hard, and it had pressed and forced its way into her and torn her apart. Before he had thrown a few extra notes on the floor next to her and left.

She wasn't able to go to the toilet, that was the worst part. The bleeding, the fever, the pain, she could handle all that. But she didn't dare use the toilet, the thought was insufferable, she held it in. Rupa refused to let Mumtaz Begum look at her, refused to see the doctor. The old woman saw through her anyway, gave her gulkand at first, rose-petal candy, followed by almond oil in warm milk to speed up her metabolism. Mumtaz knew constipation wasn't the problem here, knew Rupa was holding it in on purpose. 'If you don't go now, I'm giving you senna leaves tomorrow,' she threatened. Rupa didn't care. *It can't be worse than this*, she thought through the torrents of fever, faintly noting that the towel folded underneath her was soaked in blood.

'Is there something going on?'

Saleem looked back at Fauzia and shoved the paan further in with his tongue before answering. 'Something going on, no, why do you ask?'

They sat perched on the ground outside her shack, he had come to visit her while she ate her evening meal. Fauzia insisted on sharing the food with her brother, but he refused: 'No, didi, I have eaten, it's the truth. Give me some paan, I'll keep you company.'

Fauzia ate slowly, savouring each bite. 'It's just ... after the trouble at the women's meeting at school, people are talking.'

'Talking about what?'

He tried to keep his voice light.

'Oh, you know ...'

She stopped there, and he had to keep pushing, though he didn't like it.

'Talking about what, Fauzia didi?'

His sister slowly chewed a piece of bread. Was she hesitating, just for a moment?

'I've heard people swear that your school will be forced to close down.'

He didn't know how seriously to take it. The school and its teachers had always been under threat, along with Amina and Tamanna for running the kindergarten. And he suspected his sister might not be telling the whole truth, she could be sly like that. Portioning out her information in tiny increments, to pry out the details she wanted from him in exchange. He went on the offensive:

'That's old news. Roshan and the school have been threatened before.'

She said nothing in reply, slowly scooping up the rest of the yellow lentil stew with a piece of bread. He tried to lure her in:

'Of course, it would be such a shame if something were to happen. Now that Rozy has just learned to read.'

That sparked her attention. Her head snapped up, her jaw froze midway through a mouthful. Rozy was the only soft spot in

Fauzia's heart. It was too late for children of her own, and she was far from spoiling her niece, that wouldn't be Fauzia's style. But she saw something of herself in Rozy. The willowy girl, not especially cute or charming, always keeping her distance from everything and everyone, never beaming a smile or engaging in idle conversation. Taking a piece of chewing gum when offered, saying thank you and following orders, but staying at arm's length. Hiding behind an invisible wall for as long as she could.

'Rozy?' Fauzia looked back at her brother, confused.

'Yes.'

He knew this was emotional blackmail.

'Wouldn't it be good if she could stay in school? Learn reading and math well enough to run her own shop? Imagine that, Fauzia! Maybe a tailor's shop. Or a little candy store. You could help her get started.'

He went for the final flourish, laying down the trump card.

'She could live with us, you know. In our house. She'd be safe there. But if we don't know what will happen to the school ...'

He left it suspended in midair.

His sister examined him, long and hard. How could her brother possibly understand how she lived? Never reacting to the anguish on the girls' faces in the doorways. Nor to the shouts and curses hurled at children and dogs alike in the Town of Love, the beatings in broad daylight and behind paper-thin walls a few feet from her paan-stand. Showing nothing but indifference to the spiteful insults targeting her brother, the traitor, the constant muttering that he shouldn't get too comfortable. She couldn't react, couldn't show how she was being torn in half. She owed him everything; after all, she was sitting here behind a paan-counter on a wooden platform instead of on a chair in a doorway. But she was Nat, and so was he. Their brothers and their families, nieces and nephews, cousins, they would never escape their part in it. Of course, she had no greater dream than moving into a house with Saleem, a clean house with no one sitting in the doorway, where Rozy could come home from school with books in a bookbag and eat food that she, Fauzia, had cooked. But could she go through with it, knowing that it had cost them everything? That all ties to Prem Nagar had been severed because her brother had chosen to go against his own people?

Fauzia shook her head slowly, more to herself than to Saleem. Decided to call his bluff.

'You know as well as I do that it makes no difference,' she said, her voice heavy with exhaustion.

'You know her father would never let her go.'

Embarrassment flushed Saleem's cheeks and a slightly wounded frown crept across his mouth. Fauzia felt her throat tighten; this was her brother, he wished nothing but the best for her. And of course she wanted the house, oh, how badly she wanted the house across the river! With a real kitchen, an indoor bathroom, one bedroom for Saleem and one for her. So let them hate her for it.

'They say you're going to regret it,' she said. Fixed her unreadable dark gaze straight into her brother's eyes.

'Who ... who is saying that?'

His voice didn't tremble, just a slight clearing of his throat.

She had said too much already. She knew that the walls in the Town of Love had not only ears, but antennae. Long tentacles that snatched up every trace of gossip or ill will, every minuscule hint of treachery. So Fauzia said no more, the nod of her head was enough. A slight nod in the direction of the house up the street, where Amina's stubbornness and Kasim's threats were the least of the current problems. Fauzia's nod was directed at the two older men in the house, Kasim's big brothers. One of them had two daughters and a daughter-in-law in prostitution, the other was married to the daughter of an elder in the panchayat, the village council. It wasn't hard to guess how they felt about Saleem. The educated cousin who gave speeches and wrote petitions they could not read. The traitor supreme, the king of dhoka!

Saleem didn't want to ask, but it was impossible not to.

'What do they know?'

A tiny ripple across Fauzia's immovable face, a twitch of one eyebrow. What did he mean? So there was something going on, she thought. *Little wise, foolish brother, there is something, but you don't want to tell me what it is.* She slowly got to her feet and picked up the empty plate.

'I have to go sell paan,' she said. 'My customers are waiting.'

15

Lalita's funeral came three days after Baby's. Salma bathed her mother, pushed her sister away, turned her back to Heena and the others who had come to help. This was one thing she wanted to do alone. Her mother lay on the bed, she seemed so small, like a shell, a bird. Salma followed the rituals, washing the private parts gently with a clean washcloth. She cleaned the teeth, the nostrils, washed her mother's hair and braided it. Stood in the doorway watching as Prabir and the other men carried the corpse away, disappearing in the direction of the graveyard. Lifted Nila up with both arms, squeezed the soft, plump body against her own.

She told Prabir the next day. He had awoken earlier than usual, came gruff and red-eyed into the inner courtyard where Deeba sat on her haunches shearing the stalks off a bunch of green okra. Muttered something about tea and walked by Salma without a word. And then, as if she suddenly popped up on his radar, he turned around: 'Why haven't you made yourself up?'

Her hair hung loose and unwashed, her kurta was stained.

'No one will want you looking like that,' he said curtly. He began to turn away but something in her gaze held him back. She had always been stubborn, Lalita's eldest daughter, but this was something else. A determination that would not be compromised.

'Okay,' Salma said slowly. 'I'll get ready. I'll go earn the money. But I want something in return.'

A surge of exhaustion overwhelmed him. The problems never stopped piling up, there was always something with these women. Exhaling slowly, he took a teacup from Deeba before she turned around, her belly jiggling all the way back to the vegetables.

'I want to keep Nila,' Salma said, locking eyes with her father. 'She'll be my daughter. And she will never take a single passenger.'

He turned sharply to face her, mechanically jerking his right arm into the air. His mouth opened to swear at her, spew out a stream of threats and curses, but they halted halfway off his tongue. Salma's face, her resolve cemented like earth and steel. It made no difference who the child called Amma, he thought wearily, they all lived under the same roof. Deeba was expecting another one soon anyway, it would be easier for her if Salma took care of Nila. And when Nila got old enough ... he brushed the thought away. No need to keep today's promises tomorrow.

But he had to say something. It wasn't just Prabir Salma was challenging, it was his livelihood, all that he stood for.

'You won't be able to take care of a kid. And I'm her father.'

She narrowed her eyes at him. Oh, there was so much she could say.

'A randi's baby has no father,' she said at last. 'Only a mother. That's enough.'

Deeba sat very quietly by the brick oven, her knife had stopped chopping stalks off the vegetables. Nila's mother did not turn her head; her face showed no sign of having heard what had been said. Prabir would be the one to decide.

Slowly, he lowered his arm. 'You'll keep taking just as many passengers as before,' he said. Tried to make his voice firm and threatening, but it came out feeble and had no effect on the young woman silhouetted in the light that poured in from the street. The white sunshine blazed through her thin, loose-hanging kurta. Washed away the stains, formed a shimmering suit of armour around her body.

※

Amina was angry. She felt her blood boil beneath the moist tendrils curling around her forehead, she yanked her daughter's hand impatiently as she hurried her down the dusty road. Shifted her son further up her hip and picked up the pace as she turned onto the path towards the schoolhouse. After the catastrophic mahila mandal meeting they had agreed to keep the school and kindergarten closed for a few days to see if things calmed down. Above all, they couldn't afford to lose the trust of the parents who had faithfully been sending their children here. Amina hadn't spoken to Roshan in several days. She had a vague plan to look for him in the schoolhouse, he might be at his desk in the corner catching up on paperwork.

Amina's rage grew and sparked off in many directions. She was angry that the women's group appeared to be falling apart, angry that the school was closed, angry that Rukmini and Darya and Saleem were so cautious, so *scared!* How far would she, Amina, ever have come if she had been scared? She was angry with Kasim, angry with his brothers, angry that Baby was dead. Amina dragged her daughter up the front steps and poked her head into the quiet, shadowy classroom: 'Namaste!'

The teacher returned her greeting, gave his woollen hat a little pull and shuffled the papers on his desk. She sat down next to him; there was a momentary silence.

'When can we open the school again, Roshan bhaiya?'

His melancholy eyes fell to rest on her indignant face, her pursed lips.

He shook his head. 'I don't know. Rukmini says that …'

'Rukmini doesn't know everything, does she?'

Amina was surprised at her own shrill voice, but she had to continue: 'How long are we supposed to keep everything on hold? Wait for new training sessions that will help us find new sources of income. Wait for the food stamps we have a right to. Wait for the children to be allowed to go back to school and kindergarten. Wait for Tamanna to …'

She stopped herself in time. Didn't say 'get her daughter out'. Amina knew it was prudent to keep quiet. She was happy not to be part of the rescue operation, shuddered at the thought of her husband and his brothers. They would kill her if she were involved in this, if they even knew that she knew, she was sure of that. Still, the fury glowed inside her, the old fire that had carried Amina through days of desperation and nights of crushing defeat. She would have loved to come, to get all the girls out and have Kasim's revolting cousin thrown in jail!

'Wait for Tamanna to … what?'

Roshan's voice was as mild as his eyes. She averted her own gaze and shook her head. Heard his anticipation filling the room. Pulled herself together and looked at him:

'Wait for Tamanna to be left in peace.'

Her cheeks burned bright from the lie.

Roshan scratched his chin and leaned his narrow head back down over the stack of papers.

On the way back Amina calmed down a little. Realised that she couldn't blame the teacher, he was walking a finer line than all the rest of them: ridiculed by the Nat men, probably much more involved in the women's lives than he wished to be, idolised by the children she knew he'd do anything to protect.

There were two others waiting in line when she arrived at Fauzia's paan-stand. The first one, a man she had never seen before, bought two cigarettes and disappeared on his motorcycle. The other was Heena's daughter; the stocky girl with the vacant stare said nothing as she handed over her two-rupee coin. But Fauzia knew her customers; she gave the girl a zarda paan and two pieces of chewing gum. She shuffled back down the street towards her uncle's house, where a chair awaited her in the doorframe.

Amina nodded hello, dug out some money from her purse and pointed to a dusty packet of biscuits. Fauzia handed it to her in silence along with the correct change. Amina's irritation bubbled back to the surface: Fauzia should be supporting them! She had escaped the flesh trade herself – how could she just sit there with that vaguely mocking smile under the hooked nose, instead of helping them? Amina knew she should keep quiet, but as usual, she couldn't help herself.

'Fauzia didi,' she said in the friendliest voice she could muster. 'It must be sad and very quiet for you, now that Baby's gone.'

Was that a glimmer of something under the paan-saleswoman's half-closed eyelids? Served her right! Amina thought in triumph. Fauzia deserved to remember the horror that happened to her tenant, a fate Amina held her partly responsible for: hadn't she helped Prabir keep Baby in traffic by renting out a room to her?

Fauzia's stubborn silence pushed Amina further, she had nothing to lose.

'You know you're more than welcome to come join the mahila mandal? We're having another meeting soon,' she blurted out, untruthfully, about the women's group no one had as much as mentioned since the schoolhouse commotion. 'As soon as things calm down a little,' she added.

At last, Fauzia opened her mouth. Her voice dragged itself up her throat, the words crawled slowly over her tongue: 'Things won't calm down for a long time. And the new woman will only make it worse.'

Amina stared open-mouthed at the paan-saleswoman: 'The new woman …?'

But Fauzia said no more. She lowered her head, took out a green betel leaf from the water dish and began folding it.

Amina found Tamanna and Heena under the mango tree. It wasn't big and didn't bear much fruit, but now its colours were starting to ripen into yellow. Tamanna's mangoes were the sweet Alfonso-type, the slightly heart-shaped fruit with the meat so juicy that the smell alone made it burst and tickle inside your cheek. When Amina entered the courtyard through the flimsy gate, Heena got to her feet and vanished quickly into the house. She had always had the feeling

Amina didn't like her, and it had only intensified after she had moved in with Tamanna. Heena had cultivated the art of treading lightly her whole life; nothing could be more natural for her than to disappear from sight as soon as she sensed a hint of ill will.

Amina sank down in a chair, placing Aftaab into his five-year-old big sister's arms: 'You watch him!' Tamanna glimpsed the familiar anger in her face and waited wordlessly, knowing from experience that the reason would soon come out. She was about to offer Amina a cup of water when her friend snapped, 'Who is the new woman?'

Tamanna had no idea what she meant. As far as she knew there had been no new arrivals in the Town of Love in recent days, other than the constant flow of passengers coming and going.

'The new woman ... what do you mean?'

'That's what Fauzia said!'

Tamanna heaved a quiet sigh. How much easier it would be if Amina would just say exactly what she was so upset about!

'What did she say?'

'She said things would not be quiet again in Prem Nagar for a while. And that the new woman would make it even worse.'

'What new woman?'

'That's exactly what I'm wondering!'

Amina tugged at the dupatta around her shoulders.

Tamanna furrowed her eyebrows. Fauzia, who never said anything, about herself or anyone else, what could she have meant? The picture formed back in her mind's eye. The blue sari stretched across wide hips, the swaying gait that was unlike anyone else's. A short, pink jacket; the prettiest one Tamanna, no, Hasina, had ever seen. A pink jacket disappearing into a pickup truck with letters painted on the side. Goods Carrier.

Tamanna stood up sharply, her eyes suddenly wild: 'Come on! It's Jannati! We have to find her!'

It did not prove difficult. They scurried up the main street in the Town of Love, over the bridge where someone had finally removed the stinking dead dog from the river, past the hospital with its sad assemblage outside of hopeless patients and penniless next-of-kin. They threw themselves into the perilous task of navigating the street down to the bus station in Forbesganj on foot, weaving in and out between trucks and buses, ox-carts and speeding mopeds. Tamanna had scooped up Amina's daughter and held her in her arms as she ran, while her friend charged forward with her son glued to her hip. They didn't discuss where they were headed, Amina didn't even know whom they were looking for. She just blindly followed Tamanna, who had but one thought in her head: the buses. The wheezing, overflowing jalopies barrelling down the street with deafening blares and total disregard for anything that got in their way – they were all Tamanna could think of. It was Jannati she had seen; Jannati, who had for some reason travelled to Forbesganj to see Baby buried. How could she not have recognised her at once? Everything that had happened that day in Chhukha, every colour, every whiff of a passing smell, oh, how clearly she remembered it. Jannati comforting her on the bus, promising her a dress in Siliguri and keeping that promise. Jannati letting go of her hand and walking towards the truck, climbing in with no help. Jannati, who was in some way connected to Baby. Jannati, whom she had to stop at any cost, before she got on the bus and vanished again.

She hadn't boarded the bus yet. Jannati sat perched on a crumbling stone wall behind a row of parked buses, holding a glass of sugar cane juice. She did not seem surprised when two out-of-breath women screeched to a halt in front of her and put down the children they were carrying. Took the time to empty her glass before she spoke.

'Hasina,' she said.

Slowly got to her feet.

'I am so sorry. So very, very sorry.'

The bus station in Forbesganj was not a place they could stay. The Nat women headed back to the Town of Love, Amina carrying

Aftaab, Jannati toting a striped shoulder bag. Tamanna stared straight ahead, clutching the hand of Amina's daughter. Part of her wanted to hate Jannati. *But she wasn't the one who lured you into it*, the other voice in her head argued back. *You were kidnapped by force, don't you remember?*

She was the one who left you alone with Jabbar, the first voice replied, yellowed by years of disdain.

But she was just a child herself, how could she have known?

She stopped you from crying so you wouldn't draw attention. She actually helped Jabbar kidnap you!

Tamanna peered out of the corner of her eye at the woman next to her, took in the bulging skin between her sari's blouse and the skirt wrapped tightly around her backside. The lines framing her eyes, the corners of her mouth locked into a grimace of defeat. Something broke inside Tamanna, melting softly down through her body, made her knees quiver with tears. She had left that world behind now, she was through. To Jannati, there was no way out.

Tamanna stopped midway across the bridge, turned to face the girl who was her childhood neighbour.

'Me too, Jannati didi,' she said. 'I'm sorry too.'

Amina's cheeks were burning with questions as she sat tensely on the edge of one of Tamanna's plastic chairs. Heena roved around in the background, fixing tea, making herself useful as a non-participant in the painful memories being fished out from a twenty-year deep sea and laid out to dry underneath the mango tree.

Tamanna felt that Amina had no business there right then. Jannati and the girl once called Hasina should have had this moment to themselves, just the two of them. Should have had the chance to tell the stories they could bear to tell, leave out what they must leave out, lie when they needed to lie, without an audience. But Amina was not going anywhere, she was upset by Fauzia's cryptic comments and wanted to know what this was all about. Amina wanted to keep going forward.

But Tamanna and Jannati were travelling backwards now. Back to the day when a fourteen-year-old girl had climbed into a pickup truck on the border to India and an eight-year-old had grown into a tiny bud on a money tree in Katihar. Back to Kolkata, where no good job with a good family had lain in store for the girl in the short pink jacket. Where she had come to know, all too late, that the money in Driver's pocket had come from yet another trafficker, one with connections in many houses in many dirty alleyways in Khidderpore. Where the 'good family' had been a surly khala, 'auntie', and the job had consisted of serving passengers ten, twelve, fifteen times a day in chukri, the slave-labour arrangement where one hundred percent of the money went to Mausi, 'for room and board and clothes.'

Amina's fury was extinguished, replaced by silent, dry sobs as the two other women painted their years of horror with broad, bleeding brushstrokes. Jannati's betel-stained lips opened wide to let the stories pour out, piece by piece. The beatings, the diseases, the men, the moving from one brothel to another. The babies she had never been allowed to carry to term, the moving from one mela to the next, the girls who had been there one day and were sold the next. The family in Chhukha that she could never see again because they had come to know what she was doing. The younger sister who was married; Jannati's deepest wish was to meet her children, she knew she had two nephews aged eight and six.

'I used to have many dreams,' she said slowly. 'Now I have none. If I can, I'd like to help support my nephews. I want them to go to school, get good jobs and marry nice girls. But for myself I have no more dreams.'

They sat in silence for a while. Aftaab whimpered a little and Amina lifted him into her lap, pulled out her breast. Tamanna leaned forward in her chair, eyes glued to the ground. Jannati's story hung in the air between them, an awareness Tamanna knew she had always had. Somewhere deep inside she had always known that beyond the passenger door of the pickup truck, nothing good had lain in store for Jannati.

The sturdy woman looked at Tamanna's bowed neck, waited for her to straighten up and say something. When she finally lifted her head it was with a leaden sigh, a breath that swept away forgotten grudges. A face with no trace of Hasina from Chhukha turned towards Jannati, her eyes were calm and clear.

'What happened, happened,' she said simply. 'And it wasn't your fault.'

The questions didn't start until Amina broached the subject of Fauzia's apocalyptic warnings.

'They call you "the new woman". If you only came for Baby's funeral, why are you still here? It's been many days, why haven't you left yet?'

Intrigued and inquisitive, she stared at the woman with the ample arms and cheap henna streaks in her hair.

'Were you on your way out when we found you at the bus stop? Did you have a ticket?'

Jannati shook her head. No, she wasn't on her way.

Amina failed to understand. 'Then why were you sitting there?'

Jannati looked at Tamanna, who didn't meet her gaze. Scratched a bothersome rash on her lower arm and took her time before answering.

'I was sitting there pretending to be free. I wanted to try it, just for a few minutes. To see if I could find that feeling, if I could sense it again. The feeling of being able to go anywhere I wanted, to be absolutely free.'

Tamanna was looking straight at her now. 'Did you find it?'

Jannati shook her head slowly. 'No. I couldn't feel it. My feet would never have stepped onto that bus even if they were given the chance.'

Amina refused to give up, felt the irritation crawling underneath all this mysterious talk. What could she mean, this woman from the mela? And why was Fauzia calling her 'the new woman'?

'If you were not planning on leaving, then … why did you come at all?'

She didn't care if it sounded rude, even hostile.

'Where are you going to live?'

Amina's eyes shifted from Jannati to Tamanna, her friend's face was inscrutable. Suddenly, in a flash of lightning, Amina saw how it all fit together. The never-ending chain of supply and demand, Fauzia knowing, Prabir having lost a girl.

'Her name is Fauzia,' Jannati said. 'And the room is nice.'

Silence fell again. Aftaab had stopped feeding, his sister had fallen asleep on the ground behind her mother's chair. Jannati continued, her features were blurry in the dark.

'I don't know why he bought me. There were many younger girls there, I thought I would be moving on to the next mela.'

Another pause. No bitterness in her voice, it was only a simple statement of fact.

'My price was low. And he knows I won't get on a bus and run away.'

※

No one lifted an eyebrow when the flowery curtain was pulled aside and the man in the red T-shirt emerged. The women leaning against the brick ledge along the wall didn't stop what they were doing, some idly chatting, one of them brushing another's hair. Basanti came out from behind the same curtain a few minutes later. She wedged her feet into her rubber sandals, squinting into the sunlight that barely penetrated the narrow alley in Khidderpore, Kolkata. She wore a long, shapeless dress, her hair was scraggly and her face revealed no trace of makeup.

'Is anyone going to buy food?' she asked, looking from side to side.

One of the younger girls, with her hair pulled back and fresh makeup on, looked at her haughtily: 'Food already, Basanti didi? Are you going to eat up all your earnings before lunchtime? What if there are no more passengers today?'

The girl turned her back and took the few steps forward into the narrow passage where the alley opened out onto a teeming pavement. Positioned herself just far enough out to be seen, but not far enough to be on display.

Basanti didn't bother to respond. She knew the pecking order and its rough tenor well, she didn't care, everyone knew they were all in the same boat. The stench was the same behind every curtain in the alleyway, the mattresses were equally stained. The girls equally helpless. Why should she bother to snap back?

Basanti was going to eat early today. Wasn't going to give a damn whether more men would come through her doorway, letting go of the endless worrying about where tomorrow's meal would come from. She had a plan, she had something to do.

One hour later a robust figure hurried through an alley a few blocks away. A goat stood tied to a fence nearby, she sidestepped the droppings and held her breath through a swarm of flies. A little boy was leaning against the wall holding a bottle of milk, his oily hair lay pasted to his scalp. Basanti turned left through a half-open gate, set her course towards the innermost of two courtyard doors. Peeped quickly into the first doorway, where a scrawny man was sitting, head in his hands, on a charpoy, a bed frame with a thatched rope bottom.

Basanti began to climb the stairs to the third floor. She passed by a door with the remnants of purple sparkly paint flaking off, a fuse box gaping lethally wide-open on the landing, surrounded by loose wires. At the top of the stairs she slipped off her sandals and shoved open the door without knocking.

Pukaar's day centre had two rooms. The metal shelf along the wall of the room to the right designated the 'office'; four chairs shared the remaining space with a stack of thin mattresses that served as beds by night, as sofa with a blanket thrown over them, by day. In the room to the left three sewing machines were lined up against the wall. A few young girls sat cross-legged on straw mats with schoolbooks in their laps, a teacher bent her dark chignon over one of their books, pointing something out with a red pencil. Manjira stood by one of the sewing machines, her paan-cheek bulging towards the small woman with thick, lustrous hair who fumbled with the fabric and the side crank. 'You have to hold it tight,' Manjira instructed, grabbing onto the light blue fabric. 'Like this!'

She looked up and saw Basanti in the doorway. Surprised, she waved hello and motioned for her to come in. Manjira's forehead creased into a line of instant worry. 'Why have you come, is something wrong? Are you sick?'

Basanti shook her head, struggling to find the words. Four young girls filed in through the door behind her, said hello to Manjira and began stacking the chairs along the wall.

'Is it ... that dancing you were talking about ... is it today?'

Manjira looked at her, the sagging, weary body, the sheepish half-smile with betel-red gums. The hands she didn't quite know what to do with. Manjira nodded and made up her mind at once. If there was anyone whose life hadn't had enough dancing, it was Basanti.

At first she just sat and watched. The four young girls assembled in the centre of the room as if it was the most natural thing in the world, not a trace of shame, not a shadow of discomfort in their faces. Long, slender necks, gazes fixed forward as they glided into movement to the music that poured out from the tape player on the windowsill. Basanti tried to make herself invisible behind the homework girls, who were now pressed into a corner, she sat perfectly still and let the music engulf her. Looked down to find her bare feet tapping out the beat, the pulse radiated outward to her fingertips and she felt her breath quicken. Wide-eyed, she absorbed the sight of the dancing girls through every pore, watched their anger stomped out by the soles of their bare feet, the fear pushed back by their undulating arms. Basanti unwittingly got to her feet and suddenly the music took over, her body responding to an age-old cry. Started to sway back and forth, glide slowly along the wall as her grandmother's voice echoed in her ears: ... *danced for kings and princes ... performed for the emperor in all his splendor ... admired for their bold jumps and fearless leaps.*

Her hair fell loose down her shoulders, her arms lifted high, her eyes squeezed shut against the paint-flaking wall and the tattered insect screens covering the windows. Basanti was on the road, far ahead on the horizon were the mountains in Nepal, the forest around her was green and fertile. Fauzia walked beside her, they were singing, Grandmother was there, a young Grandmother with colour in her hair and a spark in her eyes. 'Dance, Basanti,' she said, clapping her hands so her glass bangles rattled and sang. 'You are Nat. You were born to dance!'

And Basanti danced. A shimmering afternoon light filled the grey room in the gloomiest alley in Khidderpore. A plucked string reverberated through the room, long after the music had stopped and the tape player was left humming white noise from the windowsill.

16

Rukmini was reading. The teacup on the floor next to her had long been empty; books, binders and loose-leaf sheets lay scattered all around as she sat cross-legged on the bed. She stretched her back, sighing as she slowly rolled her head from side to side, feeling the crick in her neck. The thought of calling her husband in Delhi struck her — but no, it was too late, she'd risk waking him, and her daughter would have been asleep for hours. What she wouldn't have given to be with them, to have lain in her own bed with cool, clean sheets. To have had no other worries than the workday tomorrow, pushing papers, attending meetings, eating the usual lunch with her department colleagues.

But that was no longer her life. She had enlisted as a full-time soldier in what most people branded a hopeless war against 'something that has always been there and always will'. A war she was confident could be won, but one where she had to play not only soldier but also strategist, motivator, arms supplier, and battlefield commander-in-chief. And late at night, when doubt and despair seized her in their firm hold, she was all alone.

Rukmini sighed again and began to half-heartedly gather up the papers around her. Sometimes the responsibility was just too much to bear. But there was no turning back. Tomorrow Tamanna was lodging a formal complaint. Tomorrow they were getting Rupa out.

Darya was walking. She plodded and paced back and forth on the dead-end street outside her hostel, murmured a distracted greeting to the vegetable peddler as he swept away some rotten cabbage leaves, nodded hello to the candy seller and bought a small tin of barfi before he closed up shop for the night. Nibbled on crumbly pieces of the sweet, sticky confection as her feet avoided muddy potholes in the road, pressed herself up against a wall when a nighttime goods carrier roared past.

Was it worth it, what they were setting out to do tomorrow? Could this be the end of the road for Birbal, for Rozy and the other kids who had just glimpsed the possibility of another life? Would Tamanna and Amina be sitting alone at the next meeting of the women's group?

She had invested her whole adult life in this. Her sociology degree from the university in New Delhi, her plans for further education, her brief thoughts of marriage and children, everything had been pushed aside. In the meeting with Pukaar, the first time by sheer coincidence, she had been hooked, captivated, immediately convinced. She had known it, clear as a bell: to see this, to know it, and then to walk on by as if nothing were wrong, just wasn't possible. It was that simple.

It didn't feel quite as simple tonight. Darya licked the last crumbs of barfi off her fingers, hesitating a moment outside the front door of the hostel. Should she walk the ten minutes over to the office and see if Saleem was there? She still wasn't sure if it was a good idea for him to come along tomorrow; she had a feeling the consequences might be uglier than he could imagine. She shook it off. Saleem had said he wanted to come; no one knew the Aslams better than him; he knew what he was heading into. She pushed open the door to the hostel, threw a glance towards the half-asleep night watchman, headed decisively for the staircase. Everything was set. Tomorrow they were getting Rupa out.

Saleem stared up at the ceiling. The thick, dusty curtains couldn't be drawn completely shut; flickering lights from the traffic outside danced against the wall above the file cabinet in sweeping arches. He tossed and turned, couldn't seem to find a comfortable position on the narrow sofa. There was so much that could go wrong; why hadn't he thought it through before? The thought of Jabbar's knife returned. Tamanna had told him all about it, and he knew the stories of his cousin's knife skills ran far and wide. *'Is that what you're afraid of?'* he mocked himself. *Being beaten up, being stabbed?* His sister's face rose in his mind's eye; he owed Fauzia a house. Owed her the chance to spend her remaining years in safety, behind a door to which only he and she had the key. He had awakened the dream in her, had painted the castle in the sky she never otherwise would have thought of building, let alone moving into. What if something went wrong now? What if Rupa wasn't there; what if Jabbar had been warned and they ended up looking like fools? Not only would he have made enemies for life in his own family, it would all have been for nothing. He had saved up the money, Fauzia didn't know that he had already bought the little plot of land. Pukaar had promised to lend him the money to build the house, a loan he could manage on his modest salary if he was careful.

Saleem sat up, his pupils staring out into the dark room. What if their plan for tomorrow meant the end of Pukaar in Forbesganj? He knew Rukmini was worried; he had heard and understood everything she had said. If this went wrong, both his salary and everything they had built up here could be lost.

He closed his eyes, but his mind kept churning. Fauzia's immovable face in front of him: 'They say you're going to regret it.' And then, abrupt and uninvited, another face, another sister. A face he would no longer recognise today, and which therefore bore a ten-year-old's childish features through the haze of memory: 'Saleem, when you are grown-up and have your own house, I want to live with you. Then I don't want to live in Kolkata and be married.'

He forced Basanti's face out of his thoughts. The man his mother had taken money from, Saleem knew he had had no intention of marrying his little sister. So long ago. Nothing he could do now. No one knew where she was.

He took a gulp of water from the glass on the floor. The exhaustion ached in his bones; the sorrow, the anger which soaked up so much of his energy. The shame he refused to bear, the mantra he recited to himself every day: *I am Nat. I am Nat, and there's nothing wrong with that.*

He couldn't afford to be scared. Not of the knife, not of anything. Tomorrow they were getting Rupa out.

Tamanna had decided what to tell Amina. In the endless discussions of alternative work and other means of income in the women's group, one recurring idea had been the production of incense. It wasn't hard to make, the schoolhouse could be turned into an incense factory by night, and Rukmini had a contact willing to buy as much as they could deliver in bulk. They had often discussed how they might arrange training sessions so that they could learn to operate the simple machines used to cut the sticks out of bamboo. Pukaar would loan the mahila mandal the money to purchase the machines, a loan to be paid off over several years. That's what she would tell Amina tomorrow. She and Darya didi were going to Patna to shop for incense-stick machines. Her friend would, for sure, smell a rat, Amina was not stupid. *But it's safer for her if I lie,* Tamanna thought to herself. *So that no one can claim later on that she knew.*

Tamanna knew she wouldn't be getting much sleep that night. Every thought in her head was with Rupa, *was* Rupa on the mattress on the second floor of the blue house. The moon was out, its enigmatic white light shining down on Tamanna underneath the mango tree; offering no answers, no prophecies about what would happen. Heena had stuck her head out twice already, asking if she was coming inside soon. Tamanna had answered her in vague deferrals. It was as if she had to hold Rupa up tonight, send a sky-bridge of promises and assurances over to Katihar: *It won't be long, I'm on my way! Just a few hours now, I'm coming! Tomorrow I'm getting you out!*

Rupa sat on the mattress, holding a crust of bread between her fingers, gazing at Sona with glassy eyes.

'Eat!' Sona insisted. 'Rupa, you have to eat!'

She lifted the plate of yellow curry up to her friend's nose. 'Look, chana dal, you have to taste it!'

She tried, Rupa really tried. Attempted to scoop up some of the lumpy liquid with the piece of bread. But her hand was stiff and uncooperative, she wasn't able to complete the movements through her wrist and fingers; the dal dripped out of the rolled-up bread and she looked at Sona helplessly.

'I'm not hungry.'

The words were thick and sluggish, as if said in a language she didn't speak. The pills they had given her, for the pain, for the bleeding, to calm her down, made everything distant and slow. She didn't feel, didn't think, didn't care. Time was just passing by.

Sona cautiously got up from her squatting position across from Rupa, cradling a hand over her bulging belly. She didn't know what would happen to her or the baby, had no way to defend herself against whatever they might do. No money, no backup plan. But she had made a promise. She had sworn she would carry her child to another kind of life.

She looked down at the skinny girl on the mattress. The crust of bread was pinched between her fingers, dal had dripped down onto her pink kurta and formed a round, yellow stain seeping into the fabric.

'You're going to get out of here,' Sona said. She could barely comprehend her own words, had no idea where they were coming from. 'Someone will get you out.'

17

It was not what she had thought it would be. Actually, Tamanna didn't really know what she had expected, but it wasn't this. Not this many policemen, this many cars, this many people everywhere. She had thought she would be prepared after running through it so many times, hashing out every possible outcome, taking stock of everything that could go wrong. She had been through countless conversations with the police and the lawyers, recounting her story again and again, had laid it all out on the table, blow by blow. Had told them every detail of the kidnapping, the raping, the beatings, giving birth, her escape, the other girls, the passengers, who had been involved in what and when and where.

And today she had lodged a complaint. Had filed her report at the police station in Katihar, where she had first shown up all those years ago as a terrified little girl, only to be escorted by a police officer back to Jabbar and his knife glinting up there on the shelf. The same station where she had stood in the doorway and faced rejection more times than she cared to remember. Where, this time, she had not only met a policeman who listened to her and wrote down every word of her report, but even the chief inspector with his big moustache had sat in on the meeting, silent and stern, on a chair next to Rukmini and another man, some important police sahib from Patna. She, Tamanna Khatoon, had filed a report against the people who had destroyed her life, had inscribed their names in the book of crime and punishment. She had gone far beyond her rank and status, fearlessly and foolhardily spitting straight into all of their faces, the whole vicious web of the Aslam butchers and their brotherhood. She alone had brought qayamat, doomsday, to the Town of Love. Jabbar's gleaming knife was nothing compared to what she had just unleashed.

Maybe that was the reason why she felt so oddly distanced from it all, seeing it as through a peephole. Tamanna sat quietly in the back seat of one of the dark police jeeps; Chief Inspector Laskar was riding up front next to the driver. The cars hadn't yet started their slow glide over the few miles to Kuli Pada, and the yard was teeming with officers in khaki uniform. The TV journalist crew was in place; the scratchy static of walkie-talkies filled the night air. Saleem was coming along in one of the cars, too; she saw him a minute ago and wondered why – to look his cousin in the face when the axe dropped? For one dizzying, reckless moment Tamanna let herself open the floodgates, drop all her worries and imagine the finale of this unreal performance: Jabbar and his brothers, Dolly and Mumtaz all being led away in handcuffs, her own arms wrapped around Rupa, an unscathed and beautiful Rupa who whispered 'Amma, thank you for coming.' Tamanna exhaled, blinked, and again looked around for Saleem.

Groups of spectators had gathered along the side of the road they were about to drive down, and the razor-sharp instinct awakened in Tamanna: would the news have already spread down the grapevine and reached the blue house? She bent forward and spoke straight into Chief Inspector Laskar's ear – she, Tamanna, was directly addressing the chief of police in Katihar, telling him what to do: 'We have to leave right away. Otherwise they'll escape, they'll take Rupa with them and escape!'

He didn't answer and leaned away from her, slightly irritated, and pressed his walkie-talkie to his ear.

'Yes!' he barked. 'The doctor is coming. And the woman from Delhi will ride with me in this car.'

The ride to Kuli Pada took the caravan of four cars just a few minutes, but for Tamanna it was an epic journey through the evening darkness. The enormity of what they were about to do rose up like a giant dust cloud around her, a slow-motion explosion she must be careful to steer clear of or else she'd become deaf and blind and mute and unable to do anything ever again. She pushed it away, kept it at arm's length, focusing on her only task in this expedition: to find Rupa. Only Tamanna knew what she looked like, she was the only one who could recognise her and identify her to the others.

They entered the labyrinth of narrow alleyways, barely wide enough for the convoy to squeeze its way through. Behind shutters and window bars, beneath curtains pushed aside a few inches and doors slightly ajar, countless pairs of eyes blinked in the darkness, witnesses to Tamanna Khatoon's return to Kuli Pada. Maybe they could see her silhouette through the police jeep's tinted windows, or maybe it was the size of the motorcade that spurred a stirring within the walls of the houses, threw the doors open and formed a tail of followers behind them. As the cars came to a stop outside the blue house, blurred faces were pressed against the side windows, angry fists pounded the car roof. The driver opened the door for Tamanna, and Chief Inspector Laskar snapped at her: 'Come on now! Jaldi, jaldi, they know we're here, let's go!' She stumbled out and felt the thundering roar of the mob wash over her. Like the rain, the thought whizzed through her head, like the monsoon rain wildly hammering the roof of her house.

The houses in Kuli Pada had electricity, illegally wired cables that criss-crossed along walls and over roofs, but inside Jabbar's house it was pitch black. Tamanna raced up to the front door, sensing Rukmini right behind her, briefly noticing the tall police sahib from Patna striding out of another car. Some of the policemen were carrying flashlights, they communicated in sharp shouts, some trying to block off the crowd which was growing at an exponential rate, inching closer, screaming louder.

'What are you doing here? Leave us alone!'

'Jabbar Aslam is innocent. You have no business here!'

'That woman lies, she is nothing but trouble!'

In the background, a TV camera beeped and whirred like a giant insect. The journalist's steady voice was a calm current running through the monsoon roar of shrieking voices: 'We're on the scene in the red light district of Katihar, in the state of Bihar in Northern India ...'

The door was locked and bolted shut, with no sign of life inside the house. 'Is there another way in?' the chief inspector asked, shouting straight into her ear to be heard above the fray. Tamanna shook her head. The Kuli Pada houses were all connected in an adjoining maze of walls, alleyways and dead-end streets, perfect for hiding things away, impossible to navigate for those who didn't know the pass code. 'The courtyard is fenced in,' she said. 'The only other way is over the roof.' He lifted his head, scanning the balcony with his gaze. Tamanna shook her head again. 'They're in there,' she said. 'I know Rupa's in there.'

Chief Inspector Laskar met her eyes in a firm stare for one long second before he opened his mouth and yelled to the officers: 'Get this door open! Find something to break down this door!'

The policemen pulled back slightly, perplexed and looking around for something they could use to force the door open. But Tamanna couldn't wait another second. She threw her body against the door, pounding the wood with both fists, cursing, willing it to open. Rukmini was right behind her, and now she sensed that Saleem was there too. And as the door swung open, it was Saleem's face that Mumtaz Begum hissed straight into. Old Mumtaz was the one to pull the deadbolt aside and crack open the door, but all she had a chance to say was 'What is this ... what ...' before the door was kicked in forcefully and they poured into the room as she stumbled backwards. The house was utterly black, in a split second it occurred to Rukmini that they must have flipped the circuit switch in an absurd attempt to stop them, and she dashed into the next room after Tamanna.

'Rupa! Rupa, where are you?' Tamanna's voice carried through the house bathed in darkness, ricocheting up the stairs ahead to the second floor, prising open doors, shoving barricades of furniture aside. She heard the policemen's boots thudding up the stairs behind her, and her own pulse throbbing in her eardrums. Frightened figures appeared in the doorways, pressing up against the walls, startled screams from the mattresses on the floor. Tamanna didn't even look in their faces, she knew none of them was Rupa's, knew that every cell in her body would instantly recognise her daughter. She kept running, refusing to let herself feel the pain. She was here for one reason only, the reason she just couldn't seem to find. 'Rupa!'

Tamanna had been through every room on the second floor, screaming like a madwoman, pushing aside a dozen girls standing in the way of her desperate search. She was storming back towards the stairs when a familiar voice, or was it a smell, stopped her cold: 'Tamanna didi, is that you?'

She whipped around. The full moon beamed a white ray of light down through the balcony door and across the face directly in front her, with deep-set scars running down the cheeks, the uneven bridge of the nose.

'Sona!'

Her heart skipped a beat as she realised in an instant that she hadn't imagined Sona could still be alive.

From downstairs she could hear Chief Inspector Laskar barking orders to his men and Saleem speaking loud and clear, in a strangely ice-cold tone. *'They'll kill him'*, she thought, voicing the notion several times before she could shove it aside. *'They'll kill Saleem for this'*.

Her body only snapped back to life when she heard Mumtaz's voice penetrate through the clamour. That rough, croaking voice she knew all too well, she heard it at the bottom of the stairs now, sputtering and hissing and swearing to the gods that they would regret this! What was this all about, forcing entry into her house, breaking down her door and barging in without permission? There was nothing illegal going on here, all these girls were here of their own free will, it was no one's business who came to visit them. Her sons? How dared they suggest her sons were involved in something illegal? Her sons were out of town, visiting relatives, they were not at home, what was this supposed to mean?

Tamanna felt a red-hot wave surging through her body. She turned away from Sona and stormed down the stairs, across the floor and back towards the front door, where two officers were holding Mumtaz Begum by either arm as the old woman quivered with rage. 'Let go of me, you have to show some respect, I …'

She placed herself squarely in front of Mumtaz, and there was no hint of a tremble in her voice as Tamanna Khatoon, who would never again be frightened little Hasina, spoke out: 'Can't you understand we're here to rescue her? We're here to get Rupa out, and no matter what you do, we will find her.'

She straightened her shoulders and nodded at the policemen, a merciful nod, like a medieval queen pronouncing judgement: I'm finished with her. You may take her away now. Then she turned to the chief inspector, now she was a field agent running point on a high-risk operation: 'There's more to the house than what we've seen. We have to look in the basement.'

Armed with the tools at hand – a chair, a few solid planks torn off a nearby scaffolding – they broke down the cellar door and wedged their way down the staircase. Tamanna sprinted in a frenzy up and down the subterranean corridors, past closed doors that led to more narrow passageways when they were forced open. She kept calling her daughter's name but her shouts sounded different down here, choked off by the dust, echoing off the brick walls and hitting her back in the face, like bewildered bats.

She stayed alert as she kept running, sharpening her ears to register even the smallest hint of human sound. Something's not right, she thought and stopped in a daze, the house wasn't this big, how could the cellar …

'We're underneath the neighbours' house,' the chief inspector's voice sounded behind her. 'The basements are connected, this is where they go to hide, to flee, to transport the girls to and from the house.'

You have known all this! she wanted to shout. *You have known all of this and you let it all go on* –

But before she could open her mouth one of the other policemen yelled through an open door: 'Laskar Sahib! Over here!'

He whirled around and darted back into the room they had just scanned without noticing anything, it was empty other than a few rags scattered across the floor and a metal tray with scraps of dried cement in the corner. A rough-hewn ladder with broken rungs leaned against the wall and the officer shoved it aside, pointing to the door behind it, grey and blending into the brick wall in invisible camouflage. The policeman shouted something as he took hold of the giant deadbolt on the door; the chief inspector strode quickly across the floor and grabbed hold of it with him.

At first, Tamanna thought the room was empty. No windows, no light bulb dangling from the ceiling, the only shaft of light emanating from a policeman's flashlight in the corridor behind them. No furniture, just the densely trampled dirt floor and the sealed-in stench of mould and neglect. The corners were dark, looming with empty shadows. Tamanna took a couple of steps into the room and opened her mouth, poised to sigh a short, disappointed 'no' when one of the shadows suddenly changed shape. Almost imperceptibly, a tiny patch of darkness suddenly took on a slightly paler shade of grey. A hunched-over bundle in a corner, a tiny person crouched against the wall, hugging her knees to her chest. A face buried behind skinny arms, a dupatta like a shroud over slouching shoulders.

'Rupa!'

Her own voice rang foreign to her, this was not how she had meant it to sound. The first word she had said to her daughter in eight years, and her name came out as a shout. A hoarse and ugly scream of the name that meant beauty, the name that had dwelled in her throat, in her mouth every day. 'Rupa!'

The harsh beam of the policeman's flashlight landed on the face that jolted up from behind folded arms. The girl blinked, pressing herself harder up against the wall and shuffling to her feet.

'Don't touch me!' she screamed. 'I know who you are, don't touch me!'

Tamanna halted, her unknowingly extended arm hung suspended in mid-air. She stood frozen, letting her daughter's stream of curse words flood over her.

'You stay away from me, you filthy whore! You're not my mother, you liar, don't you dare touch me!'

She vaguely sensed Rukmini's hand on her shoulder: 'Tamanna! Is it her?'

Tamanna drew a sharp gasp of breath, took a step forward, letting the torrent of insults wash over her. Grabbed on to Rupa's arm, pulled her close despite the fists pummeling wildly in the direction of her head, her face, her chest: 'Let me go! You filthy ... let me go!'

'Yes,' she said in a stranger's voice. 'Yes, it's her.'

Chief Inspector Laskar led the way up the stairs to the first floor with two policemen holding Rupa fast by the arms, her skinny body trembling feverishly. Halfway up the stairs, her curses were drowned out by Mumtaz Begum's voice, a high-pitched moan lamenting broken family trust. 'Saleem, I didn't believe it! I didn't want to believe it. Wouldn't even listen to my own sister, I couldn't believe my ears. Oh ... dhoka, dhoka, what a traitor!'

When Rupa appeared at the top of the stairs, the old woman rushed over to her. 'Rupa, what have they done to you, what ...?' But Tamanna interrupted her brusquely, she had to keep going, had to finish the job. 'Where is Jabbar?' she yelled, her pointing finger inches from Mumtaz Begum's frightened face. 'And Dolly?'

She turned towards Laskar. 'The old woman takes the money from the passengers,' she said. 'Arrest her! And the men, her sons – you have to arrest them too!'

'Where are they?' she shouted to Mumtaz, her voice reeling out of control. 'They won't get away!'

'Tamanna,' Rukmini said gently. Tamanna vaguely sensed the TV camera by the opposite wall, recording every moment. 'We found Rupa, that's the most important thing. We have to get her out of here now, you can see she's not well.'

A constant stream of curse words and obscene threats spewed non-stop from Rupa's mouth. Her body shook uncontrollably, her pupils shiny and dilated. Rukmini didn't hesitate, she grabbed Rupa with the help of one of Laskar's men. They led her towards the car, the TV camera following close behind. The noise of the crowd outside grew to a mad roar as they shoved her into the back seat, where Darya was waiting. 'Whatever you do, make sure you protect her!' Rukmini shouted as she slammed the car door shut. She felt the adrenaline surge through her body as she marched back towards the house, where the police squad had their hands full holding the mob back from pouring through the front door.

Before Rukmini could heave open the blue door, it opened from the inside and a woman staggered out. One hand resting on her bulging belly, she stumbled forward a few steps, terror gleaming like shards of glass in her eyes. 'Take me with you!' Sona knew it was now or never. She had decided to take the leap, had sworn on her life, and this was the moment, she had to get out now. 'Take me with you, didi!'

Tamanna's and Saleem's faces appeared in the doorframe behind her. Laskar had just grabbed the wheezing, sputtering Mumtaz's arm, her broken sobs over the shame showered on her family had lapsed back into a new round of threats and yelling. Rukmini could see Deputy Superintendent Vatsavani standing by the jeep with Darya and Rupa in the back seat, he discreetly pulled back when he saw Laskar striding up to assume his place up front. Tamanna got in the back with the two other women, steeling herself as more profanities and dirty curse words rained from Rupa's mouth. Rukmini and Sona got into the car behind them, and the convoy began to pull forward.

A sharp thud against the glass right behind Rukmini's head, running footsteps following the car. A face contorted in rage pressed against the window before the driver accelerated and they turned the first corner.

Tamanna had never travelled this way by car before. The road from Jabbar's house to the police station that she had stomped in a rage, fled in a panic, crawled along with an aching body battered from beatings. Now she rode down the same road in triumph, this should have felt like a victory parade. They had found Rupa. They had got her out, her daughter would never again enter the blue house in Kuli Pada. So why did she feel nothing, why was she hollow inside? Why did she just register everything as a spectator, as if nothing of this had anything to do with her?

In the car behind Tamanna, Rukmini leaned back in her seat. Sona, the unfamiliar woman seated next to her, closed her eyes and began to move her lips. Cradled her belly, speaking to someone she couldn't see.

A crowd was waiting for them when the motorcade arrived at the police station. Tamanna kept her arm firmly around Rupa, who had stopped screaming and flailing and sat with stiff, disdainful shoulders, though the rest of her body was still noticeably trembling. Her enormous pupils stared straight ahead into the back of Chief Inspector Laskar's head and Tamanna regretted not asking the doctor to ride in their car, there was no doubt that Rupa was sick.

She used her own body to shield her daughter as they scurried across the few yards from the car into the police station, blocking her off from the threatening shouts, protecting her from the ever-present TV camera lights and the accompanying gaggle of journalists. The questions hit her from all sides: *Who is this girl? What's happening with her now? Is she a minor? Is this the start of a larger strategic offensive against the Kuli Pada brothels?*

So many questions, Tamanna could only wish she had the answers. Who was this girl? What would happen to her now?

She got her answer a few hours later, at least a temporary one: not much. Hours of waiting in the police station late into the night had yielded nothing but delays, an endless string of phone calls, and a Rupa who grew more distant by the minute: cold and trembling on a chair by the wall, answering the police officers' questions, but unresponsive to her mother's gentle touches. Finally it was decided that Rupa's hearing would have to wait until the next afternoon, when the magistrate would be present in the district court. But the doctor insisted that the medical evidence had to be secured right away, and after lengthy negotiations with the hospital via phone they were granted permission to use the OB/GYN facilities and headed back out towards the car. Tamanna, Rukmini, Darya, Rupa, and Sona, an exhausted motley fivesome, arrived at the hospital in Katihar at half past two in the morning. The receiving doctor was tired and grumpy – no, no one was allowed in the room with Rupa during the examination; no, it didn't matter that the girl was terrified and most likely drugged; no, he didn't have the resources for anything beyond a standard pelvic examination. Waves of anger and desperation surged through Tamanna once again, but she couldn't muster the energy to gather the storm of words she wanted to release at the unsympathetic doctor with his arms folded across his chest. But Rukmini could. Rukmini had been on the phone for hours until her ear was red-hot, pleading with lawyers and activists and politicians, pulling every string she could think of, this was just another bump in the road.

'I'm coming in with her!' she told the doctor. 'This is a police investigation and you're responsible for gathering evidence to be used in court. This girl can't speak for herself, and critical proof has to be secured. I'm coming in with her!'

The legal scholar in her knew her assertions were treading shaky ground, but now that they had come this far, she couldn't allow this pig-headed doctor to ruin their only chance to document Rupa's state.

He didn't reply, just pouted demonstratively and glared at the wall as he stepped aside to let her enter the examination room. Rukmini helped Rupa into the chair and told her softly that she had to take off her pants, the doctor was going to examine her now, it wouldn't hurt. The girl obeyed without a word, and Rukmini positioned herself at the headboard. She took Rupa's slender hand in hers, surprised when the girl returned her squeeze.

Rupa didn't make a sound during the examination; her thin body just lay there, taut and tensed up in the chair. An avalanche of pain inside Rukmini as she glanced at Rupa's knees, the skinny, splayed-out knees of a thirteen-year-old with her legs in the stirrups: *She's a child!* She tore her eyes away and looked down at the crown of Rupa's head. Her long hair was clipped together by a barrette shaped like a butterfly.

The doctor had finished collecting the necessary samples, and a nurse carried the tray full of tiny vials out of the room.

'Well?' Rukmini looked at him questioningly.

He hesitated for a second, dwelling on his unwillingness to share anything with this persistent woman who obviously came from another India – what could she possibly know of the despair that engulfed his impoverished patients' lives? But he swallowed his doubts and decided to give in; dragging this out any further would simply cost him more valuable time off his shift.

'She has significant injuries.' He spoke slowly. 'External wounds and bruising on her thighs, tears in the vaginal opening and scrapes on the mucous membranes.'

She could hear in his voice that there was more to come.

'But the worst injuries are in the rectum. She has been abused with some sort of object, the anal sphincter muscle is torn and has sustained significant damage. She needs to be operated on by a specialist, otherwise she'll suffer the effects for the rest of her life. This will not heal itself.'

Another pause.

'And she is sedated with some form of opiate, probably morphine. It's likely she has developed an addiction.'

Rukmini took it all in without blinking an eye. The Pukaar employees dealt with thousands of women daily, many of them younger than Rupa, many of their injuries worse. But this was Tamanna's daughter. Rukmini's face betrayed no reaction to the doctor's words, but inwardly she was sobbing. *Forgive us, Rupa. Forgive us for not coming earlier. Forgive those of us on the outside looking in, letting it happen.*

She squeezed Rupa's hand, trying her best to sound heartening as she asked her to get dressed. 'Now let's find you some food and a place to sleep.'

Rukmini took the trip back to Forbesganj alone. After the hospital visit and an even longer wait back at the police station a hotel room had finally been arranged for the others, Rupa was obviously in no state to sit in a car for hours all the way back to Forbesganj. And even if they had all come along, where would they have put her? Tamanna's flimsy straw house, where the inhabitants were already shunned, with the Aslam relatives right across the street? The office where Saleem spent his nights on the couch? Darya's dormitory? Her own small room on the second floor above the office?

Exhausted and half-asleep in the back seat, she forced her thoughts ahead to the next day and the court hearing that awaited. They would need to secure temporary custody of Rupa so that they could take her with them, buy some time, get the girl the medical attention she needed. The adrenaline rush from the rescue operation, the dizzying joy over finding and freeing Rupa had faded, and she was seized with anxiety over the next move. What was really the best place for the girl now? Rukmini let out a heavy sigh and rested her head against the side window. She needed to think. She needed to sleep. She needed to find a solution.

Tamanna and Rupa took the two beds on one side of the room, Darya and Sona the two closer to the window. The room was on the second floor of a no-frills establishment a few blocks from the police station. Two female officers sat silently by the door, which was locked and guarded by two of their male colleagues right outside. Tamanna stared out into the darkness, her pounding head spinning with fatigue. Rupa was here with her, the raid had been a success, she had got her daughter out. The fact that she hadn't come willingly, that she had cursed her and blamed her for the betrayal Tamanna herself had felt unbearably guilty about over the past eight years – she pushed those thoughts away forcefully in this blessed hour of temporary safety behind the locked door. They had to move on, she knew she had to think ahead. Rupa wasn't safe anywhere in Katihar, not anywhere in Forbesganj either. The dhanda-monster's arms, visible and invisible, reached everywhere.

Tamanna turned back against the wall. Would her daughter ever be safe, anywhere?

Rupa felt sick. She was nauseous, her arms and legs convulsing. And she was scared. She was out of Jabbar's house now and anything could happen. Rupa had no illusions that Jabbar and his brothers wouldn't find her, they always found the girls who ran away, they would find her too. And Tamanna, how could Tamanna protect her? Tamanna, who claimed to be her mother, but who abandoned her all those years ago? Why had she come back to get her now? And the kajas who came with Tamanna, what did they want from her?

She had no idea who they were, these two women who were so very different from anyone she had ever met. Rupa had listened to Rukmini's voice for hours tonight, had heard her speaking to the police, talking on the phone, demanding to come in with her to the doctor. She had heard her say she would be with her at the hearing tomorrow, that they were going to find a safe place for her to live, that she was going to feel better, that everything was going to be fine. Fine? How was a stranger supposed to make everything fine? What did they have planned? And Sona – what would happen to Sona? When Jabbar found Sona he would beat her black and blue, and what would happen to the baby then?

Rupa tossed and turned in the unfamiliar bed, hearing the chair scrape as one of the policewomen by the door shifted her weight. No way could she sleep here. She was so scared.

Darya placed a hand across her eyes and tried not to think of what would happen at the hearing the next day. This wasn't over, they might only have Rupa on temporary loan. What would they do if she kept refusing to acknowledge Tamanna? What would they do if the butchers' web of influence extended to the sphere of the justice system? No, she had to get some sleep, had to force her mind to let go of the restless thoughts teeming inside her head. Tomorrow she would need all the strength she could muster.

But from the corner bed below the window a smooth, peaceful breathing could be heard. A large, swollen belly rose and fell in rhythm with the light snoring. Sona floated on the still surface of a tranquil, grey sea. She had sworn and pleaded her child out into safety.

18

She would rather not have left the house today. But Amina knew that if neither she nor Tamanna were there, waiting on the brown dhurrie outside the school when the kids arrived, it could mean the end of the kindergarten altogether. Whatever had happened in Katihar last night, she had no doubt it would reach the Town of Love within a few hours.

She spotted the worry in Roshan's face the moment she walked through the schoolhouse door to collect the rug and the basket of toys. Every morning the teacher pedalled in on his bicycle from Khwaishgram, nine miles away, and he often picked up bits of gossip on his way to Forbesganj.

'Tamanna's daughter was taken from Kuli Pada last night,' he said without preamble.

Amina inhaled sharply, hurried to turn her back towards him and tended to Aftaab, who was whimpering on the floor. Didn't want Roshan to see it in her face, didn't want him to know that this was the news she had been waiting for. When she replied, it was with a question: 'Where is Tamanna now?'

She didn't mention Rupa's name. If she spoke the name, her voice would immediately reveal her as an accomplice.

He shook his head: 'I don't know. I think they're still in Katihar.'

He tried to catch her eye: 'Saleem was there too. He was with them last night.'

In the dark flash of one second she understood what that meant. Saleem was the one who would suffer for this. First Saleem, then the school, then them, then Pukaar. And the children. The girls who came here instead of sitting in the doorways, the little kids who played and sang on the brown dhurrie instead of being ushered outside or pushed underneath the bed. For her own part Amina knew she would manage, and Tamanna had always been a barely-tolerated outsider in the Town of Love. And Darya and Rukmini were kajas, they would never dare touch them. But Saleem. Saleem had put not just himself but everything they had worked for, at risk, and Amina suddenly felt furious at him. He had known the raid would directly target his aunt Mumtaz and his cousin Jabbar – couldn't he have stayed out of it for once? She knew what Saleem had given up to be on Pukaar's payroll: family, protection, acceptance. Knew that the organisation, with its vulnerable position here in Forbesganj, wouldn't be enough to keep him safe now. Amina gathered up more toys for the youngest children as her thoughts kept racing: she knew who would be sought out for revenge. But what kind of revenge would it be?

Fauzia's face was inscrutable as always. Her fingers folded, creased, slathered, took money and placed it in the plastic box. Everything buzzed around her: Tamanna, her daughter, Rukmini, the police, Jabbar who hadn't been there, Mumtaz who had been pulled in. The story unfolded around her, assembling piece by piece until the fragments made a whole. No one asked or accused her directly, no one knew what she had or hadn't known. And Fauzia's fingers folded and slathered, revealed nothing, weren't interested in anything at all.

Birbal was hanging around her paan-stand with some older boys; his dead eye shone white against the dark skin of his face. Fauzia noticed more kids roaming the street than usual; did this mean the school was closed again? Hadn't it been open again for several days now, after the trouble at the women's meeting? A sinking feeling in her stomach as she glimpsed Rozy through the doorway of the shack across the street; her niece sat on her haunches, holding a broomstick. Rozy hadn't been to school for a long time; whenever Fauzia tried to approach her, she vanished quickly into the house.

Fauzia sighed and turned towards her brother, who was perpetually half-snoring in the shade of the bench by the paan-stand; he seemed to be asleep. She took the chance, leaned forward and motioned to Birbal, 'Come here!'

The boy approached her sideways, crab-like, his left eye glued to her face. Fauzia knew well that most of the Prem Nagar children feared her; she pulled out a stick of chewing gum and offered it to him. 'Can you go check if Roshan is at the schoolhouse?'

The boy stared at her. Showed no sign of accepting the gum. Opened his solemn mouth and delivered the message. 'Roshan Sir is at school. But there are almost no children there.'

She hesitated a moment. Fauzia was not one to ask questions; she avoided showing interest in the complicated, problem-filled lives of others. She sold her paan, kept her mouth shut, listened and observed. As for Amina, the wildcat from Jogbani who had wreaked so much havoc and turmoil in the family and down the whole street, she took care to stay far away from her. Still, she had to ask: 'Is Amina there?'

Birbal fixed his knowing eye on her face.

'Yes. But Tamanna didi isn't there. And Salma says she might never return.'

In the waiting room at the Katihar police station, Tamanna asked herself if she would ever return to Prem Nagar. She didn't even know where she would sleep tonight, and more importantly, where Rupa would sleep. Her plans had never extended beyond the events of last night, *Get Rupa Out* had been the only point on the agenda. Her mind had had no room for anything beyond the thundering panic that had engulfed her the second she saw her daughter sitting on the balcony of the blue house. From that moment on, there was just one thought that counted. Get Rupa Out.

And now she was out. Rupa was sitting here beside her for yet another round in the waiting room; the district magistrate had agreed to hold the hearing at the police station instead of at the courthouse since the witness was in need of extra protection. Rupa's pupils had shrunk since yesterday but she was still shaking, she wouldn't eat, wouldn't speak. At least she had stopped screaming curses.

Darya bent over Tamanna, 'Rukmini called, she'll be here soon, she's on her way. We won't let Rupa go in there alone.'

The thirteen-year-old heard every word, but not a muscle moved in her face.

'I'll go in with her!'

The fighting urge awakened in Tamanna again.

Darya shook her head, her voice taking on a more insistent tone, 'No no, we have to let Rukmini do it. She's a lawyer, she knows how these things work. And after all,' she caught Tamanna's eye, 'we have no right to be in there. Technically the magistrate is supposed to question Rupa alone. We have to let Rukmini present the arguments, she might be able to convince him.'

Three students sat facing Roshan on the floor of the schoolhouse. Hirkani with her gnarled Hindi letters; Zaina, who erupted in giggles whenever anyone asked her a question; and Akash, who was there to learn just enough arithmetic to collect payment for the homemade liquor he helped his father sell. The teacher sat hunched over in his chair, his face a mask of total despondency. *What have we accomplished?* Roshan thought, exhausted. *What am I doing this for?*

He recognised it all, every bit of it; he was a Nat, like them. The difference was that in the village of Khwaishgram where he grew up, it was the men's labour with the red-hot iron that had secured their bread and butter. Roshan remembered his father's enormous fists, the soot and smoke, the clanging of tools. The resignation he had seen in his parents' faces from an early age, his father wearily shaking his head: their thin and sickly youngest son, with one leg that wouldn't grow as fast as the other, would never be able to swing a sledgehammer. Roshan's thoughts lingered on the memory of his mother, a smile softly grazing his lips. *'She was the one who insisted I learn to read.'* he thought. *'She was the one who understood that my mind was I all had.'*

He had never had any kind of cohesive or consistent schooling, but had happened to be in the right place at the right time when a teacher showed up in the village, paid by an aid organisation that had come and stayed awhile before disappearing again. Sheer luck, Roshan mused, that he had faith in me, that I received a few extra months of schooling. And that he managed to solicit the money, a one-year stipend to a boarding school in Patna, for a preparatory seminar on teaching.

But the year had come and gone, the money had dried up, and Roshan had never completed his teaching degree. The homecoming had not been a hearty one, the sickly boy had been just another useless mouth to feed, so Roshan had spied an opportunity the day he heard about the kajas with the crazy idea to build a school in Prem Nagar. A school in the Town of Love, where the likelihood of getting even one student was next to none, where the pay would barely cover one meal a day, and where contempt and beatings would for sure be part of the job description. A school where well-qualified teachers certainly wouldn't be lining up to work, a school where they wouldn't be able to promise textbooks for everyone or even a certificate at the end. But it would be a school where other Roshans with no hope and no money could learn the magic of letters and numbers, where a tiny window to the amazing world outside Forbesganj could be opened, a world where people said please and thank you and washed their hands and learned to wait their turn. So he had cycled the hour-long stretch, had found the Pukaar door behind the green gate at the old rice mill, and had told Saleem he could do this job, degree or no degree.

Roshan shut his eyes for a moment, balling his fists in his lap. What was the point? Had they achieved anything at all? Kasim's threats, the evening raids of raging men who vowed to burn down the school, Prabir keeping Birbal at home whenever he felt like it.

A twinge of tenderness inside him at the thought of Birbal and his blind eye. Forget it, he said gruffly to himself. The boy would never get a chance. One step forward, two steps back, that was how they were going.

He opened his eyes when he felt a light tap on his arm. Hirkani was looking up at him. 'Are you sleeping, Roshan Sir?' Her pigtails bobbed up and down in rhythm with her words, and her nose, that was never quite clean, wrinkled up in a question mark. She held her chalkboard in front of her, displaying the tiny letters in a corner: *ka, ta, pa*. Her eyes, proud of what she had to show him, were nevertheless tinged with the ever-underlying fear. He saw the black string hanging around her neck, the cheap amulet, a metal box that could be opened. The folded-up Quranic verses inside were the only protection Hirkani had. And Roshan remembered now, everything fell back into place. This was why he was here, to bolster that protection. To hold up a shield in front of Hirkani, Birbal and the others. To assure them that there were other places and other ways, that they could have things they had never experienced, become people they had never been. That they could leave behind what everyone told them they were born into.

'No,' he said. 'I'm not sleeping. Let's look at your work.'

※

'Name?'
   'Rupa Khatoon.'
   'What is your family name?'
   Silence.
   'I don't know.'
   'How old are you?'
   'Thirteen.'
   'What is your mother's name?'
   A long silence.
   'I grew up with Dolly Khatoon. She's my stepmother.'

The district magistrate scanned the piece of paper in front of him. Decided to continue the questioning.

'Where were you born?'

'In Katihar.'

'Have you gone to school?'

Rupa's frail shoulders hunched over a little further.

'I wanted to go to school, but when I told my father, he said there wasn't enough money for that.'

She hesitated briefly but kept going.

'He said, "I'm the one who owns you, you do as I say".'

'What is your father's name?'

A quick glance over at Rukmini, who sat on a chair by the door.

'Jabbar Aslam.'

Rupa's hearing went on; Rukmini could hear some of the answers but not all. She knew she had to adhere strictly to the compromise she had finagled with the magistrate: she could be present in the room, but had to sit quietly at a distance. Still, she had to struggle to keep her face expressionless when she heard Rupa call Jabbar her father without hesitation. Why was she then calling Dolly her stepmother? When the magistrate returned to the question of her mother, would Rupa then say Tamanna's name?

The magistrate had a stern face; the dark circles around his eyes stretched outward to his temples. Still, Rupa was handling the situation much better than Rukmini had feared; she comprehended every question and took her time before answering. Now, in a low voice, she was describing her childhood with her stepmother. 'Dolly used to beat me, my grandmother Mumtaz did too. I used to tell them, "all I want is to go to school", but then they would beat me even harder. I wasn't allowed to leave the house. The other girls in the house told me Dolly couldn't be my mother since she treated me that way. I cried and asked my father who my real mother was, but then he hit me too and said of course Dolly was my mother.'

Rupa paused, and the magistrate interjected with a question:

'Who were the other girls in the house? What were they doing there?'

At last Rupa lifted her gaze from her tiny hands resting in her lap. 'Don't you know? They took passengers.'

A wave of relief washed over Rukmini. She had said it unprovoked, Rupa had said it. Now the magistrate just had to follow up, ask what had happened to her!

He did; he asked Rupa, 'Did you have passengers in that house too?'

Long silence.

The magistrate, again, 'Rupa Khatoon. Did you also take passengers in Jabbar Aslam's house?'

When she began to speak, it was nearly in a whisper. 'There was an old man. He had a lot of money in a big bundle. They said he wanted to marry me, but I said that I didn't want to. Then they beat me, and I didn't get anything to eat that night. The next day they gave me new clothes and told me I had to take a bath. When he came back in the evening, they pushed me and told me I had to go to him. Dolly said, "Your father took money from this man, you have to do what he wants". I started crying, but Dolly just told me to be quiet.'

More silence. The magistrate waited patiently.

'They locked me in a room with him. I hit him in the face, but he was very strong.'

She raised her voice, it trembled, but she spoke loud and clear.

'That man forced me. And afterwards I got ill.'

Rukmini was glad Tamanna was waiting several rooms and many thick doors away. Glad she couldn't hear the far-too-young voice uttering the far-too-grown-up words. The magistrate asked a few more questions. How many times had they forced her? Who set the price? What happened to the money?

Finally, a long silence descended. The magistrate shuffled his papers, Rupa stared silently into her lap. Rukmini began to get nervous, wasn't he going to raise the question of custody?

'Rupa,' he said at last, removing his wire-frame glasses. 'You are thirteen years old, you can't live alone, someone has to take care of you. Who do you want to live with?'

Rukmini held her breath. She wouldn't be surprised in the least if Rupa said she wanted to go back to Jabbar Aslam.

The girl with the long braid hanging down her back turned her head and peered at the woman by the door. Turned back towards the district magistrate.

'I don't know,' she said.

Sona had nowhere to go. No one was waiting for her, no one would welcome her home. She, too, had given her statement at the police station in Katihar and had been told she would be summoned again if Jabbar Aslam was to face trial. She wasn't worried about that right now, these were just words, something distant. What overwhelmed Sona in the police station's waiting room, more than her upper-belly aches and pains, more than the headache gripping her forehead like a steel claw, was the inconceivable, ominous freedom. She was relieved, she was terrified, she had a thousand questions that Darya couldn't immediately answer. As the hours went by on this first day of freedom, the world grew larger and larger and overtook Sona completely. She was not prepared, she didn't have the means to cope with this, she was totally unequipped!

Sona didn't know how many years she had lived in the blue house. Any ties she might have had to an earlier life were severed long ago, all she had was a vague memory of clear blue sky above and the sound of goats bleating. Had she been married? She felt sure she had been married, she remembered her excitement over a pink wedding costume. Could she have been ... nine? Ten? The man who had called himself her husband had been tall, and she had held his hand. She thought they had ridden the bus together; he had brought her to an unfamiliar house, she remembered that she hadn't been allowed outdoors. She recalled dark rooms, always men, and always keeping her mouth shut to escape the beatings. Now she was out of the room, out of the house, a newborn poised to navigate the universe with no map, no guide.

Sona didn't have a plan. Her only anchor was her belly, the baby, she had to find a safe place for the baby coming soon. She turned to Darya, it was obvious to her that Darya had to help her. 'Help me, behen,' she said. 'I have nothing. Help me.'

Darya turned to her with something like panic flooding her eyes. 'Sona, I …'

Her cell phone rang in her pocket and she sprang up from the chair, fleeing the impossible demand and heading for a corner of the room. 'Hello?'

Darya pressed the phone against her ear, the connection was poor and she couldn't make out what Amina was saying. Her crackling voice was agitated, and she spoke too close to the receiver. 'Amina, calm down, speak slower, I can't hear you … where are you?'

Amina had no time to explain how she had run from the kindergarten and up the street, had made her way to the telephone man and paid ten rupees for a three-minute call to Darya's cell phone. 'Darya didi, there are almost no kids at school and Salma says Jabbar Aslam is on his way. What's happened, why haven't you come back? Where is Tamanna?'

Amina turned her back to those around her as much as possible; the telephone man shot her a curious glance and invented an errand by the phone beside hers, untangling a knot in the wires.

But Darya didn't have a simple answer. 'We'll be there soon, Amina, there are a few more things we have to sort out here first.'

'And Tamanna?'

Amina was relentless. 'Will Tamanna be back?'

She pressed the black phone receiver against her ear, why was Darya pausing?

'First we have to see what will happen with Rupa.'

'Yes, but Darya didi, haven't they taken Jabbar Aslam and put him in jail?'

Darya sighed. 'He wasn't there, they don't know where he is right now. Amina, I have to go …'

Then she suddenly remembered. 'What about the kindergarten, Amina? Who is looking after the kids?'

'There are almost no kids today. And Heena is there to watch them. Heena and Jannati.'

More waiting at the Katihar police station. They had asked for a speedy processing of the custody request Tamanna had filed when she lodged her complaint, and had been told that temporary measures would be determined that afternoon. Tamanna was worried that Rupa hadn't eaten all day. Her daughter looked pale and trembling, she hadn't said a word to anyone since giving her statement and Tamanna's fear and confusion clamped down on the issue of food. Maybe Rupa had eaten something bad in Kuli Pada, could that be the reason she was sick? Oh, but what could she do? How could she soothe and feed her daughter back to her?

Darya had pulled Rukmini aside in a corner of the waiting room and recounted her conversation with Amina.

'There are rumours in Prem Nagar that Jabbar is on his way there.'

A flash of alarm shone in the eyes of Pukaar's director from Delhi: 'Where is he, then? Haven't the police got anything out of Mumtaz?' Rukmini had already turned around and was headed straight for Laskar's office. 'I'll go inquire …'

But Chief Inspector Laskar wasn't easy to get hold of; he was a very busy man and the officer outside his door stopped Rukmini with the palm of his hand. When Laskar finally emerged into the waiting room and motioned for her to come in, he didn't have much to report. 'We have not finished interrogating Mumtaz Begum yet,' he said curtly. 'We have no information on where her son might be.'

Rukmini looked at him in shock. 'What …? But we have a minor here who just testified that she was forced into prostitution in Jabbar Aslam's house. Tracking him down must surely be a top priority?'

She swallowed her words as soon as she heard them. She, a kaja from Delhi, and a woman kaja, no less, how did she think she could stand there and tell the chief inspector how to do his job?

Laskar's moustache trembled with spite. 'Madam, we have a lot to do at this station. We've done everything we can to help you, but I have other ongoing cases to deal with. Your task is to care for the girl, leave it to me to handle the police matters!'

She was struggling not to explode when they were interrupted by a skinny man with rolled-up shirtsleeves and too much grease in his hair, the assistant to the district magistrate. 'Excuse me, sir, excuse me, but the magistrate would like to speak to Madam Rukmini.'

The decision had been made.

'A rehabilitation home,' the magistrate said. 'The court feels it is in the girl's best interest given her present situation, and the home in Patna has room to take her in.'

Rukmini was startled. 'In Patna?'

He nodded. 'It's within our legal precinct, and has an excellent reputation. As the court understands it, the girl needs medical attention and likely an ongoing course of therapy; and Patna can offer both.'

'But that's still in Bihar, it's close enough that …'

She pulled herself together. 'If that's the case, measures must be taken to ensure that none of the accused from Katihar will have access to Rupa.'

He looked at her sternly, furrowing his brow.

'These things must be arranged directly with the personnel at the home. They will be assigned as Rupa's guardians. Temporarily,' he added when he saw Rukmini's mouth open to protest.

'But her mother has filed a request for custody, hasn't the court considered …'

He removed his glasses and stroked his chin with a weary motion.

'The girl has not acknowledged Tamanna Khatoon as her mother. And she has not said whom she would like to take over custody.'

Amina walked back down the street in the yellow afternoon heat. She barely moved to avoid an overcrowded van and distractedly swerved away from a goat chomping away at some rotten fruit by the side of the road. She was lost in thought; how could Salma know anything about Jabbar Aslam when not even Darya in Katihar knew where he was? Amina had sensed it immediately when she hurried past the girl in the doorway on her way to the telephone man: today was a day when Salma was going to say something. Instinctively, Amina had slowed down, and sure enough, the information had been delivered with no introduction, in a flat, dry voice. 'Jabbar Aslam has family in Prem Nagar. He might be coming by to see them soon.'

Saleem! The name struck her like lightning, again. Jabbar Aslam was Saleem's cousin. Amina didn't get a chance to ask Darya whether Saleem was still with them. She heard Roshan's voice in her head, a doomsday pall now cast over his words. *Saleem was there too. He was with them last night.*

She hurried down the path towards the schoolhouse. She didn't know what to do or who to talk to. She only knew it was urgent.

Heena was waiting on the dhurrie with Amina's son on her lap. Aftaab reached out for his mother, twisting and turning, and Amina mechanically bent down to pick him up. She saw just three or four other kids; a yellow toy truck with three wheels was being driven slowly around in circles over bumpy tufts of grass. Amina looked around: 'Where is Jannati?'

Heena nodded in the direction of the school. Amina didn't quite understand: Had Jannati gone into the schoolhouse? It was hard enough to believe that she showed up alongside Heena this morning; all of Prabir's girls were usually kept on a tight leash and were rarely seen walking around in the Town of Love. But Amina had asked no questions, and Jannati had offered no explanations. Amina got up with Aftaab in her arms and hurried over to the door.

Three children were still seated at their desks. Hirkani had filled her chalkboard with tiny, scrunched-up letters, she leaned intently over the low desk, nose buried in the chalk. Akash had a book open in front of him, but his gaze wandered out the window as he distractedly scratched an itch on his arm. Zaina spotted Amina and broke into a chorus of giggles as she fingered her pink hair clip.

Roshan's chair was angled so that his back was halfway turned to the children. He didn't see Amina in the doorway, didn't notice Akash not reading his book. Roshan's face was turned toward the window, where a robust woman in a blue and black sari sat silhouetted on the ledge. The sun sneaked a few afternoon rays through the metal bars, illuminating her heavy body in a frame of gold.

19

Manjira spotted her at once – a new woman at the back of the room. The daughter seated on her lap couldn't be more than six years old, a scrawny little thing with a frizzy ponytail and gold sandals. Her mother scanned the room with contemplative eyes; she didn't speak to anyone. Manjira cleared a path through the chattering women who filled the floor of the Pukaar shelter; it was Thursday afternoon and time for the mothers' meeting.

'Hello ... I don't think I've seen you here before?'

She flashed the newcomer a reassuring smile, shoving her lump of paan further back in her mouth.

The woman looked up at her, mumbled a form of greeting as she hugged her daughter closer.

'How did you hear about us?'

The newcomer nodded toward Laxmi, whose head was turned away from them as she chatted with two other women.

Manjira paused for a moment, but the new woman said nothing else. The women of Khidderpore's red-light district were clumped in tight circles around her, all anxious to get the meeting underway, no one here could afford to waste precious time in the workday. Manjira sat down on her haunches.

'Are you here because of your daughter? Does she need a safe place to sleep?'

The woman nodded and looked down. Manjira sighed inwardly – *how much easier it would be if people could just open their mouths and say what they've come here to say!* But she kept up her soothing smile. 'Why don't you stay after everyone leaves, and we'll talk about it.'

The meeting dragged on with wide-ranging discussions about the girls. Some of the mothers pushed for another shelter, for the boys. 'It's not just the girls who need a safe place to spend the night!' Manjira nodded and listened, but knew that the money to set up another location, no matter how spartan, just didn't exist. She tried to shift the focus over to daily activities, like the small workshops where the boys could learn simple vocational skills. The first priority, for both boys and girls, was always to get out of Khidderpore, away from the flesh trade and all its side branches. Numerous voices chimed in:

'First of all we have to move the shelter out of Khidderpore!'

'No, then we'll never see our girls! I can't afford to take many hours off and go to another neighbourhood to see my daughter!'

'The best thing would be if Pukaar had a boarding school here in Kolkata. That way our girls could live and go to school in the same place.'

'No, the girls have to go to regular schools! If they go to a Pukaar school they'll never be anything but "prostitutes' daughters", they'll always have that label.'

'But isn't that the whole point? That they shouldn't be ashamed of who they are? They didn't ask to be born into this!'

Manjira leaned back a little, content with the discussion, which usually centred on health woes and lack of medication, passengers who demanded more than they had paid for, or the women going hungry due to a dearth of passengers. She would much rather hear them discuss matters like those currently being aired: thoughts beyond the daily worries about where their next meal would come from, reflections on who they were and what hopes they had for their children. Her gaze refocused on the back of the room and settled on the newcomer. Her daughter had evidently fallen asleep, her little head with the bobbing ponytail flopped down toward her chest. The woman had Nepalese features, narrower eyes, slightly higher cheekbones. Manjira sighed again, there must be a hundred thousand Nepalese women who suffered the same fate in the brothels of India. Then her eyes widened in surprise as the new woman waved her hand in the air, requesting the floor.

'The girls need the shelter more than the boys. The last thing I want is for my daughter to end up like me – I have to get her as far away as possible! She's only six, and already my passengers look at her as much as they look at me. She's six years old!'

The room fell silent for a moment, then the buzzing resumed. None of the mothers showed the faintest sign of surprise; they had all been in this situation – this was precisely the reason their daughters had been brought to the shelter. Manjira's stomach turned. She had worked in Kolkata's red-light districts for years, but she never stopped feeling revulsion at the constant demand for younger and younger girls. For children's bodies with flat chests, skinny thighs, hairless genitals. What kind of person wanted this for sex?

Manjira stood up, clapping her hands for attention. 'There are clean bedsheets up at the front, and you're welcome to a cup of tea before you go!'

She headed straight for the back of the room toward the new woman, who sat still with her daughter asleep in her lap. There wasn't room, the shelter was overflowing as it was, but they would just have to share. If two kids could share a mattress, why not three? Manjira smiled at the newcomer, putting on her most cheerful face. 'Can you stay here with her for a few hours? Most of the girls get a little upset the first night away from their mothers.'

※

He regretted it now. Or at least part of him regretted it. Saleem was on the train, a twelve-hour ride on the Haate Bazare Express from Katihar to Kolkata, dazed and exhausted and torn by doubt and embarrassment. Should he have gone back to Forbesganj after all? Wasn't this cowardly of him, running away to Kolkata like a little boy afraid of the bullies?

Disconcerted, Saleem looked around the train car. Four bunk beds, two against each wall, and there were seven people in here. He had no idea how they secured him a ticket and a place to sleep on such short notice – it must have been the combined resources of Rukmini and the Patna police, plus the fact that the son of the retired colonel who somehow knew Darya's father was employed by the railways. In any case, he didn't expect to get any sleep tonight – the six-person family had filled every bed with their tiffins, stacks of metal lunchboxes and canteens, bags and baskets, thermoses and soda bottles, and a battery-operated toy piano that flashed red and yellow when the youngest boy pounded out a cheery, tinny melody for the hundredth time. Saleem nestled further into the corner of the bunk that in theory belonged to him, barely escaping a sea of orange soda that gushed toward him as a girl in pastel-coloured pyjamas dropped her cup and let out a screaming wail. Mother and grandmother immediately came to the rescue with washcloths and napkins; Saleem got up and escaped into the corridor.

All the bunk beds along the outer wall of the car were full; there wasn't much room for a night-time walkabout. He couldn't slip past a man attempting to press a giant cardboard box under the bottom bunk that was two inches too low, and was left standing still listening to the nocturnal sounds onboard the train. An infernal snoring droned from the bunk to his left, the boy's toy piano seemed a welcome respite in comparison. The vendors approaching from both ends of the train cried out their rhythmic, braying refrains, 'Tea! Cold drinks! Potato chips! Nuts!' A portable bazaar rolled through the sleeping car: the girl with a basket atop her head filled with nail polish, earrings and sparkly barrettes; the boy in the sweat-drenched T-shirt balancing a long pole festooned with bags of candy and popcorn through the overfilled corridor. Over the cardboard-box-man's shoulder Saleem spied the queue for the toilet at the end of the car and decided to wait until later.

A towel that read *Indian Railways* had soaked up most of the orange soda and his bunk was miraculously empty when he found his way back to his cabin in the sleeper car. He leaned back with his arms folded under his head and shut his eyes. It had not been his idea to get away for a couple of days, it honestly hadn't. He had had no plans other than returning to Forbesganj straight after the rescue raid, he hadn't imagined that turning Rupa's world upside down would also involve shaking up his own universe. Not until Mumtaz's high-pitched whining seared through his head had he understood that his own cards would now be dealt differently as well. It wasn't just Pukaar's credibility and their work in the Town of Love that was put at risk by the dramatic events in Kuli Pada; the stream of curses his aunt had spewed out in the brothel hallway also tinged his own future with a darker hue: 'How could you? Dhoka, traitor!'

But his lowly act of treachery wouldn't merely bring the furious shame of his family down on his own head. His betrayal might have even more dangerous immediate consequences. The Nats of Forbesganj had long held him in contempt, this might be the deciding factor that could propel them to shut him up once and for all. That was what Rukmini feared. That's why she had insisted he take a trip to Kolkata instead of going back to Forbesganj: 'You can be of service at the Pukaar office there for a few weeks, they could use the extra help. I'll call and tell them you're coming, they'll arrange a place for you to sleep.'

He had protested, thinking of Fauzia, the plot of land he had purchased on the outskirts of Forbesganj, the workers he had spoken to about the construction. But deep inside he had known Rukmini was right. After a night spent partly at the police station in Katihar and partly in hiding behind a wall at the bus station waiting for daylight, he had realised that returning to the sofa at the Pukaar office was no longer an option. Mumtaz had been released after giving her statement the next day and was back in the blue house. Jabbar had not shown up and Saleem shook his head in silent contempt: not a chance that much would be done to locate and arrest his cousin, he was sure of that! And even if Jabbar didn't make his own way to Forbesganj, there were plenty of those whose services could be bought. Plenty of those who would find him for a price. Saleem, the traitor.

He turned towards the wall, trying to let the soothing rhythms of the train pulsate through his veins and lull him to sleep.

Farther north of Katihar, a few hours later: another railroad journey. For the second time Tamanna sat on the train with Rupa, for the second time a police officer sat squarely facing them in the opposite seat. But this time there was no heavy, drowsy three-year-old resting in her lap, merely a black, threadbare handbag that both her hands clutched tightly.

Darya, too, was accompanying mother and daughter on their long journey to Patna. She twisted and turned on the squeaky vinyl seat, hoping to sneak in a few hours of sleep in spite of the worries torturing her overworked brain. She rubbed her throbbing temples, felt exhausted to the bone. Had they made the right decision? Would the home in Patna be safe enough? Darya pushed away, again and again, the question which tried to force itself to the forefront of her mind: Was it too late for Rupa? Had they risked everything to rescue a girl who was beyond rescuing?

Tamanna watched Darya fret, eyes closed, in the seat next to her. For her own part she had no desire to sleep. She didn't dare lift her eyes from Rupa's face, not even for a second, she couldn't take the chance of the policeman falling asleep, too – what if her daughter were to disappear again! The shock, like a punch in the stomach, that day when the train had screeched to a halt in Kursila, Jabbar's face suddenly appearing in front of her. She nervously scrutinised the young sergeant from head to toe; the police hat on his head looked oversized, what was to say that history wouldn't repeat itself? But Darya's light snoring soothed her frenzied worry. Darya didi wouldn't let anything happen to Rupa. Chief Inspector Laskar was bound by his agreement with the two Pukaar women, these two who had challenged every rule that governed the purchase and sale of a little girl. This solemn-faced sleeping young woman was her sword and shield, the young sergeant couldn't compare to her.

Tamanna was exhausted. The brief blaze of victory she had sensed when Darya had explained the temporary custody arrangement – that at least the home in Patna would be taking over as guardian instead of Jabbar Aslam – was long since extinguished, drowned beneath new worries. Rupa's health, her ravaged genitals, the morphine addiction that still made her tremble. The rehabilitation home, how well would they look after her there? Patna was too far away from Forbesganj, she would never get to see her daughter! And was it far enough from Katihar, far enough from those who had done this to her?

But even to herself, Tamanna couldn't name the deepest pain of all. That Rupa just sat there, distant and cold. Not a word, not a glance. Not a flash of recognition or a hint of relief that every thud against the train tracks was carrying her further and further from Kuli Pada. She was not surprised that Rupa wouldn't call her Mother, she could handle that, it was what she had expected. But that she couldn't even bring herself to look at Tamanna, to scan across her face in search of a familiar feature, a hint of connection between them; that Rupa bore deeper wounds than those between her thighs – that was the dark wave that washed over Tamanna and carried her out onto a black, sorrowful sea.

Motorcycles were a common sight in the Town of Love at night. They usually drove slowly, some with lights and some without. Heads turned and long gazes were cast at the girls in the doorways. Salma sat slumped over on the charpoy just inside the open door, distractedly fondling Nila's head as the baby slept beside her. She didn't bat an eyelid when a man with rolled-up white shirtsleeves slowed his two-wheeler down as he passed by; she looked right through him when he spoke to her. The man grew uncertain, hesitated for a moment before cruising onward down the street, on to the next doorway where a dangling light bulb illuminated the crown of another girl's head, her dark red lipstick.

Nila grew unsettled and began to whine and Salma bundled her in her arms, cradling the warm body against her own. She busied herself with the baby, eyes turned away from the street, when she heard another motorcycle, the engine roaring as the heavy two-wheeler zoomed over the bridge and into the Town of Love. She whipped around, hugging Nila close. Who could this be in such a rush? The brake lights flared red next to a house on the right further down the street, the house Kasim shared with his brothers. Cousins of Saleem, the weakling traitor who had stabbed them all in the back and scorned them with the deepest of insults. Two broad-shouldered figures, their faces obscured from Salma's view, parked their motorcycle and vanished into the house.

They took a motorised rickshaw from the station to the home in Patna. The policeman sat in front next to the driver, Rupa was between Tamanna and Darya in the backseat. Tamanna soaked up the town around her: the streets so much wider than in Forbesganj, the traffic, the soaring buildings, crowds of people everywhere. They turned off a three-lane road into a neighbourhood where the houses had several stories but were hidden behind thick walls, interspersed with dusty brown vacant lots. The rickshaw-wallah asked for the address once again, the policeman took out a slip of paper to double-check. They hit the brakes in front of an unmarked gate, an anonymous doorbell revealed nothing about what was inside. The officer pressed the bell, and told the rickshaw-wallah to wait outside as a bearded watchman came to open.

Rupa didn't object, but showed no interest either. She let herself be led through the gate, trailing behind the others across the courtyard and in through the frosted-glass door marked 'Headmistress'. At first, Darya couldn't tell who bore this impressive title; the three desks in the room all were roughly the same size and none of the sari-clad women looked up when they entered the room. She was just about to open her mouth when the youngest woman, the one in the sea-green sari by the door, lifted her head. As she removed her gold wire-frame glasses and got to her feet, a warm smile spread across her face. 'Namaste,' she said calmly and looked straight into Rupa's face. 'You must be Rupa.'

The officer got the signatures he needed, and with a friendly farewell slipped out the door back to the waiting rickshaw.

Darya felt the knot in her stomach loosen and dissolve. Three visitors' chairs were brought out and placed by the headmistress's desk, teacups appeared, and the whirring of the ceiling fans formed a drowsy, soothing hum. Headmistress S. Dumra stood before her aching eyes like a radiant heroine cloaked in sea-foam green. She knew what Rupa needed, she knew what had to be done and would see it through. The check-in paperwork ensured the required doctor's visit, psychologist's assessment and recreational therapy – she wouldn't be left to languish and stare at the wall, Ms Dumra insisted. Rupa would be checked in for an initial duration of three months; she would be sharing a room with another girl, healthy and full of positive energy, the headmistress assured them. Darya rolled her shoulders now that the heavy burden had been lifted and responsibility had been transferred to someone used to dealing with these things, someone who wasn't overwhelmed or paralysed. Someone who would hold the girls' hands day by day, lift them up, lead them onward.

Tamanna had barely said a word since they arrived, but she nodded gratefully when Ms Dumra asked if she would like to stay the night. 'So you can see for yourself that we'll take good care of Rupa, before you leave', she said. Tears pooled behind Tamanna's eyelids. She should have been the one to do this, she should be the one taking care of Rupa. She should have been the one Rupa smiled at, she should have been the hand Rupa reached for on the train. But Rupa smiled at no one: she gave plain, monosyllabic answers to straightforward questions. Her eyes were still expressionless, an occasional shiver ran through her body. A trembling wave of emotion swept through Tamanna. She was so exhausted, she couldn't take it anymore. Rupa was out now, Rupa was safe. She slumped back into her chair, squeezed her eyes shut and let the tears gush forth.

Darya glanced quickly at her watch, she could still catch the bus if she hurried. At least twelve hours on indescribable roads, but her bed in the simple hostel room back in Forbesganj still seemed like the most tempting place on earth right now. She wanted to get back there, take a shower, wash the whole rescue operation off her body. The horrendous brothel, the police station, the district court, scrub it all away, down the drain. But there was one more thing she had to make sure of.

'There may be people who will come after Rupa, who will come here to track her down. You have to promise that no one can see her except Tamanna and the Pukaar people.'

Darya took a deep breath, steeling herself to argue that even though the court records showed that Jabbar Aslam was Rupa's father, as she herself had testified, things were not what they seemed! Rupa had been held there against her will, they had prostituted her, she –

Headmistress S. Dumra cut her off. 'We still have to fill out the name of Rupa's guardian on her registration sheet,' she said. Took out her pen, wrote in clear, blue letters. *Guardian: Tamanna Khatoon, mother.*

Darya felt something warm filling her throat, her nose began to sniffle.

'I'll call to check in before you leave tomorrow morning,' she said to Tamanna.

※

Amina stayed in the kitchen. The tiny, tunnel-like room was barely three feet wide and she couldn't think of anything more to be done in there. The kids had eaten, she herself had nibbled on a piece of bread while cooking for them, and Kasim's evening meal, litti chokha with spicy dal, was hot and ready. Amina waited in the narrow kitchen with the door open to the staircase that led down to the courtyard, her ears perked up for sounds from below. She had seen Jabbar and his brother arrive, and Kasim had said nothing as he hurried down the stairs, down to his brother's rooms. They were all gathered there now, she was sure of it, including her mother-in-law. Amina saw her in her mind's eye: the henna-striped hair, the eyebrows knitted in perpetual suspicion. Her other daughters-in-law were probably privy to this strange meeting as well. Amina was not surprised to be left out, merely grateful that there didn't seem to be a beating in store for her, given the last few days' events in Kuli Pada. Her friendship with Tamanna, her job in the kindergarten, her far-too-close connections with Pukaar, her involvement with the women's group – Amina knew that both her mother-in-law and Kasim's brothers felt that he was letting her off the hook too easily.

She walked out onto the landing but there was nothing to overhear, they had gone inside down there and shut the door behind them. Amina would have given anything to have a cell phone at this moment, some means to contact Darya right away. Hadn't she said on the phone that Jabbar Aslam had disappeared? That no one knew where he was?

She made up her mind quickly. She, Amina, knew where Jabbar was. She threw a quick glance at the two little ones asleep under the mosquito net and hurried quietly down the stairs.

She had reached the end of Prem Nagar and had crossed the bridge without being seen, she was sure of that. If she walked fast, Darya's hostel was less than ten minutes away; surely she must be back from Katihar by now? Amina pulled her dark dupatta closer around her face, stayed in the shadows and looked away from the faces of passersby in the main Forbesganj thoroughfare. The hostel receptionist was glued to a small, flickering TV set on a low table in front of him; he barely looked up when she asked after Darya. 'She hasn't been here in several days,' he grumbled. Amina's heart sank down into her stomach, 'Oh …' He looked up, but barely caught a glimpse of her back as she rushed out the door.

She had to get to the office right now, there was no other way. Rukmini might be there in her second-floor room, or maybe Saleem had made an unexpected return? Suddenly the burden of knowing Jabbar's whereabouts felt insufferably heavy, she wanted to tell someone, rid herself of the sole responsibility! Amina was running now, weaving through rickshaws and minibuses, leaping over mud puddles and sidestepping piles of horse dung. It was dark and quiet outside the old rice mill gate; Amina hesitated a moment. If she knocked she risked stirring the cranky old chowkidar, the watchman, unnecessarily, but how else would she get through to Rukmini? She clenched her fist and knocked sharply, two times. No response. She lifted her hand to knock again when the gate creaked slightly open and she glimpsed the watchman's stubbly chin, accompanied by a voice from a window inside, 'Who is it?'

'Rukmini didi!'

Amina stumbled in through the gate, over to the door, up the staircase and into a chair in Rukmini's room. Barely noticing the woman with the bulging belly seated on the bed, she blurted out her news of Jabbar and his brother's appearance in the Town of Love. She didn't think to ask about Tamanna or Rupa, just wanted to get this unsettling knowledge off her chest and get out of here, get back home and back into bed with the kids before Kasim made his way upstairs.

Rukmini understood. 'Hurry home, Amina,' she said. 'I'm glad you came. But now you have to hurry home.'

Rukmini knew she had to think fast. Jabbar and his brother were here, in Prem Nagar. Were they looking for Rupa? For Sona? She looked towards the woman seated on the bed, both of Sona's hands rested on her upper belly. She blinked her eyes several times, as if she couldn't see clearly. Lay back on the bed, rolled carefully onto her side. The thought that she needed a doctor flashed briefly through

Rukmini's head. Sona probably hadn't had a checkup yet during the pregnancy.

But she had to think fast, think fast! Would there be any point in calling the police in Katihar, three hours away? What about the tiny station in Forbesganj, whose officers tended to stay as far away from the Town of Love as possible? Her fingers started to dial Mr Vatsavani's cell phone number in Patna, but then she halted – the force in Forbesganj could only be called into action by the Katihar police. She made up her mind and dialled the number for Chief Inspector P. Laskar.

He wasn't happy to hear from her, she could hear him sighing heavily into the mouthpiece. 'Yes, Madam?'

He spent a long time interrogating her about who had actually reported the Aslam brothers sighting, whether she had observed them firsthand, and kept asking for a detailed description of Kasim's family's house.

'The police in Forbesganj know where it is,' she cut him off. 'Can't you just order them into action?'

His tone when he replied, 'I'll see what I can do' told her all she needed to know.

Amina stayed close to the outer walls of the houses on the right as she hurried through the Town of Love. *Almost home now, please, please let Kasim still be downstairs!* She crossed the street quickly, avoiding the light from the lone bulb that dangled above the telephone man's booth. He would undoubtedly let some comment slip to Kasim about his wife roaming the streets late at night. Amina zigzagged back and forth until she had the grey house in her sights. She froze. The motorcycle was gone. Jabbar and his brother had left. A desperate hope fluttered in her chest, her heart pounding as she scurried into the courtyard and stormed up the stairs. Maybe he wasn't up there yet, maybe he was still downstairs talking to …

She had just extended her palm to shove open the door when

it was torn open right in front of her. Kasim's face was a dark mask of fury. He didn't say a word, just snatched her upper arm in a firm grip and yanked her inside. Tightened his hold with one hand as he picked up the cane with the other.

20

He had never before had this feeling of drowning in a sea of people. An overwhelming sadness filled Saleem as he fought his way along the platform, wading through human destitution, being pushed and jostled between breathless workers and screeching peddlers, heartfelt reunions and targeted elbows. He nearly tripped over an older man hunched over against the wall, a bundle that could be his wife curled up on a cardboard flap beside him, whimpering feebly. A family manoeuvered a tower of luggage by barking orders at two porters, a beggar vociferously waved his stump of an arm into Saleem's face. He stumbled through a large hall towards what he assumed must be the exit, not daring to pause for a second for fear of choking on this ocean of poverty.

He ducked out into the cruel sunlight, hesitated a moment too long and was crushed against a wall by a short porter balancing three enormous suitcases on his head. He nearly stepped on a man crouching by a faucet in his underwear, scrubbing away at a white piece of cloth. A woman with pus-filled wounds around her mouth stretched her baby out toward him. 'Please, he hasn't eaten in two days!' The child was sleeping, clad in nothing except a blue shirt and the woollen string with the tiny metal box around his neck. Saleem felt a wistful pang, thinking of Rozy back in the Town of Love, Birbal and his eye. An aching thought: Someone must *want* these kids, they must be born for some purpose, something more than crowding pavements and filling brothels!

Saleem clutched his bag tightly and elbowed his way past a cart filled with candy and rainbow-coloured balloons. Spotted the line of black taxicabs and headed straight for the kerb.

※

Rukmini was back in Delhi. Pukaar's main office was a well-oiled machine where she didn't have to worry about people doing their job. But the responsibility, the pressure to meet the constant need for funding, ultimately always fell on her shoulders. She travelled and travelled, drafted solicitation letters and requests, started new online forums, gave speeches, talked to the media, mobilised famous faces as spokespeople for the work. Coordinated with other anti-trafficking groups all over the world, climbed up on every imaginable soapbox in hopes of gathering new potential donors. The questions she used to ask herself: *Do I really want to do this? Am I ready to commit the rest of my life, all my energy?* didn't come up as often as before. She had a responsibility. And Delhi was where she lived. This was where her family was, her husband, her daughter for whom she always bore a nagging guilt. Every cuddling session with Meeta on her lap was a gift, every time she had to say goodnight on the phone was another crack in the facade of the mother she would have liked to be. But Meeta would understand, Rukmini told herself. One day she would understand why this was necessary.

The rescue raid in Katihar had been a success, she told herself over and over again. They had got Rupa out, she was safe, a new road lay ahead for Tamanna's daughter now. Rukmini was sure: they had done the right thing. But what about all the others? She heaved a sigh, replaying the phone conversation with Manjira one more time in her head. The director of Pukaar's Kolkata division had not been pleased with the raid, to put it mildly. When Rukmini had called to prepare her for Saleem's arrival, she had first been stunned, then angry and hurt at Manjira's reaction:

'Have you considered the consequences of this?'

Even now, Rukmini could feel the disappointment throbbing black and heavy in her stomach. How could Manjira fail to give them any credit? Didn't she understand how high the stakes had been? How dangerous the gamble they had taken – and won?

'What do you mean? Jabbar Aslam won't be able to touch you, all the way down in Kolkata,' she had replied.

'That's not what I'm talking about.'

Manjira had stayed calm on the phone, but the slight edge of reproach had been audible enough under her words. 'Something like this sets a precedent, it builds up expectations. When this gets out, everyone with a sister or a daughter they think we could extract from a brothel, will point to our special treatment of Tamanna's daughter.'

Rukmini had felt her temperature rising. 'So? We'll just have to save them as well! Let's not forget that our goal is to abolish the whole flesh trade, to put an end to it all!'

'I know that!' Manjira had raised her own voice slightly in return. 'But one step at a time! How many times have we said that trust-building has to be the first step? Something like this undermines the loyalty we're trying to establish, not least with the men. If the men aren't on board, we'll never get anywhere! It's not just the supply that has to be curtailed, we have to put an end to the demand! And this kind of bravado could get us kicked right out the door at places where we've worked for years to get inside!'

Rukmini rubbed her temples and shut out the memory of their conversation. Of course she knew what Manjira was afraid of. She had doubts of her own, many more doubts than she had let on. But it was over and done with; they couldn't take it back. They had gone through with the raid, they had got Rupa out. Now they had to move forward.

Rukmini had carried her worries for Sona with her back to Delhi. The pregnant woman they had rescued out of the brothel wasn't faring well. The last few days before Rukmini had left Forbesganj, Sona had complained of upper abdominal pain, she had a headache and felt ill at ease. The doctor Rukmini had taken her to had diagnosed the problem as high blood pressure, 'but that's not unusual toward the end of a pregnancy', he had said, prescribing bedrest. That had been all, no tests, no comprehensive examination. Rukmini paced back and forth across her living room floor: Should she have insisted on taking blood and urine samples? Was Sona healthy? And was she safe? She had been refusing to leave Tamanna's side: 'If Tamanna can live in Forbesganj, why can't I?' Rukmini's attempts to explain the close-knit bonds between Jabbar Aslam and the most powerful families in Prem Nagar had fallen on deaf ears, Sona hadn't wanted to accept that this was the first place he would come looking for her. 'I have no family,' she had stubbornly repeated. 'Tamanna is my family. Tamanna and you, Rukmini didi.'

But Tamanna was on guard as well, carrying around the same feeling of unease as Rukmini. Something was different in the Town of Love. Even Heena had given a cautious welcome when Tamanna returned from Patna; she hadn't been waiting in the doorway cheering for the successful rescue raid. New frontlines had formed between the small huts, sinking in behind the water pumps. Etching themselves along the vegetable patches behind the houses, cutting clear across courtyards and into bedrooms. Old grudges were being awakened, new loyalties put to the test.

'You can't live with me,' Tamanna had bluntly told Sona as they sat under her mango tree and discussed where the pregnant woman could possibly go. Her voice had been a hushed whisper of exhaustion after twelve hours on a train and a three-hour bumpy bus ride, but the words had rung sharp and clear.

'They don't like me here. They've never liked me, and it will be even worse now. They say I've stolen from Jabbar Aslam.'

Sona had opened her mouth to protest, and Rukmini had felt the dismay settle like a grey cloak around her shoulders. She had tried to collect herself and anticipate the next step: maybe she would have to bring Sona with her back to Delhi?

Suddenly, another voice in the doorway of the sun-baked room under the mango tree: 'Come with me. You can stay in my room.'

Rukmini had stared at Jannati's dark, decisive face in surprise, had heard Tamanna's protest. 'Jannati didi, you can't ... Prabir ... and the passengers ... where is Sona supposed to go when ...'

But Jannati had been resolved. 'I will talk to Fauzia. We'll make it work somehow. Maybe someplace in Khwaishgram.'

Rukmini had seen the skeptical look on Tamanna's face: Jannati expected *Fauzia* to come to Sona's aid? The anxious eyes of the bloated, pregnant woman in the plastic chair in the shade. Rukmini had forced herself to keep quiet, she had sensed the heavy determination in the voice of Tamanna's old friend. Had felt a tiny, impossible joy growing in her chest: Could it be? Khwaishgram, the village where Roshan was from?

Rukmini was left standing, staring blankly out the apartment window in the quiet Delhi afternoon. *Wasn't this what it was all about? Developing a sense of solidarity, so the women could grow stronger together?* She was used to the surprising alliances and improvised solutions by now, this was the way Pukaar had grown and evolved.

Rukmini chose to believe that Sona would be safe in Bihar. Looked at her watch and got her car keys out. It was time to pick her daughter up from school.

※

Saleem was working with the young boys. Pukaar's office in Kolkata could use help from anyone who was available, whatever they brought to the table. He had no place in the mothers' meetings, and didn't come along when Manjira and the others travelled around talking to the women in tiny rooms off dirty alleyways. And of course he stayed away from the night-time shelter, where no strange men were welcome at the door.

He worked in the office the first few days; there was accounting to be overseen and contracts to be updated, he was used to these routines from Forbesganj. But the little carpentry shop for boys on the floor below the office sparked his curiosity and, after a period of observation, Saleem became an eager assistant to Peter, the German who led the instruction in how to make simple furniture, whittling and shaving and polishing. Peter had volunteered with Pukaar for over a year, and was here in India under contract with some Christian organisation, Saleem wasn't exactly clear what his story was. The unassuming young man spent almost every morning in the workshop, where boys from ten-years-old and up learned to wield saws and hammers, chisels and awls and sandpaper. A way out of the red-light district, a profession, a leg to stand on. Pukaar had no lodging to offer the sex workers' sons, but Saleem knew that the telltale drowsy faces and mops of sawdust-filled hair belonged to those boys who had grabbed a few hours of sleep on the floor behind the circular saw in the corner. Saleem kept quiet about it and so did Peter, how could they send the boys out to sleep on the sidewalk instead?

Saleem had no experience with tools, he simply mimicked Peter's every deft motion and gesture, storing the skills at the back of his mind, attaching them to his dreams of the house in Forbesganj. He wanted a proper house of brick, pucca, but what if he could learn enough carpentry to build his own furniture! A real bed for Fauzia, a wide and sturdy bed for a good night's sleep, in a room that was all her own.

After more than three weeks in Kolkata, Manjira appeared in the workshop one bright mid-morning. 'Saleem? Could you come upstairs with me for a minute?'

He hesitated, standing just inside the office door. All three chairs were taken; he didn't know quite what to do with himself.

Manjira pointed to two cardboard boxes piled in a corner; he carefully took a seat on top of them. She jumped straight to the point:

'I would like you to come to a meeting we're having tomorrow night. A men's meeting.'

Saleem looked at her, perplexed. Men? What was she talking about? What kind of …? She spotted his total confusion before he could express it. 'All kinds of men,' she continued. 'Passengers, pimps, babus, husbands, sons, the landlords who rent out the rooms, anyone with any connection to the flesh trade here in Khidderpore.'

Saleem's face was a question mark. Why in the world should these men come to a meeting? Why should they be interested in communicating with an organisation that told the girls no one had the right to beat them? What business did they have with a group that did everything in its power to prevent new recruits to the dhanda?

She nodded and went on to explain. 'This will be our second meeting,' she said. 'The police helped us the first time, it was a chore getting them to come, but we are actually becoming a force to be reckoned with in Khidderpore.' The last sentence was accompanied by the slightest hint of a triumphant smile.

'We have quite a bit of influence over the women here by now, they're sending their daughters to the shelter and to the day centre, some of them have even sent their girls off to boarding school with our help. The men can no longer afford not to know what we're doing and what our plans are.'

'And, of course,' she added after a brief pause, 'we serve food.'

Saleem nodded, although he didn't comprehend. How was talking to the men supposed to help get more girls away from the flesh trade? And why on earth did Manjira want him to come?

Once again she answered his silent, unasked question. 'We won't eradicate the trafficking of girls simply by reducing the supply,' she said, as if discussing the sale of sugar or rice or lentils. 'We have to eliminate the demand. And the men are the source of that demand.'

One of the office girls handed Saleem a teacup and shot him a curious glance; he cleared his throat and tried to steady his voice: 'I understand.'

He didn't, but continued anyway: 'And what is it you want me to do?'

Manjira took a moment to size him up. 'Saleem,' she said calmly, 'Have you ever paid for sex with a randi?'

His cheeks grew burning hot; an uncontrollable spasm rippled across his face. How could she *say* something like that? *Him*, who …

'No!' Manjira cut off his stream of thoughts. 'Of course you haven't. Because you've seen it all. You've seen the rape, the beatings, the disease; you've seen what your mother's and sister's lives were like. You've shared their pain. That's why I would like you to talk to the men.'

He wanted to protest. To tell her that nothing he could say would stop a horny passenger from buying a girl if he had the money. Look at my brothers, he wanted to shout, they've seen what I've seen and they still do what they do. How could he, Saleem, possibly hope to influence the pimps and the purveyors of little girls?

But Manjira thought he could do it. Manjira thought he could make a difference. The assurance in her face reminded him of something. Reminded him of the trust behind another pair of eyes. Wide and glowing with excitement, with thick eyelashes casting long shadows up towards her eyebrows. A pair of eyes fifteen years ago, whose gaze locked into his as she was led out the door: 'Saleem bhaiya, you'll come visit me, right? You'll come visit me even though I'm married?'

His powerlessness as a twelve-year-old boy was replaced by the grown man's burden, his determination to meet those eyes. He was a different person now. It wouldn't be hard.

'Of course,' he replied. 'I'll speak to them.'

The hall they had rented wasn't quite full, but Manjira was happy with the turnout. She adjusted her light blue sari and took one last peek at her notes. The chattering petered out, row upon row of male eyes followed her as she walked up to the little platform at the front of the room. Suspicious eyes under bushy eyebrows, curious eyes, guarded, aggressive, haughty eyes. Manjira raised her voice: 'Good evening, and thank you all for coming …'

He waited outside for as long as possible, cringing at the thought of going in. His shirt itched uncomfortably, his pre-planned words and sentences leaped around in a confounding dance inside his head. Saleem clenched his fists helplessly, what did he, a Nat-boy from Khawaspur, have to offer? How could he fight the far-reaching web and the intricate connections of those orchestrating this trade? What could he do against the fear they spread? Against all the money sunk into their business?

He breathed heavily, tried to stop his knees from trembling. Tugged at his kurta sleeves one last time and walked decisively towards the door leading into the hall. Manjira's voice was calm and confident in there; someone interrupted her with a question, she answered it concisely without getting off track. He halted just inside the door, focusing in on her, avoiding the gazes of the heads that had turned his way.

'... save your questions for the end. But now, I'd like you to meet a man who has chosen a different path, someone who believes that human beings shouldn't be bought and sold. Saleem from Khawaspur was born into all of this, he's a Nat himself, he could have been in the same business as you. But ...' Manjira paused, her eyes urging him on towards the platform, 'But Saleem is here to tell you why he didn't do that. Why he *couldn't* do that.'

And he found the words. One after the other, in the right tone of voice, emphasising and pausing in the right places. The words that painted the picture of his childhood home, the grey-tinged poverty. His mother, his sister, the sad trips in and out of the back room. The homemade liquor splashing around in small plastic bags, the yelling and the beatings in the dangerous dark of night.

His voice did not falter. Loud and clear, it carried far and wide, carried each of them out of the meeting hall and into other rooms, small and filthy rooms without a breath of fresh air.

'I know you've been there. You've heard the whimpering behind the curtain. You've seen her face when it's done. You know she hates you and what you force her to do. But that's not the worst thing. The worst is that you make her hate herself.'

He stopped, glanced at the page of notes in his hand. Was this what he had planned to say? How far had he got? He lifted his head. It made no difference, he knew what to say. He had always known.

'It's your own women you are selling. You take money from another man, a stranger, and in return you let him undress your sister or your daughter and do what he wants with her. Or maybe *you* are that customer.'

He took a moment's pause to catch his breath.

'Buying or selling, it's the same thing. They both turn a human being into a product. You know your sister doesn't want this. The girl you've paid for, doesn't want this.'

Saleem didn't stop to notice their reactions. Didn't hear the muttered comments, the rustling and scraping when two younger men in the back of the room got up to leave. Didn't see the painful recognition in the face of the man with the scar across his temple, didn't notice the head bowing down shamefully in the second row. There were other images flickering inside Saleem's mind: his little sister on her way out the door, the man whose face he could no longer picture, grabbing her by the arm. Her eyes looking straight into his under her thick eyelashes: 'Saleem bhaiya, when you grow up and have your own house, I want to live with you. Then I don't want to live in Kolkata and be married.' Did she live in Kolkata now? Was she 'married'? Was she alive, was her name still Basanti? The thought of his sister filled his head while the words kept streaming from his lips, words about honour, family, respect.

'I'm no different from you. I've grown up eating rice bought with blood money, I've worn clothes my mother earned in shame. I have no more money than you, I haven't been any luckier than you in life, my brothers made exactly the same choice you have made.'

He was baring all in front of this audience now, throwing Saleem from Khawaspur straight at them, full force.

'I'm a Nat. The road was paved before me, I only had to start walking. Use my sisters, get a wife and daughters, let anyone with money in his hand use them. Beat them into silence if they tried to resist. But there was a bitter taste to the candy my sister bought her little brother. It wasn't easy to sleep at night when I heard her choking back tears on the other side of the wall.'

He waited a moment, he had to get through to them, had to make them listen.

'I know who has paid so that I could eat, so that I could grow up safe and sound. Who has paid so I could learn to read and write. I know who was deprived of a life so that I could have one.'

His throat closed up suddenly.

'I have a sister to whom I owe my life. You do too. We all have people to whom we owe dignity and care. The day you start to pay off that debt, you'll know that you're human. No matter where you come from.'

He stumbled down from the platform with no idea how long he had been speaking. Manjira gave him a nod, he vaguely registered her face amidst the room shaking and swaying around him. He felt dizzy and lightheaded, both happy and strangely weighed down with sorrow, he needed to get out. In the poorly lit hallway between the meeting hall and the exit, a group of women stood clumped together. They were all dressed differently, their ages were varied, some bore Nepalese features. Still, they seemed a sort of collective, they had something in common beyond the profession immediately betrayed by their weary bodies and slightly overdone makeup. They were not at work, they seemed solemn, several of them held Pukaar's pink ID cards in their hands, clutching them with life-or-death seriousness. He walked by them in a rush of fresh courage, bursting with the bravery of one who had thrown caution to the wind.

The women followed him with their eyes as he walked past. One of them, a stout woman of about twenty-five, wore a chocolate brown sari, her hair was pulled back in a makeshift bun. Her mouth, with betel-red corners, opened halfway as she tracked him with her gaze, a dark brown gaze beneath unusually thick eyelashes. A long, searching gaze, as if trying to remember something.

21

Rupa's days were glassy. Smooth, globular pearls rolling straight ahead, one after the other. Ideally, she wanted nothing to happen. Wanted the girl who shared her bedroom to go straight to class after breakfast so she could spend the morning alone in the second-floor room. Rupa pulled her chair right up to the window, narrowed her eyes and squinted at the tree outside. If she squeezed her eyes nearly shut, the green leaves blended together with the blue sky, blurring into a flickering, dancing landscape of freedom at a safe distance.

The trembling and the constant itching and crawling inside her skin went away after the first few days. They gave her pills they said would make her feel better. Rupa opened her mouth wide and swallowed, she just wanted them to leave her alone. Glimpsed the flurry of green foliage through the tiny crack between her eyelids, shut out all other thoughts.

Ms Dumra spoke to the doctor after every checkup, read the teacher and staff reports, knew the daily status of recovery for each and every girl. Knew that Rupa's surgery during the first week to repair her anal orifice had gone as well as they could have hoped; she had been back after only three days' rest in the hospital. The personnel had not been thrilled to have two police officers guarding the intensive care unit around the clock; it unsettled the other patients, Ms Dumra had been told. But Deputy Superintendent Vatsavani had insisted – as Darya had predicted back in Forbesganj, when she had recommended that the headmistress contact him – and Rupa had been accompanied back to the home by police escort.

So Rupa was safe, and her physical injuries would heal. But Rupa was silent. She was barely responsive in conversations with the therapist, showed no emotion, expressed no desire for anything at all. 'She's in a kind of holding pattern,' the therapist concluded. 'On the one hand, she's waiting for something terrible to happen, that she'll be brought back to Katihar, that someone will force their way into her room, anything at all. Rupa has no reason to believe that she'll be left alone, that the future, even the immediate future, is predictable – she has never had any control over what happens to her. But on the other hand, she's waiting for her new life to start, the one she has been promised. A life without violence and coercion, an existence where she can be who she wants to be and make her own choices.'

'But that is exactly what she's incapable of,' Headmistress S. Dumra nodded pensively.

The therapist agreed. 'How could she possibly be capable of making her own choices? She lacks the framework, the basic mental conditions. Not just to be able to see what's out there, but even to understand and apply the dynamics of the choosing process itself: to weigh options, to balance the scales so they tip in one direction or the other. She doesn't know how to do that. And so she's holding out. Waiting for the rest of her life to happen to her, like everything else has always just happened to her.'

Ms Dumra removed her gold spectacles. The wrinkles on her nose were vertical, an extension of the worry lines that ran in two deep furrows between her eyebrows.

'She has to start with smaller choices,' she said quietly, mostly to herself.

The therapist looked at her, intrigued. 'What do you mean?'

'Tiny choices,' Ms Dumra repeated. 'Choices that aren't difficult, choices where the outcome will be good no matter what.'

Rupa had said no to everything. She had discovered that if she claimed to be tired and said she needed rest, they would leave her alone. Leave her to sit in the chair by the window, observing the bluish-green flicker of leaves through half-closed eyes. But today the headmistress refused to give up. She stood stubbornly in the doorway until Rupa unenthusiastically got up from the chair and followed her down the stairs. They crossed the yard and approached the flat-roofed workshop wing, Rupa reluctantly shuffling her feet, shoulders slouched. A glass wall slid into place in front of her eyes, muted the sounds and made everything distant and immaterial.

In the handicraft workshop the ceiling fans whirred on high speed, wicker sofas with red cushions lined the wall along one side. A long table ran down the middle of the room, two sewing machines were bolted into it on one side. The girls stood by the table or sat perched on high stools; a few had curled up on the wicker couches, chatting as their hands sewed tiny neat stitches into the cloth stretched taut across circular frames.

'We've picked out a pattern for you, Rupa,' Ms Dumra said in a friendly voice. 'Since you've never done embroidery before, you should probably start off with something simple.'

She held up a sky-blue piece of fabric, a simple floral pattern drawn onto it in chalk.

'Can you see what it is?'

Rupa stared vacantly at the cloth.

'It's a piece of a top, can you see?'

Ms Dumra held it up in front of her, folding and draping it so Rupa could picture the shape of a short-sleeved blouse.

'This will be for your very own sari blouse. All you have to do is embroider this pattern on the sleeves, just follow the chalk marks. The teacher will help you with the stitches, don't worry.'

Now Rupa noticed the round-faced older woman standing behind Ms Dumra; she flashed a smile, holding a box full of embroidery thread in her hands. Rupa shifted her gaze back to the headmistress; what did she just say?

Ms Dumra's voice grew clearer, she plopped down in the wicker sofa and the creaking noise ripped through Rupa's eardrums. 'See? All you have to do is pick the colour.'

Rupa stared down at the box with bundles of yarn of every colour. Lavender, red, orange, spring green, white, navy blue, brown, sunshine yellow. Her hands stayed folded in her lap.

'They're all nice, Rupa. You can have any one you want. Just pick one.'

Ms Dumra's encouraging voice glided away, shut out behind the glass alongside the yarn-box Rupa couldn't bring herself to touch. The headmistress took out two colours, placing the red and the spring green bundles side by side on top of the fabric. 'Rupa?'

She observed the yarn from behind the glass. If she squinted, the colours flickered and blended in against the blue backdrop. Fluttering green leaves against bright blue sky. She lifted her hand, poked it through the glass wall, picked up the shiny green bundle. 'This one,' she said.

The headmistress made another visit to the bedroom on the second floor in the afternoon. Signalled to the room-mate to leave them alone and pulled a chair over next to Rupa, who sat by the window. Spoke softly but firmly, very close to her ear.

'Rupa, you have to let us in.'

Rupa did not respond. Played with a loose thread in her dupatta while Ms Dumra's voice droned on from somewhere far away.

'You're safe here, Rupa. You're on your way to feeling better, and we're going to keep helping you. It was great that you started working on your embroidery today!'

Still no reaction from Rupa, only the tiniest twitch of a muscle in her face when the headmistress softly touched her arm.

'But what you have to understand is that the most important doctor is *you*! The best medicine is the one you have inside yourself!'

The girl by the window turned her head towards the woman in the green sari. What was she talking about? She always took the medicine they brought her, opened her mouth and swallowed, ate when they told her to eat. What more did they want?

'You have to talk, Rupa! Talk to me, or the therapist, or one of the other girls; anyone!'

Ms Dumra sighed and lowered her voice.

'You're carrying around a jar full of painful memories, too big and heavy for you to carry alone. Empty it out, Rupa. Empty it out, pour all that dirty water down the drain! When the jar is empty, then you can fill it with fresh, clean water. You can walk to the pump and start all over again.'

Rupa opened her eyes wide. Slowly focused in on Ms Dumra, the calm and steady gaze behind her glasses. Suddenly she heard the trickle of the water pump in the backyard behind the blue house; she saw Sona's face in front of her. Her friend's steady, desperate plea for the child she was carrying. Start all over.

Rupa grabbed hold of the armrests on both sides of the chair. Her tongue felt dry and swollen in her mouth. But she wanted to empty the jar.

'They didn't want him to ruin me,' she said.

'There was no benefit to them in seeing me torn apart. They should have paid attention.'

Ms Dumra said nothing. Let her eyes rest on the pale face in front of her, uneven spasms rippling under the skin.

Rupa's story came in bits and pieces, involuntary spurts interspersed by long silences.

'They didn't want him to ruin me, but they weren't there. They came in when it was over. Jabbar and Dolly. They came hurrying in, and I remember I wanted to cover myself. There was blood between my legs. Slime and blood smeared along my stomach, I didn't want them to see it. But I couldn't raise my arms. I just laid back on the mattress and closed my eyes. But I didn't cry.'

Ms Dumra had laid her hand on Rupa's slender arm. Slowly she stroked it with one finger, up and down, up and down.

'Then Dolly started talking about me, bad words. She said I was ungrateful and useless. I kept my eyes closed, I just listened.'

Rupa's voice changed, a sudden, searing bitterness cut through the flat emptiness of her story. 'She didn't even ask me if it hurt!'

Her words filled the room for a minute, before being absorbed by the dusk slowly seeping in through the window. Rupa heaved for breath, she struggled for several minutes before continuing her story:

'They saw what he'd done, but it was me they were angry at. All I could think of was that I wanted to wash myself. I felt sick.'

'I don't remember exactly, I think I fell asleep. When I woke up I was lying in a bed in their part of the house; I recognised Mumtaz Begum's handbag on a shelf by the door. A plastic bag filled with liquid was tied to the top of the bed; there was a trail of bubbles moving from it through a rubber tube into my arm.'

Ms Dumra's finger stroked and stroked; she asked no questions. Rupa had to empty the jar in her own time.

'Later, they took me to the hospital; Jabbar Aslam drove me in his car. I lay in the back seat, looking out. Each time I opened my eyes there was a new picture in the side window: a branch with a white flower, or a cloud, or the top of a tree.'

Silence fell over the room. An older woman knocked on the door and poked her head in, but a quick nod from Ms Dumra made the door glide shut again, quickly and quietly. Rupa didn't budge, not even her eyes moved, her gaze fixed on the headmistress's face.

'The other girls said I had been away from the house for two months. They had asked for me, but Dolly had just told them I was "somewhere else". I don't remember much, except for how much I wanted the shots. They took me away. The needle didn't hurt at all.'

'They left me alone for a long while after that; mostly I was tired and wanted to sleep. But the day after they brought me home to Kuli Pada, I heard Dolly and Jabbar arguing about me.'

Rupa grew silent. A grimace of disgust passed over her face.

'I remember exactly what Dolly said. "It's no worse for Rupa than for the others", she said. "She's the best one we've got, she is young, her skin is nice and fair. She is scrawny right now, but that will change when she starts eating properly again".'

Rupa's eyes refused to meet Ms Dumra's, her fingers kept playing with the loose thread in her shawl.

'But Jabbar said something else. He said he would rather find me a husband. He wanted to get me married. That's what he said!'

Another long pause. When Rupa spoke again, the hard edge in her voice was back. 'But Dolly said no. She started talking about Rahul sahib and the other big, important passengers. "Rupa needs to learn how to behave", she said. "Just like the others".'

Ms Dumra felt the muscles in Rupa's lower arm tense up as she clenched her fists in her lap.

'He tried one more time. Jabbar did that, he tried one more time. He told Dolly he could get a good price for me in Forbesganj. "Then her husband can teach her how to behave", he said.'

'But I knew Dolly wouldn't give up. The door was open and I lay perfectly still; if someone came in I would pretend I was sleeping. Dolly raised her voice, she wouldn't give up. "We can't marry her off yet!" she said. "We need the money, you with your new car and all! Who will pay for that if not Rupa?"'

'The next day he came into the room where I was lying and repeated everything he had said to Dolly, that he wanted to get me married. He put his hand on my arm. It was so heavy, I couldn't breathe.'

Ms Dumra's fingers ceased their gentle stroking over Rupa's downy arm, felt the cold clamminess of her skin.

'He said, "I'll find you a husband, Rupa. A good man, so you can live in your own house".'

Her voice was tense but feeble, the dithering veins in her neck choked back the tears.

'But I knew he was lying. How could I ever get a good man after what they had done to me?'

The string snapped, the rest poured out in heaving sobs.

'I wanted to hit him, but I pretended I was asleep.'

Rupa curled up in the chair, her whole body shook as she emptied the last drops out of the heavy jar. 'I pretended I was dead. I kept my eyes closed and pretended I was dead.'

The crying began. Ms Dumra sat motionless.

The crying began. The jar was empty.

22

Nine miles was a long way by bicycle. Roshan leaned forward, the last hill up to the railway tracks was a tough one. The thought of finding his own place in Forbesganj had often occurred to him, but it had never come to pass. Where would he stay? He wouldn't dream of setting up a shed in the Town of Love – not that he considered himself any different or better than its inhabitants, but he didn't see the point of living next door to the girls in the doorways. It would be too depressing, too difficult in relation to the kids at school. *Or is it because I'm a coward?* he asked himself as his quivering calf muscles pushed him over the top of the hill, across the train tracks and past the pyramids of mangoes stacked around the fruit peddlers. *Is it because I don't want to be sitting alone in a small, defenseless house when darkness falls, when the liquor starts flowing and the embers of rage directed at the school and its employees begin to glow and ignite? When kicking down a door and beating up a puny schoolteacher won't be something to think twice about?*

Roshan's breathing got easier; this time he avoided the coughing fit after the exhausting bicycle ride. Still, he had remained in Khwaishgram, where he and his mother now lived under his eldest brother's roof. Roshan had two young nephews; he didn't foresee any school in their immediate future, but had promised himself that he would at least build them a foundation – reading, writing, and arithmetic – even if they were destined for a life as blacksmiths' helpers.

He walked the bicycle across the street by the bus stop and swerved to avoid a black hog gobbling up a sticky mass of rubbish and mud in the alley behind the hotel. His stomach lurched a little as he crossed the bridge; these days you never knew what the mood would be in the Town of Love. Roshan had one foot in the door in Prem Nagar, but the other foot was planted outside, and sometimes he found himself wholly ignorant of what was going on here, who was being talked about, which decisions were being made. Lately he had woken up every morning to the thought that today, maybe *today*, was the day he would find the school destroyed. Today could be the day he would arrive at work to find a smouldering, burnt ruin. He knew the buzz had been louder than usual since Rupa was rescued; he knew Jabbar Aslam and his brother had been in town. One rumour said that the Katihar police was looking for them; another story claimed that Jabbar had long since reached an agreement with the police, and that traffic in and out of the blue house was as bustling as ever. He knew that the acrimony over Saleem's participation in the raid ran deep; perhaps his friend shouldn't risk coming back to Forbesganj, Roshan thought to himself. He didn't know exactly where Saleem was; Darya had only vaguely mentioned he was 'helping Pukaar somewhere else'. Roshan could not fathom that Tamanna still had the guts to live in the Town of Love; the contemptuous rumours circulating about her had got uglier, the threats more apparent. Something was going to happen, Roshan was sure of that. Maybe today was the day they had burnt down the school?

But there was no burning smell today either, as he turned down the bumpy path that led to the schoolhouse. The water buffalo were roaming peacefully as usual along the yellow meadow where the grass was devoured long ago; Tamanna and Amina were standing outside the school as usual with the brown rug and the worn plastic toys between them. There was another figure with them, a heavyset figure in a blue and black sari. She looked at him, and Roshan felt a quick burst of joy as he dismounted his bike. 'Namaste,' Jannati greeted him; she nodded to the other women and turned to leave.

Her gait was slow and swaying. Halfway to the bend in the road she stopped and looked back over her shoulder.

'What did Jannati want?'

Roshan immediately regretted his question; first of all, it was none of his business. Second, it sounded like he was fishing for gossip; and third, he was worried that his voice revealed a strange amount of interest in the woman from Chhukha.

But Tamanna's answer was serious. 'We were talking about Sona. It's not safe for her here, and Jannati doesn't know what to do.'

Amina gave an irritated grunt. She had known all along that this was too dangerous! Sona had been sleeping in Jannati's room for several weeks now, and Amina knew it was only a matter of time before Kasim, and then Jabbar, would find out. They might even have come to know already – secrets couldn't be kept for very long in Prem Nagar. But it was the thought of Fauzia that concerned Amina most of all. The paan queen on her throne, you could never tell whose side she was on.

'I thought Sona was sleeping in Darya's room?'

Roshan blushed to admit his knowledge of the ongoing rumours and gossip.

'No, no,' Tamanna shook her head. 'She stays in Darya's room during the day, but the hostel won't let two people sleep there at night. Darya would have to pay extra.'

'So now she's sleeping at ...' he had to gather his courage to say her name, '... Jannati's place?'

Tamanna nodded. 'They bring her over there at night. You didn't know?'

She lowered her voice when she spotted a woman approaching, leading a little boy by the hand.

'But ...,' Roshan was perplexed. 'What about Prabir? When Jannati ...'

He didn't finish the sentence. Couldn't bring himself to utter the words that for some reason felt more painful attached to her than to the other women.

Amina made a quick gesture with her head, shushing him with her eyes. Exchanged a few words with the woman dropping off her little boy, spread out the toys before resuming the conversation with Roshan. 'That's just it! Jannati sees her passengers while Sona is in Darya's room, but of course she never knows when Prabir might show up, in the evening, in the middle of the night, whenever.'

A futile rage surged through Roshan. Prabir! He pictured the unshaven face, the limp, hulking body in a ragged undershirt. Prabir, who kept Birbal home from school and took away the boy's only chance at a different future! Knowing that Prabir came to see Jannati at night was a thousand times worse than thinking of the nameless passengers who arrived in the Town of Love every day.

'If he finds out she's hiding Sona, he'll beat her to death.'

Amina declared it as a matter of fact.

'Sona?'

What did she mean?

'Phhh!' Amina snorted. 'What does he care about Sona! But God help Jannati if Prabir thinks she's losing out on a single rupee because she's busy helping an escaped girl!'

Roshan was surprised that the kids were back in school. The first few days after the raid in Katihar only two or three children had shown up, and attendance was about the same in the kindergarten. He had tried to keep a cool exterior, had said nothing to Rukmini or Darya about how scared he was that this might actually be the end. That their fears would be realised: they had rescued one girl but missed their chance to help hundreds of others. He had kept on teaching as usual, had told the kids to bring their friends along tomorrow, and pedalled the nine miles back home each day.

And then it turned around. Slowly, slowly, they had come back, and now just four of the most regular pupils' seats remained empty. Birbal's was one of them, Rozy's another. Roshan gave the older students a writing assignment: 'Imagine that I gave each one of you a nice, brand new pen. Tell me about the very best thing you could think of to do with it!'

Some jumped into the task at once, bowing their heads and beginning to fill up their notebooks line by line. Others needed to have the assignment explained one more time, and a few were still sitting there twirling their pencils when he moved on to practising Hindi letters with the younger children. Outside, he heard Tamanna leading the kids on the rug in a sing-along; he recognised the song about a pretty little fish from his own childhood.

The kids had received their bread and milk and had gone home for the midday break as Roshan settled down with a cup of tea to read the pen stories:

'I would write a letter and send it to my sister.'

'I would sell it to get some money.'

'I would stab it into my little brother's back, because he always annoys me.'

'I would draw a great big beautiful house.'

'I would write a song for everyone at school to sing.'

'I would give it to my mother and teach her how to write her name.'

Roshan let his own pen sink down. How little it could take for the day to turn around! Light was pouring in through the doorway: *See, it works. Someone gets it. Someone has seen what you're trying to say.*

※

'We could use you as a regular here, Saleem.'

Manjira smiled widely at him and held his gaze with a challenge. 'I'm sure we could find an opportunity for you to stay on, at least for a few months. What's the matter, don't you like the hostel room?'

'No, no.' Saleem shook his head, the hostel was fine, that wasn't it. But he had to go back. Forbesganj was where his job was, more than enough work awaited him there. And he had a house to build.

Manjira furrowed her eyebrows. 'But is it safe to go back, Saleem? It hasn't been long since the raid in Katihar, and the brothel owner is still roaming free, from what I've heard?'

She paused, giving him a chance to respond, but he said nothing and she continued, 'And as I understand, these people are relatives of yours? Are you sure it's a good idea to go back so soon?'

Saleem squeezed his lips shut. He had already been through this discussion with Rukmini on the phone. Then he thought again and opened his mouth: 'I am a Nat. I have to be proof of the fact that a Nat can be something other than what *they* are.'

He smiled at her; he didn't wish to offend her or hurt her feelings: 'Everything has been great here, Manjira didi. I've learned so much. But I have a sister to take care of, and a lot of work to do. When you come to Forbesganj, you can stay in the house that I'm building.'

The paperwork had been piling up for days. Manjira was sifting through a stack of it when the four girls climbed the steps up to the Pukaar day centre, chatting and giggling as they closed the door behind them and greeted her politely. With habitual movements, one of them pulled out the tape player and placed it on the windowsill, cleared away the chairs, mused a little over the choice of music. Manjira shook her head and put on her strict voice: 'You all know how we always begin.'

The girls took their seats on the floor, at a distance from the sewing machines humming away by the wall. The youngest children were finished with their schoolday, they had had their lunch and some of them were busy with homework. A stooping old woman made her way methodically back and forth across the floor with a broom.

'What are we dancing today?'

Manjira asked the usual question.

'The happiness of being here,' one of them said.

'I want to dance the water dripping and bouncing and never stopping.'

The youngest girl with her bobbing ponytail couldn't wait to get started.

Only Dimpal's tiny, dark face was scrunched up and silent. Manjira turned toward her, 'What's wrong, Dimpal? Why are you angry?'

A gruff shake of the head.

'Is there something you're afraid of?'

The girl opened her mouth, closed it, opened it again.

'My mother is sick. I'm so scared that she'll die.'

Manjira moved closer to the short-haired girl, she had no intention of lying to her. She knew the details of her mother's illness, knew it was hopeless. Dimpal was technically too old to be sleeping in the shelter, it wasn't meant to be an orphanage, but Manjira had decided that the girl would not be thrown out when the day came. She had begun preparing the memory-book for Dimpal, the scrapbooks they assembled for the girls who lost their mothers. Quotes, anecdotes their mothers had told, whatever information they had managed to gather on family members, photographs if any existed. The mothers' own recorded stories of why their lives had turned out this way, how things had unfolded, how much they loved their children. For a girl who owned nothing, the book became more important than any birth certificate: the memory-book was a concrete artifact she could carry her whole life, an affirmation that she existed and had a story. The undeniable proof that she had been loved.

'I know ... it's not easy.'

Manjira wished she could give some tiny glimmer of hope, but she knew that Dimpal's mother's health was steadily declining. There wasn't a dance in the world that could rid her body of the disease.

The youngest girl fidgeted impatiently on the floor: 'Can we start now?'

When Manjira nodded, she jumped up and started the music, and Manjira gathered her papers and brought them to a chair by the door. She sat down and replaced her paan with a new, fresh one.

The first footsteps were prancing across the floor when something stirred in the doorway. Manjira turned around: 'Basanti!'

She smiled warmly at the heavyset, slightly reticent woman. Manjira knew that Basanti experienced true joy when she was dancing and that that kind of joy was a rare find in her everyday existence. She wondered how the girl could get away in the middle of the day, how could she afford it?

But today Basanti wasn't here to dance. She had a question.

'Manjira didi, that man …?'

Mnajira waited patiently, gentle question marks in her eyes.

'The one who spoke.'

Manjira crinkled her eyebrows. 'Spoke …?'

Basanti felt the irritation grow inside her; how could Manjira not understand who she meant?

'Yes. He spoke, that night. The night you spoke too, remember?'

Manjira's thoughts travelled back to the evening in the rented meeting hall. She had felt so proud, so moved, so strong! She hadn't had a chance to thank Saleem until much later; when she had gone outside looking for him she had been derailed by the group of women in the corridor – yes, now she remembered, Basanti had been one of them, of course. Some of the women from Khidderpore had showed up at the meeting with a sole purpose: to stand there without being displayed for sale. To stand there with a newfound identity: the pink cards in their hands. The Pukaar ID cards that told a story of being someone, having a name. Manjira had no idea how many of them had had to pay the price in beatings the next day when news of their mini-demonstration had reached every alley in Khidderpore. But that had not negated the girls' victory, nor had it diminished their courage. What a night!

After a long detour Manjira's eyes refocused on the woman in the white kurta. Basanti's face burned with an impatience she was struggling to control: 'The man who spoke. Who was he, didi?'

'Oh, yes. His name is Saleem, he's from Khawaspur in Bihar. But he lives in Forbesganj now.'

※

Thank goodness they were at Tamanna's house when it happened. Sona had just come in, sneaking in from the back tonight after crossing the field behind the school building. She had waited underneath Tamanna's mango tree until Jannati appeared with a plastic bag in her hand: 'Come on, Sona, let's go. I brought samosas, hurry up!'

Jannati had been worried about Sona for weeks; her swollen legs, hands, and face. Always the same thought: any night now, the baby would be here – but what would she do then? Ask Fauzia for help?

As Sona was about to hoist herself up, it happened. Suddenly her body convulsed, her neck whipped back and her eyes rolled back in her head. The chair toppled over and Sona fell to the ground as her arms and legs seized and spasmed uncontrollably. Jannati screamed, tried to grab hold of her arm, stop the violent shaking, but it was no use. Sona's breathing was rapid, a thin film of sweat laced her face.

'She needs ... the hospital, now!' Tamanna's voice cut through in a terrified screech.

Jannati was already out the door and Tamanna wrapped her arms around Sona's twisting body, holding her tight, repeating meaninglessly that everything was going to be okay. Jannati rushed back in, bringing Salma with her. Tamanna had no time to think of the consequences now, who was supposed to know and who wasn't, and together they managed to lift Sona up into a rickshaw. She was white as chalk and there were beads of cold sweat all over her body.

Salma sprinted into the hospital and reappeared, followed by two men with a stretcher. Tamanna and Jannati hurried after them into the dimly lit front hall, and jumped on the first white-uniformed person they spotted: 'You have to help her, she ...'

The man in the white lab coat looked right past them and pointed further down the hall. 'Talk to the reception desk. They'll help you.'

Oh thank goodness, Sona got help. Tamanna stayed at the receptionist's desk answering questions while Jannati followed the stretcher, refusing to let Sona out of her sight. She scurried down the corridors, squeezing through half-closed doors and shoving nurses aside. 'That's my sister!' she repeated like a mantra. 'I have to be with her.'

Inside an examination room at last; a stern, bony-faced lady doctor needed just a few seconds to conclude. 'She needs a C-section, immediately!'

She turned to Jannati: 'What's her blood type?'

Blood type?

'I don't know ...'

The doctor knitted her eyebrows. 'Didn't you say that you were sisters? What's your blood type?'

'I ... we don't have the same father!'

At least that much was true.

'We don't have a blood bank. If she loses too much blood during surgery, you might be her best chance. Now let's see if we can save this baby.'

Jannati gazed anxiously down at Sona, who was wearing an oxygen mask over her crooked, white, unrecognisable face. As long as the child got to live! Jannati trailed the stretcher all the way to the door of the operating theatre, but that was as far as she could go, sister or not. The door slammed shut and a man with starched shirtsleeves pointed her mercilessly towards the corridor and back out to the reception. She found Tamanna, who needed no explanation after seeing Jannati's face.

The few chairs in the room were all taken – a young woman tried to muffle her sobs with her dupatta; an older man stared vacantly straight ahead, a frayed ladies' purse resting in his lap. The night shift for the sick, the worried, and the waiting slowly neared its end. Jannati and Tamanna sank down against the wall, leaning against the greyish brick wall with stains imprinted by sweaty heads filled with anguish and hope. Now there was nothing to do but wait.

23

Rupa liked to embroider. She didn't reveal this to anyone; she betrayed no enthusiasm. The work was often slow-going, she frequently stopped and let the round wooden frame fall into her lap. But she liked playing with the yarn, the soft, simple pleasure she felt watching the colours slip through her fingers. She had extended the pattern on her blouse fabric, adding stitches of pink, brown, and bright yellow. Maybe it would be a tablecloth instead, it didn't much matter, Ms Dumra thought as she passed out bundles of yarn and scissors. Nearsighted or not, she had no difficulty seeing that Rupa had begun refilling her jar.

Rupa went to bed early every night; she exchanged few words with the lively roommate for whom the headmistress had had such high hopes. She was still thin, still even weaker than her pallid skin revealed, but she had stopped shaking and trembling. She swallowed her food and kept it down, and her system digested it normally. Rupa was gradually falling to rest.

The headmistress stood with her handbag tucked under her arm, quickly looking around before turning out the light. One last inspection before she left work for the day, most days much later than she would have liked. Samila Dumra poured a disproportionate amount of effort into this room compared to the figure on her paycheck. She walked alone across the courtyard, looking up at Rupa's dark window. The old watchman locked her out at the gate with a friendly goodnight. The moment she stepped out onto the pavement, a motorcycle roared to life at the end of the street, turned the corner and vanished.

Her cell phone rang at exactly 2:20 a.m. Darya scrambled to retrieve it from the floor and yanked out the charger as she stumbled over to the window to get a better signal. She stood upright and dazed in her floor-length, blue nightgown, trying to process what she heard.

'Yes ... hello? Yes, of course I remember ...' She shuddered at the cold awakening as she listened with the phone pressed hard against her groggy head. Struggling to find her voice, her first reaction to Ms Dumra on the other end of the line was a series of hoarse croaks: 'What? But how ... is she ...?'

'They couldn't get inside,' Headmistress S. Dumra said, trying her best to keep her voice steady. 'Nothing happened to any of the girls, Rupa is fine.'

'But how ... don't you have a security guard at the gate?'

Darya was still confused. And overwhelmed. And scared.

'Yes, and luckily he managed to raise enough of a racket that they ran away. And of course we can't be sure it was them. We don't know it was Rupa they were after.'

A brief silence as the anxiety buzzed through the wires from Forbesganj to Patna and back again.

'Yes,' Darya said decisively. 'We do know that.'

There was no doubt in her mind. The men on the motorcycle had come from Katihar.

'Rupa is making progress,' Ms Dumra said after another pause. 'But she still needs time. And naturally, she cannot be left vulnerable to things like this. I'm not even sure if she knows what the commotion at the gate was all about, but ...'

'But she is not safe,' Darya said. 'Rupa is not safe in Patna. It's not far enough away.'

'No,' Ms Dumra admitted in a heavy voice. 'Rupa is not safe here.'

While still on the phone, Darya had pulled her nightgown off over her head and replaced it with a salwar kurta. When she hung up she was ready to head out, but remained frozen for a moment by the door: Where should she go first?

Saleem. Saleem first. Darya didn't know how they would make it happen, but two things were clear to her: Rupa had to get out of Bihar, and Saleem had to help her. She had to talk to Rukmini and she had to talk to Tamanna, but first of all she had to find Saleem. And it couldn't wait. Ms Dumra wanted to get Rupa out of Patna as soon as possible, preferably before daybreak.

She knew the route to the office so well that she could run it blindfolded, weaving in and out through the trucks. She had a key to the green gate, no need to wake up the guard. She knocked on the office door as she pushed up against it and sharply whispered his name. No answer, the door was locked and refused to budge. Darya called out louder: 'Saleem!' She rattled the doorknob, knowing that her colleague worked late nights and usually collapsed exhausted on the sofa. 'Come on! You have to wake up!' She was about to shout even louder, almost recounting the whole scenario for him through the door: 'You have to take Rupa with you to Kolkata! Talk to Pukaar there and find a safe place for her!' But she collected herself, thought of the watchman, he didn't need to hear and know everything.

Either Saleem was lost in a deep sleep, or he wasn't in there. Darya pulled out her cell phone and dialled Rukmini's number in Delhi as she hurried back out to the street.

The Town of Love was completely bathed in darkness. The few electric bulbs dangling over the girls in doorways late into the night were long since extinguished. Not many passengers came by after nightfall, and the last few had finished long ago. Darya had no problem navigating in the dark, but she needed to catch her breath after half-jogging the thirty-minute stretch. Finding a rickshaw so late in the night was never easy and she had no desire to draw attention to a nightly visit to Tamanna.

But the second she made it across the bridge she sensed that something was awry. There was no loud commotion, no screaming or shouting, just a muffled agitation casting long shadows in the moonlight. She hurried closer, trying to move speedily but invisibly along the walls, but how could she do that when she didn't know where the staring eyes were hiding? The dormant fear, nestled in her stomach ever since the phone rang at the hostel, grew larger as she made her way deeper into the Town of Love; ballooned into a panic fumbling hastily along the walls of the darkened houses. Terror pounded in her ears as her feet carried her past Tamanna's house, further down the street, mixing with the ominous mumbling that rose and fell from the black, shapeless clump she spied in the distance. When she got close, she recognised the faces, the mumbling separated into voices and words. At the edge of the circle billowing back and forth, Darya spotted Heena and rushed forward, 'Heena – what's going on?'

As the terrified face turned around, the buzz of voices died away; Darya watched one dark figure after another withdraw into the shadows. Heena glided away as well, and suddenly Kasim's eldest brother stood before her; in a cold déjà vu Darya watched his mouth open and knew exactly what he was about to say. 'You should have left us alone! If you had never come to Prem Nagar, none of this would have ever happened!'

Stormy waves of panic rolled through her; the rumbling grew to a fever pitch. What was he talking about? Darya elbowed her way in towards the middle of the circle, the unruly mass of bodies parted to let her through. A woman's back was arched over a dark bundle on the ground. Her sari was grey with large flowers in purple and brown, flickering splotches that exploded in Darya's face as the back suddenly straightened:

'This is all your fault! If you hadn't come here and got involved in our lives this never would have happened. He would have found a job, a regular job!'

Fauzia's long face was drawn out in horror, a mask of rage and desperation.

'He could have done well! He wanted to build us a house! A house!'

Darya knelt down and swept Fauzia aside in one swift motion. Saleem lay on the ground, a pool of blood spreading underneath his hip.

The panic rumbled through her – what were they waiting for? 'Lift him up!' She shouted, nearly kicking his sister aside. 'Can't you see he's bleeding to death? He needs to get to the hospital fast, hurry up!'

The trip across the bridge seemed eternal, every yard a never-ending mile. Saleem lay on a woven bed with a wooden frame; brothers and cousins, neighbours and enemies now elevating the limp, unconscious body overhead in a nocturnal mourners' procession. Darya ran ahead, squeezing her cell phone in her hand like a lucky talisman. She alternated between dialling Rukmini's number in Delhi and Ms Dumra's in Patna – oh God, what would she do? Rupa had to be moved right away, preferably tonight. Saleem's blood was dripping into trails along the dusty road in the Town of Love. What had happened to him? Who had done this? But he was still breathing, she was sure of that, he was breathing and he had a pulse when she leaned down over his face.

And Tamanna, she suddenly remembered. She had been on her way to Tamanna's house. She turned around; her gaze sweeping the melancholy procession behind her. Where was Tamanna? Fauzia's flower-patterned sari flickered back and forth through the darkness; Saleem's sister had no reaction whatsoever when Darya threw out the question: 'Tamanna? Has anyone seen Tamanna?'

Was she imagining things, or had the clatter surrounding her changed for just a moment? Had she seen some of the heads turn towards each other, exchange a few quick glances under the unwieldy wooden frame? Darya looked frantically around, was Heena here? Who could she ask, who could she trust here? In this surreal, nocturnal horror where Saleem lay stabbed on a charpoy,

Darya felt everything unravel around her. What was she doing here? What had they done, that it should come to this?

Did we get everything wrong? she thought, stopping dead in her tracks. The conclusion was numbingly simple: If they don't *want* us to be here, what are we doing here at all?

Her gaze suddenly struck Heena in the crowd now approaching Referral Hospital. The tiny woman kept her eyes fixed on Saleem stretched out on the charpoy, an old mask of resignation in a grimace across her face. Darya ran towards her, 'Where is Tamanna? Heena, you have to tell me! Did they get her as well?'

Hearing the panic in her own voice, Darya realised that this had been her innermost fear all along, ever since they got Rupa out of the blue house. Tamanna, she knew their sentiments towards her. The pigheaded, impossible randi who had gone so far as to steal Jabbar's daughter out of his own house. *Tamanna,* Darya thought in exasperation, *how could I not have seen how dangerous it was for you? How could I have thought they'd let you get away with it?*

But Heena shook her head. Blessed, wrinkled, reticent Heena shook her head, Tamanna had not been attacked. A crooked finger pointed towards the brightly lit rectangles in the building up ahead. 'She's in the hospital. With Jannati and Sona. Sona's time has come, but she isn't feeling well.'

Darya could not take any more. Stayed by the side of the road as the charpoy-led procession made its way up to the front door of the hospital. Reflexively pressed 'Answer' when her cell phone rang, numbly registered Headmistress Dumra's voice. 'I can't take the responsibility for keeping her here any longer. We've rented a car. I'm bringing Rupa back to Forbesganj.'

Tamanna sat hunched by the wall as Darya came charging into the reception area. Fauzia followed, ignited in a desperation no one had ever seen across her haughty features. Heena, stumbling and disoriented. Kasim and his elder brother, their clothes splattered with dark spots, who were they carrying between them? Right behind them, a train of spectators packed into the main reception of Referral Hospital. Mostly men, a crowd shouting in agitation, but still somehow tinged with a subdued sense of shame. Oh God, it was Saleem – *Saleem*! Tamanna leapt to her feet but couldn't fight her way through to the lifeless body before it was surrounded by nurses, two men carrying a stretcher, the receptionist and a doctor barking orders. The stretcher vanished out the same door Jannati and Sona had passed through, and the receptionist began the task of shooing out the unruly entourage from the Town of Love. 'You'll have to wait outside … you can't all be in here at once! You have to …' At last she managed to clear the little space in front of her desk with the help of a waiting patient's relative, grateful for the diversion from his countless hours in the plastic chair, and a weary stillness settled back in over the reception area. Tamanna followed the crowd outside to learn what had happened, but Jannati would not budge. As long as Sona was inside, she wasn't going anywhere.

Tamanna located Heena but couldn't get a sensible word out of the petrified old woman, and she started to look around for Amina. She was nowhere to be found, and Tamanna knew better than to approach her husband, Kasim, right now. But Salma was there. Salma was there, and Tamanna suddenly remembered she hadn't seen her since Sona was pulled out of the rickshaw. Where had Salma been in the meantime? What did she know?

Salma's expressionless eyes were fixed on Tamanna for a long time before she opened her mouth.

'A knife,' she finally said. 'They stabbed him with a knife.'

Numbly, Tamanna sensed a prickling in her cheeks, her lips quivered and she struggled to form the words: 'Who was it? Who stabbed him?'

Salma shook her head. 'They came on a motorbike,' she said. 'They were gone before anyone could get a good look.'

At the same moment, Tamanna felt a hand on her arm; she turned around and found herself peering into Darya's grey, frightened face. 'Tamanna, there you are! Rupa …' Darya cut herself off, taking a half step backwards when she saw Tamanna's reaction. Tamanna's eyes widened, her lower lip shot forward, 'Rupa! What's happened to Rupa?'

Darya opened her mouth to answer, knowing full well the nightmarish picture her words were painting in front of the terrified mother's eyes. 'They tried to break into the home in Patna. Ms Dumra is in the car on her way here with Rupa now.'

Tamanna felt her knees weaken. *Not after everything we've been through!* It couldn't happen, not now, when Rupa was finally safe.

She sank down in a heap at Darya's feet, hearing a whimpering voice that must be her own. 'No no, not here! Please, she can't come here, that's the most dangerous of all! Oh please, not here!'

Darya crouched down to face her and grabbed her by the shoulder, shaking her hard: 'Stop, Tamanna, stop it! We'll make sure Rupa is safe. We'll find a place for her, I promise you, Tamanna, I'll ...'

But truthfully, she had no idea what to do next. The hopelessness wrapped itself around Darya like a stifling cloak; she was exhausted from performing magic tricks, finding quick fixes, improvising new solutions every minute. *Where are we now*? she thought wearily. They had got Rupa away from the horror of the blue house, but where were they now, months later? Rupa still wouldn't acknowledge her mother, she was still sick in body and mind. And now she was again fleeing her abusers.

Darya pulled Tamanna close to her. *I'm sorry*, she cried on the inside. *I'm sorry, Rupa. We thought we could do it. We meant well.*

Her cell phone ringtone, a happy little melody, blared from her pocket. Darya jolted and frantically pressed the answer button. 'Hello?'

The signal from Delhi was poor, but Rukmini's voice was clear and pronounced. 'Manjira is getting on a train in a few hours, she'll be in Katihar tonight. Arrange for a car to meet her at the station, make sure you send someone whose face the Aslams won't recognise.'

Her mind refused to work. Darya squinted her eyes, squeezing the last fragments of concentration to the front of her overworked brain. 'Manjira?'

'Rupa needs to get away from Bihar.'

Rukmini spoke slowly and calmly, her words left no room for discussion.

'Manjira will take her to Kolkata. She'll stay at the shelter there until we find a more permanent solution.'

Even the longest of all nights is eventually graced by morning. The timid, pink shimmer of a new day spread softly over the gulmohar tree by the main entrance to Referral Hospital, casting delicate shadows over the two tired women on the brick ledge along the wall. A black goat sauntered by, pausing to sniff at Tamanna's sandal. She pulled her foot away, glancing over at Darya, who slept with her mouth half-open and her head against the wall.

All of a sudden, Jannati just stood there. Her eyes flashed with dark denial, her fingers fumbling with the headscarf she held in her hands. The words she tried to utter were lodged in her chest; she desperately swallowed and grabbed to reach them, yanking and tearing them out of her mouth: 'Sona! Oh Tamanna, she's dead! Sona died. They said it all happened so fast, something about her blood pressure ... or was it her kidneys ... and the placenta broke apart. She ... they took out the baby, but Sona died!'

Jannati halted and looked down at them, bewildered, her eyes roving back and forth between the two. Was she really standing here, saying this? Was this her own voice, were these her own words?

Darya got to her feet and wrapped her arms around Jannati. They stood there motionless for what seemed an eternity as the new day awakened around Referral Hospital. A car rolled into the yard, an insistent woman haggled with a rickshaw-wallah. The first puri halwa-vendor wheeled in and parked his cart, the aroma of deep-fried bread and coconut-sprinkled sweets drew in a breakfast-hungry crowd around him. Smells and sounds coloured the morning, made it familiar and manageable for the citizens of the Town of Love. Many of them sat resting in the shade under the gulmohar tree waiting for news of Saleem, the regal orange blossoms in the foliage forming a mighty crown above them. The first day in the life of Sona's baby.

Jannati breathed in, slowly and shakily.

'It's a boy,' she said. 'A tiny little boy.'

At the intersection by the rickshaw stand a bicycle turned into the road leading down towards the bridge. The two women, still locked in their embrace, tracked the spindly figure with the blue woollen hat from the corners of their eyes. He pedalled slowly down towards them, veering left before the bridge, and turned into the hospital yard. Jannati turned around and walked towards him as he jumped off the bicycle. Darya could not see her face, she didn't have to. Jannati's shoulders softened, her footsteps grew lighter. She placed her hands between his on the handlebars.

He was alive, that was the only thing she heard. Fauzia had settled down outside with the others when the boisterous Town of Love crowd was thrown out, but it had felt impossible. Impossible to just sit there and think of nothing else, no images in her mind but his dangling head, his dark green sweater stained black with blood. No one had tried to stop her when she ran back inside, no one had greeted her with a single word as she quietly sank down against the wall.

She could see it in the doctor's face as he entered the reception area and looked around. Instantly knew her brother was alive, that his heart was beating and he was going to come home. That they would build their house and move in together. She was already on her feet when the receptionist pointed in her direction and felt the relief burn behind her eyelids.

'Saleem is going to be fine,' was all the doctor said. His voice was solemn, lips moving up and down, she couldn't understand why he wasn't smiling. But Saleem was alive, that was all she needed to know.

'Go home now and get some sleep,' she finally heard – was that a tiny, weary hint of a smile at the corner of his mouth after all? 'You can come back and visit him this afternoon.'

She didn't pause in front of the clump of people in the shade underneath the tree. Lifted her long Fauzia nose up in the air, sinking her eyelids halfway so that she could just barely see the road ahead. Ignored the shouts, only vaguely registered the calling questions about her brother. If they wanted to know, they could go in and find out for themselves. Fauzia had somewhere to be. Fauzia wanted to speak to Amina.

'Did you see them?'

She cut to the chase.

'See who?'

Amina was kneeling in front of the water pump in the yard. Aftaab dangled down her front over her shoulder, wearing nothing but a red T-shirt, his tiny rear flinching at the spurts of water as Amina vigorously scrubbed him with soap.

Fauzia waited, frozen in the sunlight, until Amina turned around to give her full attention.

'The people who stabbed Saleem.'

Amina fussed with her son for a moment before setting him down on the ground.

'No,' she said at last. 'I didn't see them.'

Fauzia kept waiting, she would stand here all day if she had to. Didn't say a word until she managed to catch Amina's eye.

'But you know who they were.'

This wasn't a question. And there was no reply. Amina bent down and took off her rubber sandals. Restarted the water pump and rinsed her feet under the glittering stream, first one, then the other.

'I didn't see them,' she repeated.

The green metal gate in front of the old rice mill clanged shut behind the car from Patna. Rupa and Ms Dumra had been on the road for nearly ten hours, it was a blistering hot afternoon in Forbesganj.

Tamanna had had a long wait in the Pukaar office. All of last night's emotions had been spent, drained, had floated to the bottom of her stomach like fine-grained sand, a layer of sludge covering the bottom after the floods have receded. Darya had gone back to her hostel to catch a few hours of sleep this morning, but Tamanna hadn't closed her eyes for a minute. And now Darya was back out there on the well-trampled patch of dirt used as a parking lot, Tamanna could hear car doors opening and closing. She slowly lifted herself up, holding on to the bleary, grey exhaustion that formed a protective membrane around her thoughts, careful not to let a single emotion through. Rupa wanted nothing to do with her, Rupa felt nothing for her, Rupa would never call her Amma. It didn't matter, Tamanna told herself. As long as Rupa wasn't sitting on the balcony in the blue house, with ruby-red lips and glittering earrings, nothing else mattered.

'Namaste!'

Hand motions, polite greetings, weary smiles. The couch in the corner of the office had room for three, but Rupa sat down just close enough to the middle so that there was no space for Tamanna to sit between her and Ms Dumra. Darya automatically placed herself in the swivel chair behind the desk, and Tamanna followed suit by taking a seat in the visitor's chair.

'So ... Rupa, are you feeling better?'

Darya tried to fight off her hazy fatigue. She wanted to have some kind of orderly transition, to thank Headmistress Dumra for going above and beyond for this odd, quiet girl. A tiny irritation gnawed inside her, seeing Tamanna and her daughter sitting there in silence – would it kill them to say something, too? It would be nice if Tamanna could at least thank Ms Dumra for all her extra work!

But Rupa looked down at the floor and fidgeted with her fingernails, and Tamanna stared straight ahead, lips pursed tight. It was Ms Dumra who finally spoke up – yes, Rupa was feeling better, she was. The external wounds from the rape had healed after surgery, and they had weaned her off the morphine addiction. Rupa was a smart girl, Ms Dumra emphasised, she was convinced she was going to be all right. But – she hesitated for a split second – Rupa should probably stay in therapy for a while, some sort of counselling … could their organisation in Kolkata provide that?

Darya nodded. Breathed an enormous sigh of relief knowing that Manjira was on the way, her train due to roll into Katihar in just a few hours. Manjira could talk to Rupa, could find out what she needed. 'Rupa will be going to Kolkata tomorrow. She'll be safe there.'

The thought on all of their minds. She would be safe there.

Suddenly Rupa lifted her head. Her voice was thin, like silver bells.

'Where is Sona?'

Darya was dumbstruck. This was one question she wasn't prepared for. Ms Dumra looked vaguely quizzical, she had never heard of the other woman who was rescued the same night as Rupa. Darya frantically searched her brain for something to say, something that wasn't a lie, something that wouldn't unleash a new torrent of pain.

Tamanna turned a pair of calm, brown eyes towards her daughter. Pronounced the words with a voice beyond tears.

'Sona died this morning. She gave birth to a little boy and then she died. But the boy is alive.'

No tears for Rupa either. Just the slender fingers fiddling and fidgeting. Repeating the words slowly, distantly.

'The boy is alive.'

She added, her voice a touch more stable, a profound fact: 'She had thought it would be a boy.'

Manjira arrived just before midnight. Rupa was sleeping on the office couch; Ms Dumra had closed her eyes for a few hours in Darya's hostel bed before waking up for the long-awaited night-time meeting. Manjira was pale and drained after a demanding twelve hours on the overcrowded train, plus three more in a bumpy back seat. 'And in the bathroom at the end of my train carriage was a goat. A goat! Tied to the doorknob!'

Too exhausted to laugh, she shook her head and sucked at the paan wedged inside her cheek.

Darya had sent the guard to buy some food for them; they ate their silent midnight meal in the dark, shabby office now engulfed in the delightful scent of roti gosht, the aroma of freshly baked bread with mutton in spicy sauce wafting through the air. The quiet, contented stillness remained after the plastic bags of food were emptied; none of the weary women could muster the energy to take the next step and think of what needed to be done. Darya had closed her eyes and nearly drifted off to sleep in the stiff-backed office chair when a cautious knock on the door startled her.

'Sorry, so sorry …'

The guard's voice: 'The Begum from Patna, her driver wants to go. He's asking if she's almost ready.'

Manjira and Darya escorted Ms Dumra out to the car, and Manjira finally posed the question she had saved until they were out of Rupa's earshot. 'Psychologically speaking … what does your therapist say?'

The director shook her head. 'There's still a long way to go. He says Rupa is waiting. Sitting there waiting for the rest of her life to happen.'

Darya's mind twisted and turned, trying to find places for all of them to sleep as they climbed the stairs back up to the office. Rupa couldn't be moved outside these walls, of course. Hopefully they could find a bed for Manjira at the hotel, she needed to sleep a few hours before getting on the bus and then the train back to Kolkata with Rupa. Darya was worried about the journey tomorrow, what if someone in Katihar had sniffed them out, what if news of Manjira's arrival had spread down the grapevine to the Aslams, what if …?

She sighed and tried to clear her drowsy head. Sleep first. Rupa had to sleep here, on the office couch. Tamanna could go home to Prem Nagar, and then maybe she could … her train of thought ceased abruptly as she opened the door. Tamanna sat next to Rupa on the couch. The glowing desk lamp cast a cone-shaped spotlight on her lap, onto a sky-blue piece of cotton cloth. Two hands, one slim, the other coarser, darker, slowly traced the tiny stitches in a simple floral pattern. Fingers glided across the colours, springtime green, pink, brown, and bright yellow. Stroked over a leaf, slowly outlined a curlicued vine. They did not meet, these hands, never once touched each other's fingers. Just explored, quietly, the roads travelled, their footsteps in the dust. Gently charting a pattern without words.

Manjira and Darya quietly slipped away from the room.

※

Amina had seen nothing. Had heard nothing, had no information to share. But in the days that followed, she felt underneath her skin the mood in the house changing, new glances exchanged between her husband and his brothers. After Sona's sad little funeral, which no one wanted to organise but Jannati and Roshan finally took care of, Amina hadn't asked Kasim about anything. Not a word about what had happened that night, nothing about Jabbar and his brothers. Whatever he knew, he would never tell her anyway.

Tamanna asked her too: 'Did you see anything?'

No, she had seen nothing.

'Do you know anything?'

No again. But they both knew it. The knife was safely back in place on the shelf. The knife that stabbed Saleem in the stomach and by some random miracle failed to sever his lifeline, was back on the shelf in Katihar.

'Aren't you afraid they'll come after you next time?'

Amina's strong eyes bored straight into Tamanna's.

Tamanna took her time answering, meditating on the question, her voice oddly light. 'No, I don't think they will. If they can't go through me to get to Rupa, they have no use for me.'

She let her words settle in, feeling relieved and ancient at the same time. Rupa was safe. She had spoken to her on the phone, and Darya kept passing on updates from Manjira. Rupa was far away from the blue house, and was never to return.

Give birth to a daughter, Tamanna thought. Heena watching her girl grow up in the shadow of the doorframe in her brother's house. The inheritance Lalita had passed on to her daughters. Rozy, who had stopped coming to school.

Give birth to a daughter. Condemn a life.

24

Amina stood in front of the school building, impatience written across her face in large letters. What was taking them so long? Tamanna and Heena would definitely show up; several other members of the women's group had barely been seen since that dramatic night with Sona and Saleem. Rampant rumours had rolled through the Town of Love like tidal waves, the stamp of treachery had grown commonplace. But Jannati had sailed through unscathed, it seemed. The stocky woman who had kept Sona hidden behind Fauzia's door had somehow avoided the beating that Amina had been sure would be Prabir's first response.

But what was taking them so long? Amina swatted at a persistent horsefly. She wanted to get on with the meeting!

They had been at it for a while, discussing whether the monthly bank contribution should be increased from ten to fifteen rupees, and whether they should submit an article about the launch of the mahila mandal in Forbesganj to Pukaar's quarterly newsletter, printed in Delhi. None of the women had any writing skills to speak of, but old, toothless Munni was fired up at the thought: 'We could have Saleem write it for us!'

Amina immediately shot down the suggestion: 'Saleem? No, we'll ask Darya! How could we have a *man* write about our women's group?'

Heena tried to mediate: 'But he will only write what we tell him to, it wouldn't be …' The shadow that fell from the doorway stopped her midsentence and made the buzz of voices in the schoolhouse fall silent. Jannati had materialised, filling the doorway with her wide hips and her peaceful face. Without speaking or acknowledging the silence that surrounded her, she took time to size up the group, letting her gaze scan across the eight women gathered on the threadbare rug for the first time since that tumultuous night in the Town of Love. Tamanna was the only one to nod in her direction, and Jannati took a seat on the outer edge of the circle.

Amina was baffled: Prabir ... how could Jannati just show up here in the middle of the day? But she didn't ask, didn't let her face betray a glimmer of the newly sparked flame of solidarity between Jannati and her. Jannati was still earning money for Prabir. And she had promised to take responsibility for Sona. Loyalty was not an easy concept in Prem Nagar.

The next point on the agenda was the incense project, once again. Darya wasn't here today, but she had explained the technicalities many times in the past. The sticking point in the discussion was, as usual, the projected income: how much could they expect to earn? How long would it take to pay off the cost of the equipment? The heart of the question: could they make as much money rolling aromatic incense powder onto sticks for six, eight, ten hours a day as they would make from seeing passengers behind straw walls in the same amount of time?

Tamanna opened her mouth, but shut it again. She had said it so many times, she couldn't bear to repeat it again: *It's not about making more or less money. It's about owning yourself.* She looked around at the weary bodies, the henna-red fingertips, a dupatta pulled across one woman's neck to hide the bruises. Suddenly, a surge of empathy burnt in her throat. Manufacturing incense for a few paise per stick, what good would that do? They still had such an endless way to go! Rupa at the shelter in Kolkata; Sona dead and buried. A bitter wave of helplessness swept over Tamanna; eight women on a frayed carpet, what power could they hope to have? At this very moment, new trucks were rolling across the border in Jogbani with eight-year-old, ten-year-old, twelve-year-old girls hidden under tarpaulins in the back. Girls who thought they would be working as maids in Delhi or at restaurants in Mumbai. Girls who would be raped in other blue houses tonight.

Tamanna had closed her eyes, her body rocked mindlessly back and forth in an inexpressible anguish. She didn't sense that Jannati had moved in right next to her, had fixed her dark eyes on her, waiting to say something.

'I'm leaving.'

Tamanna was dumbfounded by Jannati's announcement as her eyes snapped open. She turned sharply toward her friend, perplexed by her own violent reaction. 'Are you …? Prabir … is it …?'

But Jannati's face showed no sign of alarm. Her neat, shiny braid rested peacefully on her shoulder; the plump arms were folded in her lap as she rested solidly on the corner of the green rug. Jannati's voice was soft, but her words contained heaven and earth as she announced, 'I'm going to Khwaishgram.'

She was looking at Tamanna, but her words were directed at the whole group. The little village nine dusty miles away was every bit as destitute as their own, the houses just as flimsy, the daily portions of roti sabzi just as meagre. Jannati saw the question marks on the faces around her, Amina already had the words on the tip of her tongue: What are you going to do there? What will you eat? Prabir – you can't just *leave*, he'll …

But the lines in Jannati's dark face were oddly relaxed, a small, brave hint of courage quivered in the betel-red corners of her mouth. *Everything will be fine*, her brown eyes whispered. *It's my turn.*

Tamanna understood it all in a flash. Before she turned to look out the window, before she spotted the skinny figure with his hands on the bicycle handles, it all dawned on her. The prince with the knitted woollen hat and the stubbly chin was waiting out there. It was Jannati's turn. Finally, it was Jannati's turn. Nineteen years after she climbed into the truck in Phuntsholing, she had paid off the cost of her ticket.

Jannati slowly got to her feet, gathered her sari around her with a dignified motion. 'We will pick up the baby today,' she said. 'He's eating well now, and screaming loud. Strong, healthy lungs. We'll pick him up later today.'

Silence washed over the carpet as Jannati left. Eight pairs of eyes followed the odd couple as they vanished down the path towards the Town of Love; the woman with the wide hips and the swaying walk, the man with the narrow shoulders and the dark blue hat on his head. Jannati's voice rang in Tamanna's ears, 'For myself, I have no more dreams.' How strange and wonderful things could be. Despite having no more dreams.

The afternoon sun hung low over the fields behind the schoolhouse, pouring its generous rays over the day labourers on their way home. The women in the schoolhouse lingered in the dusty light for a while, each with her own silence. No one brought up the subject of incense sticks again. It was not every day that the women of Prem Nagar Mahila Mandal witnessed a miracle.

It was Amina who finally said it out loud.

'She can't just *leave*. She is Prabir's property. He's going to come and get her back.'

The group nodded slowly and reluctantly, but no one said a word. This was what they all wanted, too. They wanted this miracle for Jannati and Roshan.

Old Munni was the first to get up, driven by the unspoken feeling that the meeting was over. Tamanna followed her, then Heena and the others; Amina brought the carpet outside to shake it out.

And there she was. Salma stood leaning against the brick wall by the front steps, cradling Nila in her arms. Her earrings dangling long and glittering flashy, her kurta was shocking pink and adorned with sequins. But it billowed softly and cheerfully around the little girl in her arms, fluttered playfully around the two chubby fists flailing in the air. Salma rested her head against the wall, closed her eyes for a moment while her face glowed softly in the sun.

She said nothing to the women leaving the house. Salma simply stood there, in the middle of the workday, showing off the tiny branch she had broken off Prabir's money tree. The second miracle in just a few minutes. Salma didn't come to their meeting today. But it was just one short step up to the door.

※

'I'll be back, didi.'

She nodded slowly. Fauzia had no reason to doubt her brother's words, but she didn't like it. Saleem had just got back on his feet; he wasn't strong enough yet; she didn't think he was ready for another trip to Kolkata. Nevertheless, she knew her brother would be safer there; they still hadn't arrested anyone for the stabbing in Prem Nagar. Fauzia saw Kasim and his brothers every day, along with their women, the aunt with the stringy hair. They passed by her paan-stand with a quick greeting, everyone pretended as though nothing was wrong. She folded the next betel leaf into a neat little triangle. Looked over at her own brothers playing cards in the shade. *You knew,* Fauzia thought. *You always know.*

'I have to go,' Saleem repeated. 'I have to see how Rupa is doing; they're trying to find a permanent place for her to live.'

Fauzia nodded again. She pictured Tamanna in her mind's eye, the outsider who had caused nothing but trouble since she came here. Still, a little voice inside her said – *wouldn't you have done the same? If you knew you could give Rozy a future outside the dhanda?* The thought of Tamanna flew out of her head, replaced by an image of a house. Not a big house, no, a small, white-painted brick house with a solid door, real windows with bars across them, a bed in a room of her own. She looked at her brother, knew it wasn't her place to pester him. But he read her mind:

'And I have to go see Peter, you know. The carpenter I told you about?'

He looked at her, a feeble smile in his pale face: 'I haven't forgotten that I'm going to build you a good bed for our new house.'

Fauzia felt a pressure behind her eyelids and quickly wiped her hand under her nose. She averted her eyes, concentrated on tightening the lids on the jars in front of her. Of course, he hadn't forgotten their house. Of course, Saleem would be back. He had shown her the land he had purchased, a small, rectangular plot beside the train tracks. Sometimes Fauzia walked by there at night, without stopping, without breathing a word to anyone. Simply walked by, feeling its presence: A house. Brick walls, tin roof. *My own piece of earth.*

The bus to Katihar, and then the night train to Kolkata. Saleem held a ticket to the Haate Bazare Express for the second time in just a few months. He and Darya were travelling together to Katihar; she wanted to speak to Chief Inspector P. Laskar in person about the complaint against Jabbar Aslam, his brothers and his mother. Saleem winced at the thought. He knew that the inexorable, unyielding aid worker's fiery tone could help her far along the way in some cases, but it could also backfire when faced with self-righteous arrogance and aggressive territorial impulses.

'Let it go, didi.'

Darya looked at him sharply, lightning flashed behind her glasses: 'What do you mean, let it go? These people have been buying and selling girls for years, drugging and raping and abusing them. You saw what they did to Rupa – how can you tell me to let it go?'

He fidgeted in his seat. 'Nothing, it's just….'

Saleem couldn't find the words to go on. How could he convey that justice was the last thing he expected, that the world didn't work that way when you were a Nat? The best you could hope for was escape, the wildest dream was a tolerable life for those you loved. Lofty principles, equality in the eyes of the law, fair treatment regardless of class and caste – that was simply not how it worked! He knew he shouldn't think that way, at least he shouldn't say it, but the knife in his stomach had spoken loud and clear. Those with the power and the means must not be challenged. Don't think you can change the way things work.'

'It's nothing,' he said reluctantly. 'I just don't think they're going to lift a finger to lock up Jabbar Aslam.'

Darya looked at him sombrely and pushed her glasses up the bridge of her nose. 'You may be right,' she said. 'But we can't allow ourselves to give up. We got two women out of the brothel. A new, little person will grow up outside Kuli Pada because of what we did.'

'In Khwaishgram,' he pointed out wearily.

She nodded. 'In Khwaishgram. In poverty. But still, in a kind of freedom.'

She fell silent, her gaze roamed the fields flickering past outside the bus window. The dusty grey sky, the winding, well-trodden path towards a clump of rickety houses on the hill under some trees. 'There will always be shadows of sorrow looming over our road,' Darya slowly uttered. 'But there is some peace in resting under the trees that cast them.'

They parted ways as they stepped off the bus. Saleem headed straight for the railway station. The train didn't leave for another three hours and he already had his ticket, but he was taking no chances. He would rather take cover there, in the teeming crowd, visible and surrounded by people, until the train departed. Kuli Pada was just around the corner from the station, less than two minutes away by motorcycle.

Saleem put his bag down on the dirty brick floor in the ticketing hall. Plopped himself down on top of it, peeled the wrapper off a piece of sticky jalebi and took a bite of the bright orange confection. Chewed and savoured every mouthful of syrupy sweetness as travellers' calamities and joyful scenes unfolded around him: farewells and reunions, hopes and disappointments. Maybe it was just the sugar coursing through his bloodstream, but he actually felt excited at the thought of the journey ahead. Rupa, he knew how important it was for Pukaar that he followed up on her progress.

Peter, he looked forward to seeing the boys again and smelling the sawdust in the workshop. Manjira, who believed in him, who had pushed him into the meeting hall and up to the podium.

His conversation with Darya on the bus played again in his mind, and a gust of shame crept in alongside the sweet anticipation in his mouth. She was right, of course. They could not allow themselves to give up. If Manjira wanted him to, he would speak to the men, again and again. If it could stop even one of them from spending fifty rupees on a few pitiful minutes of pleasure.

Darya hurried from the bus stop to the police station. She had an appointment with P. Laskar, but was kept waiting a long while in the all too familiar waiting room with the worn plastic chairs. When he finally let her in, she sensed a touch of impatience, but he still greeted her politely from under the bushy moustache.

She gave him a moment, but when he didn't take the initiative, she launched in:

'I ... we would very much like to know the status of the charges against Jabbar Aslam and his brothers. Rupa is in Kolkata now, and if the issue of testifying comes up ...'

She had everything prepared, had planned to use their concern for Rupa to lead into the larger issue.

'What charges?' he cut her off. 'No charges have been brought against any of them, as far as I know. But you'll have to take your questions elsewhere.'

Darya lost track, what did he mean? Was he talking about a court case? Had Jabbar been brought in for questioning? This was the first she had heard of that!

Laskar noticed her bewilderment and softened up a little: 'Jabbar Aslam was apprehended and questioned six days after the rescue of Rupa Khatoon.'

Darya was even more confused. Why hadn't anyone told them?

'He was released on bail a few days later.'

'Bail? Who ...?'

He shook his head. He couldn't say. Or he didn't want to say. In any case, he was never going to tell her who had secured the bail, Darya thought wearily. Besides, she knew the answer all too well. With all the money from the money trees, in Katihar and other places, it was always possible to squeeze out the necessary amount to open a back door.

'And now ... is he back in Kuli Pada?'

Laskar looked at her sharply. 'No one can stop a man from living in his own house. As far as I know, the question of bringing charges against him or any of his family members is not yet settled. And you know as well as I do, it could be years before it ever ends up in court.'

A glimmer of compassion – or was it respect ? – in his eyes: 'But I understand that your organisation will be following up this case?'

She nodded. 'Absolutely! We'll be following up, and we will keep pushing for an indictment.'

He examined her for a moment before standing up to indicate that the meeting was over. 'Yes,' he said. Was that a hint of an appreciative smile underneath the moustache? 'I would not be surprised if you succeed.'

Darya stood up, thanked Chief Inspector Laskar and left the office with a befuddled sense of not knowing exactly what to think. Jabbar was out on bail. She had no doubt that the threat to Rupa in Patna and the attack on Saleem in Forbesganj could ultimately be traced back to the blue house in Kuli Pada. But he had been apprehended. He had been questioned about Rupa and Sona. And the police just around the corner knew well that Pukaar was a force to be reckoned with. 'I would not be surprised if you succeed.'

The sky was a little bluer above Darya's head as she walked back towards the bus station. She thought of Tamanna's mango tree by the water pump. Tonight they would share one of its ripe, yellow fruits.

Darya bought her ticket; the bus didn't leave for another hour and she wondered if she should get something to eat before the long trip back. A bus pulled up beside her, she swiftly jumped onto the kerb as the wheezing jalopy let the air out of its weary brakes. The door slid open and Darya stayed still, observing the flow of passengers. The sign in the windshield read that the bus had come from the south. Young men with light luggage hurried swiftly away, women with heavier loads crowded around the baggage compartment to gather their belongings.

A stocky woman in a chocolate brown sari was one of the last people to step off the bus. She carried a bulky bag and a purse, glanced timidly around her and adjusted the bun at the nape of her neck. No one was there to meet her, it seemed. Darya's gaze followed the woman as she took a few reticent steps forward and stopped again. Then she made up her mind and steered her footsteps towards the kerb, heading straight for Darya.

'Namaste, didi,' she said with an apologetic smile, pressing her palms together in greeting. Her eyes were anxious and decisive at the same time, like someone who had made up her mind to jump overboard and risk everything on the life jacket. Darya took note of her eyes, framed by unusually long, thick lashes.

'I'm on my way to Forbesganj, do you know which bus I should take?'

'Namaste,' Darya said in return. 'I'm going to Forbesganj as well, I can show you.'

She hesitated a moment, but couldn't resist asking, 'Forbesganj is quite far from here. Do you have anyone there? Family?'

The unease in Basanti's face disappeared, was replaced by a firm conviction settling in across her heavy features; her lips parted in a smile.

'Yes,' she replied. 'I have someone there.'

AFTERWORD

BY RUCHIRA GUPTA

Sometimes a chance encounter produces outcomes you could never have imagined. The story you hold in your hands is the tangible result of a casual invitation I extended to Anne Ostby in a Tehran garden in 2007, to come to Forbesganj in India and meet the Nat women I was working with there. Neither of us knew that this would lead to several visits, a close cooperation, a lasting friendship, and ultimately, this book. All because Anne experienced, as I had, that once you have listened to these women's stories and witnessed their courage, you cannot simply turn the page on their lives.

For me, it began as a routine assignment, triggered by a journalist's nose for news. While walking through the hills of Nepal in 1994 I stumbled upon a sloppy, dogged and cruel flesh trade – a system to procure girls and carry them in trucks, buses and trains to brothels in India. I saw procurers on the prowl, money changing hands, and tin-roofs and radios in Nepali homes with daughters in Mumbai, Kolkata, Delhi …

I badgered everyone I knew to get word out about human trafficking and finally got a commission for the Canadian Broadcasting Corporation to field-produce a documentary.

Months were spent hanging around the Mumbai brothels, getting to know the women, building trust and slowly gaining access. I didn't go through anyone in the power hierarchy in the area. No police, politicians or NGOs. I had to make friends with the women in prostitution, talk to them on terms of equality and portray the story from the point of view of those affected. I told them intimate details of my life before I got to know theirs. I promised them that they could walk off camera whenever they wanted, reveal only what they wanted to and ask me to stop filming at any time.

Certain politicians were involved and the mafia did not want us to continue; we were stopped on the road, our helicopter was denied permission to land, our car was stoned, a knife was pulled out at me, but the shoot was finally completed. Later, I won an Emmy for Outstanding Investigative Journalism for the 47-minute film called *The Selling of Innocents*. The shoot was over, but I realised that I couldn't walk away.

I continued to keep in touch with the women in the red-light areas of Mumbai who had helped make the documentary. They asked me to help them change their situation and protect their daughters from prostitution. However, my helping out, once or twice or even ten times, could not entrench a long-term obstacle to these crimes. I asserted that they had to help themselves and I would facilitate. And so Apne Aap, the organisation on which the book's fictional Pukaar is based, was born. Apne Aap means self-help in Hindi.

Apne Aap began to mobilise and mentor small communities of trafficked and vulnerable girls and women to rescue and empower each other by talking, healing and accessing legal, educational and livelihood rights in safe spaces in Mumbai. It also began working in my hometown Kolkata and, of course, in my home village Forbesganj in Bihar. It helped women find sustainable and dignified livelihood. It helped girls into schools. It brought out a newspaper, *Red Light Dispatch*, to give voice to a small but swelling women's movement against trafficking.

President Bill Clinton awarded me the 2009 Clinton Global Citizen Award for my leadership in improving the lives of people by helping them see their own potential. This book is about such people – girls, women and men in a small low-caste squatters' settlement on the Indo-Nepal border, resisting inter-generational prostitution. The book tells of the courage of a few girls, women and men against a whole system of powerful people, trying to question all excuses for hierarchies – caste, class, and gender – with every act of assertion. Sometimes the girls, women and men do not themselves recognise the dent they make in this armour of slavery, with the strike of each brave dream made true.

Saleem's story in the book tries to digest the dichotomy of this country that is India, and its historical present. Through his character the dichotomy of his life's context comes out with lucidity. Saleem, who works in Pukaar, is an idealist who works to end trafficking in his community, and in the world. He is educated and a committed worker in Pukaar. But here comes the irony of his life: the education that has equipped him to fight for justice was paid for 'through endless trips behind the dirty curtain', his sister paid for his education through prostituting herself. So here is Saleem, with another euphoric dream that he lets us dream. His character is one that we as activists fighting against trafficking want a man to be. To fight not just in the community against injustices, but to fight and defeat even the ideals of masculinity that make a man the supplier or the buyer of women and sex. He is a kaleidoscope and he makes us see, in this book, a universe that was, that is, and that we wish will be. Tamanna's heroic claim to her daughter, Rupa, eventually rescued from a brothel, takes us into the injustices of a corrupt police force which will not listen, and a casteist society that will scorn and snub her attempts. It takes us into the complex relationship of a mother and her daughter – a relationship conceived in a brothel and abandoned by a mother seeking to survive by running away from that brothel. It takes us into the world of solidarity, built by Pukaar, in which other oppressed women in the 'Town of Love' help their friend reclaim her daughter. The women are nothing but revolutionaries.

The book shows how movements for justice are contagious. Tamanna's journey helps Amina help Salma help Jannati help Sona help Basanti … With this book perhaps, this journey will never end and Basanti's journey will help Anne to help Rachel to help Gloria to help Pamela to help Sonali to help …

Anne Ostby's book is an important voice in the history of slave resistance. I have heard and experienced so many stories, and with every step I am constantly reminded of a poem written by Maya Angelou – *Still I Rise*.

> *Out of the huts of history's shame*
> *I rise*
> *Up from a past that's rooted in pain*
> *I rise*
> *I'm a black ocean, leaping and wide,*
> *Welling and swelling I bear in the tide*
> *Leaving behind nights of terror and fear*
> *I rise*
> *Into a daybreak that's wondrously clear*
> *I rise*
> *Bringing the gifts that my ancestors gave,*
> *I am the dream and the hope of the slave.*
> *I rise*
> *I rise*
> *I rise*

The women of *Apne Aap* want a world in which it is unacceptable to buy or sell another human being, and they want to imagine an economy in which one is not forced to sell oneself. This book is about such women, and also shows that any one of us could be a Rukmini or Darya.

Ruchira Gupta is an Indian sex trafficking abolitionist, journalist and activist, and founder and president of the NGO Apne Aap (www.apneaap.org). She has been honoured with the Clinton Global Citizen Award in 2009, the UK House of Lords' Abolitionist Award in 2007, and an Emmy in 1997 for her documentary *The Selling of Innocents*. In 2012, she was named 'Amazing Indian' by *Times Now*.